The Capture
of the
Earl of Glencrae

BY STEPHANIE LAURENS

Cynster Novels
The Capture of the Earl of Glencrae
In Pursuit of Eliza Cynster
Viscount Breckenridge to the Rescue
Temptation and Surrender • Where the Heart Leads
The Taste of Innocence • What Price Love?
The Truth About Love • The Ideal Bride
The Perfect Lover • On a Wicked Dawn
On a Wild Night • The Promise in a Kiss
All About Passion • All About Love
A Secret Love • A Rogue's Proposal
Scandal's Bride • A Rake's Vow
Devil's Bride

The Black Cobra Quartet
The Reckless Bride • The Brazen Bride
The Elusive Bride • The Untamed Bride

Bastion Club Novels
Mastered By Love • The Edge of Desire
Beyond Seduction • To Distraction
A Fine Passion • A Lady of His Own
A Gentleman's Honor • The Lady Chosen
Captain Jack's Woman

Coming Soon
The Lady Risks All

The Capture
of the
Earl of Glencrae

Stephanie Laurens

HARPER LUXE

An Imprint of HarperCollins*Publishers*

THE CAPTURE OF THE EARL OF GLENCRAE. Copyright © 2012 by Savdek Management Proprietary Ltd. All rights reserved. Printed in the United States of America. No part of this book may be used or reproduced in any manner whatsoever without written permission except in the case of brief quotations embodied in critical articles and reviews. For information address HarperCollins Publishers, 10 East 53rd Street, New York, NY 10022.

HarperCollins books may be purchased for educational, business, or sales promotional use. For information please write: Special Markets Department, HarperCollins Publishers, 10 East 53rd Street, New York, NY 10022.

FIRST HARPERLUXE EDITION

HarperLuxe™ is a trademark of HarperCollins Publishers

ISBN: 978-0-06-210725-1

11 12 13 14   ID/OPM   10 9 8 7 6 5 4 3 2 1

The Capture
of the
Earl of Glencrae

The Cynster Family Tree

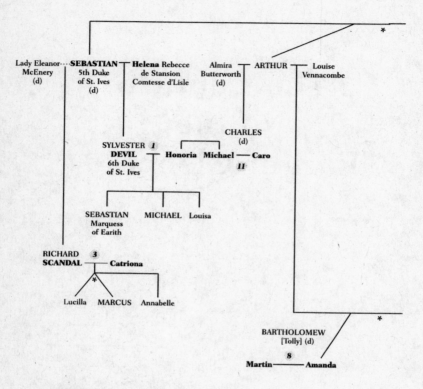

MALE Cynsters in capitals   * denotes twins
CHILDREN BORN AFTER 1825 NOT SHOWN

THE CYNSTER NOVELS

1. *Devil's Bride*
2. *A Rake's Vow*
3. *Scandal's Bride*
4. *A Rogue's Proposal*
5. *A Secret Love*
6. *All About Love*
7. *All About Passion*
8. *On a Wild Night*
9. *On a Wicked Dawn*
10. *The Perfect Lover*

Cynster Special—The Promise in a Kiss

CBA#1—Casebook of Barnaby Adair #1—Where the Heart Leads

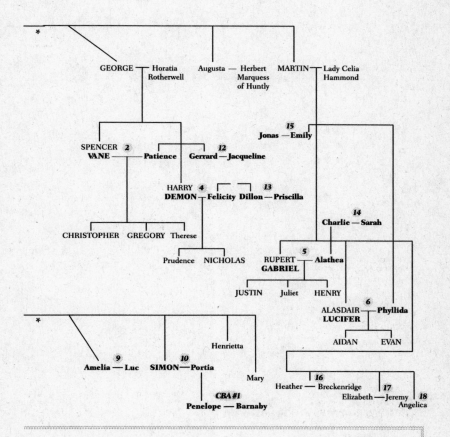

Chapter One

June 1, 1829
Cavendish House, London

"Oh. My. God." Angelica Rosalind Cynster, standing to one side of Lady Cavendish's salon with the bulk of her ladyship's chattering guests at her back, stared at the long windows giving onto the unlit terrace and the dark gardens beyond, at the reflection of the gentleman who was staring at her from the opposite side of the room.

She'd first felt his disconcerting gaze some thirty minutes before; he'd watched her waltz, watched her laugh and chat with others, but no matter how discreetly she'd looked for him, he'd refused to show himself. Irritated, with the musicians resting she'd worked her way around the room, moving from group to group, exchanging greetings and comments, smoothly shifting until she'd got him in her sights.

Eyes wide, barely daring to believe, she whispere "It's *him!*"

Her ill-suppressed excitement drew a glance fro her cousin, Henrietta, presently standing beside he Angelica shook her head, and someone in the group the side of which she stood reclaimed Henrietta's atten tion, leaving Angelica with her gaze locked on the mo riveting man she'd ever beheld.

She considered herself an expert in the art of as sessing gentlemen. From her earliest years she'd bee aware of them as "other," and years of observation ha left her with a sound understanding of their feature and foibles. When it came to gentlemen, she had very high standards.

Visually, the gentleman across the room trumped every one.

He was standing with six others, all of whom she could name, but she didn't know him. She'd never met him, had never even set eyes on him before. If she had, she'd have known, as she now did, that he was her one, the gentleman she had been waiting to meet.

She'd always been unshakably convinced that she would know her hero, the gentleman fated to be her husband, the instant she saw him. She hadn't expected that first sighting to be via a reflection across a crowded room, but the result was the same—she *knew* it was him.

The talisman that The Lady, a Scottish deity, had gifted to the Cynster girls to assist them in finding their true loves had passed from Angelica's eldest sister, Heather, to her middle sister, Eliza, who on her recent return to London with her new fiancé had handed the necklace to Angelica, the next in line. Composed of old gold links and amethyst beads from which a rose-quartz pendant hung, ancient and mysterious the talisman now lay beneath Angelica's fichu, the links and beads against her skin, the crystal pendant nestling in her décolletage.

Three nights ago, deeming her time, her turn, had come, armed with the necklace, her instincts, and her innate determination, she had embarked on an intensive campaign to find her hero. She'd come to the Cavendish soiree, at which a select slice of the upper echelon of the ton had gathered to mingle and converse, intent on examining any and all prospective males Lady Cavendish, a lady with an extensive circle of acquaintance, had inveigled to attend.

The talisman had worked for Heather, now engaged to Breckenridge, and had brought Eliza and Jeremy Carling together; Angelica had hoped that it would help her, too, but hadn't expected such a rapid result.

Regardless, now she had her hero in sight, she wasn't inclined to waste another minute.

He hadn't noticed, from his position on the opposite side of the room possibly couldn't see, that she was studying him. Her gaze locked on his reflection, she visually devoured him.

He was stunningly impressive, towering half a head taller than the men around him, none of whom were short. Elegantly attired in a black evening coat, pristine white shirt and cravat, and black trousers, everything about him from the breadth of his shoulders to the length of his long legs seemed in perfect proportion to his height.

His hair appeared solidly black, straight, rather long, but fashionably styled with windblown, slightly ruffled locks. She tried to study his features, but the reflection defeated her; she couldn't make out any details beyond the sharply defined, austere planes of his face. Nevertheless, his broad forehead, bladelike nose, and squared chin stamped him as the scion of some aristocratic house; only they possessed such hard, chiseled, coldly beautiful faces.

Her heart was thumping distinctly faster. In anticipation.

Now she'd found him, what next?

If it had been in any way acceptable, she would have swung on her heel, marched across the room, and introduced herself, but that would be too forward, even for her. Yet if after thirty and more minutes of watching her he hadn't made any move to approach her, then he wasn't going to, at least not there, not that night.

Which didn't suit her at all.

Shifting her gaze, she scanned the gentlemen in the loose circle in which he stood. He'd been listening to the conversations but rarely contributing, merely using the interaction to cloak his interest in her.

Even as she looked, one of the other men saluted the group and moved away.

Angelica smiled. Without a word, she quit Henrietta's side and glided into the crowd thronging the salon's center.

She caught the Honorable Theodore Curtis's sleeve just before he joined a group of young ladies and gentlemen. He looked around and smiled. "Angelica! Where have you been hiding?"

She waved to the windows. "Over there. Theo, who is that gentleman in the group you just left? The very tall man I've never met."

Theo, a friend of her family who knew her far too well to entertain thoughts of her himself, chuckled. "I told him it wouldn't be long before the young ladies noticed him and came swanning around."

Angelica played the game and pouted. "Don't tease. Him who?"

Theo grinned. "Debenham. He's Viscount Debenham."

"Who is?" She gestured for more.

"A capital fellow. I've known him for years—same age as me, came on the town at the same time, similar interests, you know how it goes. His estate's somewhere near Peterborough, but he's been away from the ton for . . . must be four years. Left because of family and estate business, and has only just returned to the drawing rooms and ballrooms."

"Hmm. So there's no reason you shouldn't introduce him to me."

Still grinning, Theo shrugged. "If you like."

"I would." Angelica took his arm and turned him to where her hero, Debenham, still stood. "I promise to return the favor next time you want to steal a march with some new sweet young thing."

Theo laughed. "I'll hold you to that." Anchoring her hand on his arm, he led her through the crowd.

While they tacked past various groups, nodding and smiling, pausing only when they couldn't avoid it, Angelica conducted a rapid inventory of her appearance, checking that her pale teal silk gown was hanging straight, that the lacy fichu that partially filled in the scooped neckline was sitting properly and adequately concealing the necklace. At one point, she paused to redrape her teal-and-silver silk shawl more elegantly over her elbows; she'd elected to make do without a reticule or fan, so she didn't have those to fuss over.

Her hair she didn't dare touch. The slithering red-gold tresses were swept up in a complicated knot on the top of her head, anchored by innumerable pins and a pearl-encrusted comb; from experience she knew that even a little jiggling could bring the entire mass cascading down. While no gentleman had ever minded her transformation to a clothed version of Venus rising from the waves, that wasn't how she wished to appear before her hero for the first time.

He knew she was coming; she caught a glimpse of his face through the crowd. His gaze still rested on her, but even though she was now closer, she couldn't read anything in his expression.

Then Theo pushed past the last pair of shoulders, drew her to the group, and presented her with a flourish. "Heigh-ho! See who I found."

"Miss Cynster!" came from several throats in tones of pleased surprise.

"I say, delightful fashionable ladies always welcome, don't you know." Millingham swept her a bow, as did all the other men in the group, bar one.

After acknowledging the greetings, Angelica turned to Debenham; Theo had helpfully inserted her into the group by Debenham's side. She raised her gaze to his face, eager to see, to study, to know . . .

From her other side Theo said, "Debenham, old son, allow me to introduce the Honorable Angelica Cynster. Miss Cynster—Viscount Debenham."

Angelica barely registered the words, captured by, trapped in, a pair of large, well-set, heavy-lidded eyes of a stormy, pale-greenish-gray. Those eyes held her entranced; the expression, not in them so much as behind them, spoke of shrewdness, assessment, and cool, clear-headed cynicism.

Her hero was still watching her, coolly studying, examining, and assessing her, and she couldn't tell whether he was impressed with what he saw or not.

That last snapped her back to the moment. Lips curving lightly, her eyes still on his, she inclined her head. "I don't believe we've previously met, my lord." She extended her hand.

His lips barely relaxing from their noncommittally straight line, he raised a hand from where both rested, folded over the silver head of a cane—something she hadn't seen from across the room—and clasped her fingers.

His grip was cool, yet not impersonal, too definite, too firm to shrug off as the usual. She inwardly wobbled, some inner axis tilting as, still locked in his eyes, she absorbed the unexpected sensation—and the subtle but undeniable impression that he was in two minds over letting her go. Lungs suddenly tight, she curtsied.

Those disconcerting eyes remained on hers as he bowed with a fluid grace unimpaired by the cane. "Miss Cynster. It's a pleasure to make your acquaintance."

His voice was so deep his tones sank into her and wrapped sensuous fingers around her spine.

Combining with the effect of the cool fingers still clasping hers, that voice sent warmth sliding beneath her skin, set sultry heat unfurling in her belly. Close to, her hero was a sensual force, as if he exuded some elemental male temptation that was directed at her and her alone . . .

Good Lord. She quashed an impulse to fan her face. She was tempted to give thanks to The Lady there and then, but instead corralled her wits and retrieved her hand, sliding her fingers from between his. He allowed it—but she was intensely aware that he'd made the decision. Certain alarms rang in her head, but she would be damned if she acknowledged, even to herself, that she might be out of her depth with him; he was her hero, ergo she could go forward with confidence. Drawing in a tight breath, she said, "I understand you've only recently returned to London, my lord."

As she spoke, she turned toward him, away from the group, compelling him to reciprocate; the adjustment left them still attached to the group, but able to converse more privately, leaving the others to their own amusements. Theo took the hint and stepped in to ask Millingham about his newly acquired acres.

Debenham, meanwhile, continued to look down at her, his heavy lids and lush black lashes largely veiling his gaze. After a fractional pause, he replied, "I returned a week ago. Debenham Hall is no further than Cambridgeshire, but business has kept me away from the ton for some years."

Tilting her head, she openly studied his face and let the questions that were crowding her tongue—impertinent and unaskable—show in her eyes . . .

His lips curved—not a real smile but an unequivocal sign of understanding. "I've been managing my acres. I take the responsibilities that are mine very seriously."

Despite the lightness in expression and drawling tone, she felt certain he was speaking the absolute truth. "Am I to assume that your estates are now prospering sufficiently that you no longer feel the need to monitor them constantly, and so have returned to the diversions of town?"

Again he considered her, as if his strange eyes could see straight through her confident, sophisticated social mask. Devil Cynster, Angelica's cousin, and his mother, Helena, both had pale green eyes, and they, too, had penetrating gazes. Debenham's eyes were paler, more changeable, more gray mixed in with the pale green, and for Angelica's money, his gaze was even more incisive.

"You might say that," he eventually conceded, "but the unvarnished truth is that I've returned to London for the same purpose that drives most gentlemen of my age and class to haunt the ton's ballrooms."

She opened her eyes wide. "You're looking for a wife?" It was utterly shocking of her to ask, but she absolutely had to know.

His lips curved again, a touch deeper this time. "Indeed." His gaze held hers. "As I said, the most common reason of all for returning to the capital and the ton."

Because of the press of bodies, they were standing only inches apart; due to his height and her lack of it, she was looking up into his face, and he was looking down, into hers. Despite the proximity of the other men, their stance was peculiarly close, private . . . almost intimate.

His largeness, the sheer power of his body, albeit disguised in elegant evening clothes, impinged on her senses; a tempting warmth, his nearness reached for her, wrapped insidiously around her, tempting her closer yet.

The longer she stared into his eyes . . .

"Angelica—I thought I spotted you through the crush."

She blinked and turned to see Millicent Attenwell smiling at her from across the group, as Millicent's sister, Claire, insinuated herself on Debenham's other side.

"I declare, even though it's June these events are still unmitigated crushes, don't you think?" Claire angled an inquiring gaze upward at Debenham, then smiled coyly. "I don't believe we've met, sir."

Theo glanced at Angelica, then stepped into the breach. He introduced Millicent and Claire, then had to perform the same service for Julia Quigley and Serena Mills, who, seeing the Attenwell girls had found a devastatingly handsome new gentleman, hurried to join the expanding circle.

Although not pleased with the interruption, Angelica seized the moment to cool her overheating senses and reclaim her wits, suborned by Debenham's too-handsome face, mesmerizing eyes, and disconcertingly tempting body—a novel occurrence for her. She'd never suffered such an *enthrallment* before. She'd certainly never got lost in a man's eyes before.

Admittedly, he was her hero, which presumably explained his marked effect on her. Nevertheless, that he could so effortlessly capture her senses and steal away her wits left her wary.

Millicent, Claire, Julia, and Serena had claimed the conversation, animatedly performing, their bright gazes flicking again and again to Debenham, clearly hoping to engage him, yet while he paid polite attention, he made no response.

Angelica slanted a glance at his face. The instant she did, he looked down and their gazes touched . . . locked.

A heartbeat passed.

She caught her breath and looked away—at Julia, presently relating some thrilling story.

Debenham's gaze lingered on her face for a moment more, then he, too, looked at Julia—and shifted fractionally closer to Angelica.

Her heart leapt, then thumped heavily.

He felt it, too. He was as intrigued by the link between them as she was.

Well and good. Now how to capitalize, how to gain them an opportunity in which to explore further?

A hidden violinist tested his strings.

"At last!" Millicent all but jigged. "The dancing's starting again." Her shining eyes shamelessly implored Debenham to ask her to dance.

Before Angelica could react, he brought his cane forward and leaned more heavily on it.

Millicent saw, realized she shouldn't force him to explain an injury that prevented him from dancing; enthusiasm undimmed, she turned her encouraging gaze on Millingham.

Who accepted the cue and solicited her hand.

The other gentlemen stepped up to do their duty by asking the ladies beside them to dance; accepting that Debenham wouldn't be swirling about the space clearing in the salon's center, Claire, Julia, and Serena accepted with alacrity, and the group dispersed.

Leaving Angelica standing between Debenham and Theo, and facing Giles Ribbenthorpe. Theo met her eyes, smiled and saluted her, nodded to Debenham and Ribbenthorpe, and moved away into the crowd.

Ribbenthorpe, who could read the signs as well as any other man, nevertheless arched a brow at her and, lips curving, inquired, "Will you dance, Miss Cynster?"

"Thank you for the invitation, Ribbenthorpe, but I believe I'll stand out from this set. However, Lady Cavendish will be thrilled to see you on her floor, and Jennifer Selkirk"—she tipped her head toward a young brunette standing alongside her dragon of a mother— "could do with rescuing. I suggest you play St. George."

Ribbenthorpe turned to survey the Selkirks, then laughed, bowed, and, still smiling, walked off. Angelica was pleased that he acted on her suggestion and drew Jennifer onto the floor.

Finally alone with Debenham, she dropped all pretence of acceptable social distance and pointedly directed her gaze at his cane.

He hesitated, but then obliged. "An old injury from before I first came to town. I can walk, but can't risk dancing—my knee might well collapse under me."

Raising her head, she studied his face. "So you've never waltzed?" She loved to waltz, but if he was her hero . . .

"Not never. I was old enough to have learned and indulged at country balls prior to the accident, but I haven't waltzed since."

"I see." Leaving that disappointment aside, she turned to more immediate concerns. "So if you haven't been circling the floors at Almack's or anywhere else, what avenues have you been pursuing in your quest to find your bride? You're not easy to overlook—given that I, and Millicent and company, too, were unaware of your existence until this evening, I would own myself surprised if you'd attended any of the major events this past week."

His eyes again held hers, as if gauging what would be acceptable to tell her.

She tipped up her chin. "Don't tell me—you've been haunting some gaming hell, or carousing with friends."

His lips curved in wry amusement. "Sadly, no. If you must know, I spent several days organizing to have some rooms in my London house refurbished, after which my first social forays were, unsurprisingly, into the clubs. Given I've been absent from town for so long, it was . . . unexpected, but gratifying to find so many still remember me." He paused, then added, "Then Lady Cavendish's invitation arrived, and I thought it time to test the waters."

"So I've caught you at your first ton event."

"Indeed." He heard her satisfaction. His eyes searched her face. "Why are you preening?"

"Because, in ton parlance, that means I've stolen a march on all the other young, and not-so-young, ladies."

He looked down at her as if inwardly shaking his head. "As much as I find your candor refreshing, are you always this forthright?"

"Generally, yes. Creating unnecessary complications through overnice adherence to the social strictures has always struck me as a waste of time."

"Is that so? Then perhaps you'll tell me—in all candor and without any overnice adherence to the social strictures—why you inveigled Curtis to introduce us."

She opened her eyes wide. "*You* were hunting *me*."

He held her gaze. "So?"

She'd expected him to deny it; the look in his eyes, an expression she associated with an intent and focused predator, made her breath tangle in her throat, but she evenly replied, "So now I'm hunting you."

"Ah. I see. That must be some new twist in the customary matchmaking dance." He glanced briefly around, then returned his gaze to her face. "Although I confess I haven't noticed any other young ladies being quite so bold."

She arched her brows. "They're not me."

"Clearly." He looked into her eyes for a moment more, then said, "So tell me about Angelica Cynster."

His voice had lowered; along with his changeable, mesmerizing eyes, it lured her on, as if reeling her in. She decided it wouldn't hurt to let him think he was succeeding. "Anyone who knows me will tell you that I'm twenty-one going on twenty-five, and am commonly held to be the most confident, stubborn, and willful of all the Cynster girls, and none of us could be described as wilting flowers."

"You sound like a handful."

She arched a challenging brow at him and didn't deny it.

The musicians launched into a second waltz. He hesitated, then said, "If you would like to dance, please don't feel obliged—"

"I don't want to dance." She glanced around. The attention of all those not waltzing was focused on the dance floor, on the couples now whirling. "Actually . . ." She looked up and caught his gaze. "I'm finding it rather warm in here. Perhaps we might stroll on the terrace and get some air."

He hesitated; again she got the impression that he was inwardly shaking his head at her, and not in an approving way. However . . . "If that's what you wish, by all means." Gracefully, he offered her his arm.

She put her hand on his sleeve, felt steel beneath the fabric, and smiled delightedly, as much at herself as at him. Her pursuit of her hero was underway.

His cane in his other hand, he very correctly escorted her to the open French doors that gave access to the terrace and the gardens beyond. Stepping over the threshold onto the terrace flags, she breathed in, savoring the near-balmy night. A wafting breeze caressed her nape, her throat.

The Cavendish House gardens were old, the trees large and mature, their thick canopies shading the steps at either end of the long terrace and deepening the general darkness of the night. She looked around, noted several other couples strolling in the faint light of the quarter moon, and steered Debenham in the opposite direction.

He noticed; although he obliged, when she glanced up, into his eyes, despite the shadows she sensed his disapproval, underscored by the set of his chiseled lips.

She widened her eyes. "What?"

"Are you always this . . . for want of a better term, forward?"

She tried to look offended, but her lips wouldn't oblige. Regardless of any disapproval, he'd fallen in with her suggestion; they were slowly strolling further down the terrace that ran the full length of the salon. "I realize that gentlemen like to lead, but I'm impatient by nature, and also direct. I want to get to know you better, and you want to get to know me, and that requires being able to converse in private, so"—she waved at the expanse of deserted terrace before them— "here we are."

"We've only just been introduced, and you've engineered a private interlude." His tone held more resignation than complaint.

"I see no point in wasting time, and"—she glanced pointedly at the salon's wide windows—"trust me, there's nothing the least illicit about this. We're in plain sight of the entire room."

"All the occupants of which are facing the dance floor." He shook his head. "You're as bold as brass." His gaze rose to her hair. "Just like your curls. Your brothers have my sympathies. You have two of them, I believe."

"Indeed. Rupert and Alasdair—or Gabriel and Lucifer, depending on whether you're within hearing of our mother or aunts."

"I'm surprised neither of them is here, lurking in the shadows, ready to step in and ride rein on you."

"I grant you they would try were they here, however, happily, these days they have better things to do—wives to attend, children to dote over."

"Nevertheless, you strike me as the sort of mettlesome female who requires a permanent keeper."

"Strange though you may think it, not many would agree with you. I'm generally held to be remarkably sane and thoroughly practical—not the sort of female any perspicacious gentleman would attempt to take advantage of."

"Ah—so that's why no one seems to be keeping any close eye on you."

"Indeed. It's an outcome of being viewed as twenty-five, rather than twenty-one."

He glanced back along the terrace; she did, too, noting the two other couples still strolling near the door.

When she looked back at him, he said, "You said you wanted to talk. About what?"

She studied his face, taking in the telltale features, the clean, strong lines that unequivocally placed him in her social class. "I'm puzzled that I can't place you, that I can't recall ever having seen you. When were you last in London? Theo thought it was four years ago."

"It was five. I first came to town in '20, and the last time I graced London's ballrooms was in June of '24. I've visited the city on business over the intervening years, but had no time for socializing."

"Well, that explains it—I wasn't presented until '25. But perhaps you remember my sisters?"

He nodded. "Yes, I remember them, but in those days I wasn't interested in *young* ladies. I spent more time avoiding them than chatting with them, and I don't believe I ever spoke with your sisters. We were never introduced."

"Hmm . . . so your return to the ballrooms in search of young ladies is something of a novel endeavor for you."

"You might say that. But tell me, what of you?"

They'd reached the end of the terrace; halting at the top of the steps leading down to a gravel path, she glanced out into the gloom of the garden. The light thrown by the salon's windows ended several yards back; the spot where they now stood was enveloped in dense shadows cast by nearby trees.

Drawing her hand from his sleeve and turning to face him, putting her back to the garden, she met his gaze and arched a brow. "What do you want to know?"

"You're clearly very much at home in this sphere. Do you spend all your time in London?"

Looking into his shadowed face, she smiled. "As a Cynster, I've been a part of the ton for all my life, so it's hardly surprising that I'm at home within its circles. That said, I spend only the months of the Season in town, and perhaps a month during the Little Season. For the rest of the year I'm in the country, either in Somerset, where I was born, or visiting family and friends."

"Do you prefer the country, or town?"

She paused to think.

He glanced back along the terrace.

Idly following his gaze, she saw the last of the other strolling couples returning inside.

Then he looked at her again, and she refocused on his eyes. "Whether I prefer town or country is not easy to answer. I enjoy being in town with all the associated amusements and entertainments, but if, in the country, I had other things to occupy my time, my energies— other challenges to satisfy me—then I suspect I could be entirely content remaining far from London."

He looked into her eyes for a long moment, then glanced down and propped his cane against the balustrade. "I have to admit"—straightening, he met her gaze—"that that's something of a relief."

"A relief?" She wanted to know, so she asked. "Why?"

He looked into her eyes, and she looked into his. Time seemed, oddly, unexpectedly, to suspend, to thin and stretch. Slowly, gradually, puzzlement rose and grew; she let it show in her eyes.

"My apologies." The words fell from his lips, soft and low, so deep they were almost a caress.

She frowned. "What for?"

"This."

Clapping one hand over her lips, wrapping his other arm around her, he picked her up. Holding her against him, he went swiftly down the steps and into the garden.

Shock, complete and absolute, held her frozen as he carried her into the deep shadows under the trees.

Then she erupted.

Behind his hand, she screamed, then wriggled and fought against his hold, but his body was as hard as rock, and the arm locking her against him might as well have been iron for all the give in it. Realizing the futility, she abruptly went boneless, slumping in his hold.

He halted in a small clearing along the path, screened from the house by thick shrubs, and eased her down until her feet touched the gravel; she held to her pretend-faint, waiting for her moment.

He released her suddenly, whipping his hand from her face, but at the same time spinning her around so that she teetered, tottered. Eyes wide, she flung out her arms, wildly tipping as she fought for balance. Raking the darkness—where had he gone?—she steadied, straightened, and sucked in breath to scream—

A silk handkerchief whipped over her head, across her lips and cinched tight; her scream was reduced to a muted shriek. She felt him knot the material at the back of her head. Jerking away, she whirled to face him, simultaneously reaching up to drag the gag away.

He'd moved with her; from behind, he caught both her hands, one in each of his, and drew them out, around, back and down. Ruthlessly locking her wrists in one hand, he held them low, her arms pulled straight, and stepped close behind her; she was about to drop to the ground when his other hand closed about her upper arm. "Don't fall—you'll wrench your arms if you do."

She tensed to struggle again.

"Calm down. Despite all appearances, I'm not going to harm you."

She responded with a tirade, smothered by the gag; furious, she squirmed, tugged, tried to break free, but that was hopeless. She tried to kick him, but he was too close, and all she was wearing was ballroom slippers. She couldn't even hit him in the face with the back of her head because he was so tall.

Throughout her efforts, he stood like a rock, his grip on her hands unbreakable.

Her breath coming in pants, the muscles in her arms starting to ache, her hair tumbling around her face and neck, she quieted.

He bent his head, his voice falling through the darkness from above and a little to the side. "I repeat—I'm not going to harm you. I will explain this, but not here, not now. Rest assured I need you hale, whole, and healthy—I'm the last person who would hurt you, or allow anyone else to, either."

He was supposed to be her hero! She hauled in a huge breath, felt her breasts rise dramatically. While one part of her, the furious, betrayed, ready-to-do-murder-or-at-least-scratch-his-eyes-out part, wasn't prepared to believe a word he said, the more pragmatic and practical side of her listened to his tone, rather than his words, and suggested that she at least hear him out.

He believed what he was saying.

When she stood and waited, he went on in the same definite and faintly dictatorial tone, "I need to speak with you at far greater length. I'm going to carry you out of this garden and put you in my carriage. No, I'm not going to release you then—I'll have you driven to my house. We can talk there."

"Vul-oo-ntt-mm-gum-afa-da?"

Silence, then, "Will I let you go after that?"

She nodded.

He hesitated, then said, "Actually, that depends on you."

She tried to look back and up at his face. Frowned direfully in that direction. "Wa-sis-sis?"

"You'll learn all soon enough." He leaned back, then she felt her shawl being untangled from about her elbows. It slid away.

The next instant, she felt the soft material being looped about her wrists. The fiend was tying her hands with her own shawl! There was nothing she could do to prevent him tugging the binding tight.

Before she could even tense to break free and race back to the house, he bent and swept her off her feet and up into his arms.

She cut off her squeal, squirmed, then realized that his hold, the fingers of one hand perilously close to the side of her breast, the fingers of the other burning her thigh through the silk of her skirts, was best left as it was. She subsided in smoldering silence. And tried to gather her wits enough to think.

The path cut through a small open area; in the faint light, she saw him glance at her face.

She narrowed her eyes, hoped he could feel the fulminating glare she bent on him.

If he did, he gave no sign. "My carriage is in the alley." Looking ahead, he ducked under a low branch. For all the difficulty he had in carrying her, she might as well have been a small child. "And just so we understand each other, I had no intention of kidnapping you tonight—the soiree was supposed to be purely reconnaissance." He glanced down at her again. "But you set the stage so perfectly, what was I supposed to do? *Not* take advantage, let you go, and pray that fate granted me another chance, at some other time?"

So it was *her* fault he'd kidnapped her?

He stepped out from under the trees, and the faint moonlight touched his face.

Eyes narrowed to shards, from behind the gag she gritted out, "Ou. Ill. Ay. Pfh-is."

He'd glanced down at her. He studied her face for a moment, then arched his brows and looked ahead. "Indeed. I suspect I will."

The path ended at a wooden gate set in the garden's high stone wall. Debenham juggled her, unbolted the gate, swung it open, and carried her through, into the alley that ran beside the house.

A carriage was waiting in the darkness. She glimpsed a coachman on the box and a groom jumping down. The latter hurried to open the nearer door.

Trussed and gagged, and in the presence of three large men, she didn't bother struggling or trying to resist as Debenham, the fiend, lifted her into the coach; he set her on her feet, spoke briefly to his groom, then climbed in after her—which left very little space for her to do anything at all.

One huge hand on her shoulder eased her down until she sat on the leather bench seat. She sniffed. The carriage smelled musty. Was it hired? She glanced at Debenham as he sat across from her; his legs were so long that his knees flanked hers.

Then he bent, captured her feet between his hands, and raised them, tipping her back against the seat. Ignoring her outraged shriek, he swiftly bound her ankles with . . . his groom's kerchief?

"Mmurgh!" She tried to kick at him, to no avail.

"Wait." Smoothing down her skirts, he rose; her feet slid to the floor. "If you'll allow it, I'll retie your wrists in front of you. Otherwise you're going to be rather uncomfortable until I get you into my house."

She glared at him, but, as before, that had less than no effect. She was still trying to make sense of what was happening, as if her wits were still catching up with the action. She couldn't imagine what he was about; he was supposed to be her *hero.*

When he simply stood, staring down at her and waiting, making a grumbling, grudging sound—one promising hellish retribution—she swung on the seat and presented him with her bound hands.

He bent over her. She tensed, waited, but in untying her wrists he gave her no chance to wrench one free and strip away her gag; he was large enough, his arms long enough, to reach over and around her. One of her hands in each of his, he brought them forward and retied them even more securely, wrapping and trapping her fingers in the folds of her shawl.

Bah! How the devil was she to get out of this?

Presuming she wanted to get out of this.

The errant thought struck with such disconcerting force that she was momentarily distracted.

Long enough for the fiend to lift down a carriage blanket from the rack above her head, shake it out, solicitously wrap it about her shoulders . . . then he swept her knees up and sideways, tipping her lengthwise onto the seat.

She shrieked, then futilely fought as he ruthlessly wrapped her securely in the blanket, then settled her on her side on the seat, rolled and trussed, her arms held down, her legs straight. "*Va-a-ou-ouing?*" From her ignominious and utterly helpless position, she scowled blackly up at him.

He stood towering over her, his head bent because he was too tall for the carriage; he looked down at her for a moment, then calmly—in that deep, utterly sinful voice—said, "If you have the slightest sense of self-preservation, you'll stay as you are. Once the coach starts to move, as it will in a moment, if you try to wriggle you'll end on the floor. I'm sending you on to the mews behind my house—it's not far. I'll rejoin you there as soon as I can."

He was leaving her? "Wrr-rar-rou-rooing?"

"Back to the soiree. I'll leave once your disappearance has been noticed and enough people see me still there." He looked down at her for a moment more, then turned to leave. "Trust me," he said. "You'll be perfectly safe."

He stepped down from the carriage and closed the door.

Straining her ears, she listened to him speak to his coachman. She couldn't distinguish the direction he gave—that damned voice of his was so smoothly deep—but she heard the coachman's reply.

"Air, m'lor."

She froze. *Aye, my lord.* Except that wasn't how it had sounded.

The coachman was Scottish. And not from anywhere civilized, like Edinburgh, but from the wilds of Scotland.

A coincidence?

Primitive sensation swept over her nape.

The carriage rocked, then rumbled slowly off. Her mind abruptly racing in a dozen directions, she barely registered the turn out of the narrow alley into a larger street.

Black-haired, large, a nobleman. *A face like hewn granite and eyes like ice.*

But it couldn't be. The laird was *dead.* He'd fallen off a cliff and plunged to his death. They hadn't found his body yet, but . . .

And Debenham was well known among the ton. He wasn't Scottish . . . yet she knew several Scotsmen who spoke perfect, unaccented English.

Debenham was known to have a badly damaged knee. No one had mentioned the laird limping along with a cane . . . but Debenham had left his cane on the terrace, and she hadn't noticed him limping as he'd trapped her and carried her to the carriage.

And his eyes . . . she wouldn't have said they were cold, not as she'd seen them, but she could imagine that, if he so wished, their expression might grow chilly . . .

She dragged in a strangled breath. She could barely believe what her wits were screaming.

She'd been kidnapped, possibly by the laird.

Definitely by her hero.

Chapter Two

The carriage rocked and rattled over the cobbles. Angelica lay on the seat, grappling with the realization of what had just happened. Of what was happening now.

She dragged in a breath, held it, then wriggled and fought furiously against the restraining blanket.

It eased not at all; her fiendish captor had tucked the ends in tight. The carriage rolled around a corner, and his prediction nearly came true; flinging herself back, she only just saved herself from falling off the seat.

Abandoning all thought of immediate escape, she huffed out a breath, lay still, and tried to think. Tried to decide what was what, so she could then decide what to do.

She'd been kidnapped by a man who bore a striking resemblance to the supposedly dead laird, the mysterious nobleman behind her older sisters' kidnappings. Heather had been kidnapped first, then several weeks after Heather had escaped, Eliza had been snatched from inside St. Ives House. Angelica tried to imagine what Heather and Eliza had felt on realizing they'd been captives. Shock, horror, terror, fear—some combination of those?

Studying her own roiling emotions, all she could find was anger, in several shades, some of it directed at herself, various threads of incredulity and disbelief, and beneath all else an incipient feeling of betrayal. Debenham was her hero, yet he'd trussed her up like a package and stolen her away. Just the thought sent her temper spiraling. If he truly was the laird come back to life, then, as she'd warned him, he would pay.

The carriage turned ponderously again, and the light from the streetlamps faded. Darkness closed in. Tipping back her head, she shook her hair off her face and peered out of the window in the nearer carriage door. The carriage slowed, then halted, settling on its springs. Eyes adjusting, she saw a shadowed wall of old stone.

Debenham had said his house wasn't far; given the very short distance the carriage had traveled, he'd spoken the literal truth, and said the house was near Cavendish House, which in turn was just around the corner from Dover Street. She had to be within minutes of her home.

The coachman and groom remained on the box, quietly talking. She listened, but couldn't make out their words.

Debenham had said the carriage would take her to the mews behind his house, that he would come to fetch her after her disappearance from the soiree was noted.

She'd gone to Cavendish House with her mother, Celia, her aunt Louise, and her cousin Henrietta. Given the crowd in the salon and the nature of the gathering, she doubted any of the three would notice her absence until they were ready to depart; only then would they look for her.

Which meant she had at least an hour in which to decide how to react to Debenham when he reappeared.

Should she be frightened?

No matter how deeply she dredged, she couldn't find any fear. Even in those minutes when he and she had wrestled beneath the trees, she hadn't been afraid. Shocked and furious, yes; fearful, no. At no time had her instincts, until that night invariably reliable over alerting her to men with undesirable intentions, detected any threat emanating from Debenham; they had detected what she'd read as sexual interest, but no threat.

She thought back to the moment she'd first seen him, when he'd been watching her so assessingly . . . she inwardly squirmed. She'd interpreted his interest in her as personal, while he'd been studying her as a target.

Ouch. She grimaced around the gag, felt heat warm her cheeks. *How embarrassing.*

His disapproval of her forwardness now made sense; he'd seen her as a flighty, mindless, tonnish miss taking an incomprehensibly stupid risk. She'd all but thrust herself into his arms and invited him to make away with her.

That didn't mean he had to take me up on it.

But he had, which meant there was something wrong somewhere. She'd only acted with such brazen boldness because she'd been beyond convinced that he was her hero. But he couldn't be her hero and be her kidnapper as well. *That's impossible. I refuse to accept that I'm fated to fall in love with a kidnapper.* No. Either he'd made a mistake, or she had.

Decide whether to be afraid, first. She thought back over all he'd said, compared that with what she'd learned of Heather's and Eliza's kidnappings; in both instances, the laird had ordered his henchmen to take excellent care of their captives.

Debenham had assured her several times that he intended her no harm of any kind. Closing her eyes, she replayed his words, carefully considered his tone. He'd been absolutely sincere. More, even though he'd ruthlessly subdued her, bound her, carried her off, and placed her in his carriage, she doubted she'd sustained so much as a bruise. Even now, while she wasn't exactly comfortable, she wasn't in pain, not even true discomfort.

Not physically. Mentally . . . she was in a *state*, something she rarely, if ever, endured.

She was angry, confused, and curious. While the first and the last were widely regarded as her besetting sins, confusion was not something she normally indulged in. Confusion had no place in her world, a world she managed, organized, and ruled. Confusion meant a lack of knowing, and she always knew—what she wanted, what she felt, how her life should be.

Her confusion lay entirely at Debenham's feet.

He couldn't be her hero. She tried to tell herself that her instincts had been wrong, that The Lady's charm had failed. That somehow the signs had been twisted or corrupted. She reminded herself that he hadn't responded to her in any encouraging way—she might have thought at the time that he had, but that had just been him leading her on . . .

The minutes ticked by as she lay in the dark and argued with herself.

She had no idea how much time had elapsed when she finally gave it up as a lost cause.

Her instincts remained unmoved, her confidence in The Lady and her talisman unshaken. She *knew* exactly what she had known when she'd set out to arrange an introduction to Debenham. Nothing that had happened since had altered that knowledge or changed the unassailable conviction stemming from it.

He *was* her hero.

Which meant that everything else was wrong.

All right. Lips thinning behind the gag, eyes narrowing, she nodded. *So I'll wait until I learn what this is all about, and then I'll change it.* Change the situation, change him. Remake him if necessary. *Whatever it takes, he* will be *my hero.*

She'd always hoped securing her hero would be a challenge; it appeared she'd got her wish.

So. She blew out a breath. *No fear, not unless I discover some reason to be frightened. I'll find out what's going on and go forward from there. As The Lady and I aren't* wrong, *then there has to be a way, and clearly it's up to me, and entirely in my best interests, to find it.*

Debenham had said that he would explain all. Once he did, she would take charge.

She settled to wait. Waited.

Waited some more.

Where the devil is he?

She'd reached the point of muttering dire imprecations when the coachman and groom abruptly fell silent, then the carriage rocked as the groom jumped down. Stilling her tongue, she listened, yet she didn't know Debenham was there until he opened the carriage door. For such a large man, he moved all but silently.

She stared stonily at the dark silhouette that was him, all but filling the doorway. "Ou-t-u-tine."

He looked at her for a moment, then climbed into the carriage. "Matters took longer than I'd hoped. Your family didn't leave until nearly the end of the soiree, then I was waylaid by a friend as I left." He slid one large hand, then his arm, beneath her, and hefted her up.

Still wrapped like a mummy, she bit her tongue and held still as he maneuvered her out through the door.

When he had her free of the carriage, he hoisted her over his shoulder.

"*Mmph!*" Wriggling furiously, she glared down the long length of his back.

His arm tightened about her legs, trapping them against his chest. "Just wait. I'll carry you into the house and untie you there."

She recognized his tone. His voice was even deeper, but he might have been one of her brothers talking to some female they were resigned to protecting.

Resigned?

Her temper boiled again.

A corner of the blanket had fallen over the back of her head, but she could see to either side. As Debenham started walking, she glimpsed the coachman and groom, but they were merely shadows in the gloom.

Debenham ducked and carried her through a gate in a high stone wall into what appeared to be an extensive back garden. She looked about, trying to get some idea of where his house was. What she saw didn't definitively answer the question, but from the areas she glimpsed—kitchen garden, small orchard, various outbuildings, paved courtyard outside the back door, with raised gardens of lawns and shrubs stretching to either side—this was one of the old mansions still to be found in some of London's best streets.

The restricted glimpses she caught of the house confirmed that; old carved stonework surrounded the windows, and the house rose three stories and more above the rear gardens, its massive bulk outlined against the night sky.

She was still deep in the heart of the ton.

Both Heather and Eliza had been whisked directly out of London, but neither had been kidnapped by the mysterious laird himself. Angelica was increasingly certain that the broad shoulder over which she lay belonged to that elusive nobleman.

She was looking forward to the moment when he removed her gag.

He carted her into the house via the back door. The huge room beyond was warm, comfortable, and well lit. Chairs scraped; the instant Debenham walked into the light, exclamations erupted from several throats.

"Merciful heavens! Is that her?" A woman with a Scottish accent.

"I thought you were planning on just looking tonight." An older man, also Scots.

"The countess's rooms are ready, my lord." A much more refined individual, not, Angelica thought, Scottish. "The candelabra are lit—I thought you might wish to view the refurbishing."

"Good. Miss Cynster and I will talk up there." Her captor handed something—his cane?—over, then proceeded to walk through the room.

Angelica caught fleeting glimpses of the three she assumed were members of his staff—a neatly dressed maid, an older man whose attire suggested he was a majordomo, and a short, slightly rotund individual who bore all the hallmarks of a gentleman's gentleman, and now held the cane. All three looked surprised, but pleased, positively *happy* that their employer was returning from his evening's entertainment with a kidnapped lady wrapped like a package and slung over his shoulder.

Debenham ducked through another door and into the corridor beyond; as the servants' hall fell behind, Angelica frowned. What the devil was going on? He'd kidnapped her and his staff thought that was wonderful?

Were she to attempt an escape, clearly she could count on no assistance from them.

Debenham pushed through a swinging door and continued into a large front hall. She saw a wealth of fabulous paneling, impressive Jacobean doorways, arches, and leadlight windows, but all were wreathed in dust and cobwebs, suggesting that the house had been closed for years. Reaching the bottom of a massive staircase, Debenham turned and started up. He didn't seem to even register the extra weight of her, riding like a rolled rug over his shoulder.

He stepped onto a wide landing, turned left, and went up another flight. The balustrade was of dark, heavily carved wood; everything she saw—the table on the landing, the ornate flambeau flanking it—

was of excellent quality, but outdated. Long out of fashion.

Gaining the first floor, her captor turned into a gallery, then paused before a door, opened it, and walked through. He turned to close it, allowing her a quick survey of the room. If what she'd seen of his house thus far had made her wonder, the elegance and expensive comforts of this room banished any doubt that Debenham commanded wealth as well as station.

Lit by two silver candelabra, the large room was a lady's sitting room. A pretty chaise covered in gold-and-ivory silk sat facing a delicately decorated marble fireplace. The gold framed mirror above the mantel was huge, reflecting ivory silk wallpaper stamped with small gold fleur-de-lis. A mahogany writing desk sat before one window, a fine straight-backed chair before it. An enormous Oriental carpet in gold, browns, and cream covered the polished floor.

A door in the wall alongside the fireplace stood open, giving her a view of the room beyond and the massive four-poster bed it contained. She recalled the valet's words. These were the *countess's* rooms. Which presumably meant that there was, or had been, a countess, and the house was most likely still owned by an earl.

Two large armchairs upholstered in gold velvet sat on either side of the hearth. Debenham walked to the chair further from the door, stooped, then lifted her from his shoulder and sat her in the chair.

She shook the blanket back from her head and, ignoring the hair cascading over and around her face, *glared* at him.

His lips thinned. "Yes, I know. I apologize unreservedly for my methods, but bear with me."

She let her expression convey her response: She didn't have much choice.

He hesitated, then slowly, carefully, lifted the hair that had fallen over her face and smoothed the silky strands out of her eyes, off her cheeks. His fingertips touched, faintly brushed, her forehead, her cheeks, and she battled to suppress a sudden shiver of awareness.

Lips even more compressed, he reached around her, loosened the blanket, and began unwinding it. She shifted as required; between them, they unwrapped her. Finally drawing the blanket away, he tossed it behind the chair.

Spine poker-straight, gaze fixed forward, her bound hands resting in her lap, she waited for him to undo the gag still firmly over her lips.

Standing between her and the fireplace, he looked down at her. Finally, she glanced up at him, eyes narrowing in clear warning.

Impassive as ever, he studied her face, then said, "This house is very large and sits in its own grounds. If you scream, other than me and my staff, no one will hear. But, I repeat, I have no intention of harming you, not in any way. I've brought you here because I need to talk with you. Privately, and at length. I need to explain to you what's going on." He held her gaze. "And why I need your help."

That last phrase altered everything. It shifted power from him to her, in six words transforming him from kidnapper to supplicant. She searched his eyes, confirming that he'd uttered the words deliberately, that he wasn't the sort of man who didn't understand the consequences of such a statement. Curiosity welled anew, along with impulses significantly more commanding. He was waiting for some sign; eyes locked with his, she inclined her head, signaling her willingness to listen.

He reached for the knot in the silk handkerchief. A moment later, he peeled the fabric from her face. She went to speak, and discovered her lips and mouth were bone-dry.

"Wait." Stuffing the handkerchief into his pocket, he unpicked the knot in the shawl about her hands, then leaving her to free them, he crossed to a cabinet along the wall, a feminine version of a tantalus. He poured a glass of water and brought it to her. "Here."

Laying the shawl over the chair's arm, she took the glass in both hands, raised it . . . and stopped. She considered the liquid inside the cut crystal, then looked up at him.

His lips thinned again. He took back the glass, drained half in one gulp, then held it out to her. "Satisfied?"

His tone made her lips want to twitch, but she kept them straight and with a regally gracious inclination of her head, accepted the glass, sipped, and nearly sighed.

"My feet." She held them out. They were still bound.

He crouched beside her to work at the knot.

She hadn't intended *"my feet"* to be her first words, but having him remove the restraint gave her an extra minute to marshal her thoughts. If he needed her help . . . she couldn't imagine how, but if that was what this kidnapping was about, then perhaps he wasn't so far from her hero-ideal as she'd thought.

Courtesy of her struggles, the knot in the kerchief had tightened; while he concentrated on loosening it, she studied his face, closer and better lit than before.

What she was looking at was a mask, a rigid, uniformly uninformative shield. Whoever Debenham was, he kept his emotions, his self, locked away, completely concealed behind that distractingly attractive screen.

The binding about her ankles fell away. He fluidly rose.

"Thank you." She clung to the graciously civil, sensing it pricked him; she was a long way from forgiving him for treating her as he had.

Glass in one hand, she settled into the comfort of well-padded luxury.

He considered her for a moment, then, crossing to the other armchair, he sat, effortlessly achieving an ineffably graceful, elegantly masculine pose.

She sipped again and stared at him over the rim of her glass. She'd grown up surrounded by large, graceful, physically powerful men, yet Debenham put all those others to shame; he was undeniably the most gorgeous male she'd ever seen. It wasn't just his face—so harshly handsome and framed by that black mane that suggested barely restrained wildness—nor was it merely the coldly sculpted planes of his cheeks or his fascinating eyes and lips that riveted her. It was all that he was—all the above coupled with a body that was perfectly proportioned, his long legs those of a man who rode frequently, his shoulders almost impossibly broad, yet all of a piece with the width of his chest and the heavy muscles of his upper arms. His hands were large, blunt fingered, and strong, yet she knew he was capable of using them gently; she got the impression he was a man very aware of his strength, and used to being careful with it.

If she'd thought to physically design her hero, she wouldn't have done as well. He sat in the armchair, his gaze on her face, his expression impossible to read—a dark Adonis with changeable eyes, and he was hers.

And she might as well start as she meant to go on. Her eyes on his, she demanded, "Who, exactly, are you?"

A frown passed behind his eyes, but he answered. "Dominic Lachlan Guisachan, eighth Earl of Glencrae." Her eyes widened. He searched her face. "Do you recognize the title?"

"No." She frowned. "Should I?"

Slowly, he shook his head. "I just wondered if you did."

"And Debenham?"

"One of my lesser titles."

She frowned more definitely. "Why be the viscount rather than the earl?"

"Because the earl is from the highlands, while the viscount is not." He paused, then went on, "I'd assumed I'd have to slink around the ton's fringes to track you, but when I reappeared in London a week ago, I discovered the ton still thinks I'm Debenham. My late father withdrew from London forty years ago. The ton has forgotten him, and the title, too. His death passed largely unnoticed down here. During the years I spent in London, I *was* Debenham, an English title with an estate outside Peterborough. I'd seen no reason to advertise either my Scottish background or that I was heir to an earldom—I had trouble enough beating off the matchmakers as it was. Presumably because of all the above, my succession to the earldom hasn't registered, so as Debenham I can circulate in society, and as long as I avoid the other Scottish peers—Perth, Dumfries, all those who would recognize me as Glencrae—no one will think to connect me with the attempts to kidnap your sisters."

She stared at him. "Just to be clear—you *are* the laird? The Scottish nobleman behind these tiresome kidnappings?"

"For my sins, yes."

He didn't look happy about it, yet in openly approaching her, he'd taken what seemed to her an inordinate risk. "Avoiding all Scottish peers . . . what if one of them had glimpsed you and mentioned it, and it got back to my family, as such things are wont to do? A Scottish peer of your size, coloring, and age—that's exactly what my family have been combing the ranks for."

"Luckily for me, the majority of Scottish peers prefer Edinburgh society. If they do circulate here, it's generally not in the same circles as the Cynsters. On top of that, most Scottish peers will by now have retired to their estates for the summer hunting. All of which left me reasonably safe hunting you here."

"What about Breckenridge, and Eliza and Jeremy, too? All three saw you, albeit at a distance."

"As newly affianced couples, your sister Heather and Breckenridge, and Eliza and Jeremy Carling, are not presently gracing the ballrooms. Hoping to avoid them while tracking you was an acceptable risk."

"But everyone in the family has heard descriptions . . ." She broke off.

"Precisely. Being tall, heavily built, and black-haired isn't enough to raise suspicions, not when I speak without a Scottish accent and am widely known as an English viscount."

"And the cane." She glanced at his left leg. "Is your injury real, or a convenient fabrication to aid your disguise?"

He didn't actually sigh, but she got that impression. "Nothing I've told you this evening has been anything other than the literal truth. My original injury was serious and long-lasting—I used a cane through all my earlier years in London. I haven't used it for the last four years, but I recently jarred my knee, so I've had to resort to the cane again, at least while in society. So it's true that I don't waltz. But, fortuitously, having the cane only strengthened everyone's view that I was Debenham come back." He paused, then said, "Not even you suspected. When did you realize?"

"When I heard your coachman's accent." She considered him, then said, "I have one, highly pertinent, question. Why aren't you dead?"

He regarded her, then frowned. "Why would anyone imagine I'd died?"

"Possibly because you fell off a very high cliff when you rescued Eliza and Jeremy from Scrope."

His frown evaporated. "I fell onto a ledge about twenty feet down. Scrope missed it. He fell to his death, not me." Apparently instinctively, his hand stroked down his left thigh. He noticed and stilled the hand. "It was the fall that jarred my old injury." The black slashes of his brows drew down again. "But when only one body was found at the base of the cliff—"

"The bodies—body, apparently—was retrieved by drovers, and those tracking them haven't caught up with them yet. So no one connected with the family knows that there was only one body, not two."

"So your family thinks I'm dead." He refocused on her face. "And that's why there wasn't any guard watching over you."

"Dead men pose no danger. Of course, my disappearance will throw the family into an uproar again." She sipped, then added, "And eventually the drovers will be found, and the family will realize you're still very much among the living."

"And then they'll want my head."

"At the very least. However, they still don't know who you are." She let a moment pass, then, trapping his gaze, arched her brows. "So why am I here?" She spread her hands, indicating their surroundings, including him. "You said you would explain."

His eyes fixed on hers. She got the impression he was ordering his thoughts. After a moment, he said, "I could explain the whole, but that will take hours, and for our purposes tonight, all you need to accept—"

"No."

He blinked. "What?"

"*No.*" Jaw firming, she held his gaze. "No, I am not going to let you give me half an explanation. Or even less!" She flung out an arm. "You've just *kidnapped me from a soiree* in order to speak with me, 'privately and at length.' I suggest you get to it, and don't think to skimp."

His face locked. She couldn't be certain, but she thought faint color touched his cheeks.

Meeting his gaze, maintaining her own in the face of the not-so-subtle aura of power—old, aristocratic power—emanating from him, she was reminded yet again that he was a man of her class, one who ruled, whose ancestors always had.

"For a twenty-one-year-old chit, you're a bossy little thing."

She smiled, falsely sweet. "Indeed. And I believe you said you needed my help."

Silence ensued. She knew he could move with startling speed, as he had on Lady Cavendish's terrace, but in common with other large, strong, and very intelligent men she knew, he also had the ability to remain totally still, and often did.

It was a ploy, but not one that would work with her. She now knew what he was, appreciated what he was capable of, but she wasn't about to be intimidated. Ensconced in the armchair, she held his gaze and boldly broke the silence. "I would suggest, my lord earl, that this interview will go very much better if you start at the beginning."

After a very long moment, he drew a deep breath. "The beginning? In that case . . . what do you know of your mother's life in the months before she wed?"

She blinked. "Your story starts there?"

Temper severely reined, Dominic Guisachan, eighth Earl of Glencrae, nodded. He hadn't been looking forward to this interview, and given his captive was proving very different from the spoiled, pampered, ton princess he'd expected, he was anticipating enjoying the experience less with every minute. Spoiled and pampered Angelica Cynster might be, but she was also sharp-tongued, quick-witted, more observant and insightful than was comfortable, and he was starting to suspect she had a spine of honed steel. She'd told him no. He couldn't remember the last time anyone had . . . other than his mother.

When she stared at him uncomprehendingly and made no reply, he gritted his teeth and rephrased his question. "What do you know of the circumstances of your parents' wedding?"

A line appeared between the perfect arcs of her brows. "They eloped and married at Gretna Green." She blinked. "Is that why you had Heather taken there?"

"Yes, and no." He waved the point aside. "That's much later. I thought you wanted the beginning?"

"Yes, well." She waved imperiously back at him. "Get on with it, or we'll be here all night."

They'd likely be there all night anyway . . . "Do you know why your parents eloped?"

"Yes. Mama's parents had organized a marriage to some nobleman—some old earl—but Mama had fallen in love with Papa. Her parents, however, preferred an earl over a duke's fourth son and were pressing Mama to accept the earl, so she and Papa eloped and married over the anvil at Gretna Green."

"Do you know the name of the earl your mother refused to wed?"

The line between her brows reappeared. She studied his face. "You're going to tell me he was the Earl of Glencrae. Your father?"

He nodded.

"And . . . ?"

Her impatience touched a nerve. "As I believe I mentioned, I hadn't expected to kidnap you tonight, so I haven't prepared any neat dissertation." When she made no reply, just met his gaze steadily, he swallowed his temper and began. "Mortimer Guisachan, seventh Earl of Glencrae, was in his early forties when he met Celia Hammond, a young English beauty. Barely nineteen, she captivated him, almost certainly unwittingly. Mortimer doted on her. He wanted nothing more than to have Celia for his wife. He approached her parents, who were entirely agreeable, and all was progressing— or so Mortimer thought—toward the altar. Being a strictly conventional man, Mortimer hadn't spoken to

Celia directly, leaving it to her parents to inform her of her good fortune, as was common in those times. A week later, Mortimer received word from the Hammonds that Celia had eloped with Lord Martin Cynster and had married St. Ives's fourth son at Gretna Green."

Angelica's eyes had widened. He paused, but she waved for him to continue.

"You need to comprehend that Mortimer was not a passionate man. I didn't say he loved Celia. His was an avuncular, even patriarchal regard. Consequently, understanding that she loved Martin Cynster, and seeing the couple together on their return to the capital, Mortimer accepted that Celia was truly happy and withdrew—not just from her life, but from the ton, and from London. He closed up his house"—*this house*—"and retired to his castle in Scotland."

"In the highlands?"

He nodded. "Courtesy of Mortimer's father's long reign, the estate was prosperous, the clan faring well. Mortimer went home and left Celia and Martin to their lives. However, his fixation with Celia didn't wane. He discovered he couldn't live without knowing how she was, what she was doing, and isolated in the Scottish highlands by his own choice, he turned to living vicariously through her. He inveigled old friends to write to him of her exploits, and within a few years he had paid observers among the ton who regularly—at least every week—sent letters north, telling Mortimer of every little detail of Celia's life. Celia's, and eventually her children's, because Mortimer's obsession extended to them."

This time when he paused, she simply waited, eyes glued to his face, for him to resume the tale. "But Mortimer was head of the clan and needed to marry and get himself an heir. His younger brother had never been groomed to be the laird, the earl, so Mortimer accepted the duty, took himself to Edinburgh one Season, and found a wife. Mirabelle Pevensey was from a lowland family, of excellent birth but limited fortune, spoiled beyond all reason, and widely lauded for her startling beauty. Although much older, Mortimer was yet a handsome man. His obsession with his lost love was common knowledge in Edinburgh at the time, but Mirabelle viewed that as a challenge, one that, once successfully overcome, would gain her a certain social accolade. She determined to conquer Mortimer, to wean him from his fixation with a distant English lady and make him her devoted slave. She set out to secure his love and every last iota of his attention for her own, and with her undeniable beauty, she was confident of success. She married him and happily went with him into the highlands, fully expecting to have him wrapped around her little finger if not within the month, then certainly within the year.

"Instead, she discovered she couldn't compete with Celia, and even less with Celia's children." He held Angelica's gaze. "Mortimer knew every minute detail of your brothers' lives—he knew their grades at Eton, what sports they favored, what their interests were as they matured. He knew every ailment they ever contracted. He forgot Mirabelle's birthday if she didn't remind him of it, but he never forgot Celia's, or Rupert's, or Alasdair's. Assuming it was the children Mortimer most fixated on—for how could he remain devoted to Celia when she, Mirabelle, was so much more striking and there in the flesh—Mirabelle decided to do her duty, and so she bore Mortimer a son."

Angelica regarded him steadily. "You."

He nodded. "Me. But sadly for Mirabelle, although Mortimer was a kind and affectionate father and paid as much attention to me as I wished, my advent did nothing to alter his obsession with Celia and her brood." He glanced down at one hand, fingers spread on his thigh. "I gather my birth was difficult. Consequently, in producing me Mirabelle felt she'd paid her dues, not just to my father but to the clan, as well. She waited for what she considered her just reward, but it didn't eventuate. I can only guess, but I believe she thought that if she simply waited, then as I grew, Mortimer's affection for me would continue to grow, and ultimately would shift to include her, too.

"So she found patience, and waited. Although Mortimer had no interest in rejoining society—Celia and her family were all the society he needed—he had from the first been happy to allow Mirabelle to use the house in Edinburgh and join society there. She never did, which puzzled everyone, until much later when, as a young man, I moved among Edinburgh society and discovered that she'd been corresponding with her bosom-bows from soon after her marriage, telling them she'd broken Mortimer from his obsession with Celia, and that he now doted on her. Her letters had painted her life as she'd wanted and wished it to be, not as it was. Consequently, even though she was free to visit Edinburgh, she couldn't, not without Mortimer fawning at her feet. So she was stuck in the highlands, waiting, still waiting, and growing increasingly bitter.

"Eventually, she realized her strategy was never going to bear fruit. Your sisters, and you, had been born by then, and Mortimer was in alt. He constantly prattled about your exploits—if he'd doted on Celia, he was positively besotted with her daughters."

Glancing at Angelica's face, he found her frowning at him.

"You must have hated us—all of us."

"No. Not at all." He paused, then, accepting he had to make a clean breast of even that, went on, "The truth was I was perfectly happy to have my father distracted by Cynsters. That left me free to range as I would, and with the clan all around me I never lacked for either companionship or mentoring. I had cousins and uncles to teach me riding, hunting, fishing, shooting—every activity a boy could wish for. I had aunts and pseudo-aunts to feed me soup and tend my scrapes. Because of Celia and her offspring, I had a much more . . . colorful and satisfying childhood than I otherwise would have had, and for that"—he inclined his head—"I thank you and yours."

"But your mother . . ." Angelica was sincerely shocked. "That must have been painful."

He held her gaze, after a moment said, "Mirabelle wasn't exactly maternal—she never saw me as anything other than a pawn in her game, and children notice things like that. Even as a young boy I didn't trust her, but you don't need to pity me for that—I had clan all around me, and no one could have had better care." He paused, then added, "The right sort of care—I wasn't spoiled. I was just one of a dozen of us who ran wild through the summers and always had dozens of adults watching out for us. That's what clan is, what it's for.

We're all family." He exhaled. "Which brings me to the next development in Mirabelle's tale.

"When she gave up all hope of claiming my father's regard, she tried to reclaim me—more or less from the clan. I was twelve at the time. She hoped to make me her puppet so that when Mortimer died—he being so much older than she—she would be able to control the clan, and the clan's purse-strings. So she tried to draw me back under her wing, and discovered she couldn't. Mirabelle was from the lowlands and didn't understand—had never tried to understand—how the highland clans work. When she suddenly tried to own me again, the clan closed around me and wouldn't give me up. No one openly opposed her, but whenever I was home from school, she could never find me—I was always out, about, never where she could catch me, drag me into her sitting room, sit me down, and try to control me.

"After a while, she stopped trying. I—we all— assumed she'd finally accepted her lot. She'd never made the slightest effort to be a part of the clan—to be the laird's lady in any real sense. She looked down on the clan and had no one as a friend to help pass the years. She grew even more bitter, more resentful and withdrawn." He paused to draw breath. "Then, when I was twenty and home from university, I fell and badly hurt my knee. I was laid up for weeks, a captive, and Mirabelle tried once again—this time to turn me directly against my father."

He paused. Angelica wondered if he knew his eyes had turned not just cold but to a shade that fully justified the description *"eyes like ice."*

"I don't know how far she would have taken things, because I cut her off—corrected her mistaken impression that I harbored any ambition to accede to the title before my father died an entirely natural death—as soon as I understood her direction. She was at first utterly disbelieving, then furious, but there was little she could do. I warned my father and those around him, and that was largely that. Once I recovered, as soon as I could I left for London and for the next five years spent much of my time down here. When I went home, I spent my time with my father, with clan, and out and about the estate. I already knew much of what I would need to when the earldom passed to me, so there was little reason to stay in the highlands for any length of time."

He paused, then leaned forward; resting his forearms on his thighs, he refixed his gaze on her face. "That's all necessary background, but the events that led to my present predicament—and the reason I need your help—start here. During the period I spent largely in

London, the seasons turned bad, the crops failed, and times grew hard for the clan. In '23, my father came to London for the first time in over thirty years to ask for my blessing for a deal he'd worked out to save the clan. I listened, and I agreed with his scheme."

His gaze fell to his hands, hanging between his knees. "The scheme hinged on a goblet my family has had in our keeping for centuries. The tale of that goblet is unconnected to the present situation, and other than satisfying your undoubted curiosity, will explain nothing more than why the goblet holds great value for a coterie of London bankers." Linking his fingers, he glanced at the mantelpiece clock, then met her eyes. "If you will accept that the goblet is fabulously valuable, we can avoid the distraction."

She searched his eyes, then nodded. "You can tell me the tale of the goblet later."

He straightened, then leaned back in the chair. His gaze returned to her face. "Very well—so we're in late '23, with the goblet in hand and my father desperate to keep the clan's businesses afloat. Although the earl, the head of the clan, owns and manages the lands and businesses, by custom all clan members draw income from said businesses, so if the businesses fail, the entire clan fails. It wasn't only his family's future at stake." He paused, then went on, "The deal he'd devised and sought my approval for was with a group of London bankers. In return for the goblet, they'd agreed to hand over a significant sum, more than enough to reestablish the clan's finances. However, as I mentioned, my father was a deeply conventional man. Because of our family's history with the goblet, he couldn't bring himself to hand it over—I, however, had no such qualms. So the deal was set, signed, and the money handed over, and my part in it is to hand over the goblet to the bankers on the fifth anniversary of my father's death."

He studied her eyes, then abruptly stood. He walked to the tantalus and poured himself a drink. Angelica used the moment to take a sip of her water. His story had held her mesmerized; if she was parched, he had to be, too.

"My father was neither a good laird, nor a bad one." He spoke without turning around. "He was a relatively gentle man, no saint, but he always did the best he could for the clan. Over his time as laird, he did little anyone might complain of, but conversely he did nothing to actively further the clan's holdings, to grow the businesses. If he hadn't made that deal, the clan would have been destitute. It shouldn't ever become that vulnerable again—I've spent the last five years ensuring that—but it's primarily my grandfather's legacy I've built on."

He drained the glass he'd filled, then refilled it, turned, and walked back.

She raised her gaze to his face. "When are you due to hand over the goblet?"

He let himself down into the chair. "On the fifth anniversary of my father's death—the first of July this year."

"And . . . ?"

His gaze locked on hers; there was a chilling coldness behind his eyes. "In January this year, the goblet went missing. It was kept in the estate safe, and I checked it every month. Only I and my steward had the combination, and neither of us had told anyone, let alone moved the cup." He paused, sipped, then, his gaze shifting to rest, unseeing, on a point beyond her chair, he went on, "The next day my mother informed me that she had taken the cup and had hidden it. I have no idea how she'd opened the safe, but the family jewels are also kept there. Presumably at some point my father had opened the safe for her and she'd noted the combination."

Angelica did not envy his mother; his tone had changed to one of icy control, reined menace lending every word a cutting edge.

"Mirabelle has her own agenda—she informed me that she'll return the goblet, allowing me to complete the deal and save the clan, provided I give her what she wants."

When he rested his head back against the chair but didn't go on, Angelica prompted, "So what does she want?"

He lowered his gaze to her face. "She wants revenge on your mother."

"My mother?" Angelica frowned. "Why? And how?"

"Why? Because she holds Celia responsible for all that's gone wrong in her miserable life. And because Celia won—despite everything Mirabelle did, your mother retained her hold over my father until the day he died, even though she'd never known anything about his obsession." He paused. "As for the how . . ." Raising his glass, he sipped, then locked his gaze with hers. "All I have to do is seize one of Celia's daughters, and ruin her."

Angelica stared into eyes that showed no hint whatever of any mental disturbance. He was utterly serious. "Ruin how, exactly?"

He nodded. "I asked her that. Apparently I was to kidnap one of you—she didn't care which one—and take you north to the castle, and by that act you would be socially ruined, and Mirabelle would have her revenge through knowing she'd caused Celia untold pain by wrecking the life of one of Celia's daughters, in return for Celia wrecking hers."

Angelica studied him, his eyes, his expression, then asked, "Is your mother insane?"

"On this subject, so I would suppose. However, she's otherwise perfectly lucid, and more than clever enough. Wherever she's hidden the goblet, no one has been able to find it. We've searched high and low, multiple times. But the castle is huge, and old, and . . . we're running out of time."

"If she doesn't give you the goblet, and you can't give it to the bankers on the first of July, what will happen?"

He hesitated, then, voice lower, replied, "The way the deal was done, the account, as it were, can only be settled with the goblet—no amount of money can stand in its place. If I don't hand over the goblet on the first of July, I, and the clan, lose the castle and all clan lands—glen, loch, and forests—and all the clan businesses, too. The clan will be dispossessed and destitute. The collateral on which the deal was based was all clan assets."

"Good Lord—*all?*"

"All." His expression grew harsh. "It didn't seem any great risk at the time—I had the goblet to complete the deal." He refocused on her. "Now I don't—which is why I need your help."

Her head was spinning; there was so much to take in. "Assuming I believe all this"—which she did; it was too fantastical a tale to concoct, and the man before her was anything but fancifully inclined—"how, exactly, do you see me helping you?"

"I never intended, and still do not intend, to bow to my mother's dictate. I initially searched for every possible alternative other than acceding to her demand. However, there is no way to save the clan other than by handing over the goblet . . . so I looked for a way to make it appear that she was getting what she wanted, without that actually being the case."

"You set out to trick her. Good. How?"

He searched her eyes. His lips fleetingly eased, but then his expression closed again. "The only way I could think of was to capture one of Celia's daughters and make a deal with her—essentially throwing myself and the clan on her mercy." He held her gaze. "I was prepared to argue with whatever weapons I had, and in order to set the stage to make such a bargain with one of you, to tip the scales my way as much as possible, I arranged to have one of you kidnapped and brought to me in Scotland—and it had to be a real kidnapping because how else was I to get one of you appropriately alone, away from your family and in my keeping long enough to persuade you to my cause? I could hardly present myself in Dover Street, beg an audience, and make my case. Your family would never have allowed any of you to come north with me alone. And it had to be alone. While Mirabelle might be unhinged over Celia, she is otherwise sane. If she sees any Cynsters or even a maid from your parents' household around, she'll know there's no real 'ruination,' so the kidnapping itself had to be real." He paused, studied her eyes. "I first hired Fletcher and Cobbins—you know about them?"

She nodded. "They kidnapped Heather."

"And took her to Gretna Green. And yes, I chose that location because it fitted with your parents' story, and also because it might have been useful in inducing whichever Cynster sister was brought there to . . . accept the deal I intended offering her. But Heather escaped, so I sent Scrope after Eliza, but she escaped, too." Their gazes locked, he hesitated, then said, "I had thought that if I, personally, wasn't involved in the actual kidnapping, then whichever of you was snared, you'd be more inclined to at least hear me out, and perhaps be more amenable to accepting my offer."

Given her reaction to him treating her as he had, even for so short a time, she had to agree with his reasoning. "One question. Why did you pull back when Breckenridge rescued Heather? Why did you do even more, and risk your life to help Eliza and Jeremy get away from Scrope?"

He hesitated. When she faintly arched her brows and simply waited, he exhaled, then said, "At the time each of your sisters was kidnapped, she was known *not* to have developed a partiality for any gentleman. I have my sources, and that was confirmed. My plan couldn't have proceeded if that hadn't been the case, if she'd already been attached to another. Once an attachment formed . . . my only concern was to see the pair safely away." He met her gaze. "Given you pursued me tonight, I assume that, in your case, you haven't fixed your interest on any gentleman as yet."

She had, but he didn't need to know that.

He was studying her face closely. "From what I've gathered about your sisters' recent betrothals, betrothals consequent on being drawn into my plans, they haven't been harmed by my actions—by being kidnapped by my hirelings."

She stopped herself from nodding. Considered, then allowed, "I don't believe they would hold their adventures and subsequent betrothals against you, if that's what you're asking."

Relief was a fleeting shadow in his eyes, then those changeable eyes refocused on her face. "Which brings us to the here and now."

"Indeed." She held his gaze. "So what was the offer you intended to lay before the Cynster sister you snared?"

Her, as matters had fallen out.

His eyes locked with hers. She returned his gaze steadily and waited.

"Clan means everything to me—it's my life, and I would give my life for it, and every one of my people would do the same. There is, however, one thing that stands above clan, a line I will not cross even in this instance. The family motto encapsulates it: 'Honor above all.' " He paused for a heartbeat, then said, "I planned to ask for your help, to ask you to travel to the highlands, to my castle, with me, and once there to play out a charade to convince my mother that you're ruined, a charade sufficiently convincing for her to be satisfied and hand over the goblet. I can't tell what such a charade might entail, but as I mentioned, she apparently believes that you simply being kidnapped and taken north will be sufficient to do the deed."

"For most young ladies, that would be enough. However, in my case, my family will conceal my disappearance until they discover what's happened to me . . . and then they'll devise some other tale so that I won't be ruined and socially ostracized regardless."

"You and I know that, but thankfully, my mother doesn't. She has little real notion of English society, and no concept of the ways in which a family such as yours operates."

She studied his face. "So what's your part of this bargain? What do I get in return for such assistance?"

He met her gaze. "To balance the scales, and to ensure that you aren't, in fact, ruined in even the slightest degree, should you agree to help me in this, I will make you my countess, give you the protection of my name in marriage, and agree to abide by whatever—any and all—arrangements you wish to stipulate as to our future lives."

He'd spoken slowly, clearly, his tone measured and even; Angelica knew she'd heard every word correctly.

He'd offered her himself.

His eyes searched hers, then his jaw firmed. "I tried for your older sisters first because I know you're only twenty-one and presumably still have starry-eyed notions of love and a white knight who'll sweep you off your feet. Against that, as you haven't yet formed any attachment to another, I'm hoping that, coming from a family such as yours, you'll recognize the advantages of what I can, and will, offer you as my wife."

His gaze locked on her face, he shut his lips and waited.

She sat and stared back at him, reacting not at all, held back by unprecedented inner chaos. Her dominant bold and confident self wanted to beam with delight and seize his offer with both hands, but a less familiar, cautious self had reared her head, screaming at her to wait, to *think*.

For once, she listened to that rarely heard voice of reason.

She searched his eyes; she could only hope her own expression gave away as little as his did. He held her gaze levelly, steadily, fearlessly, even though she knew he was fully aware that his entire life hung on this moment, on how she elected to respond. She was the last Cynster sister available for his plan.

That plan . . . was outrageous, but could—and if it was in her hands, would—work. It didn't take much thought to confirm that.

He was a wealthy earl and had already told her enough to answer all the usual pertinent questions. In ton terms, he was a highly eligible suitor for her; she didn't need to know more on that score.

She could feel her heart thudding, but it wasn't excitement that had her in its grip.

He *was* her hero. Nothing he'd said had altered that conviction, only underscored it. And he'd just offered to marry her and allow her to dictate how they lived their future lives . . . on the surface, that appeared an offer she should leap on, grasp, and later, after, use to demand . . . what?

That he love her?

He'd offered her his name, his title, his purse, his houses, along with his body and a certain regard, but that was all.

She knew men like him, knew love wasn't something any lady could demand from them. More, love wasn't an emotion men like him fell victim to readily; he would instinctively guard against it, resist it if it struck, and shield himself from it as far as he was able.

Yet he *was* her hero. She might not love him yet, but if she believed in her instincts, in The Lady's guidance, at all, then if she spent much time with him, she would.

She couldn't be so foolish as to close her eyes to the fact that he was proposing to marry her in cold blood— just as his father had married his mother. Did he see the parallels? What he was offering was in essence a dynastic marriage, which given the situation, for him was a necessity, but for her was a choice.

His offer left her facing a decision more fraught than any other Cynster female of her generation, or the previous one, had faced.

If she accepted his bargain, she would fall in love with him, but would he fall in love with her?

If she accepted his bargain, fell in love with him, then discovered that he couldn't love her . . . what then?

What of the life of love and shared happiness she'd always imagined would be hers?

She could refuse the bargain. Refuse to help him. Couldn't she? Eyes still on his, she quietly asked, "What if I refuse?"

His face didn't alter, but his eyes grew bleak. His voice, however, held to the same measured and even tone as he replied, "If you can't see your way to assisting me, I'll return you to your home within the half hour. Your family will have concealed your absence thus far, and you arriving home with whatever tale you wish to tell will ensure that you take no lasting harm from my . . . interference with your evening."

He was speaking the truth, as she suspected he had throughout. But if he returned her to her home, she would never see him again. And if she ever whispered anything about him to her family, the males, at least, would ferret out the truth and try to force a marriage, which would be infinitely worse.

She wanted him as her hero, wanted him to love her, needed him to grow to love her, and the only way forward was, apparently, to take the risk—to lay her heart on the scales, to risk it, risk all, and trust that everything she'd ever believed of love would come true.

Blind, unconditional trust . . . in love.

She'd wanted a challenge—here it was.

Was she brave enough, courageous enough, to accept it? To take him on, fight for his love, and win?

She'd been staring into his mesmerizing eyes. She blinked, then locked her gaze with his again. "I have . . . a few questions."

He arched a brow, inviting her to ask.

"Should I refuse, and you send me home, what will you do after that?"

He held her gaze; several moments ticked by before he replied, "I don't know. I haven't thought beyond this moment."

Because he understood, as she did, that this was his last, final, and ultimate throw of the dice.

Raising the glass she still held, she drained it, then set the empty glass on the small table by her chair. "First, I want a promise from you that, before we reach your castle, you will tell me anything pertinent that you've not yet revealed, as well as anything and everything I wish to know about your mother, the castle, and your clan." Looking up, she met his gaze. "I don't wish to find myself in a situation where you've withheld information because you thought I didn't need to hear it, or that you didn't need to sully my ears with it, or any similar excuse."

His lips tightened, but he inclined his head. "Granted. All of it."

"And I wish to rephrase the bargain—are you willing to consider my terms?"

His gaze grew intent, sharper and more incisive. "As you're perfectly aware, you have me over the proverbial barrel. Whatever you ask, if it's in my power to give, I will give it."

She tipped up her chin. "In that case, my terms are these. I will agree to help you save your clan. Specifically, I will travel to your castle with you and enact a charade sufficient to have your mother return the goblet so that you can complete your late father's deal with the bankers and save your clan and its holdings." Watching his eyes, she saw confusion creep into the gray-green; he thought she'd agreed to everything. Drawing breath, she continued, "However, as to the matter of marrying you, I reserve the right not to make that decision until after you have the goblet in your hands."

His black brows drew down. He regarded her with what she could only interpret as suspicion, with a healthy dose of disapproval behind it. Eventually he said, "If you travel north in my company—even if you remain here for the rest of the night—your family will demand a marriage between us as the only acceptable outcome."

"Yes, they may—or at least, the men will. But we've already touched on how the social strictures can be circumvented if families like mine put their minds to it." Holding his gaze, she felt increasingly confident that in this she was taking the right tack. "Those are my terms—take them or leave them. I'll help you get back the goblet and save your clan, but the question of a marriage between us will remain unresolved until later, your offer to remain on the table until I decide whether to accept or not."

Chapter Three

Dominic Guisachan, Earl of Glencrae, a highland laird accustomed to absolute rule, absolute command, stared at the diminutive female sitting in the armchair opposite and fought an irrational impulse to scowl. He had no idea what she was up to.

He rapidly replayed the exchange, but could see nothing in it to account for the determination that had slowly infused her, for the resolution he could see in her expression, in the set of her chin, the curve of her lips . . .

Nothing to account for the instinct that was screaming at him that he'd just, somehow, stepped into some snare.

What snare? It was his plan. And how could her *refusing* to agree to marry him possibly be a trap?

He shook off the feeling; perhaps it was some strange symptom of inexpressible relief.

He looked at the mantelpiece clock. It was nearly three o'clock. He and she had been talking for hours. He glanced at her. She didn't look overtired, but focused and aware. Engaged, alert, and subtly challenging in a way he found viscerally alluring—

He blocked the sudden awareness of his half-aroused state. Complications of that ilk he didn't need. "Very well. I accept your terms." He paused, then tipped his head down the room to the desk before the windows. "If you wish to write a note to your parents, I'll have it delivered. As you've no doubt guessed, their house isn't far."

"Hmm." Her lips, rosy and full, firmed, then relaxed. "I appreciate the offer and would prefer to let them know I'm safe, but I'm not sure where they'll be—at home, or will they have gone to St. Ives House by now, or perhaps to Horatia and George?" She arched her brows, then met his eyes. "If you'll agree to have a note delivered in the morning after breakfast, I suspect that will be preferable. It will also give me time to think of how best to phrase it."

He studied her face, wondering . . .

"No, I'm not imagining that I'll change my mind." She regarded him measuringly. "And I'm assuming you realize that you can't send any note in my stead. It'll have to be in my handwriting. Anything else risks escalating the family's collective anxiety, and that's precisely what we need to allay." She wrinkled her nose. "As best we can."

He had been thinking of sending a note if she didn't, but . . . she was correct. "It's late." He rose, set his empty glass on a side table, then looked down at her as she raised her gaze to his face. He hesitated. He didn't want to give her a chance to change her mind, but . . . "Sleep on your decision. If you're still of the same mind in the morning, we can discuss the matter further and work through the necessary details."

"I won't change my mind."

"Nevertheless." Turning, he headed for the door; he needed to get out of there—to somewhere without any distractions, so he could think. Grasping the doorknob, he looked back at her. "I'll send up a maid to attend you. You should find all you'll need in there." With his head, he indicated the bedchamber next door.

"Thank you." She paused, then inclined her head. "Good night."

He responded with a curt nod, then went out and shut the door. Releasing the knob, he stood for a moment, then shook his head. He couldn't understand why he felt so off-balance; he should be rejoicing.

He exhaled. Experience had taught him to distrust anything that came too easily, especially if it came via the hand of fate. *Everything* about the evening had gone far too easily, too pat, almost as if his plan had grown legs and run away with him—only to be brought up short when she'd rescripted their bargain.

Inwardly grimacing, he turned for the stairs. He could do nothing but accept her counteroffer and go forward. Too much was at stake for him to even waver.

Reaching the front hall, he strode for the servants' hall. He wasn't surprised to find lamps burning and his entire staff sitting about the central table waiting to learn of the outcome of his meeting with Miss Cynster, their prospective savior. The five numbered among his most trusted people: Griswold, his valet, Mulley, his majordomo, Brenda, the senior maid, Jessup, his coachman, and Thomas, his personal groom.

He halted, met their expectant gazes. Nodded. "She's agreed."

A fervent "Thank God!" was the communal response.

"Brenda—go up and help her to bed. And please sleep on the truckle in the dressing room. I don't think she agreed just to sneak out later, but I don't want to take any chances."

"Aye, m'lord." Brenda rose, picked up a candle, lit it, and went.

Dominic looked at Jessup. "It seems we won't be needing the carriage again tonight. However, by dawn tomorrow I expect the Cynsters to have thrown a cordon around the entire town. I want you and Thomas to set out at first light and carefully check how tight it is. We're going to need to find some way through it, but initially all I want to know is that it's there, and what form it takes—how they watch, through whom, and where."

"Aye, m'lord." Jessup nodded, as did the much younger Thomas. "We'll put the carriage away and turn in."

Dominic nodded a dismissal. As Jessup and Thomas rose and headed for the kitchen door, he transferred his gaze to Griswold and Mulley. "Despite her agreement, we should keep watch on the front and back doors through the night. Just in case."

"I'll take the front," Griswold said.

Mulley nodded. "I'll stretch out here, then."

"Thank you." Dominic turned and walked back into the house, canvassing his arrangements, looking for anything he might do that he hadn't already done. Angelica and her agreement to help him were too important—to him and to so many others—for him to risk leaving any opening or having any weakness in his plans.

He knew she'd agreed, yet his instincts weren't convinced, weren't yet ready to accept that, after all the dramas and mishaps, the missteps and unforeseeable calamities of the past five months, he'd finally succeeded in securing what he and his clan needed to survive.

He'd finally got a Cynster sister in his keeping and had persuaded her to aid him.

That the Cynster sister in question was the one of the three with whom, had he had the choice, he would have preferred not to deal was neither here nor there.

That she was already showing signs of being significantly more assertive and unpredictable than he'd anticipated was much more troubling.

An hour later, Angelica slid from beneath the crisp new sheets and freshly plumped feather-quilt on the countess's bed. Clad in the pretty, if modest, white cotton nightgown the maid, Brenda, had pulled from the chest of drawers, she slipped through the shadows to the window.

This room, too, had been refurbished. Glencrae, evidently, knew how to plan.

Quietly, so as not to disturb Brenda, who was peace-fully sleeping on the truckle bed in the adjoining dress-ing room, Angelica slowly drew back the heavy velvet curtains, careful not to let the rings rattle.

Courtesy of Brenda's ready tongue, loosened by Angelica's assurance that she was indeed committed to helping Glencrae regain the goblet, she'd confirmed that everything he'd told her of the situation had indeed been true; if anything, he'd downplayed the serious-ness, the devastation that threatened not just the clan but him as its laird.

She doubted she had as yet truly grasped how deeply the threat affected him. She didn't know that much about highland clans, but from what Brenda and he had let fall, Angelica had gathered that clan was like a very large extended family, one even more intricately interdependent than a family like her own.

If clan was family taken to the extreme, then Dominic's position was equivalent to Devil's taken to extreme . . . and Devil, and how he would feel if such a situation threatened the welfare of the entire Cynster family . . . that, she could imagine well enough.

Luckily for Dominic, fate and The Lady had ar-ranged for her to be his helpmate. Easing back the latch on the casement window, she carefully pushed the pane wide. Breathed to herself, "Just as well for him that he got me, and not Heather or Eliza." Heather wouldn't have wanted to do it, and nor would Eliza, for the simple reason that he wasn't their hero. They were also significantly less qualified for the role, being far less bold, adventurous, and inventive, and also less histrionically gifted.

Also far less steely in resolve, one quality that was going to be essential, both in the quest to regain the goblet and in her personal quest to capture the Earl of Glencrae.

Her natural confidence had reasserted itself. Nevertheless, she stood at the open window and couldn't explain the impulse that had driven her there.

Regardless, she leaned out, looked down and around. Fading moonlight shivered in the thick leaves of an old creeper; it covered the wall, reaching up and around the window, and had obviously been recently trimmed away from the window frame. For anyone with a little gumption, the old, gnarled stems provided ready access to the ground.

Looking further, she traced a path across a small square of overgrown lawn to a section of stone wall that, from its position opposite the rear gardens, had to border a main street. Old ivy grew in a straggling ladder up and over that wall.

If she wanted to escape, the path lay before her. If she wanted to leave her reckless bargain with Dominic Guisachan behind, run home, and keep her heart safe and intact, she could. It would be easy.

Bathed in the luminosity of the fading moonlight, she leaned on the windowsill and waited. Gave her heart permission to choose as it would, to consider again, to reassess.

She was fully aware of the risk she'd taken with said heart, with her life, with her future. Once Dominic had left, she'd waited for panic, or at least some uncertainty, to rise and swamp her, but neither had.

Drawing the old necklace free, she held up the pendant; in the faint light, it almost glowed. "He is my hero." The words were nothing more than a breath as she turned the crystal in her fingers. "He needs my help—help only I can give. So no matter what his vision of our marriage, I will go forward with faith that, just as I will learn to love him, he will learn to love me."

She remained at the window for several more minutes, then, finally tucking the pendant away, she drew back, quietly shut the casement, closed the curtains, and padded back to the bed.

She'd made her choice. For good or ill, she'd taken the first step, turning from the comfort and safety of her family to embark on her own adventure, her own quest for love; she wasn't going to refuse fate's challenge.

Sliding back beneath the sheet, she lay on her back and looked upward into the darkness. Boldness, confidence, and faith had got her through most of life's challenges to date. They'd get her through this one as well, and see her triumph.

The worthy things in life rarely came easily, but . . . "I'm not widely regarded as the most forceful, willful, and determined Cynster girl for no reason."

Settling beneath the sheet, she closed her eyes.

Her sole regret of the evening was that she hadn't been able to send word to her parents. She knew they would be frantic, but, quite aside from the quibbles she'd advanced to Glencrae, real enough in their way, she hadn't wanted to write until she was absolutely certain that she knew what she was doing, and that she wouldn't need to be rescued; that missive might have been her only chance to alert them to her whereabouts. But now she was convinced that her path was correct, she would send them word in the morning.

She was trying to think of appropriate phrasing when sleep crept up on her and drew her gently down.

"I don't understand." Lady Celia Cynster clung to the hand of her husband, Lord Martin Cynster, and looked at Devil Cynster, Duke of St. Ives. "How can this be? The laird is dead. So who has taken Angelica?"

Standing before the fireplace in the drawing room of Martin and Celia's Dover Street home, Devil shook his head. "We assumed the laird was the instigator of the kidnappings, but perhaps he, too, was a pawn. Regardless, I've sent men to the posting houses on all the major roads leading out of the capital. If Angelica's been taken out of London, as Heather and Eliza were, we should hear something before dawn."

It was the small hours of the morning. Standing beside Devil, Honoria, his duchess, gripped his arm. "I know it seems unlikely, but we should consider that she hasn't been kidnapped but left the soiree for some other reason. And no," she continued, as everyone looked at her, "I can't imagine what reason that might be, but we all know Angelica—it's possible."

Silence fell while the others, including Angelica's elder brother, Gabriel, and his wife, Alathea, considered Honoria's words.

Heather, Angelica's eldest sister, seated beside her fiancé, Breckenridge, pulled an expressive face. "If this had happened before we—me, and then Eliza—were kidnapped, would we have jumped to the conclusion that she—Angelica—has been kidnapped?" Heather looked around the circle of concerned faces. "Or would we have thought, as Honoria says, that she must have left the soiree for some reason and hasn't yet been able to send word?"

Alathea sighed. "There is that. Angelica is the last young lady I would imagine being kidnapped and the kidnapper managing to make away with her, not in such a setting. She would fight tooth and nail, and she's not one to be taken lightly."

"She's far more . . . well, *physical* than either me or Heather," Eliza put in from the chair in which she sat, Jeremy Carling seated on the chair's arm, his arm around her.

Devil glanced at the faces, met Gabriel's gaze, then looked at Martin. "We'll keep our searches discreet, just in case she turns up an hour from now with a perfectly reasonable excuse."

"And we ladies," Honoria said, meeting Celia's eyes, "will put our minds to thinking up some tale to cover her absence, just in case she doesn't."

Devil looked at his wife, then covered her hand on his sleeve with one of his. "If this is a kidnapping, then one way or another, we'll know by midmorning."

"Mmm . . ." Mirabelle Guisachan, Countess of Glencrae, lolled on her side, pleasantly exhausted, and gave thanks, yet again, for her lusty lover.

Of course, he was a good few years younger than she, but she'd kept her figure and her skin was still fine, especially when viewed in flickering firelight, the only way she allowed him to see her unclothed. As he generally only visited her after midnight, that was easy enough to arrange.

He lay on his back on the bed behind her, getting his breath. One large hand idly stroked her naked flank. "Have you had any word from Glencrae?"

When she didn't respond—she didn't want to think of her son, a sure way to destroy her pleasant mood— her lover came up on his elbow and pressed a heated, teasing kiss to her bare shoulder while his hand caressed the lush curves of her derriere. "Is he any closer to getting you your revenge?"

"No . . . well, perhaps he is. I don't know. I told you he left for London two weeks ago."

"But what do you think of his chances given there's only one sister left unclaimed?"

"Actually, that fact—that she *is* his last chance— seems to have finally spurred him to take a personal interest in my cause." Men always liked to have their egos stroked, so she half turned and murmured, "But I'll never forget that it was you who reminded me of the goblet. If you hadn't, I doubt I would ever have found a way to bend Dominic to my will . . . and, dearest"—raising a hand, she caressed her lover's lean cheek, then stretched up and placed a kiss on the curve of his jaw—"I *do* so like forcing that intractable son of mine to do my bidding." Smiling into her lover's eyes, she purred, "Rest assured I'll never forget your part in gaining me the revenge I so deserve. I will, I suspect, be forever in your debt."

Her lover smiled. Knowing his face was in shadow, he didn't bother making the gesture reach his eyes. Yes, he'd reminded Mirabelle of the goblet her son had had in his custody, and he'd urged her to take it, but he'd wanted the blessed thing himself . . .

He forced the hand that had been fisting at her hip to relax, forced himself to stroke her ageing skin. She'd been easy to seduce, easy to bend to his purpose, but then she'd seized on the goblet as a way to force Dominic to enact her ridiculous revenge, and had hidden the damned thing.

Bending his head, he cruised his lips over the curve of her shoulder. "You never did tell me where you've hidden the goblet. Are you sure it's safe from his people?"

She grinned. "Trust me, it's hidden in a place where no one will ever think to look. They've ransacked the castle, searched high and low, and haven't even come close."

His lips tightened. She had, for some reason, been utterly resistant to his every approach to learn where the goblet was. His hours in the castle were too short, and too fraught with the danger of exposure, for him to mount any search of his own; he couldn't afford for any of Dominic's loyal clan to see him within the walls.

"Still," she murmured, her mind drifting down its own path, "if he doesn't get me the revenge I want—doesn't bring me one of Celia's daughters and ruin her—then I will ruin him." Her voice strengthened. "Him and his precious clan. I will *laugh* as they're turned out of this place and driven from this valley."

Her words dripped vicious vindictiveness like venom.

Which, he had to admit, suited him well enough. He couldn't imagine the Cynsters wouldn't guard their daughters well. Perhaps they might even catch Dominic and string him up, plunging Clan Guisachan into abject disgrace. That prospect was one he could savor. Who knew? Mirabelle's crazy scheme for vengeance might spell disaster for Dominic and his clan on a scale even more dramatic than he himself had planned.

Regardless, when, as seemed highly likely, Dominic failed in his bid to kidnap the last of Celia Cynster's daughters and bring her all the way north to the castle, then, courtesy of Mirabelle's vindictive streak, her lover would gain all he'd ever sought in seducing her in the first place.

He would see Clan Guisachan evicted from this place, from all the fertile fields they currently possessed, from their ownership of the teeming loch and the surrounding richly timbered forests. He would see them leave, and be there, poised and ready to seize their lands.

And he would see Dominic Lachlan Guisachan devastated, derided, and left a broken man.

Slumping back in the bed, Mirabelle's lover draped one arm over her and let himself relax. With his ultimate goal all but assured, he could afford to be patient and let the silly bitch use the goblet to pursue her ludicrous revenge.

Chapter Four

In the breakfast parlor the next morning, Dominic sat and worked his way through his usual hearty meal, and brooded on why he didn't feel happy, or at the very least content.

By any standards, last night had been a coup. He'd gone to the soiree expecting to do no more than observe Angelica; this morning, she was under his roof, and had agreed to his bargain, the critical first part of it at least, and once she climbed down off whatever high horse she was on, she would see the sense in the rest and agree to that, too.

He should be ecstatic, or at least ecstatically relieved. Instead, he was unsettled, somehow unsatisfied.

"Good morning."

He looked up and watched the source of his disquiet glide into the room. She'd attempted to restrain the red-gold silk of her hair in a neat bun, but tendrils had already escaped to lick like tiny, gilded flames about her forehead, cheeks, and alabaster throat. She was, perforce, wearing the silk gown she'd worn to the soiree; the blue-green shade suited her, perfectly framing her creamy skin. Much more of the latter was visible this morning; she'd left off the lacy neckpiece that, last night, had filled in the gown's scooped neckline.

The result was potently distracting, yet, as had happened the previous evening when he'd first seen her across the Cavendish House salon, it was the way she moved that transfixed his senses.

After glancing at him, she'd halted and looked around the room. Completing her survey, she smiled at Mulley as he hurried to draw out the chair at the opposite end of the table. With an effortless, intensely feminine grace, sleek, subtle curves shifting beneath the silk gown, head held proudly, her very posture, her every gliding stride ruthlessly holding his awareness, she walked to the chair and sat down.

He was a natural hunter, born and bred to stalk, to circle, to study his prey with cold calculation until he knew just how to bring it down. It wasn't only game he hunted in that fashion, with that same cool deliberation.

The way she moved brought his hunter's instincts roaring to life, and locked them on her.

She picked up her napkin, shook it out, and laid it in her lap.

He breathed in, slow and deep, and seized the moment to reaffirm his previous assessment. By any man's judgment, she qualified as *fair*, using the word in all its romantic glory. Her skin was flawless, a milky alabaster, her cheeks tinted the faintest rose. Every line of her face, every feature, from her pale forehead, delicately arched brown brows, her large, lushly fringed green-flecked golden eyes, her straight little nose, her lips, the upper provocatively bowed, the lower lusciously full, to her firm, rounded chin, might have been drawn by a master artist intent on conveying the elemental female—graceful, elegant, delicate, yet intensely feminine, vital and alive.

She was shorter than her sisters, but with her burnished copper hair an all but living flame added to the impression of sheer feminine force she projected, her lack of inches barely registered.

No one viewing her would imagine she was mild. Meek didn't even enter her equation.

Passionate did. Also willful. Expensive, too, but that didn't concern him.

Finally looking up the long table at him, she arched a brow. "I take it this house isn't normally kept staffed."

Her voice was low-pitched for a woman, faintly husky—one tone away from sultry; another aspect of her that stirred him regardless of any intent on her part. "No. It was shut up when my father retreated from London and hasn't been opened since."

"You didn't use it while you were here?"

"It's a trifle large for a bachelor's abode." Before she could ask, he went on, "I had lodgings in Duke Street during those years."

He studied her face, then returned his gaze to her eyes; they appeared brighter, her gaze more definite and assured than it had last night. "I take it you haven't changed your mind."

"No, I haven't. I did tell you I wouldn't."

Mulley had left the room; seizing the moment, Dominic asked, "Not even about accepting my offer?"

"Especially not about that."

Mulley came back in. Dominic subsided, watching as his majordomo presented her with a rack of toast.

"As per your request, miss. Just out of the oven, so they're a wee bit hot."

Angelica smiled. "Thank you, Mulley. And my compliments to Brenda, too."

Mulley blinked, surprised but pleased that she'd known his name. She'd grilled Brenda about the household that morning, and later the maid had asked what she'd fancied for breakfast so it could be made ready.

After making sure the butter and strawberry jam were within her reach, Mulley said, "The teapot will be here momentarily, miss."

"Lovely." Angelica helped herself to a thick slice of toast from the silver rack that needed a tad more polishing. Rather like the room in which they sat. Although a nice size for a breakfast parlor, with morning sunlight streaming in through windows overlooking an overgrown garden, while someone had made an effort to make the room habitable, cobwebs still hung in the corners and dust lingered in the air and in the crevices of the ornate sideboard.

The table, however, had been thoroughly cleaned and polished, and laid with crisp new linen, while the crockery was an exquisite Sèvres with which no one could find fault.

Slathering her toast with jam, she reviewed her plans. Other than writing to her parents, she'd decided today would be a fact-finding day. She needed to learn as much as she could about Glencrae-Debenham-Dominic, in all his incarnations, and they needed to work out the next stages of his plan.

Brenda appeared at her elbow with the teapot. Mulley was hovering by the sideboard.

Mouth full, Angelica smiled her thanks and relieved Brenda of the pot. As she poured, from the corner of her eye she saw Dominic direct a look at Mulley, who, somewhat reluctantly, left the room, taking Brenda with him.

Dominic transferred his gaze to the confounding female at the other end of the table—the one he was committed to marrying, regardless of her present equivocal stance. As he watched, she took a sip of her tea, then, setting down the cup, lifted her slice of toast and took a neat bite. A tiny globule of jam decorated the corner of her lush lips; with one fingertip, she caught it, then stuck out her tongue and licked the sweetness from her finger. Slowly, as if relishing the taste . . . then she leveled her bright green-gold gaze at him and arched one delicate brow.

His face he could control. The rest of him was less manageable. Resisting the urge to shift in his chair, he forced himself to remain absolutely still, unmoved and unmoving.

He had no intention of playing such games with her, not until she agreed to their marriage, and perhaps not even then. Ladies like her needed no encouragement to use their wiles; he had no doubt that, inexperienced or not, she would attempt to wrap him around her little finger. She wouldn't succeed, but she would try; he suspected that instinct ran in her blood, just as somewhat different instincts ran in his. He hadn't forgotten that she hadn't explained *why* she'd decided to, by her own admission, hunt him last night. For some reason, she'd set her sights on him; experienced as he was, he fully intended to use that—whatever had sparked her interest, her agenda, with respect to him—to his own ends.

Ultimately, she would marry him; neither his honor nor hers would allow any other outcome. In reality, the only question remaining was when she would deign to agree.

Holding her gaze, he lifted his coffee cup, sipped, then lowered the cup.

Before he could speak, she waved her toast. "One thing that's puzzling me—you said you hadn't expected to kidnap me last night, but why, then, was your carriage in the alley, waiting?"

It took him an instant to shift mental tracks; by the time he realized that was precisely why she'd asked, he already had. He inwardly sighed; dealing with her clearly wasn't going to get easier. "Because I'm not as reckless as you imagine. I didn't know whether your brothers or cousins would attend the event as guards. If they had, I would have slipped away before they caught sight of me—having my carriage in the alley gave me an extra escape route. While as Debenham I might have been safe from the scrutiny of the rest of the ton, from them? Alerting any of them to the identity of a man even *like* the laird they were seeking wasn't part of my plan."

She swallowed, nodded. "Very wise. If they'd set eyes on you, they would have asked questions. Pointed, pushy questions, and they wouldn't have let be until they knew every last little thing about you."

"Indeed, but as I've successfully avoided their attention while managing to recruit you to my cause, perhaps we can address more pertinent issues. Such as"—he captured her gaze—"that the journey from here to the castle takes at minimum seven days. I've sent my coachman and groom to scout out your family's response to your disappearance—as I'm sure they'll be watching the roads north, we won't be able to leave immediately, certainly not today. You will, consequently, be in my company, living under my protection, for several weeks at least before I'm likely to regain the goblet. Before, according to our revised bargain, you will make your decision whether or not to accept my offer of marriage."

He paused, but could read nothing in the politely interested face she showed him. He went on, "As per our bargain, when you make that decision, the choice of where and when we wed will, naturally, be yours." Holding her gaze, he asked, "Given the lengthy time in which, as matters currently stand, you will not have the protection of my name, and that every day of that time will carry the risk of discovery, of exposure in ways that your family might not be able to manage and suppress, are you sure you don't wish to reconsider the timing of your decision?"

She frowned.

Before she could speak, he went on, "For instance, if you came to a decision today, or even tomorrow, then we could significantly reduce the risk to your reputation by marrying here, in town, before we start our journey north."

Her eyes had widened; she looked faintly shocked. "No. Oh, no." Lips and chin firming, she vehemently shook her head. "Absolutely not." Over the length of the table, her green-gold eyes flashed; lowering her teacup, she narrowed them at him. "*Should* I decide to become your countess, our wedding will occur once this matter is settled, once you've handed the goblet to those bankers and reclaimed full command of all that is yours, castle and estate. The ceremony will, indeed, be held here in London. It will be a huge, lavish, ton affair, and, I promise you"—she flashed him a sharply edged smile—"it will be lauded as the wedding of the year."

He kept his gaze steady, refused to react when she arched both brows at him, inviting his comment. She knew—of course she did—that what she'd just described ranked among his worst nightmares . . . and that he had no choice but to agree.

She wasn't bluffing, and he got the distinct impression that in breaking the news as she had, she was paying him back . . . perhaps for wrapping her in that blanket.

And, of course, she wasn't going to let him walk away from the exchange without acknowledging defeat; her eyes locked on his, she was waiting . . .

Stiffly, he inclined his head. "As you wish. Just remember I made the suggestion."

She merely smiled and resumed sipping her tea.

He studied her, once again assessing her, as he did most people in his life, working out how they thought, how to control them. At one level or another, he managed most of those around him; learning the ways was ingrained. With her, he'd expected to be dealing with a flighty flibbertigibbet, temperamental and spoiled, someone easy to get to know, to predict, easy to manipulate. Instead, he was looking at a woman unlike any he'd previously met, and he'd yet to gain so much as an inkling of how to manage her. He had no idea what was in her mind, what was driving her, what she sought in her dealings with him. What she ultimately wanted from him.

And she'd already laid her hands on his straightforward bargain and twisted it into something convoluted, something he no longer controlled. More than anything else, he didn't approve of that.

If she'd been any other woman, he might have decided she was too difficult, too potentially resistant to settling under his reins, and walked away.

He couldn't walk away from her.

His gaze slid from her face, down over the creamy flesh exposed by the lack of her neckpiece. "What happened to the rest of your gown?"

She glanced down at the mounds now on display above the gown's scooped neckline. "My fichu? It was terribly crushed—I gave it to Brenda to wash and iron."

Her breasts had to be the same as they'd been last night, but without the lacy covering they were a lot more . . . evident. He could also now see the fine chain of gold links and amethyst beads that circled her slender neck, a pink stone pendant depending from it. The tip of the pendant dangled in the shadowed valley between her breasts, drawing his eye . . .

Mentally, he shook himself, then gave in to the urge to shift to a more comfortable position in his chair.

Munching the last morsel of her toast, Angelica reached for her teacup, congratulating herself for having listened to the instinct that had prompted her to

rescript their bargain. The more she learned of Dominic Guisachan, the more certain she grew that bringing
him to his knees in the appropriate way wasn't going
to be any simple matter. His resistance was a palpable
thing, etched in every implacable line of his handsome
face. While her determination to make him fall in love
with her had only strengthened, trying to do so *after*
she'd agreed to be his wife would never work. Yet as
long as she continued to withhold her agreement, he
would, as he'd just demonstrated, work to gain it.

Her instincts had bought her time; it was up to her
to use it.

"So." Setting down her cup, she met his eyes. "My
letter to my parents. Is there a desk somewhere?"
Dusted and with supplies went without saying.

He pushed back his chair and rose. "I'm using the
library as a study. You can write your missive there."

She waited for him to pull out her chair, then rose
and walked beside him out of the room and down a
long corridor. She looked about her as they went; the
house truly was huge. Revealing its secrets, exposing
them once more to the full light of day, and redecorat-
ing fit for this century held very real appeal.

At the end of the corridor, he opened a door, held
it as she walked through, into a long room lined with
floor-to-ceiling bookshelves. A huge fireplace occupied

the center of one long wall, while the opposite wall hosted three pairs of long windows looking out onto a square of overgrown lawn edged with tall trees. Only the nearer end of the room had been cleared of the omnipresent cobwebs and dust. A heavy, ornately carved desk faced down the room, with an admiral's chair behind it, and two armchairs angled before it. Further down the room, holland covers still swathed all the furniture.

Resisting an urge to go and peek under the covers—later—she walked to the desk. Rounding it, she looked at the welter of papers scattered over it.

Dominic walked past her to the other side of the chair, reached across, and swept the papers to one side. "Estate business. I've been attending to what I can while I'm here."

Opening the central drawer, he drew out a fresh sheet of paper and laid it on the blotter.

"Thank you." Sinking into the admiral's chair, she reached for one of the pens in an onyx-and-ormolu holder. The inkstand looked like something her brother Alasdair would enthuse over. Now she thought of it, he would enthuse over most of the objects in the house.

Smiling at the thought, she flipped up the lid of the ink pot, dipped the already nicely sharpened nib in, paused, then bent to her task.

Rather than couch her words with any degree of formality, she wrote as if she were speaking; the missive would, she hoped, be more effective that way.

While she scribbled, Dominic—she'd be damned if she thought of him as Glencrae—walked to the nearer window and stood looking out. Giving her privacy, although he would, no doubt, want to read what she wrote.

When she'd written all she thought wise, she read through the whole, then signed and carefully blotted the sheet.

Setting the pen back in the holder, she flipped the ink pot lid shut. The sound had him glancing around. Picking up the letter, she held it out. "Here."

He met her gaze, then walked to the desk and took the sheet.

Leaning back in the chair, she watched him read it.

She'd opened with an abject apology for not contacting them sooner, explained that she'd been forced to leave to help a friend in desperate need, asked that they concoct some tale to cover her absence, an absence she'd assured them would be temporary, but might perhaps stretch for several weeks, then closed with an assurance that she was absolutely and utterly safe, and in no danger of any kind.

By the time Dominic reached the end, he was frowning. "'Forced to leave'?"

"I thought that skated rather nicely around the reality." When he arched a black brow, she said, "You'll also notice I've said nothing about *where* I've gone. As you've noted, they'll most likely have assumed that this is something to do with the earlier kidnappings and have blocked the roads north, but the possibility that I'm still in town, and seem to have no expectation of leaving, should at least start them wondering. And the more they wonder, the more likely they'll pull back and start searching somewhere else. Given we have to travel to the highlands, I would prefer to do so without my brothers and cousins on our heels."

Dominic couldn't argue that. He read the letter again, confirming that her composition was perfectly gauged to, on the one hand, reassure her family, and on the other, to deflect them. Further proof that the woman beside him had mastered skills he hadn't expected her to have. A dab hand at manipulating others, he recognized that talent when he met it.

Glancing down at her, he met her wide, green-and-gold eyes. "You are twenty-one, aren't you?"

"I turn twenty-two in August." She smiled up at him. "I'll have to put my mind to what your present to me should be." Her brows rose. "Perhaps we'll have time to look in at Aspreys before we leave town."

Studying her eyes, he realized she was teasing him; he couldn't remember when last anyone had. He grunted and handed back the letter. "Address it, and I'll have Mulley arrange delivery." Crossing to the bell-pull, he tugged it.

She folded the sheet, then reached for a pen. "And how do you see this delivery being effected? I'd wager someone from the family will be watching the door in Dover Street."

"So I would expect. I'll have Mulley give it to one of the street-sweepers in Piccadilly. The lad will deliver it, Mulley will watch to make sure it gets into your parents' butler's hands, then Mulley will vanish. There won't be any way to trace the letter back here."

Finished with inscribing the address, she blotted the letter, waved it, then handed it to him. "Excellent."

Mentally rolling his eyes, he took the letter and went to the door. When Mulley arrived, he explained how he wanted the note delivered and handed it over. Shutting the door, he turned, and discovered she'd shifted to sit in one of the armchairs facing the desk.

Elbow on the chair's arm, delicately rounded chin propped in that hand, she was gazing out at the tangle beyond the windows.

Rounding the desk, his gaze on her, he reclaimed his chair.

She turned her head and met his eyes. "So with that taken care of, we should consider how we're to reach your castle. Where is it, exactly?"

"West and a little south of Inverness." He hesitated, then reached into a drawer and pulled out a map. "Here." Spreading the map on the desk, he showed her. "However, until my men return and we know what sort of net your family has placed around London, we can't make any definite plans."

Sinking back into the armchair, she compressed her lips slightly, something he'd noticed she did when thinking. Then she lifted her gaze to his face. "I agree we'll need to wait until they pull back from actively searching every coach, but even once they do, they'll have the people at the posting houses watching for me. Whatever route we decide to take, however we decide to travel, we'll need to devise some way around that."

From that unarguable conclusion, to his silent surprise they embarked on a freewheeling discussion, first listing, then evaluating all the possible routes and modes of transportation between London and Inverness. Of course, she led, but before long he found himself engaging in an energetic back-and-forth exchange the likes of which he'd never imagined having with any woman, let alone her—his kidnapped angel-cum-savior-cum-bride-to-be.

As a man who valued control, he disliked surprises, but with her, they just kept coming.

Lady Celia Cynster walked into the library of St. Ives House in Grosvenor Square waving Angelica's missive. "She's written, thank God!"

Celia was followed into the room by her husband, Martin, her daughters Heather and Eliza, and their fiancés, Breckenridge and Jeremy Carling. Celia's elder son, Rupert, better known as Gabriel, and his wife, Alathea, currently residing in the Dover Street house, brought up the rear.

They'd sent word ahead, so they weren't surprised by the gathering awaiting them in the library. In addition to Devil and Honoria, Vane Cynster and his wife, Patience, were there, as were Martin's older brothers, Arthur and George, and their respective wives, Louise and Horatia, along with Helena, Dowager Duchess of St. Ives.

Celia swept around the room, touching cheeks and receiving supporting hugs, then she handed Devil the folded note. "It arrived just as we were finishing breakfast."

Devil glanced at Gabriel. "Who delivered it?"

"A street urchin. By the time Abercrombie registered it was Angelica's handwriting, the boy had vanished."

Devil grimaced. "No doubt paid to make himself scarce."

"Yes, no doubt—but get to the point," Helena said. "Read the note. Aloud, if you please."

Thus adjured, Devil unfolded the note, briefly scanned it, then did as he'd been bid and read the contents aloud. He concluded with, "And this certainly looks like her signature."

Gabriel nodded. "It is. And the letter entire is in her hand, too."

Devil lowered the letter to the desk. He stared at it for several moments, then raised his gaze to Heather and Eliza, seated on the chaise beside Celia. "Do either of you have any idea who her 'friend in desperate need' might be?"

Both shook their heads. "But you know what she's like," Heather said. "She's gregarious. She's friends with a lot of young ladies, and quite a large number of the younger gentlemen, too. It could be any of them, yet . . ." Breaking off, Heather exchanged a glance with Eliza, who grimaced and shrugged. Turning back to Devil, Heather said, "To be perfectly honest, it sounds as if she's set off on some adventure."

"Disappearing from a ton event without trace isn't setting off on an adventure," Vane growled. "At least not one she'd planned."

Devil, grim-faced, nodded. He studied the letter again. "She could have been forced to write this."

"Do you think so?" Head tilted, Helena considered, then shook her head and turned to Celia. "Me, I cannot see it. Can you?"

"Well . . ." Celia was clearly torn by a mother's concern.

But Heather shook her head. "I can imagine her being forced to write the words, but if that were so, she'd be furious, and she'd have made sure to smudge something, or misspell a word, or scratch the paper, or something to show she was upset and acting under duress. Instead"—she waved at the note—"that's written in her usual neat hand, perfectly spelled, and with not so much as an ink splatter."

Eliza nodded. "I think she wrote it as it appears—of her own accord, and she meant every word, most likely literally."

"Which," Horatia said, "means she is indeed up to something."

Helena nodded and folded her hands in her lap. "That is how it seems to me. At least at the moment."

None of the ladies dissented. As one, they turned back to the big desk around which their men had congregated.

Only to discover said men had come to quite a different conclusion.

"So we'll continue our search," Devil stated. "Or, more accurately, our lying in wait. As there've been no sightings of any female who could possibly have been her at any of the posting inns for at least three stages out from the capital, she's almost certainly still within our cordon—still in London."

The other men responded with grim nods.

"But who could have taken her? And why?" Jeremy Carling glanced at the other men. "Are we correct in assuming her disappearance is connected to the attempts to kidnap Heather and Eliza? Or is this something else entirely?"

"That," Honoria said, rising from her chair, "is something we can all try to discover. Discreetly, of course."

"I suggest," Alathea said, also rising and resettling her shawl, "that we take her assertion that she's gone to help some friend and use it to explain her absence. It won't be hard to imply that her 'friend' is somewhere in the country, and as Heather just mentioned, Angelica does, indeed, have a lot of friends."

Using the cane she'd recently taken to wielding, Helena got to her feet. "Indeed. So now we will each, in our own way, try to identify this so-desperate friend."

Leaving the men to their various plans, the ladies headed for the drawing room to devise their own strategies.

Following the others down the corridor, Eliza linked her arm in Heather's and quietly said, "I just thought—I wonder if Angelica was wearing the necklace at the Cavendish soiree."

Heather raised her brows. "You gave it to her, didn't you?"

"Yes, when Jeremy and I returned to town. She wore it at our engagement ball."

"Hmm . . . no point asking Mama. She's upset, and might not remember clearly. Who else from the family was there, do you know?"

"No, but Henrietta should have been, don't you think?"

"Yes, she should. We can ask Louise. And if anyone would have noticed if Angelica was wearing The Lady's charm, it would be Henrietta—"

"Because she's waiting for it to be passed on to her." Eliza nodded. "We should find her and ask."

Angelica's sisters halted outside the open drawing room door. Drawing apart, they met each other's eyes.

Heather arched her brows. "Strange and dramatic events seem to overtake whoever wears that necklace."

"True," Eliza returned. "But thus far the results have been very much worth the drama."

"Perhaps Angelica's off on her own adventure."

"Let's hope so, and that her hero is there to rescue her, too."

Heather nodded and waved ahead. "Meanwhile, let's see what we can do to help cover her tracks."

Dominic and Angelica were debating the merits of riding all the way to the castle when a rap on the door interrupted them. Surprised to feel irritated by the intrusion, Dominic glanced across the room. "Come."

The door opened to admit Jessup and Thomas.

Sitting back, Dominic beckoned them nearer. "What did you find?"

Coming to stand beside the desk, Jessup shot an uncertain glance at Angelica; eyes downcast, from beneath his lashes Thomas simply stared at her.

Dominic waved. "You may speak openly before Miss Cynster. She's agreed to help us and needs to hear what you've learned as much as I do."

Jessup tipped his head toward her, then looked at Dominic and grimaced. "Everywhere, they are. They've got men watching every posting inn, literally hanging about in the yard with nothing to do but watch every single carriage and check every single passenger. We chatted with the ostlers at a few places—seems other men, some nobs, came around before dawn asking questions about anyone spotting a young lady with red-gold hair."

Dominic glanced at Angelica, saw her grimace. "What was the outcome?"

"Well, o'course, they've had no sightings, so they've left men watching, but one of the ostlers told me he'd heard from one of the guards coming down on the mail that there were men checking as far out as Buntingford. That's three stages. No carriage could do that distance, not without stopping to change horses."

"What about the roads west and east?" Dominic asked.

"Same story. They've got men watching up to three stages out." Jessup glanced at Angelica. "Your family seems determined not to lose you."

She lifted both hands, palms out. "If you knew them, you wouldn't be surprised." She looked at Dominic. "Is there any chance of going south and around?"

Dominic glanced at Jessup.

Who shook his head. "We checked that, too, but they've got even that covered. I did wonder if, on horseback and at night, it'd be possible to slip through and head cross-country for a-ways, but even to do that, you'd have to pass several posting inns before you reach open fields, and they've got watchers in those yards, and at night, most like, they'd hear the hoofbeats on the cobbles and come out to check. Too risky all around." Jessup grimaced again. "Long and the short of it, they've got all of London locked down tight, and no way to get out."

Angelica blinked. "No way to get out—not if you're a young lady with red-gold hair."

Jessup frowned, nodded. "Aye—that's it."

Slowly, she smiled, then looked at Dominic. "I believe I know how we can slip out of London."

"I don't like it." An hour later, having dismissed Jessup and Thomas, both of whom had demonstrated an unhelpful susceptibility to a pair of green-gold eyes fired with enthusiasm, Dominic was fighting a rearguard action. And losing. "Even with the disguise, it's too dangerous. We can't risk them spotting you."

He couldn't risk her family sighting her and hauling her out of his hold.

He was pacing behind his desk; he rarely paced, but she'd driven him to it. He'd even resorted to a scowl, much good had that done him. Others quaked; she seemed utterly immune.

She was pacing, too, sweeping back and forth on the other side of the desk, her vibrant female energy causing him even more problems. Fully half of him wanted to forget the argument, round the desk, and embark on an entirely different sort of exchange.

In reply to his assertion, she waved dismissively. "You can't simply say you don't like it—not unless you come up with a better plan."

And that was the rub; he couldn't. Her plan—the one he'd at one stage found himself drawn into helping her embellish—was so damned unlikely it just might work.

"I concede that we'll have to wait until they pull back the family's own men from watching at the inns—that would be too dangerous. As I ride all the time, whether in the country or here, I doubt there's a groom or stable lad, or even a gardener from any of the households, who wouldn't know me by sight."

That was a concession; she'd started out wanting to leave tomorrow.

He halted. If he didn't get her to sit down, this wasn't going to end the way she thought it would. In fact, it was going to have to end the way she hoped so that it wouldn't end any other way. Swinging to face her, he waited until she glanced up, saw him looking at her, took in his expression, and came to an abrupt halt herself.

"What?"

He pointed to the armchair, reached for his desk chair. "Sit. And let's see if we can hammer out the details."

Her smile of triumph was a wonder to behold. She dragged the armchair closer to the desk, then, with a swish of her skirts, sat on its edge, spine poker-straight, enthusiasm and more lighting her eyes, her whole countenance. "I was just thinking that, given we need to return with the goblet by the first of next month, perhaps we should work out how long we can afford to wait in town before making our move."

Telling himself that her use of *"we"* and *"our"* was worth the cost, he sat in his chair and, across the desk, met her gaze. "Even if we take the mail, it'll still be a minimum of seven days traveling to the castle."

"And, therefore, back."

He nodded. "We have a bare four weeks in hand, so that's two of those weeks fully accounted for. In addition . . ." He glanced at the papers piled on his desk, thought, then shook his head. "I can't pass through Edinburgh without dealing with some of these—they won't wait. That will take . . . at least another day, possibly two."

"We'll have to stop in Edinburgh, anyway." When he looked at her, she waved at herself. "Gowns. I'll need gowns for traveling on from there, and for later. I can't arrive at the castle with no appropriate changes of attire."

He frowned. "As we need to spend days here waiting for your family to ease back enough to allow us through, you could get gowns here."

"I can't. Anything decent will need to be fitted, and there's not a single London modiste worth her salt who won't recognize me and promptly send the bill to my father. Besides, when I consent to become your countess, I'll need a modiste in Edinburgh—I can use the opportunity to try some out, and there's no reason I can't wait until then to get more gowns . . . in fact, it would be preferable. We won't want the extra luggage while traveling on the mail." She widened her eyes at him. "I'm perfectly certain you know the directions of any number of modistes in Edinburgh."

His face utterly impassive, in a bland, emotionless voice, he said, "There are several in Edinburgh whom I've heard described as exceptional."

"Indeed?"

He could hear the impertinence hovering on her tongue: How did he come to know which modistes in Edinburgh were exceptional?

But she thought better of it and simply smiled. "So, how many days does that leave us?"

"Allowing a day leeway for each of the journeys, plus two days in Edinburgh . . . that leaves us ten days in all."

"Ten days we can divide between here, waiting for the men in my family to call off their high alert, and the castle, convincing your mother that I'm ruined and getting back the goblet." Propping her elbow on the desk, setting her chin in that hand, she tapped one slender finger across her lips . . . drawing his gaze to the full, ripe curves. "How long do you think we should allow for the latter?"

He blinked, had to think to remember what her "latter" was. "I haven't the faintest notion. Mirabelle might take one look at you, be utterly satisfied, and race off to fetch the goblet. More likely she'll want at least a few days to absorb and reassure herself that you're real, that I've actually brought her what she demanded." After a moment, he said, "We might have more luck defining how long your family can keep their men at the inns. You know their households. How long can they operate stripped of most men? How long before they're forced to cease and desist?"

"That's not going to depend on the lack of male staff so much as on how long the ladies in the family take to persuade the men to listen to reason and accept that I am, as I've told them, safe, but . . ." Her eyes on his, she considered, weighed. "I should send another letter at some point—not tomorrow, that would be too soon, but perhaps the day after—to help things along, but . . . three or four days?"

"As you mentioned, even once they do pull back, we should assume that they'll enlist the posting-house owners and staff to keep their eyes peeled for you by offering a sizeable reward."

"Indeed, but that's where my disguise will come in. But timing-wise, if we wait for four days, then depart on the mail, that will still leave us six days in which to convince your mother that I'm ruined."

He stared at her, at her eager eyes. "No. I don't want to risk being premature and learning too late that your family's still watching. We'll wait here for five days. Today's the second of the month. We'll leave on the night mail to Edinburgh on the evening of the sixth." If he didn't get her safely out of London, nothing else would matter. "That will leave us five days to convince my mother and reclaim the goblet."

She studied his face, then nodded. "Five days should be enough."

He got the distinct impression that she was thinking, making plans about something, but before he could probe, her expression brightened.

"Now—for my disguise." She waved beckoning fingers. "Two sheets of paper, if you please—I need to make two lists."

Bemused, he complied, then watched her busily write Youth's Clothes at the top of one sheet.

"All right. If I'm supposed to be a respectable youth traveling north with my tutor, I'll need a shirt, breeches, jacket, and neck cloth. And perhaps a great-coat, given we're going all the way to Edinburgh." She neatly wrote the requirements on the sheet. "Now . . ." Studying the list, she tapped the end of the pen against her lower lip, distracting him again, then she glanced down at her feet. "My feet are so small, getting boots might be difficult. Perhaps I should wear hose and shoes?"

He blinked. "Boots. No hose." Deciding he wasn't up to explaining the significant visual difference between her exposed calves and ankles and those of any youth, he added, "I'll go with Griswold. We'll find boots for you somewhere."

She nodded and bent to make another note on the list, leaving him staring at her shining hair, at her bright, so highly identifiable, crowning glory. As if sensing his regard, she said, "And a hat, of course. I'm sure Griswold will know what sort, but it must be sufficient to cover my hair completely."

And shade as much of her face as possible, including those far too feminine lips. No youth ever born had lips like hers, another point he wasn't about to mention.

"Right." She blotted the list, then presented it to him. "See if there's anything I've missed." Dipping the pen in the ink again, she wrote on the second sheet Things I Need Now. Catching him looking, she said,

"These are personal items I'll need in addition to my disguise. If Brenda could go out this afternoon and fetch these, I'll be able to manage well enough for the moment."

Leaving her to compose that list unassisted, he gave his attention to the other. Noted that she'd included an extra linen band, possibly a cravat; he was about to ask what she wanted that for when he realized. He looked at her breasts, tried to imagine . . . shook his head and refocused on the list. One pair of silk drawers was also, sensibly in his view, listed.

He closed his eyes, tried to imagine how a woman dressed as a man might look, ended up thinking of the necessary steps to undress said woman . . . he opened his eyes as she sat back, apparently satisfied with her list of personal items.

He tossed the Youth's Clothes list toward her. "Belt, and gloves. You'll need to cover your hands."

"Ah! Thank you." She pounced on the list and made the additions.

When she finished, he reached out and took it from her. "Griswold and I will see what we can find for you tomorrow. The boots will be the most difficult, but we'll manage something." He already knew that her feet, like her hands, were small and delicate; he'd been able to circle her ankle with the fingers of one hand.

"Excellent." Eyes shining, she propped both elbows on the desk, laced her fingers, and rested her chin on them. "Now, how do we go about procuring passage on the night mail to Edinburgh?"

He thought of resisting and sending her off, but he wasn't quite sure how. Telling himself it was so close to luncheon that there was no point trying to return to his papers when he'd be interrupted again so soon, he surrendered and let her quiz him. As he was learning to expect, once she grasped the basic approach, she made several sensible suggestions as to how to best avoid her family's notice should they think to check the mail's passenger lists, suggestions he accepted without argument.

"Well," she said, apparently finally satisfied. Smiling, she met his gaze. "Now all we have to decide is how to fill in our time from now until the evening of the sixth."

He looked into her eyes, and couldn't tell whether she was teasing or not.

Chapter Five

It was, Dominic thought, like learning to hunt a new type of game. One had to learn the quarry's habits, all the nuances of their behavior; one had to learn to read the signs.

All of which was even more critical if the hunter suspected he might, at some point, discover himself the hunted.

That evening, as he held the chair at the foot of the table in the breakfast room for Angelica—he'd seen no point in opening up the huge dining room—he looked down at the glossy curls tumbling from a knot on the top of her head, at the expanse of creamy skin exposed by the continued absence of her fichu, and suspected that his hunter's instincts weren't wrong in their unabated insistence that he should be wary of her and her motives.

Once she sat, he walked down the table and took his own seat as Mulley, assisted by Brenda, brought in the soup course. They came to serve him first, but he waved them to Angelica.

And watched as she, with bright eyes and smiles, charmed them. Neither Mulley nor Brenda was an easy mark, yet both had appreciably thawed toward . . . the lady who, regardless of her present intransigence, would shortly be their mistress. He didn't know why she'd put off accepting that part of his bargain, but he entertained no doubt that she eventually would. He didn't know what game she was playing, but equally didn't doubt that at some point she would tell him.

As for his staff, regardless of her timetable, it was shrewd of her to make them hers. After Mulley and Brenda had served him, Dominic dismissed them and lifted his spoon.

For a minute, he and Angelica supped in silence, then she glanced up the table. "You said the castle was huge—do you have a large staff?"

He took another spoonful of the creamy soup, then said, "Your cousin, St. Ives—think of his country house, of the number of staff required to run it, then double that number."

"That many?"

"Not, of course, because we actually need that many, but it's a case of more hands make lighter work, and it's a way to . . ." He couldn't immediately think of the right words.

"Keep people busy in a way that makes them feel they contribute to the clan?"

"Yes." After a moment, he went on, "Brenda, for instance. She lost her husband in an accident five or so years ago. The castle's housekeeper, Mrs. Mack, decided she could do with another upstairs maid, so Brenda came to live and work in the castle."

"So she's not just a pensioner thinking herself a drain on the clan."

He nodded; soup finished, he sat back and studied her. They'd lunched in this room, then he'd stated he'd had business to attend to in the library . . . he'd been a little surprised that she'd allowed him to escape. But she had, and, he now suspected, had spent the afternoon with his people instead.

She finished her soup just as Brenda returned to whisk the soup plates away, while Mulley brought in the first course.

As if to confirm where she'd been that afternoon, Angelica exclaimed over the fish, complimenting Brenda, who was doubling as cook. Preening, Brenda withdrew. Mulley was smiling as he served the dish.

Dominic considered Mulley's smile, saw the pleasure and pride his majordomo took in performing the minor duty. He, himself, knew how to gain respect and inspire loyalty, but he was a man; he didn't have the appreciative knack Angelica clearly had.

He'd assumed that a spoiled, pampered, ton beauty wouldn't so easily bridge the social divide . . . but then Cynster young ladies were doubtless reared to manage ducal mansions and the like.

When they were once more alone, she glanced up the table. "Mulley told me he's your majordomo. Do you have a separate butler at the castle?"

"No, Mulley performs those duties when necessary."

Angelica gave her attention to the fish and to considering what next to ask him. She'd spent the afternoon in the kitchen, helping Griswold, Dominic's valet, polish the silver cutlery they were using; rather than immediately push the master further, she'd elected to get a better idea of his staff. Wisely, as it had transpired.

Thinking of what she'd learned, she looked at Dominic. "Clan staff aren't the same as . . . well, staff normally found in English households, are they?"

He arched a brow. "I wouldn't know. Tell me."

She frowned. "The interaction between master and staff is different. Your clan folk don't behave as if they're your equal, yet neither are they as . . . I suppose the word is subservient, as English staff." She paused, then offered, "The hierarchy is much less marked."

He nodded. "The word *master* to us is more equivalent to 'leader,' not 'owner.' "

"Yes. That's it in a nutshell." Returning her attention to her plate, she applied herself to consuming the delicious sole, pleased to have had her observations and deductions confirmed. While she might not yet have agreed to be his countess, she wasn't foolish enough to pass up the chance to learn from the small staff he'd brought to London before finding herself swamped by the clearly much larger castle staff.

With luck, the less rigid separation between master and staff would allow her to achieve more than she otherwise might have during the days of their enforced sojourn in the capital.

Brenda arrived to remove the plates. As soon as Mulley carved the roast beef, served them, then withdrew, Angelica caught Dominic's eye. "I outlined our plan for getting to Edinburgh to your people—they all thought it inspired. Griswold is putting his mind to what style of clothes will best disguise me as a youth. Meanwhile, have you thought of any reason to change our minds about leaving on the sixth?"

He stilled. "No. Have you?"

"No—I just wanted to confirm the date." She waved at the platters before them. "Brenda needs to know to get in the right amount of food."

That she was thinking of household logistics and had talked of their plan to his staff slew the last lingering uncertainty lurking at the back of Dominic's mind; she wasn't going to suddenly realize just what she was doing, balk, and demand to go home.

She knew *precisely* what she was doing, what she'd agreed to, and was marching ahead with what he was starting to suspect was her typical confidence.

He chewed, swallowed, then volunteered, "The Edinburgh mail leaves from the Bull and Mouth, near Aldersgate, at eight in the evening. We can dine at the inn so Brenda and the others won't have to feed us here, then rush to get packed and across London."

"That would definitely be best."

"I'll send Jessup and Thomas to Aldersgate tomorrow morning to secure our seats. Thomas can buy the papers for us—you and me—as if he's a footman in some lord's household, then Jessup can secure the other five seats, the two left inside and the three up top. Other than the coachman and guard, we'll have the coach to ourselves." Thinking further, he added, "We should arrive at the Bull and Mouth separately, too." He met her gaze. "I'm in favor of doing anything and everything we can to throw your family off the scent."

She smiled in agreement. "It's like a real-life game of hide-and-seek."

"I'm hoping that by then they'll be seeking elsewhere."

"Griswold said he'll hold himself ready to accompany you tomorrow morning." As if unaware of any temerity in thus organizing his day for him, she went on, "If you manage to gather all that's required for my disguise, and Jessup and Thomas are successful in their quest, then by lunchtime tomorrow we'll have everything we need to slip past my brothers and cousins and successfully reach Edinburgh."

Her confidence—shining in her eyes, in her expression—was contagious. He felt his lips ease. "With luck, we will."

While Mulley cleared the table, and Brenda carried in a flummery and served them, Angelica blithely informed him of her preference in colors, the quality of fabrics, and sundry other details he was, apparently, required to bear in mind when shopping for her disguise. He contemplated telling her he would remember none of it and recommending she tell Griswold instead, but didn't. By and large he had a better memory than his valet, and . . . he was unabashedly intrigued by how she—and apparently Griswold, too—imagined they were going to effectively disguise such a vibrantly, elementally feminine person as a youth. He had to believe they knew what they were doing, that they would pull it off, at least well enough for their purposes, but as she talked and waved her hands, with eyes, expression, and gestures all so innately female, he suddenly realized that no matter how brilliantly effective her disguise, he, and his libido, wouldn't be fooled. Not in the least.

And he, and his increasingly overactive libido, would be sitting next to her all the way to Edinburgh.

His inner frown must have shown in his eyes. She stopped talking and looked questioningly at him.

He shifted, pushed back his chair. They'd both finished their dessert. "I . . ." Rising, he looked down the table at her. "There are documents I need to deal with in the library."

Laying aside her napkin, she smiled and rose, too. "Yes, of course."

He'd assumed that, as she had after luncheon, she would part from him in the corridor and go off somewhere, perhaps to the sitting room upstairs, but no. Blithely talking about Scotland in general, informing him she'd never been further north than Edinburgh, she led the way to the library, opened the door, and swept in ahead of him.

He halted on the threshold, then, lips firming, stepped inside and shut the door.

She'd paused to glance around the room. Now she picked up the candelabra left on the table by the door and started strolling down the shelves, deeper into the room, scanning the books' spines.

He inwardly sighed. "What are you looking for?" He would help her find it; the sooner she did, the sooner she would leave.

"I'm just looking." Without glancing back, she waved him away. "Don't mind me. I won't disturb you."

The look he cast her held equal parts disbelief and resignation. He hesitated, then walked to the desk. The contracts and orders he'd been working on through the afternoon lay waiting. He adjusted the flames of the desk lamps Mulley had lit earlier but had left turned low, then he sat and attempted to focus his mind on the intricacies of running the Guisachan estate and the numerous businesses associated with it.

Somewhat to his surprise, he succeeded. At first.

When the clocks chimed, and he realized half an hour had passed, he glanced up—and discovered Angelica curled sideways in one of the armchairs across from the desk, a footstool she must have unearthed from under one of the holland covers propping up her small feet. Her gaze was fixed on the pages of a massive red leather-bound tome she was holding balanced on her lap.

Her absorption was complete; she didn't notice or react to his gaze.

Which left him free to indulge in a perusal he'd been reluctant to attempt before. Slowly, he let his gaze travel from the crowning glory of her hair, noting the coppery-red glints gleaming amid the gold, over her face, features relaxed and . . . angelically perfect. Visually, she was well named. Her finely arched brown brows elegantly framed her eyes, large and well set, presently downcast as she read, the fringe of her long, lightly curling lashes casting lacy shadows across her delicately molded cheekbones.

Her nose was small but uncompromisingly straight, her lips the very opposite; lush, the upper well-bowed, the lower distractingly full, those lips were temptation incarnate, promising all manner of sensual delights.

Overall, her face was an oval, her chin, presently in repose, a sculpted curve, but he'd seen that chin firm, knew it could.

His gaze drifted lower, down the long sweep of her throat, over the links of her curious necklace to the ripe swell of her breasts . . .

He told himself he should view her dispassionately, that he could be excused for being curious enough to gauge her attractions against those of the highland, lowland, and society beauties he'd bedded . . . but all those others had faded from his memory; he couldn't dredge up any visions to compare to the angel curled in the armchair.

And *dis*passion wasn't a state to which he could lay claim, not while viewing her.

Resisting the urge to shift in his chair, to ease the discomfort that only increased as his gaze, beyond his control, skimmed further down, over the indentation of her waist, largely hidden by the drape of her gown, past the evocative swell of her hip and down the sleek length of her thigh, both outlined beneath the fine silk pulled taut by her position, he reminded himself that she'd committed herself to his plan, to their now shared enterprise . . . which meant that, ultimately, regardless of any quibble over timing, she would be his.

For the first time, he allowed that realization to fully form, to rise in his consciousness, then sink to his bones.

His instincts, still wary but now watchful, too, calmed.

Mentally shaking free of the spell, the entrancement she'd unwittingly cast, it occurred to him that perhaps he was more like his father than he'd thought.

Celia's daughter fascinated him in a way no other woman ever had. She was in truth like a bright and sparkling angel; she swooped and glided, and amused, entertained, and intrigued him. He couldn't recall ever before feeling a need to divine how a particular woman thought.

That left him wondering if the old saw "Like father, like son, like mother, like daughter" actually held true. He couldn't deny that the attraction he felt toward Celia's daughter held elements of enthrallment; he had no intention of falling victim to it, yet he knew the propensity was there.

A wise man acknowledged his weaknesses, at least to himself.

He was about to drag his gaze from his most recent weakness when the question of what subject had held her attention so thoroughly that she hadn't sensed his prolonged appraisal made him angle his head and focus on the gold lettering on the book's spine.

Robertson. *The History of Scotland.*

He looked at her face, confirmed her concentration, then looked down at his papers. Picked one up and pretended to read it.

Of the hundreds of tomes in the library, she'd chosen the Robertson. Without any fanfare, she'd set out to learn about the world he was taking her into—the world, he suspected, she intended to make hers.

That was one element of her character he shouldn't forget.

The damned woman was intelligent.

Ergo, dangerous, especially to him.

Late the next morning, Dominic returned from his shopping expedition with Griswold, a pair of boy's riding boots under one arm. Griswold carried several brown-paper-wrapped parcels. It had taken three hours of tramping London's streets visiting tailors and outfitters catering to the youth of the ton, but they'd managed to acquire every item on Angelica's Youth's Clothes list.

Dominic held the rear garden gate—the only entry they were presently using—for Griswold, who was balancing his burdens, to angle through, then followed Griswold to the back door, opened it, waved Griswold through, and followed his valet into the servants' hall . . .

Halting, he stared. The place had been cleaned—no, *scoured*, to, as the saying went, an inch of its life. The copper pans above the fireplace gleamed. The deal table, scrubbed and polished, glowed, and the dresser, previously devoid of all objects, now displayed neat stacks of clean plates and dishes upon its polished shelves.

Not a single speck of dust, much less any cobweb, remained.

Setting his packages on the scrubbed table, Griswold surveyed the room with patent approval.

Brisk footsteps approached from the kitchens, off one side of the big hall. A vision emerged, dusting her hands.

Angelica saw them and smiled. "Good—you're back. Did you get everything?"

Dominic stared. "Yes. But where did you get those clothes?"

"From Brenda." She looked down at the full skirt and loose cambric blouse. Both were overlarge, the voluminous wide-necked blouse exposing one delicately rounded shoulder, the skirt rolled over several times at the waist and secured with a length of cord. A striped kerchief tied over her hair completed the outfit. "She had the extra, and these will do for today . . ." Her gaze rose, fastened on the parcels, and her eyes, her face, lit.

Dominic watched her descend on the parcels, undoing string, unfolding paper, and peppering Griswold with eager questions.

She looked like a saucy barmaid from a tavern by the docks—except she was too clean.

Too blindingly beautiful.

He shook his head, hoping to shake his brains into place. It was the contrast, that was all—the disorienting disconnection between the clothes and what was in them. He'd remained where he'd halted, by the end of the table. She was holding up a white shirt, gauging the size, chattering about cravats with Griswold; belatedly remembering the package he carried, he held it out to her. "Your boots. You might have to stuff rags in the toes, but they should at least stay on."

Face alight, she accepted the package. "Thank you." Stripping off the paper, she held up one of the boots, considered the size, then balanced on one foot, slipped off one dancing slipper, and compared its sole to that of the boot. "They're almost the right size."

Sitting on one of the kitchen chairs, she proceeded to try on the boots. Griswold assisted. Dominic forced himself to remain where he was. He didn't need to see her ankles again.

Boots on, she sprang up, strode a few paces back and forth, then, with a delighted smile, she danced a little jig. "They're perfect!" Rounding the table, lifting her skirts halfway up her calves, she halted so Dominic could see.

Then she looked up, into his face, and smiled—a blindingly brilliant smile. "Thank you. You must have had to hunt for them, but rest assured the result was worth it. I'll even be able to run if we need to."

Silently clearing his throat, he managed an uninflected, unrevealing "Good."

Sounds outside had him turning to the door. It opened, and Jessup, followed by Thomas, came in. Both nodded to Dominic, looked past him, swallowed their surprise, and, a touch warily, nodded politely to Angelica, too.

Dominic understood their caution. "Did you get the seats?"

"Aye," Jessup replied. "But only just. Gent behind us was a tad irate about having to change his plans. Offered me a good bit extra for two of our seats. I told him we were sailors and had to be in Edinburgh to catch our ship, so couldn't oblige him."

Dominic nodded approvingly. "Good story."

More footsteps approached from the kitchen. Brenda appeared, wiping her hands. Seeing Jessup and Thomas, she smiled. "Perfect timing—lunch is ready."

Mulley, wearing a long butler's apron over his customary attire and carrying a tray loaded with plates and cutlery, followed Brenda into the hall.

Brenda turned to Angelica. "If you want me to help you change, miss, Mulley'll set up the dining parlor meanwhile."

Angelica looked at her new youth's clothes, then at Brenda and Mulley. "We've been working hard all morning cleaning down here, and you're right, I'm in no fit state to sit in the dining parlor. But luncheon is just a cold collation—is there any reason we can't all eat here, around this exceptionally clean table? That will be easier for everyone, I should think."

Mulley exchanged glances with Brenda and Griswold, then looked at Dominic. "That would let us get on more quickly with what we've planned for the afternoon—if you're agreeable, my lord?"

Dominic waved to the table. "By all means." Mulley was only asking for show, in front of Angelica. Prior to her arrival, Dominic had taken all his meals in the servants' hall, with his people—just as he did at the castle, in the great hall.

He moved to his place at the head of the table. Angelica gathered her new clothes and piled them in one corner of the dresser while Griswold whipped away the discarded wrappings. In the bustle as crockery, cutlery, and mugs were set out, she gravitated toward the foot of the table, but Brenda headed her off, then Mulley intervened and gently conducted her up the table to the place on Dominic's right.

She glanced at him, not quite questioningly, yet he could all but see the wheels in her mind turning as she allowed Mulley to seat her.

Once she was settled, Dominic pulled out his chair and sat.

For masters to eat with their household staff was, he was well aware, unthinkable in tonnish English houses, yet she had suggested it. He wondered if she'd read something in Robertson about how the clans generally shared their meals, laird and people all breaking bread together, or if she was simply feeling her way.

Brenda and Mulley set large platters of cold meats, as well as sauces, fruits, breads, and nuts on the table, then all took their seats, and the meal began.

As they ate, conversation flowed freely. Brenda and Mulley told tales of their discoveries as they'd cleaned the servants' hall, the kitchens, and butler's pantry. Apparently the housekeeper's room, the scullery, and the linen and laundry rooms were next on their list.

When Jessup asked what had prompted the cleaning frenzy, Dominic learned that the suggestion had come from Angelica. When he arched a brow at her, she lightly shrugged.

"We'll be returning later this month, and while the dining parlor and library are habitable, they and the other reception rooms need work, but the rooms most used—and most necessary to a functioning household—are those down here, behind the green baize door, so I thought that, given we've days to wait before we can leave London, we might as well make a start on setting the place to rights for when we return with the goblet."

She glanced up at him, meeting his eyes as if warning him not to read too much into her actions; she didn't appear to notice the resulting pause as the others around the table took in and digested her words, along with her unstated yet patently obvious confidence that they would, indeed, be back in London at the end of the month, with the goblet in hand.

Thomas, young, eager, and now enthused, turned to Jessup and asked if they shouldn't help with the cleaning.

Dominic left Jessup to decide that while, from beneath his lashes, he watched Angelica. He hadn't yet defined what her underlying purpose was, what her private goals, immediate or otherwise, were.

That she had such goals he did not doubt; she was too definite a personality—she was too much like him. He and she were not the sort of characters who let life toss them where it would; they always knew what they wanted, and as far as possible took the most direct route to that end.

He looked at her and could see neither head nor tail of her direction.

At the end of the meal, she declared her intention of trying on her disguise and conscripted Brenda and

Griswold to assist. Leaving Mulley, Thomas, and Jessup to clear the table, Dominic escaped to the library.

An hour later, Angelica descended the stairs, one deliberate boot step at a time. She was pleased with the way her legs looked in the corduroy breeches and fitting leather boots. Until she'd pirouetted before the cheval glass in the countess's bedchamber, taking in her appearance in her youth's attire, she'd had no idea her legs, relatively speaking, were so long, or her hips quite so womanly. Luckily, the latter were concealed beneath the skirts of the jacket Griswold had selected.

She was getting on well with Dominic's valet. At first he'd been cool, distinctly reserved, but he was coming around to seeing her as an ally, at least where his master's interests were concerned. Brenda had more rapidly come to the same conclusion and was now a ready source of information on Dominic, the castle, and the clan, all matters on which Angelica needed to cram.

Knowledge was the key to managing anything; she needed to learn much more about Dominic.

Including those insights only she could glean.

Reaching the front hall, she stepped onto the tiles and turned down the corridor to the library. Dominic had bought her the disguise—it was only fair she show him the result.

And learn what he thought of it.

Opening the library door, she walked in.

Dominic looked up—and had to battle to keep his jaw from dropping.

Battle to keep from scowling, from reacting at all as she—the minx—swanned in. Swinging around, she shut the door, causing the skirts of her jacket to fan out, giving him a glimpse of her derriere neatly outlined in brown corduroy.

His mouth dried. He was conscious of stilling—of his hunter's instincts taking hold and locking his muscles in that preternatural stillness all predators assumed when stalking prey . . . he told himself that she wasn't prey, but to that more instinctive side of him she most definitely was.

She walked to stand before the desk, the shift of her hips distractingly evident. Gracefully spreading her arms, she posed and waited while he raised his gaze—slowly—up the slender length of her, past her ruthlessly restrained breasts concealed behind a linen shirt, the wide lapels of her brown jacket, and the ends of the colorful red-striped neckerchief artlessly wound about her throat, to her face, to her eyes. She captured his gaze and, lips curving, asked, "Well? Do I pass muster?"

As what? An angel from one of his more salacious dreams?

When she arched a brow, the curve of her lips deepening, he gave up on impassivity and frowned. "You need to learn to walk like a man—a male." Not even a drunken sailor would have missed the elementally feminine sway of her hips. "And . . ." He felt his frown darken. "What have you done with your hair?"

For one horrible, gut-churning instant, he thought she'd cut it off.

"Oh, it's all up here." Angelica tapped the crown of the wide-brimmed black hat Griswold had insisted would shade her face sufficiently for her to pass as a youth—if she kept her head down. "Griswold had the clever notion of using a net to keep the strands in place, and we've pinned the hat to the net so it won't blow off or shift."

She kept her eyes on Dominic's. She'd come there intending to flirt with him, to confirm for herself that she could, that him being her hero did indeed mean that he was susceptible to her in that way. But the way he was looking at her . . . suggested that further flirting would be akin to dancing between a dragon's teeth.

Some gentlemen would have reacted by undressing her with their eyes. He hadn't. His slow perusal had felt like an inventory taking—the way a sheik might assess a new slave—and from the moment his eyes had locked on hers, what she'd sensed called to mind a large, wild carnivore, presently reined and content to watch, but who might, at her next tempting move, pounce as fast as lightning, catch her in an unbreakable grip, and devour her.

She'd never thought herself fanciful, but staring into those mesmerizing eyes . . . the question of whether he had an animal on his crest—and if so, what—flashed through her mind.

Gazing into the turbulent greeny-gray, she drew a shallow breath, one further constricted by the band binding her breasts, and decided that, for today, she'd learned enough. Headstrong and willful she might be, but she rarely precipitated situations she might not be able to control.

She smiled with no teasing in the gesture. "So my striding needs work?" She glanced down at her boots. "The freedom of no skirts does take getting used to."

"You might try observing Thomas—try copying him."

Dominic got the words out, heard the crispness of his diction, the deeper tone . . . if she didn't get out of the library soon, he would very likely do something they both might later regret.

Her expression brightened. "An excellent idea."

Her gaze returned to him, to his eyes . . . he wondered if she had any inkling how close she stood to . . .

Cutting off the thought, he nodded curtly. "I believe he and Jessup are helping the others."

In the rear of the mansion, far away . . .

With a tilt of her head, and a lingering—measuring and just a touch wary—look, she started to turn. "I'll go and find him."

Never turn your back on a predator . . .

Teeth gritted, he managed to keep himself seated behind the desk. She opened the door, cast him a last, assessing glance, then slipped out and closed the door.

He tried to exhale in relief, and couldn't.

"Damn woman!" He looked down—at the letter he'd been writing. At the pen in his hand, at the nib with the ink dried on it. Stabbing the pen back into the ink pot, he reread the sentence he'd been inscribing. It took a full minute before his mind obeyed enough to supply the next words.

Settling to complete the missive, he told himself he was glad she'd had the sense to leave—and in terms of managing the relationship that would, eventually, develop between them, he was. No point jumping the gun and potentially scaring her. Regardless of when she consented to their union, that aspect—that subject—could wait until later, until after he'd got the goblet back, and they'd discussed how she wanted their married life to be.

Later.

Of course the wanton chit had come to the library expressly to provoke him, but at least she'd had sufficient wit to withdraw . . .

For now, for the moment. But he'd still be sitting next to her, with her in her damned disguise, all the way to Edinburgh.

Pen pausing, he realized that even though she'd come no closer than the other side of the desk . . .

He wondered if Griswold knew of a cologne that smelled like male.

Angelica found Thomas helping Brenda clean the laundry by using a long-handled broom to sweep down the cobwebs festooning the ceiling. She watched the lanky youth walk about the room, then, realizing the poor boy would feel dreadfully embarrassed if he caught her staring, she picked up a feather duster and did what she could about the cobwebs within her reach while watching Thomas from the corner of her eye; she tried to mimic the way he moved . . . she wasn't at all sure she was getting it right. She needed to practice in front of a mirror.

Then Brenda sent Thomas to clean the ironing room; Angelica debated, but remained and asked Brenda, "His lordship, the laird, mentioned the housekeeper at the castle—a Mrs. Mack. What's she like?"

Brenda replied readily, "Nice old duck. Mind you, she comes off all stern and rigid, but she has a heart o'gold and there's no one better in a crisis. She keeps us all in line, but she stands up for us, too." Brenda rubbed at the window she was wiping. "Dotes on the laird, she does—something fierce."

Angelica made a mental note to court Mrs. Mack's good graces once she reached the castle. Before she could ask who else among the staff there was of special note, Griswold appeared to beg for her opinion on a canteen of silverware he and Mulley had unearthed in the housekeeper's room—the third set of cutlery they'd thus far discovered.

Following Griswold to the butler's pantry, and identifying the latest set of forty-eight as the one most likely reserved for major dinner parties, she concluded, "The set of twenty-four will be for normal use in the dining room, and the set of sixteen we're currently using must be the breakfast parlor set."

"Should we leave both dining room sets here, miss?" Griswold asked.

"For the moment—no need to start polishing them. We'll bring down maids, and hire others, when we return later in the month." She looked up at the shelves above the butler's bench, at the array of silver dishes, urns, bowls, and vases. All were tarnished, but . . . "They've been as they are for decades—they can wait another month."

"I might just polish another tray or two, miss— we're rather low, and Mulley's nearly finished in the housekeeper's room . . . unless there's something you'd rather I do?"

"No, no. By all means." Angelica hesitated, then said, "In fact, if you have another cloth, I'll help."

"Oh, no, miss—you don't need to do that."

"I know, but I'm not used to being idle, and as Glencrae is busy with his correspondence, I might as well help here." Spying the stack of polishing cloths, she picked one up. "Give me that platter."

They settled on chairs to rub industriously. While buffing the plate Griswold had consented to let her attack, she learned how he'd come to work for a Scottish laird who passed for an Englishman, except . . .

She looked up. "Except when . . . ?"

Griswold primed his lips, then admitted, "When he loses his temper, miss—which doesn't happen often, but when it does, well, you're left in no doubt as to his homeland then."

She grinned. "He swears in Scots?"

Griswold bent over the platter he was polishing. "I've always understood people revert to their mother tongues in extremis, miss."

"Indeed." Letting that subject drop, she continued her questioning; eventually she said, "He told me his leg was badly injured some months before he came to town that first time."

"Oh, dear me, yes. At first I thought him permanently lame, yet over the years his knee slowly improved. But it was only when we returned to the highlands for good, and he spent more time walking the hills, that it healed well enough for him to do away with the cane." Griswold sighed. "But he jarred it recently, so now he needs the cane again."

She recalled that Dominic had been carrying the cane when he'd walked into the servants' hall, but had left it leaning against the wall there. "He doesn't use it indoors."

"He says it helps strengthen the joint if he doesn't, and if he falls here, there's no one to see."

And no one to help—stupid man. She bit back the words; men would be men, and in matters that touched their dignity, they were invariably stupid.

By dint of a few more questions, she learned something of how Dominic spent his time in the highlands. She was careful not to ask about anything Griswold might deem encroaching on his master's privacy, but, naturally enough, his staff considered her interest in their master entirely appropriate.

She'd debated holding herself aloof from the household, underscoring her refusal to allow him to consider her his countess-to-be, not yet, but as she fully intended to eventually claim the title, along with him, she'd decided that as far as his staff and this house were concerned, and even the castle and his people there, there was simply no benefit in behaving toward them other than as she intended to be. In other words, as his countess-to-be. Not picking up the reins of his household, not learning how to deal with his staff, not taking the lead in getting this neglected house into some sort of livable order would have been, in multiple ways, far harder on her than on him.

More, his people and staff were important, both to him and to her as his future wife. That was something she innately understood. Learning about his people, and then shouldering the part of their care and guidance that should fall to his countess—something her character inclined her to do regardless—would, she felt certain, be a predisposing factor in inducing him to fall in love with her, and that, after all, was her aim.

And if along the way her tack added to his confusion, as she rather thought it would, well and good.

Eventually leaving Griswold polishing another plate, she trailed into the kitchen to discover Brenda wiping down the table there.

"Is there anything I can do to help?" She felt compelled to make the offer, although her kitchen skills were sadly lacking.

Brenda smiled. "Not really. I'll manage, and Mulley'll be out in a moment to help. Besides"— Brenda nodded at Angelica's hands—"I suspect the laird would rather those stayed just the way they are."

Spreading her fingers, Angelica studied her palms. "I have to say I share the sentiment." Glancing at Brenda, she asked, "If I go out of the garden gate and across to the stables, will all hell break loose?"

"I don't see why." Brenda looked at her. "You're not planning to slip away and run off home, are you?"

Angelica smiled. "No—that I can promise. Word of a Cynster."

"Well, can't argue with that, can I?" Brenda said. "But what do you want in the stables?"

Angelica was already heading for the servants' hall. "I want to talk to Jessup. About horses."

She reached the stables without any drama and found Jessup brushing down one of the pair that presumably had drawn the carriage in which she'd been brought to the house.

Jessup glanced up at her, then turned back to the horse. "Just getting these nags ready to take back to the jobbers. No sense having them eating their heads off here."

Angelica leaned on the stall door. "I've heard that the laird rides a massive chestnut. I wondered if he'd brought the horse to town, but I see he didn't." Beyond the second carriage horse, the stalls stood empty.

"Aye. You'd not miss Hercules if he was here—he's quite a sight."

"Hercules?" She grinned. "Ah—I can imagine how he came by his name."

Jessup humphed. "The laird is no lightweight— ever since he turned fifteen it's been difficult finding a mount that can carry him for any length of time."

"Where did he find Hercules?"

"Brought him up from London. Apparently he had him off some other gentleman who couldn't handle the brute. Mind you, in those days Hercules was quite a handful, but he's steadied with the years." Jessup—the most taciturn and, Angelica judged, least charmable of Dominic's staff—shot her an appraising look. "So, do you ride, then—or is it just an amble in the park, and nothing more than a canter?"

"Oh, no—I ride. A lot. I love to gallop and race— you could say it's in the blood."

"Oh? How's that?"

"My cousin, Demon Cynster, is one of the foremost trainers of racing Thoroughbreds. He has a stud and stables at Newmarket."

Straightening, Jessup blinked.

And Angelica knew she had him.

Slowly, Jessup nodded. "Now I think on it, I've heard the name." He looked at Angelica with latent respect. "So you know something about horses?"

"Not so much the theory as the practice. Demon supplies all the family's horses—given our family, that's the equivalent of saying he supplies all the clan's horses. Carriage horses, riding horses, hunters—he sees the best in all fields and can take his pick. Everyone connected with the family calls on him for horses—well, why wouldn't we, when we know he can get the best?"

Jessup nodded, calculation in his eyes, but as he returned to currying the horse, he studied her, more measuringly this time. "You're a little thing, not much weight to you, but if you say you can handle a mount with spirit—"

"I can."

"—then we'll have to see what we can find for you. The terrain is testing—lots of climbing as well as long runs. Strong legs and stamina are a must. I was thinking you might have one of the ponies, but if you're likely to ride with himself—"

"I am."

"—then the pony won't do." Jessup smiled crookedly. "Which will suit the scamps well enough—they've been eyeing off the beast for months. I should probably start them off once we get back to the castle."

"Scamps?"

"Gavin and Bryce—the laird's wards."

He has wards? Angelica swallowed the words, then forced her parted lips into an O, denoting recollection, and nodded as if she understood, as if she'd known all along that Dominic had wards. Little boy wards. Whom Jessup labeled scamps.

Said scamps hadn't featured in Dominic's bargain, not that, on reflection, that truly surprised her; men were wont to forget such inconveniences. Brenda, no doubt, could fill her in.

Still leaning on the stall door, she quizzed Jessup about the rides around the castle, and the size of the castle stables and what carriages were kept there.

By the time she crossed the mews and returned to the house, she had another at least partial conquest in Jessup, and all in all counted her afternoon well spent.

Entering the house, she headed for the countess's suite. It was nearly time to dress for dinner. Not that she had any decision to make regarding which gown to don.

She debated wearing her youth's costume to the table, but revisiting those moments in the library—recalling *exactly* how Dominic had looked at her—she decided against it. Thought better of it.

He made her breath hitch and seized her senses without even trying. It might, she decided, be better to grow accustomed to the effect before she tempted him further. She had weeks to tame him; she didn't need to rush.

That she'd dreamt of him last night was neither here nor there.

All in all, she thought, as she stripped off her boy's clothes, fate's challenge lay before her—and she was looking forward with considerable relish to every coming minute.

Dominic had steeled himself to withstand, at least to remain outwardly unaffected by, whatever games Angelica thought to play on him—on his senses, on his increasingly unruly interest in her—that evening.

Instead, he found himself looking down the dining table at a pensive face.

During the meal, they'd chatted about the theater. Entirely innocuously. She'd inquired as to the frequency of productions in Edinburgh. He'd told her what he knew, and also of the traveling companies that visited Perth, and Inverness, too.

But over dessert she'd grown . . . inward looking.

And he, entirely irrationally, found himself resenting whatever topic it was that had drawn her attention and her awareness so completely from him.

Irrational, yes. Deniable, no.

Lips firming, he asked, "What is it?"

When she met his eyes, he wondered if he'd just fallen for another of her ploys, but then she raised her head and, a frown forming both in her eyes and on her brow, said, "I should send that second letter to my family."

"Now?"

Griswold was helping Mulley wait on them; both appeared at that moment to draw the covers.

Dominic would have waited until they'd departed, but Angelica pushed back her chair, caught his gaze. "Come on." Griswold drew back her chair and she rose. "I'll write it now. It won't take long."

Turning, she glided out of the door.

He caught up with her as she entered the corridor leading to the library. "What are you going to tell them?"

"You'll see when you read it."

Jaw clenching, he reached around her and set the library door swinging wide. He followed her through and shut the door.

Ten minutes later, with her seated at his desk, he stood beside her and read the short, distinctly pithy note she'd written and handed to him a second time, this time aloud.

" 'I've told you that I'm in no danger, and therefore there's no reason for you to be looking for me, but I fully expect you haven't taken the slightest notice. If that is, indeed, the case, permit me to repeat: I am perfectly all right. I am, indeed, helping someone and cannot at this point explain further without breaking their confidence. I promise I will write and reveal all as soon as I can. Until then, you will simply have to possess your souls in patience. Angelica.' "

He shifted his gaze to her gold-and-green eyes. "Isn't that a tad terse?"

She made a scoffing sound and plucked the sheet from his fingers. "You don't know my brothers and cousins—and even that won't work."

He frowned. "Then why are you sending it?"

"So later they can't say I didn't warn them. Obviously."

He could see nothing obvious about it; her view was clearly a female-only perspective.

"Also, getting a second letter from me at this point should make them realize that I'm still in London and that nothing I've said suggests I'm expecting to leave." Having neatly folded the sheet, she picked up the pen and dipped the nib in the ink pot. "In addition, I'm sending this communication direct to the seat of power. To Devil. That way Honoria will read it, too, and might be able to exercise some duchessly measure of control." Nib poised, she paused. "Possibly."

Looking down, she inscribed her cousin's title and direction on the missive, then blotted the sheet, leaned back, and held out the letter. "If Thomas goes around to Grosvenor Square now, there'll be plenty of urchins about waiting to earn a penny holding the carriage horses—easy enough to get one to deliver this to the front door."

Dominic took the letter, considered it for an instant, then tugged the bellpull.

While he waited for Mulley to appear, Angelica pushed back from the desk, rose, and went to the armchair beside which she'd left Robertson's *History*. Picking up the tome, she sank into the chair, adjusted the footstool, then opened the book and settled to read.

To continue to read about the history of Scotland.

He'd wondered, at first, if she'd chosen the book merely to appear interested, but she truly was reading it, and he knew the contents were neither riveting nor entertaining.

He glanced at the note he held. Its contents shrieked of blatant manipulation. Her wording made it plain that her family, at least, knew her forcefulness, her forthrightness, well.

Like her, he couldn't imagine St. Ives and her brothers and other cousins paying any attention to her directive, but their wives? Angelica's expectation that the Duchess of St. Ives might exert influence over her powerful husband in such a matter was . . . eye-opening didn't begin to cover the effect that revelation had on him. Yet Angelica's expectation of a noble lady's power with respect to her husband explained many things.

Such as her transparent assumption that he, Dominic, would consult her in all matters affecting them both, and, more, listen to any suggestions she might make.

Hearing footsteps approaching, facing setting, he walked to the door. Truth be told, if her suggestions were sensible and advanced his—their—cause, then he wasn't such a nincompoop that he would stand on his dignity and refuse to accept her advice. He'd already done so several times . . . which, he now realized, might make him more like the Cynsters, more like her cousin Devil, than he'd supposed. That he might well be fated to have more in common with the males of her family than he'd expected.

Mulley tapped and entered.

Meeting him, Dominic handed over the letter. "Grosvenor Square. Thomas might be best, this time, but tell him to make sure he's not spotted and followed." He glanced at Angelica; she hadn't looked up from the book. "Apparently there will be plenty of urchins in the square at this hour."

"Indeed, my lord. I'll see Thomas off with this immediately." Mulley departed, closing the door behind him.

Dominic turned. His gaze on Angelica, he hesitated, then walked slowly back to the desk.

He was accustomed to wielding power—in his case more or less absolute power. He'd been head of the clan for the past five years, and none had either challenged that or sought to introduce their will alongside his. Not even his mother had bothered attempting that, not over the last five years. Angelica, however . . .

Sinking back into his chair, he re-sorted the papers she'd pushed aside to make space to write her note.

She didn't make demands. She *expected* him to see the sense in what she said, and be intelligent enough, wise enough, to modify his plans.

To modify his role to accommodate what she saw as hers.

He considered how he felt about that. It wasn't so much that the reins of his life were slipping from his grasp as that there was another—much lighter, less powerful—hand settling on the ribbons. One that only occasionally tweaked them.

The clock ticked on while he pretended to read a letter. Overall, he decided, he couldn't complain. She was clever, observant, refreshingly quick-witted, and she had strengths he lacked. Most importantly, she'd thrown herself into helping him save his clan. Even though her exercising her feminine wiles made him uneasy, she was exercising them on his and his people's behalf. And if he were truthful, he would have to admit that together he and she were a more powerful team—a more effective entity—than he alone had been.

That was a difficult truth to swallow—and his more resistant self still wasn't inclined to give it credence—yet on a deeper level, he knew. And accepted.

Accepted that he was better off with her than without her. That now she'd joined her abilities with his, they stood a much better chance of succeeding.

And for that, he had to be not just grateful but thankful.

With that much resolved, he reapplied himself to the task of vetting the contracts for the upcoming year for the output of the clan's distillery. Yet even as he switched from document to document, comparing clauses, inserting notes, he was intensely aware, at some level that ran just beneath his skin, of her sitting in the armchair, immersed in the history of his people, slowly but steadily turning pages.

He glanced at her more than once. And wondered if, between him and her, this was the calm before the storm.

Lord Martin Cynster ushered his wife into the library of St. Ives House. Across the crowded room, he met the eyes of his nephew Devil. "What have you heard?"

Over the hubbub and bodies filling the room, Devil waved them nearer. When they reached the desk, he handed Celia a note. "She's written again, but damned if I know what to make of it."

Celia unfolded the single sheet and read the note aloud.

The others in the room—all those who had been at the meeting the previous day, as well as Demon Cynster and his wife, Felicity, who had traveled down from Newmarket as soon as they'd heard the news—quieted as she did.

Reaching the end of the note, Celia frowned. "She's up to something."

"Exactly!" Seated on the chaise, Helena thumped her cane for emphasis. "It is perfectly obvious that she is pursuing . . . how does one say it? Ah—I have it—*an agenda of her own.*"

All the ladies nodded in agreement.

"But this time, there's more," Devil said. "Sligo answered the door and was quick enough to collar the urchin who'd brought the note. The boy swore a man—a young man, a groom, perhaps—had given him the note, but when he and Sligo searched, the man had disappeared. However, one thing the boy had noticed—the groom, or whoever he was, spoke with a Scottish accent. Of that, the boy was quite sure."

"Scots," Vane said. "So it is this business with the laird, but clearly it can't be him, since he's dead."

"Hasn't Royce learned anything yet?" Demon asked.

Grimly, Devil shook his head. "He and Hamish are still chasing the drovers who removed the bodies. However, in light of this latest kidnapping, we have to give credence to some ongoing threat."

"Perhaps it's some family vendetta," Gabriel said. "And with the death of the laird, the sword, as it were, has passed to his heir."

"Who can tell?" Lucifer ran a hand through his hair. "Hell's bells—this is so frustrating. What can we do—what *should* we do?"

"For my money," Honoria said, her voice cutting cleanly through the several conversations, "you should all do exactly as Angelica says, and wait. Or, as she puts it—knowing you all as she does—possess your souls in patience."

Devil met his duchess's eyes. "We can't do that."

Patience, Vane's wife, shifted to stand beside Honoria. "The tone of that note makes it abundantly clear that Angelica considers herself in control, at least as far as she herself is concerned. It's entirely possible that the last thing she needs is for us—meaning all of you—to raise a dust over this. She's already asked us to cover up her absence, and that we will do, but you running rampant, searching all over and causing a ruckus, might harm her more than help her."

"Much as I'd like to shake her," Alathea, Gabriel's wife, said, "simply because it's so hard not knowing, she would never intentionally cause a problem like this—and I can't see her having done so now, not without having a *very good reason.*"

"Which is to say," Felicity—better known as Flick—concluded, "that much as it pains you, you will just have to accept that there's nothing you can immediately do."

A long pause ensued, then the men gathered around Devil's desk once more, intent and urgent, and the ladies shifted to form a circle around Celia, now sitting on the chaise beside Helena, with her daughters, Heather and Eliza, beside her.

The ladies were all agreed, and therefore calm; even Celia saw the latest note as reassuring.

Their men, however, were, as the ladies also agreed, beyond reasoning with, and would simply have to be left to grump and growl and rattle their sabers until more was known.

"For if there's one thing we can be certain about," Heather said, "it's that there's no point searching for Angelica if she doesn't wish to be found."

Chapter Six

"I suggest we start in the front hall." Once more in her borrowed clothes, Angelica led Mulley and Brenda through the green baize door. Griswold was busy doing laundry, and Jessup and Thomas were putting the stables to right in anticipation of their return later in the month.

Halting before the stairs, tipping her head back, she surveyed the cobwebs festooning the ceiling. She would have preferred to be with Dominic, but circumstances—specifically the papers on his desk—had forced her to find something else to do.

Withholding her consent to their marriage had only one purpose—to give fate and The Lady time to work their magic and induce him to fall in love with her. Her refusal to agree would also, she hoped, focus him on what was required to gain her consent, namely irrefutable proof that he loved her; if he dwelled on the point for long enough, she was sure he would work that out.

He wasn't, however, likely to fall in love with her if they didn't spend much time together. She needed to get him to herself, without a dining table or a desk piled with papers between them, and without his staff hovering.

But the previous evening, when she'd shifted his papers to make space to write her note, she'd seen that said papers were legal documents—contracts and agreements of various sorts. Although she'd never dealt with such things herself, her brothers and cousins did; she'd recognized the style of document well enough. Enough to realize that Dominic's "clan business" was substantial.

If, despite his focus on reclaiming the goblet, he'd brought such affairs with him, then he truly needed to deal with them. Noting the rate at which the piles were reducing, she'd calculated that if she left him alone for the whole day, she would have a much better chance of claiming him tomorrow.

Needing to occupy her mind and energies, she'd elected to lead the assault on the front hall. "For a house that's been shut up for more than forty years, it seems remarkably sound."

Mulley leaned the ladder he'd carried in against one wall. "Was a caretaker couple lived here until earlier this year. They'd grown old and wanted to retire, so the laird pensioned them off. He hasna had the time since to find any replacement."

"And now he won't need to." Scanning the hall, she said, "Everything here looks cleanable. Even those tapestries look sturdy enough. But before we start, let's take a look at the reception rooms—I want to get a more complete idea of the scope of work needed to bring this place up to scratch."

Walking to the pair of massive double doors to the left of the front door, she turned the ornate knob and pushed the doors wide. "The drawing room, I assume."

Beyond the threshold, all lay in dimness, the furniture swathed in holland covers.

Brenda stepped past and headed to the windows. "Best let in some light if we truly want to see." Grasping the heavy canvas curtains put up in place of any velvets or silks, she drew them apart.

Early summer sunshine streamed into the room through diamond-shaped panes. The windows were wider than they were tall, their sills at waist height; there were two sets spaced down the room, and at the far end, Brenda dragged long curtains aside to reveal an alcove containing a deep bow window offering a view over the side garden.

Surveying the room, Angelica was reminded of Elveden Grange, the Duke and Duchess of Wolverstone's manor in Suffolk; that, too, was Jacobean. But this . . . this was much grander, a proper London mansion rather than a country manor.

Mulley had gone to examine the fireplace. Angelica joined him. While he checked the flue, grate, and hearth, she examined the heavy, ornately carved— fantastically carved—mantelpiece. She wouldn't have chosen it, but it suited the room to a tee.

"All seems in order." Mulley straightened. "Once we have the sweeps in, we shouldna have a problem."

"Sadly the same can't be said for these chairs." Brenda had lifted one of the covers and was looking beneath. "Such a pity, too—they must have been so pretty."

Angelica went to look. The chair beneath the cover looked solid and nicely carved, but the upholstery had all but disintegrated, the silks faded and halfway to dust.

"See here." Brenda pointed to where the bottom of the cushioned back met the seat. "You can see what the original color must have been. Such a beautiful shade."

"Turquoise." Angelica knew it well. A sensation like cool fingertips ran up her nape. She glanced around, then walked to the wall and peered at the silk hanging, also much damaged by the passage of time. From what she could make out, it had been ivory embossed with small turquoise fleur-de-lis.

An elusive memory tickled, floated forward . . . when she'd been a toddler, barely able to walk, Celia's sitting room in Dover Street had had the same wall hanging.

Turning away, she joined Brenda and Mulley in a more detailed inspection of the furniture—each chair and chaise, every side table, sideboard, occasional table, and footstool—noting what needed to be done to restore the room to its necessary glory.

Then Mulley retrieved two elegant candelabra from a sideboard and set them on top, and again she felt that odd sensation.

She stared at the candelabra—gilt with solid turquoise stems. Her father had given her mother a pair exactly the same for a wedding gift; they were still one of Celia's most treasured possessions. Her brother Lucifer had told her the pair was rare and valuable. Turquoise of that quality wasn't, apparently, easy to come by.

She glanced again at the chairs. The damage to the upholstery hadn't been from wear but from the passage of time. She turned to Mulley. "Do you know who decorated this room?" He was in his late fifties; he might know.

"I heard tell it was the old master had it done— couldna really have been anyone else. Heard he had all the main rooms done up for some lady he was expecting to marry, but something happened and instead he closed up the house and never came here again."

With a brief nod, she turned and walked to the bow window so they wouldn't see the emotions chasing over her face.

This room had been decorated as a temple for her mother, one Celia had never entered. But now, years later, Angelica was there, her feet already on the path to marry Mortimer's son and claim this room, this house, as hers.

Almost as if, a generation later, she was stepping into her mother's shoes . . . except for one very pertinent difference. Mortimer had never been Celia's hero. Dominic, however, was hers.

Refocusing on the scene beyond the window, she went closer and peered through one pane. "We'll have to get a team of gardeners in as soon as we come back to London. Taming the wilderness out there will take months."

Turning back into the room, she waved at Mulley to replace the candelabra in the cupboard. "They might as well stay hidden for the nonce."

She helped Brenda resettle the holland covers, then followed Mulley through a connecting door into a gallery running down the side of the house.

Whatever Dominic had told his staff of the reasons he'd had to kidnap her, he hadn't given them the entire story. In light of the lingering peculiarity she felt over effectively stepping into her mother's shoes, she decided she was glad he hadn't.

She waited until after dinner that evening, when they retired to the library, to beard her husband-to-be. But by the time she'd settled in her chair and mentally ordered her questions, he'd settled behind his desk and become immersed in his papers. Although the piles had shrunk significantly, she decided to bide her time; picking up Robertson's *History,* she opened the tome to the page she'd last read and settled to continue.

In between paragraphs, she glanced at Dominic, watching the way the lamplight gilded his black hair, waiting for her moment.

He could feel her eyes on him, sense her wanting his attention; lips tightening, Dominic signed the last of the most urgent agreements, blotted it, set it aside, then, replacing the pen in the inkstand, raised his gaze to her eyes. "What is it?"

She paused, then asked, "Did you know that your father decorated this house for my mother, to her specific taste?"

He hid his frown. "Why do you think that?"

She told him, concluding with, "The color alone is telling, but the candelabra put the matter beyond doubt."

"I wasn't aware he'd done that, but I can't say it's much of a surprise."

"You told me he didn't love her. Decorating one's house in the colors and style favored by one specific lady is usually interpreted as an expression of love."

He considered, then shook his head. "In his case it was adoration, adulation, infatuation—call it what you will, it wasn't love."

Her eyes caught his. "Do you know love so well, then?"

A vision of Mitchell and Krista bloomed in his mind. "I know love when I see it." After a moment, he added, "My father only dreamed, he never acted. Your father did."

Her brows rose, but she inclined her head. "I concede the point. My questions, however, continue. Does your mother know about the decoration of this house?"

"I doubt it. She's never mentioned it, and she would have had she known. There was a gap of several years between my father leaving London and him courting her."

One delicate finger tapped the chair arm. "What about your Edinburgh house?"

"He didn't touch that. It's as my grandmother left it—Mirabelle's never resided there, not as the Countess of Glencrae, so she hasn't changed it, either." When she continued vaguely frowning, he asked, "Why these particular questions?"

"I'm trying to get some idea of what specific factors drove your mother to seek such a peculiar revenge. Learning about the decoration of this house would have been a severe blow to a young bride who had set her heart on winning her husband's, but if she didn't know about it, it couldn't have contributed."

He couldn't fault her for seeking to learn what drove his mother's madness, but the impulse to tell her more clashed with the desire to keep such unedifying family secrets close, and not sully her ears or mind with them. Yet he'd promised to tell her all, and she'd seen him clearly enough to phrase her demand wisely.

He captured her gaze. "To understand Mirabelle, there's one aspect you need to accept as absolute truth. She didn't love my father any more than he loved her.

There never was any 'heart' involved, not on either side." He paused, then went on, "As for what drives her in seeking revenge—on everyone, on the world, on fate itself—via you and your mother, it's malicious vindictiveness, plain and simple, not any convoluted eruption of unrequited love."

He paused, then, still holding her gaze, added, "Trust me—I've had a lifetime to study her, and there is nothing in her that remotely resembles love, not for any other, possibly not even for herself."

After a moment, Angelica nodded and looked away.

He waited for several heartbeats, then asked, "Is that all?"

"No." She returned her gaze to his face, a frown in her eyes. "When I asked Mulley what he knew of the decorating, while he knew your father had expected to marry some lady, he didn't know who that lady was. He and the others don't know that I'm her daughter."

He shook his head. "I didn't need to tell them, so I haven't. All the clan folk presently alive, save me and Mirabelle, know only that my father remained devoted all his life to some English lady who married another. Even if any had heard him refer to her, it would have been only by her given name, but he usually didn't mention her to others. He kept that part of himself very private—literally held to his heart. He would tell me everything, and Mirabelle would pry and learn more than she wished, but no one else at the castle was privy to the details of his obsession."

He paused, then went on, "Beyond the clan, among wider society, both in Scotland and England, certainly up to the time of my father and Mirabelle's wedding, Celia's identity—that it was she he was obsessed with— was, I've been told, more widely known, but that was thirty and more years ago, and memories have faded. To my knowledge, the information is no longer current. It isn't of relevance to anyone anymore, only to Mirabelle.

"As for Mirabelle's scheme for revenge, because of the distance she preserves from all clan members, all they know is that she requires me to kidnap a young lady from a particular family and fetch the girl to the castle before she'll hand back the goblet. None of the clan was involved in your sisters' kidnappings, so they know nothing of those attempts beyond that they failed." He searched Angelica's eyes. "Mirabelle's motives and the ton mores involved in her gaining her revenge are both entirely foreign to clan folk. If they think of such matters at all, they decide that it's some Sassenach or lowland peculiarity and as such beyond them, and they shrug it off as one of those things they don't need to understand."

"So what, exactly, do they know about me?"

"They know I needed to persuade you to help me, that gaining your assistance is the only way I can meet Mirabelle's demands, but beyond that . . . frankly, I doubt they think beyond that. For them, that's reason enough for what I have asked, or might ask, of them." He hesitated, studying her face, then said, "I hadn't intended to broadcast your connection to the lady who was my father's long-ago obsession, or why you, of all the young ladies in the ton, are the one Mirabelle now wishes to see at the castle." Capturing her gaze, he asked, "Do you wish me to?"

She held his gaze. A moment ticked by, then she shook her head. "No. Aside from all else, it will make it rather awkward when Mama and Papa come to visit."

He hadn't thought of that. "Indeed." He let another moment elapse, then asked, "Is there anything else?"

"Yes." Angelica waited until his gaze returned to hers. "Have you told your people that as part of your bargain to gain my assistance you would offer to marry me and make me your countess?"

"No." Lips thinning, he searched her eyes. "I've told them nothing of how I planned to gain your necessary support."

"So those here have leapt to the conclusion?"

"It's not such a great leap." His voice grew harder, his tones crisper. "Those here have been with me for years, and none of them are unintelligent. They know what sort of man I am, and Griswold at least appreciates exactly what sort of lady you are. On top of that, you've been behaving as my countess-to-be—learning about them, me, the clan, and this house. That a marriage between us is pending isn't an assumption they've been given any reason to question." His eyes narrowed on hers. "So no, I didn't seek to force your agreement by letting it be known that I would offer or have offered for your hand."

Despite being pinned by those gray-green eyes, she appreciated his candor. She nodded. "Very well. Now, tell me about your wards. Gavin and Bryce." He blinked, and she explained, "Jessup mentioned them."

The change in him was palpable, visual—real. Under her fascinated gaze, the tension in his shoulders eased; his face, that hard, impassive, tell-nothing face, softened in a way she hadn't suspected was possible.

"They're my late cousin's sons." He smiled.

At the sight of that smile, her heart turned over. He was utterly charmed by and devoted to his wards, protective, caring . . . *loving*. That was what she saw in his face.

My God. The expression of mingled pride and love lighting his countenance, which had banished every cloud from his eyes, was identical to the expression she saw in her brothers' and cousins' faces whenever they looked upon their children.

Utterly entranced, she sat and listened as, with little further prompting, he told her of the pair—how they'd been orphaned, how their guardianship had fallen to him, how he'd been their surrogate father since they'd been just two and three years old. How, just as he and their father had done, they now ran wild in and about the castle; it sounded as if Jessup had been nothing more than accurate in labeling them scamps.

"Gavin—he's the elder—is the master of the clan. My heir." Dominic glanced at her. "At least at the moment."

She let the comment slip past but couldn't resist testing him. "What color are their eyes?"

"Blue, and blue—Bryce's are a touch paler."

"Hair?"

"Lighter brown and darker brown, either side of the middle."

She'd never met a man who could answer such questions without even pausing to think. "Jessup mentioned that they'd been badgering him to start them on their first pony. He was contemplating doing so on returning to the castle."

"That's been a sore point—they've been limited to the donkeys until now." Across the desk, he caught her eye. "Once you see the land around the castle, you'll understand—it's not the sort of terrain you want two boys with inflated notions of their equestrian abilities to be racing over. As those two would. But . . ." He leaned back in his chair, fingers idly turning the seal ring he wore on one finger. "Jessup's right—that's a bridge we'll need to cross soon."

She nearly offered to help, but a niggling doubt over whether he'd welcome her assistance in an arena he clearly held so close to his heart—at least not until he and she had grown closer and he'd learned to trust her—held her back. There would be plenty of time later, once they'd reclaimed the goblet and she'd met the two terrors. She shifted in the chair; one leg was going numb. "Given Jessup and Mulley are here with you, who's looking after them? I assume they're not nestling under your mother's wing."

He muttered what sounded like a Scottish curse and shook his head. "Not likely." He hesitated, then, lips thinning, said, "She can't abide them. They're too noisy, and yell, and run, and track mud inside . . ." He spread his arms in an all-encompassing gesture, then looked at her as if suddenly wondering what her stance would be.

She grinned. "Good heavens—they're *boys*. Surely she knows that's how such beings are? Well, she had you, after all, and I'm sure you and your cousin Mitchell were even worse."

His grin was unabashed and utterly boyish; for the instant it lit his face, she saw the boy he once had been. "True. But at that age I was her golden-haired—figuratively speaking—boy and could do no wrong. And Mitchell always hid behind me." The grin faded, to be replaced with a look she interpreted as looking north, far north, in his mind. "Mrs. Mack, and Gillian, their nurse, will have them in hand indoors, and Scanlon, my gamekeeper, and his lads will keep them close outside the keep."

She blinked. "You have a keep?"

He met her gaze. "I have a castle."

"Yes, I know, but . . ." Most castles she knew didn't have keeps, or if they did, said keeps had long been buried within the expanding structure, but she didn't think that was what he meant.

The clock on the mantelpiece further down the room whirred and bonged. Eleven times. She glanced at the papers on his desk. "Have you finished with those?"

He looked down. Grimaced. "No."

She shut her similarly neglected book. "I'll let you get back to them."

He looked at her as she rose, arched a questioning brow.

"My questions about the castle and the keep will . . . well, keep. We've a long journey in a few days' time, plenty of hours in which you can tell me all I need to know."

He nodded. "Good night."

Smiling, she headed for the door. "Good night."

Letting herself out, she walked to the front hall and slowly climbed the stairs. Over the last minutes, when they'd been talking of his wards, he hadn't bothered to keep his rigidly impassive mask in place. He'd lowered it and had allowed her to see the man behind it.

She hadn't realized she'd been waiting for that moment, for him to stop seeing her as someone to be held at a distance and allow her within his circle.

Allow her to see the huge heart he hid behind the rigid mask.

With the insight, the realization, had come a nearly overpowering temptation to reach out and touch . . . but it was too early yet.

No. In the matter of stalking and capturing her very own wild, highland earl, she, of all ladies, knew the value of patience. Tonight she would retire satisfied with knowing she'd made very real progress, and looking forward to what tomorrow might bring.

Half an hour later, Dominic signed the last of the agreements his manager at the distillery had sent him for approval. Putting down his pen, he raised his arms, stretched . . . and let out a long sigh.

Lowering his arms, he leaned back in his chair. Shifting his gaze to the chair facing him, with the Robertson lying closed on the table alongside, he finally let his mind change tracks—to his coconspirator.

That he thought of her as that testified as to how far his view of her had changed. Over her, his coldly rational, logical side and his instinct-driven side were rapidly reaching agreement. In all that was to come, not simply in their immediate future but later, too, she would be an asset, a major one. Instead of the long-term disaster his mother's scheme might have wrought—forcing him to take to wife some sweet ninnyhammer utterly unsuited to meeting the needs of the clan, or his own—he'd been handed Angelica. Difficult or not, fiery-tempered or not, she was a boon, one he hadn't in the least expected.

He still wasn't certain he trusted fate, that something wouldn't arise to throw everything askew again, but for now he had to take the situation at face value and move forward, which meant he had to learn how to deal with her, how best to . . . he supposed the correct term was negotiate with her.

Stretching out his legs, he crossed his ankles, crossed his hands behind his head, and stared upward. With every hour he spent in her company, he felt increasingly drawn to her, increasingly caught in the web of her attraction; he now felt the effect as an almost physical tug.

Another issue they would have to negotiate at some point, but luckily not until later.

Tonight she'd revealed another dimension, another aspect to her allure.

Her interest in the boys had been genuine. If he was any judge, she would take them under her wing— would without question stand beside him in rearing them, in giving them the love and sense of belonging they'd lost with Mitchell and Krista's deaths.

That meant a lot to him.

In all honesty, he couldn't think of anything more he could ask of her. She'd done what she could to deflect her family, had helped work out a plan to elude them and reach the castle, and had thrown herself into the arrangements. She was interacting well with his staff, taking appropriate interest in his house, in learning all she needed to go forward, and, given her recent questions, she was already turning her mind to the challenge of dealing with his mother and her mad scheme.

Admittedly, she'd refused to simply agree to their wedding, but that was merely a temporary quibble. He couldn't fathom her reasoning—presumably another of her female-only perspectives—but even tonight, she'd tacitly acknowledged that she would eventually agree.

Which meant he was going to have to give more thought to what she might want of him. To what he was prepared to give her in return for all she was giving him.

If there was one truth his years of business dealings had taught him, it was that successful negotiation required give as well as take.

He suspected he would be wise to define what he was willing to give, before she decided what she would take.

Chapter Seven

"I'm going to go out and wander the streets to practice passing as a male."

Dominic raised his head and stared down the breakfast table at Angelica, seated as usual at the other end. Her reply was definitely not what he'd expected in response to his query about her plans for the day.

Admittedly, he'd asked because she was dressed in her disguise.

An authoritarian veto burned the tip of his tongue, but when she glanced up and met his gaze, he swallowed it. "You can't risk being seen by your family."

"True. But there are only so many of them, and I know where they spend their days. There's a lot of London where they never go." She looked down at the porridge she'd elected to eat. "I'll just go there."

"The areas where your family never goes—" He cut off the sentence. Telling her such areas were dangerous for young ladies wasn't going to get him anywhere. He scooped up a mouthful of porridge, just to give himself time to think. "Your disguise is good enough as it is— during the journey, you won't need to pass any terribly close scrutiny, not while you're beside me."

"Not from any females, perhaps, but we discussed the likelihood that my family will have alerted or even paid the staff at the various inns to keep an eye on all coach passengers, and while said staff might be looking for a young lady, there's no saying one of them won't spot some telltale mistake I make, and so see through my disguise."

She'd rehearsed—prepared all the arguments she needed to win this one. He realized he was frowning, that he'd set aside his usual impassive mask, but he didn't care. "You can't seriously imagine that you'll be safe wandering London's streets and staring at unknown men."

Aside from all else, she made a far too attractive youth.

"Of course not." Laying aside her spoon, she lifted her napkin and dabbed at her lips—those outrageously feminine curves—and his unruly body reacted. "I'll take Thomas with me. He'll be able to protect me."

Down the length of the table, he met her gaze, read her determination. Ungraciously growled, "All right. I'll go with you. As we both know, Thomas isn't an appropriate companion for a youth of your supposed station, especially not in areas where such youths congregate, and those youths, after all, are the ones you need to mimic."

The smile she bent on him was equal parts triumph, approval, and pure pleasure. "Excellent! I knew you'd see my point."

And if that wasn't an admission of blatant manipulation, he didn't know what was.

She capped her performance with a cheery "So! When can we leave?"

The hackney Dominic had sent Jessup out to hail so he could bundle her into it in the mews without anyone seeing her became Angelica's initial classroom.

The first thing she learned was that Dominic's house was in Bury Street. "Good Lord!" She stared at him in shock. "We're just around the corner from my home!"

He didn't say anything, just looked at her.

She grinned and looked around. "No wonder you didn't want me heading out on my own." She examined the carriage's interior. "Are all hackney coaches like this?"

"You've never ridden in a hackney before?"

She shook her head.

Inwardly sighing, he replied, "More or less. Some are bigger, others smaller, but they operate on the same system . . . one you clearly do not need to know."

"A well-bred youth would know about hackneys."

She was teasing him again. Rather than respond directly, he viewed her critically, then sat up. "First lesson." Leaning forward, he closed his hands, one about each of her breeches-clad knees, and spread them apart. Saw shocked surprise flash across her face. "No youth sits with his knees together. Not unless he's forced to."

"Oh." The word was breathless. Eyes locked with his, she licked her lips, then nodded. "I see."

The feel of her quintessentially female knees under his palms, the way her breeches had pulled taut across her lower hips . . . he nearly closed his eyes and groaned. What was he doing? The answer came instantly: Paying her back.

Slowly, his long fingers caressing, he drew his hands away and leaned back against the seat. Kept his gaze on her face, saw the faintest of blushes tinge her cheeks.

But she refused to look away. "All right." Her chin tipped up a fraction. "What else?"

If she wanted to joust . . . "Your hands." She had them folded in her lap. He dropped his gaze to them. "You should rest them at your sides, on the seat, or palms down on your thighs. Never in your lap like that."

Angelica chose the latter option, spread her fingers slightly, then moved her palms back and forth a fraction and saw him tense. "Anything else?"

"Not at the moment." His voice had dropped half an octave. His gaze—at that moment not remotely cold—lifted to her face, rested there. "For the moment, you'll do."

She inclined her head, looked out of the carriage window, and started plotting his downfall.

Twenty minutes later, the carriage rocked to a halt in the shadow of the Tower. Dominic stepped down to the pavement first; she bit back her frustration when he just stood there, blocking her way out while he checked their surroundings. Eventually, he moved. While he paid the jarvey, she clambered down the steps by herself, remembered to shut the door—no footmen there—then waited on the pavement, closer by the wall.

She felt oddly exposed without skirts to screen her legs; the unsettling feeling hadn't afflicted her in the house, but the open and very public street west of the Tower was a different matter.

Determined to show no hint of her sudden attack of missishness, she flashed Dominic a bright smile as he joined her.

He halted directly before her, his height and width effectively screening her from passersby. Like her, he was dressed in breeches and riding boots, in his case with a severely cut topcoat over a plain waistcoat; in attire, at least, he could have passed for a well-heeled tutor. He studied her, then said, "You're going to have to keep your head down, the brim of your hat tilted down. There is no way in hell anyone getting a good look at your face is going to imagine you're male. And no smiling. No youth ever born smiles like you do."

She started to smile again, fought to straighten her lips. She nodded, obediently tipping her head down. "All right." She waved to the street ahead of them. "Let's go."

He hesitated just long enough for her to remember that giving direct orders to men like him didn't work, then he swung around and started strolling.

Slowly, so she could keep up.

Her first task was to learn to walk like him. Or at least well enough to pass. After having studied Thomas, then having checked in the mirror, she was well aware that her normal stride—which she reverted to the instant she stopped thinking about it—would immediately identify her as female, no matter her disguise.

Quite aside from wanting to spend the day with Dominic, she'd been sincere in demanding to go out so she could observe, adjust, and practice. If she could work at being a youth for a whole day while in her male clothes, she'd be a lot less likely to forget and revert to being feminine when in them.

And they had a whole day to spare.

Having got what she wanted—her pacing a public street with Dominic beside her—she put her mind to accomplishing the more urgent of her goals.

By the time they reached the Custom House, Dominic was seriously questioning his sanity in having agreed to—allowed himself to be jockeyed into—the outing. She was, he had to admit, diligently applying herself to copying his walk, modifying his stride to suit her shorter legs, but that laudable endeavor required her to glance constantly at his legs, his hips. Which wasn't helping his stride in the least.

A result that in turn made her continued scrutiny even harder to nonchalantly ignore.

"You know," his tormentor said, "you're going to have to make some adjustments yourself if you want anyone to believe you're a tutor."

He didn't glance at her; she'd been keeping her head tipped down. "Why?"

"Because you walk like a nobleman, talk like a nobleman, and you positively radiate arrogance."

"I'm the scion of a noble house come down in the world and forced to earn my living."

"And the arrogance?"

He didn't reply. His arrogance, what she meant by the term, was an innate part of him; he couldn't pluck it out . . . but perhaps he could mute it somewhat. Making a mental note to bear that in mind when dealing with others while in his role of tutor, he paced on.

Increasingly aware of her, a burr under his skin, and a peculiarly titillating temptation in her youth's garb.

He should have sent her out with Mulley or Jessup . . . no, he couldn't have. Neither would recognize danger approaching . . . speaking of which. Halting at the corner of the Custom House, he looked at what lay ahead.

She'd obediently halted beside him, more or less in his shadow.

"The market." Billingsgate Fish Market lay ahead on their left, filling the area between the street and the river. "Your brothers, cousins, and their wives might not be there, but what about their staff?"

From beneath the brim of her hat, Angelica viewed the bustling throng filling the market and spilling out into the street. It was one of the well-known places in London no young lady would ever venture into, which was the reason she was keen to walk through there. "What's the time?" She didn't look at Dominic; from observing other men talking to each other, she'd realized they rarely looked each other in the face as they did.

Women almost invariably watched each others' faces when conversing.

Dominic consulted his fob watch. "Almost eleven."

"There's no danger, then—if any of the staff had come to buy anything, they'd be gone by now. But most of the households have their fish delivered to the back door."

He hesitated, then nodded. "All right. But we walk straight through and out the other side, and on over London Bridge."

She set off, pacing along, letting her arms swing. She was getting into the way of it, and she'd been right; the practice was helping.

They'd agreed on a route that would keep them away from the streets her brothers and cousins, let alone their wives, might for any reason walk or drive down.

She'd expected the market to be busy and noisy, but it proved to be more crowded than a duchess's drawing room, with humanity, largely unwashed, jostling on all sides, and wincingly loud, raucous screams, yells, and exhortations vibrating through the air. Long before they reached the exit, she was inexpressibly grateful for Dominic's large presence beside her, supporting her and shielding her from the worst of the melee.

Jaw clenched, Dominic caught her arm and literally hauled her out, into the less crowded area around the church at the market's western end. He released her. Watched as she shook herself, then readjusted her jacket and checked the stability of her hat and the hair it concealed. "Satisfied?"

Somewhat to his surprise, she didn't flash him a teasing smile; she just nodded. "At least I've seen it—and now I understand what's meant by 'screeching like a fishwife.' They *do* screech."

Without prompting, she walked on.

Pacing side by side, they rounded the church and walked on to London Bridge.

They halted for lunch in a tavern south of the river, not far from the docks. Dominic thanked his stars that he'd been able to steer her away from the rougher, dockside haunts, yet as he led the way into the tavern's main room, he felt instinct roil just beneath his surface.

If he'd had any doubt that his inner self already considered her his, the impulse to snarl and figuratively show his teeth to the men sitting supping ale at the other tables slew it. But he couldn't even look at them in silent warning; even that would mark him as what he truly was. She'd been right in stating he'd have to adjust, but it wasn't only his arrogance he had to rein in.

Reaching a table by the wall, he pulled out a chair and forced himself to drop into it before she sat. Treating her like a youth would have been much easier if he could have seen her as a youth, but his imagination balked at the task.

A slatternly serving woman slouched to the table. "Right then, what'll it be?"

"Two servings of your pie, a pint of ale for me, and"—he glanced at Angelica; her eyes met his beneath the brim of her hat—"watered ale for my charge."

The serving woman grunted and left.

His "charge" glanced swiftly around, then, mimicking one of the other men, propped her elbows on the table and clasped her hands.

It had been her suggestion to go strolling along the docks. As it transpired, it had been safe enough, just like their slow amble across London Bridge. Regardless, for the entire time he'd been hyper-alert, trying to

watch every way at once while simultaneously appearing to be a bored tutor accompanying his charge on a
day's outing.

She'd halted in the middle of the bridge, leaned on
the railing, and looked eastward down the river; only
he'd been close enough to see the pleasure in her eyes,
in her face, as she'd drunk in the scene. The sight had
gone some way to placating him for all the tense moments she was putting him through. And he had to
admit that even on the docks, she'd been watching the
men—the messengers, the navies—as they'd swarmed,
picking up traits here and there, trying them out, in-
corporating some into her new persona. She was definitely improving, which was why he'd agreed to bring
her into the tavern.

Leaning on the table, she murmured, "What do
men generally talk about at a venue such as this?" Her
natural voice was a faintly husky contralto; by lowering
the tone, she could make it pass for a youth's.

He considered what he and Mitchell would have
talked about in such a setting . . . almost anywhere.
"Women."

She met his gaze. After a moment said, "There must
be other subjects of passing interest to males."

"Horses. Gaming. None of which a tutor would discuss with his charge."

The serving woman appeared with their plates and pint pots. For several minutes, silence reigned while they sampled the tavern's offerings, and discovered them palatable enough.

"I know," Angelica said, struck by inspiration. "You can tell me about the goblet—about why it's so valuable to those bankers."

He hesitated, then said, "You know of Sir Walter Scott, the novelist?" When she nodded, he went on, "Scott is a patriotic Scotsman, and in '18, was also great friends with Prinny, who at that time was in dire need of something—anything—to appease the populace. Scott, like my father, had an obsession, in his case centering on the Regalia of Scotland, also known as the Scottish Honours. The regalia dates from James IV's time, but had been lost early in the eighteenth century, roughly a hundred years ago. No one had taken it—it had simply been misplaced and no one knew where it was. The history of the regalia appealed to Prinny— when Cromwell ruled, he specifically set out to destroy all the regalia, the symbols of monarchy. He melted down the English regalia, and all the other royal crowns he could find, then came north to seize the Scottish Honours, but he never found them. But the regalia was only hidden—it promptly resurfaced after the Restoration, and was used for many state occasions at Scone and Edinburgh, but then . . . nothing more was known of it."

Dominic paused to scoop up the last mouthful of his pie, chewed, swallowed, then went on, "Scott was convinced the regalia had simply been put away in Edinburgh Castle, and all those who knew where had died. He convinced Prinny to mount a thorough search of the castle—a massive undertaking—and the regalia was discovered in an old chest in a long-forgotten robing room. Prinny was in alt—he now had the oldest surviving British regalia restored to the Crown. There was much made of it at the time, which helped a trifle in balancing the public's view of their regent, at least for a while."

"I remember something of that." She waited while he downed a draft of his ale, then prompted, "How does that connect with the goblet?"

"The regalia found by Scott comprised the crown, the scepter, and the sword. What was missing was the coronation cup."

"The goblet." She only just remembered to keep her voice low.

He shot her a warning glance, then nodded. "It's a jewel-encrusted goblet of solid gold, about eight inches high. Centuries ago, the cup had been entrusted to Beauly Priory, which is near Guisachan lands, and during an upheaval within the church in the late sixteenth century, the cup was passed to my ancestors for safekeeping. The cup remained with my family throughout the subsequent turmoil, then later, after the Restoration, it was called for whenever it was required to complete the regalia for a state occasion, but was always returned to us. We became the protectors of the cup, and the charge placed upon us was that we should only hand it over to complete the regalia. During the years the rest of the regalia was lost, we held the cup.

"But although we had it, we more or less forgot about it as it was never called for, not for over a hundred years. When the rest of the regalia was rediscovered, no one knew to send for the cup. I knew it existed, but along with my father, I saw no need to hand it over to shore up public support for an unpopular Sassenach prince."

"Naturally not."

He paused, then said, "My father's scheme was inspired in a way. We would have surrendered the cup at some point, but he saw the potential and, sure enough, the bankers he contacted were so keen to get into the good graces of the ex-regent, now George IV, that they were happy to hand over a massive sum just to have the chance, at some point, of presenting the king with the Scottish coronation cup, a goblet very few people know exists, to complete the regalia George now holds so dear."

She stared at him. "That's an amazing story."

He sipped his ale, then drained the pot.

"One thought." She met his gaze as he set down the pot. "If we need more time to reclaim the original, would it be possible to make a replica and give that to the bankers, to hold them off?"

"If we had the original to copy from, perhaps a duplicate could be made, but even then the pieces of the regalia are all of similar vintage. Trying to match gold that old, let alone the jewels . . ." His lips set. "Regardless, we don't have the original, and once we do, we won't need a copy." He nodded to her pint pot, from which she'd barely sipped. "We should go. If you've finished?"

When she nodded, he tossed coins on the table, then rose.

Remembering her guise, she immediately rose, too, then followed him to the door.

They walked east along the river to Tower Bridge. There, Dominic surrendered to Angelica's pleading, and they took a boat from under the bridge's southern end to Greenwich. The park around the observatory was filled with nurses, governesses, and tutors escorting their charges on outings in the fresh air, but none of those present were from society's elite.

As they strolled along the paths, Dominic gradually relaxed—a little. Enough to turn some of his attention to his supposed charge. After watching her for a while, he murmured, "You're improving."

Pacing alongside him, her hands clasped behind her, she responded with a tip of her down-bent head.

They strolled for nearly an hour. Courtesy of various comments and observations, he learned that, despite appearances, she'd been a tomboy and could skip stones over water better than most males. She could also fly a kite; after helping three youngsters untangle the strings of theirs, she showed them how to get the kite aloft, then make it swoop, soar, and swoop again.

Watching from a distance, he saw the children's joy, heard their delighted squeals, switched his gaze to Angelica's face, and felt his heart clench. The ability to enjoy simple pleasures was a facility to treasure. It was one he had lost, but he knew its worth.

Something shifted inside him, settling deeper, more definitely anchored.

A Cynster princess who knew her own strengths, her own worth, who was willful, headstrong, fearless, and a tomboy to boot . . . guarding such a lady, protecting her from all harm, would never be a simple matter.

Eventually leaving the three children, she returned to his side. His inner self approved.

"Well. Now what?" Beneath her hat, her cheeks were aglow, her eyes bright.

Strolling on, he considered. She hadn't made any stupid mistakes. And while he sensed she was aware of his protective streak, of the tension that gripped him whenever she did anything potentially dangerous, she hadn't played the tease but instead had toed any line he'd drawn, accepting his strictures, at least as long as they'd appeared reasonable to her.

And despite that moment of flaring desire in the hackney, she hadn't retaliated. He'd expected her to, but she'd made no move to pay him back. Perhaps because she, too, was susceptible to that unsettling leap of pulse, that disconcerting distraction; she couldn't distract him without distracting herself. She hadn't tried but had instead remained focused on learning how to pass as a youth.

He was still feeling his way with her, learning how to deal with her. Dealing with another as an almost-equal wasn't something he'd had to do often, much less on a daily basis. All things considered, he suspected that this was a moment to give a little.

Glancing at her, he murmured, "As your disguise has improved so much, is there anywhere you'd like to go that you could only go if disguised as a youth?"

Beneath the brim of her hat, he caught a glimpse of shining eyes. "Oh, yes—indeed there is."

The pit at the Theatre Royal late that afternoon was a seething, shifting mass of men and youths, with the occasional prostitute thrown in for good measure. Cheers erupted on all sides when the heroine or hero trod the stage; when the villain appeared, boos and hisses abounded.

Dominic stood more or less in the middle of the good-natured, jostling throng gathered to watch the late matinee performance. Angelica, hat crammed low over her brow, stood directly before him, shielded from the worst of the press, but clearly visible from three sides.

The only positive in their position was that all eyes were fixed on the stage. Except for his. He continually scanned the crowd, alert for any sign that someone had noted the unusually fine skin of the youth in front of him, or that said "youth's" eyes were uncommonly fine, with long curling lashes, and a brightness to them that was inherently . . . not just effeminate but feminine. Or that the youth's lips left the question of gender beyond doubt.

Thus far, the lure of the stage had won out.

He had no idea what the play was about. The risk of discovery, and the likely result if anyone did realize that a lady in disguise stood in their midst, was more than enough to fill his mind. To have every instinct on high alert, and turn every muscle to steel.

His mind wasn't so much in thinking mode as reacting mode. Ready to react to the danger when it flared. And he couldn't even lay the blame for his state at her boot-shod feet.

He'd brought this on himself. Jaw set, he silently swore he would never again fall into that trap. Next time he would inquire as to her wishes without making any, even implied, open agreement. Her desire to visit the pit at Drury Lane had stunned him, but he'd gone too far to retract; he'd already complimented her on her much improved disguise.

So here he was, stiff as a post in every way, with every nerve alert and tension literally thrumming through him.

The play must have reached some critical point; engrossed, the crowd surged forward, pressing closer to the stage. He stood like a rock and the crowd parted on either side, leaving Angelica protected from the jostling flow, but as the crowd before her thickened, it pushed her back. She edged back, and back, then, on a smothered gasp, she was shoved back—and plastered against him.

He tried to step back, but there were multiple shoulders locked behind him, and on either side; courtesy of the surge of humanity, he was trapped, too.

Angelica caught her breath and tried to ease away from the male body scorching her back, but the crowd before them grew even more dense, pressing her even more firmly against him. She tried to edge sideways—

"*Don't. Move.*"

The words, gritted out through clenched teeth, froze her; his voice had dropped to such a gravelly growl that she'd only just made them out.

Drawing in a tight breath, she stayed where she was and, with outward calm, continued to stare toward the stage while her senses rioted.

His body was rock-hard. All of it. When he'd man-handled her during her kidnap, she'd noticed the hardness of his chest, the solidity of his shoulders, but . . . this was hardness of quite a different stripe.

This was arousal. His thighs were granite pillars on either side of hers, his erection a solid ridge against her lower back. She was pressed against him from shoulders to knees, which presumably explained why he didn't want her shifting; as she understood things, his present condition might be bordering on the painful, and her sliding against him would only make matters worse.

So she stayed where she was, only to discover that being plastered against him affected her, too. He felt scaldingly hot, and that heat transferred to her. She grew increasingly warm, as if subtle flames were spreading beneath her skin. And that skin somehow grew more sensitive, until any little shift of her clothing registered as a sensual abrasion. As for her breasts, they swelled beneath the band she'd used to restrain them . . . until she was in discomfort, if not pain, too.

Until the question of how long she could bear it and *not* move became a very real concern . . .

In unison, the crowd let out a long sigh, then a second later, erupted with whoops and cheers, followed by rowdy applause.

Finally, after another interminable few minutes, the curtain swished closed, and the play was at an end.

"Stay where you are."

Another order from above, but in the next instant the big doors at both sides of the pit opened and the crowd started to stream away to either side.

The instant the pressure of bodies eased, Dominic stepped back and ended the torture.

As the departing crowd thinned, he tweaked Angelica's sleeve. Head down, she fell into step alongside him; together they joined the rear of the departing horde.

They stepped outside into deepening dusk. He glanced at her face, despite the fading light saw the bloom of a blush still high in her cheeks, washing down the side of her throat . . . she'd been as affected as he.

Hauling his mind from dwelling on that, he scanned their surroundings, then halted.

She looked around as if enthralled by the hackneys and the noise and confusion. "Well! That was an adventure."

He cast her a look, waited until she glanced up and met it. "The next time I take you to the theater, we'll be getting a private box."

He held her gaze for an instant, then looked around, forcing his mind to deal with the moment, to gauge their chances of grabbing a hackney.

"Come on." He stepped out along the pavement heading toward Covent Garden; there would be plenty of hackneys there. "The others will be wondering where we've got to."

He was wondering the same thing.

A hackney proved hard to come by, but eventually they returned to the mews in Bury Street. Dominic held open the gate in the garden wall, then followed Angelica up the path to the house.

It was past eight o'clock when they entered the servants' hall. Brenda and Mulley were sitting at the table; both rose as Dominic and Angelica appeared.

"There you be." Brenda smiled, then her expression grew concerned. "Have you eaten, miss? My lord?"

Dominic shook his head. "We ended at the theater." Brenda and Mulley would be up at dawn; he noticed the glance Angelica threw him, hoped he read it correctly. "Just a light supper will do."

"Indeed, yes." Angelica smiled at Brenda. "We had game pie for lunch, so whatever you can put together quickly will do."

"I'll set the table in the dining parlor, shall I?" Mulley reached for a tray.

Angelica hesitated for only a second. "Yes, that might be best."

Having the length of the dining table between her and Dominic struck her as a very wise move. Ever since those fraught moments in the pit—moments she couldn't get out of her head—he'd been watching her . . . she was starting to feel like a hunted deer.

He was a highlander; she was quite sure he hunted deer.

Despite her very real desire to learn more about that side of their pending relationship, the side she was perfectly certain was on his mind, she was heart-thumpingly sure that she wasn't up to dealing with more revelations on that subject tonight. She had no idea why she was so skitteringly nervous; she only knew she was. For once—possibly for the first time in her life—*all* her instincts were urging caution and retreat.

She followed Mulley to the breakfast parlor they'd been using as a dining room. Every step of the way she was intensely aware of Dominic prowling behind her. Mulley set her place and moved up the table. She walked to her chair and felt Dominic draw near; he was so damned huge, all hard muscle, that he literally radiated heat enough for her sensitized nerves to detect.

He halted. She felt his presence like a warm wash down her back.

Moving slowly—as her senses reminded her he had on the terrace when he'd almost been ready to pounce—he drew out her chair.

She sat, let him settle her.

Waited until he walked, long-legged stride fluid and slow, to the other end of the table before she exhaled.

She told herself her reaction was nonsensical, but, after sitting himself, he looked down the table and met her gaze . . . she looked into his eyes, sharply intent gray-on-green, and knew she hadn't misread the direction of his thoughts.

He and she were destined, at some point, to be man and wife, after all.

Brenda hurried in with a soup tureen. Mulley followed with two plates made up with bread, sliced roast beef, and portions of an egg, bacon, leek, and cheese flan.

"Lovely—thank you." Angelica found a smile for Brenda as the maid ladled a rich broth into her soup bowl. "This will be more than enough."

"Aye, well, we've only got breakfast and lunch tomorrow, and then we'll be gone, so I want to use up all that we have."

After serving Dominic, Brenda withdrew, following Mulley out and back to the kitchen . . . leaving Angelica alone with her prospective husband.

She kept her eyes on her soup as she supped, but she could feel his gaze. Could feel the silence thicken— could all but sense their mutual awareness reaching over the table, colliding, twining, then his reached for her while hers reached for him—

"I enjoyed today. I have to thank you for going with me. You were right—it wouldn't have been the same with Thomas. The fish market was such an experience—not one I have any ambition to repeat, but still not one I would have liked to have missed. The crowds, the smells—let alone all the noise. Why . . ."

Dominic ate, watched, and listened. Whenever she paused—only ever for a second—as if expecting some comment from him, he hmmed, or grunted, and, apparently satisfied, she rolled on with her catalog of the day's highlights.

He wondered if she knew she was babbling.

And if she knew how revealing that was.

He seriously doubted she was a female who often babbled, but the intensity of the desire that—courtesy of their adventure at the theater—was now all but crackling between them had reduced her to it.

Despite knowing that that sensual storm wasn't emanating from him alone, her reaction to it gave him pause.

He recognized her response—it was very like that of a half-broken filly shying at the saddle. She wanted to step forward and learn what it was like, but simultaneously was leery over what she might lose, of what accepting might mean for her.

In that, she was wise. Becoming his wife in fact would change her life irreversibly and irrevocably.

And while that result would be the same regardless of when they consummated their now-fated union, it was, he suspected, her very intelligence—a characteristic for which he had to give thanks—that had her stepping back. Wanting to look before she leaped. Wanting to think things through, first.

He couldn't blame her for that.

Although he wanted nothing more than to stand, walk down the table, haul her up out of her chair, and kiss her until she melted against him, until she didn't just allow but welcomed him—nay, begged him to sink his throbbing shaft deep into the hot haven of her body—he reined the near-brutal impulse back.

Only to discover how much effort that took. Normally his appetites, although as large as he was, nevertheless remained entirely under his control. Tonight, with her, after the too-tantalizing day, that control was . . . tenuous. He wanted her more than he'd ever wanted any other, perhaps because she'd agreed to be his wife.

Regardless . . .

Lifting his gaze from his empty plate, he looked down the table.

She'd finished her meal, laid her cutlery down. Hands in her lap, she was staring at a spot midway down the table while her tongue ran on. "And"—she paused to draw a tight breath, which only succeeded in focusing his attention on her severely bound breasts, a situation his ravenously sexual self wanted to rectify *now*—"of course, I've always wanted to visit the pit at the Theatre Royal."

The thready neediness in her voice, the way she shifted in her seat . . . his hunter's instinct to seize— seize *now*—bucked hard against his control.

"Stop." His voice was deep, raw with suppressed passion, but he couldn't do anything about that.

Startled, she looked up, met his eyes.

He held her gaze, then, as evenly as he could, stated, "It's late. I suggest you retire. We have a long day ahead of us tomorrow."

Fixed on his face, on what she could no doubt sense, if not see, her eyes had widened. She hesitated for only a heartbeat, then nodded. "Yes. Of course. You're right." Gripping the table, she edged her chair back. "I'll . . . ah, go up."

She rose without taking her eyes from him. Then she turned and walked to the door. She opened it, paused, then, without glancing back, said, "Good night."

And left.

He watched the door close behind her. "*Good night?*" She wouldn't have understood the word he said next. He waited until he heard her footsteps climb the stairs, forced himself to remain seated until he heard the door of the countess's sitting room close.

Only then did he rise. Grim-faced, he crossed to the sideboard, hunted inside, and found a bottle of whisky and a glass. Bringing both back to the table, he flung himself into his chair, opened the bottle, and poured himself a dram. Or two.

Restoppering the bottle, he reached for the glass, drank, and felt the smoky burn slide down his throat. On a sigh, he leaned back.

And considered his options.

He could have her anytime he wished—tonight if he so desired. Her interest in him, in having him bed her, was all but palpable; if he pushed, she would yield.

But all things considered and appropriately weighed, was that the best way forward, for him, with her?

Or was waiting for her to come to him—for her to agree to marry him, make the first move, and invite his possession—a preferable path?

He sipped, debated; it didn't take much consideration to conclude that, for him, with her, the latter was the wiser choice.

Given her character, which he was increasingly aware was disturbingly similar to his own, then him going to her—essentially taking the decision out of her hands—would leave that decision undeclared.

She was in many ways his equal; he had to keep that in mind. Defining their future joint life, and how they were to live and interact with each other, was indeed going to be a complex negotiation; the last thing he needed was to leave her with the advantage of not having openly declared her wishes vis-à-vis the physical side of their union.

His best way forward was, unquestionably, to wait for her to make the first move.

So now, tonight, would be a strategic blunder.

And possibly not only on that front.

Reclaiming the goblet was too important for him to allow himself to be distracted, and while he might not want to admit it, even to himself, although he'd never been distracted by any bed-partner before, she was different.

And not only because she would be his wife.

"And that," he said, reaching for the bottle, "is a very troubling fact."

Resupplied with whisky, he sipped, thought.

Finally, he drained his glass, set it on the table, pushed back his chair and rose.

She'd left him when he'd told her to, and in that she'd been wise.

And in doing so she'd given him the opportunity to exercise some wisdom of his own.

Until they won back the goblet and he had it once more in his hands, he and she would simply have to live with the itch that had flared and now afflicted them.

And even after that, he would play safe and wait for her to give in and openly declare that she wanted him in her bed.

Much safer on all counts.

Leaving the parlor, he climbed the stairs, passed the door to her room, and headed for his own, although he still couldn't see even the remotest prospect of him having anything resembling a good night.

Chapter Eight

They reached the Bull and Mouth Inn off Aldersgate as dusk was tinting the sky. The yard was a-bustle with people rushing everywhere, some leaving, others arriving, all lugging bags and portmanteau. Horses and coaches stood at points around the roughly square yard, some disgorging passengers and luggage, others being loaded up. The inn itself surrounded the yard on three sides, a four-story structure with open galleries on the upper floors overlooking the chaos and cacophony of the yard.

Angelica came to an abrupt halt just inside the open end of the yard. Her bag in one hand, eyes wide, she looked this way, then that, trying to take everything in; the Bull and Mouth was another noisy and colorful pocket of London she'd never seen or even known existed.

"This way." Grasping her elbow, Dominic propelled her on—the first time he'd touched her since those moments in the theater. She nearly tripped; he held her upright, but immediately she caught her balance and started forward, he released her. "The door beside the office."

Lips tight, she changed tack, avoiding the long queue snaking out of the office; just as well they'd purchased their papers earlier. With Dominic alongside her subtly clearing the way, they tacked through the crowd.

They'd avoided each other all through the day; what words they'd exchanged had been purely practical. Yet the instant he'd touched her, when she'd heard his voice low and close, now he was so near once more, her senses had flared again, every bit as hotly as before.

A quick look at his face confirmed that the rigidly impassive mask he'd redonned that morning was firmly in place. Determined not to allow her unsettlingly uncharacteristic uncertainty to show, she ruthlessly suppressed her reaction and forged on. Reaching the door, she opened it and walked through—into the inn proper.

An even more intense cacophony assaulted her. The large main room was packed with humanity, eating, talking, laughing, shouting. Even the smells were manifold, but she couldn't halt and take stock; with

Dominic at her back she moved into the melee, but then he tweaked the back of her greatcoat. She turned, then followed him as he pushed through to where a harassed-looking clerk sat at a window set in the wall shared with the adjacent office.

Dominic set their papers on the counter. "Two for the Edinburgh mail."

The clerk inspected the papers, ticked two places on one of a plethora of lists, then handed the papers back. "You're on. Keep an ear out—we'll call passengers about eight o'clock. If you don't answer the call within ten minutes, your seats go to one of those waiting."

Dominic retrieved the papers, then turned and nodded into the room. "Let's see if we can find a table."

She hung back and let him take the lead. With a greatcoat over her youth's clothes, and her wide-brimmed hat firmly in place, she felt confident her disguise would fool most observers, but a youth would follow his tutor, not the other way about.

A guard stepped into the room, raised a bullhorn, and bellowed for the passengers on the mails to Norwich, Newcastle, and Leeds. Several groups stood and quickly gathered their bags.

"Over there." Dominic tipped his head toward a table in one corner of a wide alcove running along the back wall. She followed as he pushed past the previous occupants now on their way to the door.

The vacated table had benches for four on either side.

He waved her in. "Take the corner."

She slid along the bench while he turned and looked back at the door. Then he swung back and sat beside her. Given their current state of mutual avoidance, she'd wondered if he would. Then again, now they were once more in public, she doubted his protective tendencies would allow him to preserve any distance to speak of.

Protective men tended to hover close, and possessively protective men—she was fairly certain he would be one—were even worse.

Griswold, Brenda, and Mulley appeared out of the crowd and, after inquiring politely about the vacant seats, joined them. Jessup and Thomas arrived shortly after.

On leaving the house, they'd split into three groups and had taken separate hackneys to Aldersgate as if they weren't all one party. If she was supposed to be a youth traveling with her tutor on the mail, then they wouldn't have an entourage.

As soon as they'd all settled, a serving girl bustled up to take their orders; as all passengers needed to arrive early to ensure that their seats remained theirs, the inn did a roaring business feeding them while they waited. Angelica chose the mutton stew. With all orders taken, the girl whisked off, and the group settled to chat and pass the time.

At first the talk was of Scotland, the highlands, and the castle; Angelica drank in the details, but then the conversation fragmented and turned to people and places she didn't know. Her attention shifted to the room, to its myriad occupants.

Aware her attention had wandered, Dominic briefly searched her face, hesitated, then said, "Does the experience live up to your expectations?"

Without looking at him, she murmured, "My expectations were uninformed, and therefore very tame compared to the reality. There's so much going on, and it's so intense, so full of energy." After a moment, she glanced at him. "I've never traveled by mail, and it's unlikely I will again, so"—she looked back at the room—"I'm looking my fill and am eager to experience all there is to it."

"I've never traveled by mail either." When she glanced at him, puzzled, he caught her gaze. "I'm an earl, remember."

"I hadn't forgotten, but . . . not even in your misspent youth?"

"I'm not sure I had a misspent youth, not in the sense you mean."

She shifted to face him, leaning one elbow on the table and propping her chin on that hand. Her attention was now wholly his, which some part of him regarded as how things should be, despite his wish to keep a non-arousing distance between them.

After a moment of studying him, she frowned. "I really can't see you as the sort *not* to have a misspent youth."

At least they were talking again. "But I had clan, remember? I didn't have to travel to find like-minded souls with whom to carouse. My equivalent to your brothers' and cousins' misspent youths was spent in the highlands, or at school or university in Edinburgh. There were few mail coaches about for us to commandeer and try our hands at driving. For the most part, we rode, or drove gigs, and later curricles."

"But you came to London. You must have gone back and forth several times."

"True, but that was after the accident. I was already twenty-one and beyond the reckless hellion stage, and as Debenham, I had a private coach, which I used because of my knee. So I've always traveled privately, never on the mail."

Her frown returned. "I forgot about your knee—you haven't been using your cane." She blinked. "And you didn't have it with you all day yesterday."

Her clear disapproval made something in him ease. He shrugged. "This time it's recovering much faster. I jarred the old injury, but it was nowhere near as bad as the first time."

She glanced down at the bags at their feet. "You haven't brought a cane with you."

"It's too distinctive—just in case your family starts looking for Debenham."

Still frowning, she opened her mouth—

"Here you go."

He turned to see the serving girl lifting plates from a tray. She handed them around. "Drinks'll be with you shortly."

They fell to, and conversation largely ceased.

Once he'd cleared his plate, he cast about for some safe topic while Angelica was still eating. "We've spoken of my misspent youth—what of yours?"

"Young ladies don't have misspent youths—they have Seasons."

"And yours were . . . ?"

Gaze on her plate, she considered, then said, "Surprisingly uneventful, now I look back on them. There really is very little to relate. It was all exactly as I'm sure you can imagine—the balls, soirees, parties, and the like. Nothing of any significance."

She looked up, then focused past him. He turned.

Jessup was unfolding a map. "Let's see . . ."

A discussion ensued as to their route, of the towns the mail would halt at, and how much time the journey would take.

"Edinburgh Mail!" a stentorian voice boomed across the room. "Leaving in ten minutes, west side of the yard. All those with papers report to the guard by the boot."

"That's us." Thomas leapt up.

They quickly gathered their bags. Standing, Dominic threw a handful of coins on the table, then, clamping down on the urge to assist Angelica off the bench seat, waited until she'd slid over, stood and retrieved her bag, then with a commanding tip of his head, he led her toward the door.

The others had gone ahead, reporting to the guard in their different groups. The papers he and Angelica held entitled them to two of the inside seats. They were joined by Brenda and Griswold. Mulley and Thomas had clambered up to the passenger seat on the roof, while Jessup had claimed the seat beside the coachman.

With everyone aboard, the coachman climbed to the box, and the guard swung up to his position above the boot, alongside the sacks of mail they would deliver along the route.

Angelica peered out of the window; although her excitement was distinctly childlike, she embraced it. As she'd said, she was unlikely to have the chance to experience this ever again.

Briefly, she glanced at Dominic, seated alongside her. He was staring out of the opposite window, watching, appraising—searching for any sign of recognition or pursuit—but he was also, like her, drinking in the scene. That this journey would be a first for him, too, that they would be sharing the novelty, added interest to her anticipation.

She and her hero were about to set off on a journey to conquer a metaphorical dragon and regain a treasure vital to him and his people—what more could a young lady bent on love, adventure, and challenge ask for?

Clarity and *certainty* popped into her mind.

She'd expected to feel a lot more certain, a lot more definite about how to make him love her, a lot more sure of the route to that shining goal.

The guard's horn sounded, a long clarion call signaling the coach's departure. Thrusting her uncertainty deep, she reached instead for her excitement, for the thrill of the moment; regardless of her confusion and the disarray of her plans, in every way, on every level, this moment was indisputably the beginning of the rest of her life.

The carriage jerked and started ponderously rolling, then it turned out of the yard and into the street.

Riding the upswing of emotion, she leaned toward Dominic and murmured, "We're away!"

Glancing at her, Dominic took in her shining eyes, the reined enthusiasm in her expression. He said nothing, simply nodded, then turned back to watching the pavements.

He remained tense, alert, and watchful, a part of him expecting to meet some Cynster-inspired hurdle with every passing mile, but the coach rolled out of London unimpeded, and out along the Great North Road.

Twilight deepened, then darkness closed in. By the time they reached Enfield, it was full night. The change of horses was rapid and practiced; passengers were discouraged from alighting as the instant the traces were tightened, the coachman would drive on. While the fresh horses were being put to, Dominic noted several ostlers glancing at the occupants of the coaches in the yard, but their attention was focused on the two private carriages waiting behind the mail for their horses to be changed.

Minutes later, they were on the road again, rattling north at speed. He relaxed a fraction, leaning back, watching as the others settled to get what sleep they could.

As the miles rumbled by, he dozed. Beside him, Angelica shifted frequently, trying to get comfortable without touching him; every time she did, he had to consciously suppress the urge to reach out and draw her near, to have her lay her head on his chest and relax against him. An irrational and irritating urge. Quite aside from the unwisdom of touching her, she was supposed to be a youth, and they were still too close to London to risk someone inadvertently glimpsing her and seeing through her disguise.

When she finally fell more deeply asleep, he glanced at her. Moonlight slanted through the coach's window; despite her hat, its glow limned her profile, relaxed in slumber, and outlined her lips, so impossible to imagine on any male's face. Asleep, tongue stilled, eyes closed . . . it wasn't hard to see how she'd come by her name.

Facing forward, he leaned his head back against the seat and closed his eyes.

The rest of the night passed uneventfully, if not comfortably. Dominic shook Angelica awake as the coach rolled into Huntingdon. "Breakfast—and we'll need to eat quickly."

She'd been sleeping curled in the corner, her cheek resting on one hand. She opened her eyes, looked at him, slowly refocused, then straightened her legs and sat up, mumbling, "I thought it was just another change."

In addition to Enfield, they'd stopped to change horses at Ware and Buntingford, but as at Enfield, those changes had been effected swiftly, with no real halt. At both Ware and Buntingford, he'd seen unusually alert ostlers scanning the coaches, but while some had glanced at their windows, none had shown any real interest in them.

As Buntingford was the third stage north from the capital, it seemed that they had indeed successfully slipped through the net the Cynsters had cast around London. That didn't, however, mean that there wouldn't be other watchers further on.

Angelica yawned, then glanced at the window. "Oh—what time is it?" Not even a hint of dawn had yet lightened the night sky.

"A little before four o'clock. We're on schedule."

Brenda stirred, then woke. Griswold was already alert. "I'll change with Mulley, my lord—give him a chance to catch a wink."

Dominic nodded. "We'll be able to stretch our legs, at least, but eat first—we won't stop again for hours."

They all took the warning to heart. As soon as the coach halted, they all climbed out and, joined by the other three, made their way into the inn. As soon as their orders were taken, Angelica, with Brenda to stand guard, slipped away to the facility located at the end of a narrow passage. By the time they returned, the innkeeper and his wife were setting platters of ham, eggs, and sausages on the table, along with freshly baked bread and jam, coffeepots, and a teapot.

Angelica applied herself to the fare, but she'd never been a big eater, especially not at breakfast. Not even to pretend to be a youth could she force anything more down. Her meager appetite sated, she considered going for a walk . . . but then realized that if she did, Dominic would feel compelled to go with her, and he, and the other men, too, and even Brenda, were plainly much hungrier than she.

So she sat and sipped her tea, and waited.

Too soon, the coachman and guard who had driven them thus far came around, apparently for a customary tip. Dominic must have been forewarned; he had the coins ready, as if they'd been gathered from the whole table and hadn't come solely from him.

And then the new guard was calling them to reboard.

Thomas, the last of the men to do so, rushed down the passageway after begging the rest of them to make sure the coach didn't leave without him. They dawdled and stalled for as long as they could, until Thomas came streaking out of the inn and scrambled up to his seat, just in the nick of time.

The new coachman cracked his whip, yelled to the horses, the guard sounded his horn, and they were off again.

They made a luncheon stop at Stamford, only marginally longer than their breakfast halt. Angelica, Dominic, Mulley, and Jessup squeezed in a short walk, but the very real risk of the coach driving on without them restricted the excursion. At least they succeeded in properly stretching their legs.

On the road again, the coach rattled past Grantham, then on to Newark, where they were allowed half an hour for a rushed dinner. Then it was back in the coach, rolling north past Doncaster and on toward York.

The rattling, rumbling progress, the frequent blaring of the guard's horn as notice to other carriages to give way, the unpredictable pitching, and the constant, repetitive thunder of the horses' hooves all combined to make conversation well nigh impossible; the four of them inside the carriage quickly sank into a somnolent state, silently watching the scenery drift past.

Angelica had intended to use the hours to tease more information out of Dominic; instead, her normally active, alert, and inquiring mind sank into a miasma of . . . watching trees and fields slide past. She'd often traveled long distances with her family, although rarely at such a breakneck pace, but the Cynster carriages were much better made and better sprung, so the swaying and the noise were much reduced.

By the time the coach rolled into York, she'd made a firm resolution that she would not be traveling by mail again.

The cheery scene that met her weary eyes when their group walked into the York Tavern revived her somewhat, and the excellent supper laid before them further assisted said revivification.

Half an hour later, the call came for them to reboard. She rose from the bench on which they'd been sitting. "I can't believe it's going to take another whole day just to reach Berwick."

"The roads aren't as well surfaced and are not as direct." Having stood alongside her and stepped over the bench, Dominic reached for her hand—and only just stopped himself from completing the revealing action.

She arched a brow at him, then stepped over the seat.

He met her eyes, then turned and strode out. She followed, unexpectedly satisfied that, while she was a lad to everyone watching, she remained a lady to him.

They'd been preserving their wordlessly agreed mutual distance; as she settled in the coach alongside him, she remembered quite clearly why. Those moments in the pit, and even more the fraught minutes over the dinner table, were indelibly etched in her mind. Yet while she hadn't been able to focus well enough to interrogate him during the journey, her mind, it seemed, had been turning facts, notions, and ideas over and around, reexamining and reevaluating, and the time in the York Tavern had allowed the conclusions to rise to the forefront of her brain.

Clarity was hers again, and while uncertainty still lingered, she now accepted that a degree of uncertainty was unavoidable at this point.

At this point in her campaign to induce Dominic to fall in love with her.

Her principal problem, as she now saw it, was that when it came to experience of the opposite sex she was, indeed, twenty-one, not twenty-five. She seriously doubted Heather would have reacted to that scene over the dinner table with the same skittering nervousness that she had. While she was clever and observant, and in many respects had a sound understanding of men and how they thought, the one aspect to which she as yet had had little exposure was lust.

She had absolutely no doubt that the cauldron of hungry awareness she'd sensed across the table had been an eruption of lust, both his and hers. It had definitely been lust that had burned in his eyes, lust that had heated her from the inside out.

Which, as she understood the matter, was by no means a bad thing. Her problem lay in having no idea how to take that lust and convert it into love.

From what she'd observed, that was, more or less, what happened; lust overtook couples, then, either simultaneously or arising out of indulging said lust, love blossomed and bloomed.

What she had yet to learn was how the transformation, connection, or whatever it was, occurred.

Admittedly, ignorance alone wouldn't have done more than give her pause; if matters had been different, she would have been tempted to leap in with her usual confident abandon, commence her education, and trust that she would muddle through.

But the power of what had erupted between them had shaken her to her toes.

That was why she'd panicked.

The maelstrom that had manifested between them last night had been so turbulent and strong, so elementally powerful, she'd been instinctively sure that if it had broken loose, she—and possibly not even he—would have had any hope of controlling it.

People thought her impulsive, but she rarely leapt into situations she couldn't control. And while she imagined that he, stronger and even more accustomed to exercising control, would have assumed he'd be in control, would he have been?

Admittedly he'd had sufficient control to allow her to escape, but if he'd seized her, kissed her? Would he have been able to hold the tide back then?

Regardless, the critical issue she now faced was whether she could risk not being in control if her aim was to take charge of their lust and convert it into love. How could she channel it, or influence it, if she couldn't control it?

Her uncertainty sprang from her conclusion that she would have to accept the risk, or else risk running out of time.

She'd agreed to give him her response to his offer of marriage after he'd reclaimed the goblet and saved his clan; that translated to after the first of July. She now knew him well enough to guess that he would demand her answer by the second of the month at the latest, and neither he nor her family would readily countenance further delay.

Which meant that her window for inducing him to fall in love with her ran from now until then. But in a week's time, he and she would reach his castle and have to deal with whatever waited for them there; she wasn't silly enough to imagine that convincing his mother to return the goblet would require nothing more than her turning up and curtseying.

Once they reached his castle, he and she would have other matters demanding their attention, other issues claiming their minds.

Realistically, the best time for her to engage their combined lusts and shape them into love was from now until they reached the castle. During that period they wouldn't have any other major distractions, any urgent calls on their attention. In Edinburgh they would be staying at his town house, and from Edinburgh to the castle they would be riding and stopping at inns every night.

All of which confirmed that she'd been correct in viewing the journey to the castle as a deity-given opportunity to draw closer to him; her mistake had been in assuming that "closer" had meant through talking.

Thinking over the whole, her resolve firmed. She'd recognized from the first, on that night she'd agreed to help him, that her way forward would require unconditional trust in love. It was time to stop being a control-coward, to trust in love and take the risk. A risk that, as she wanted him as her husband, she couldn't avoid taking at some point.

Their future, the nature of their marriage, lay in her hands. It was time to act and move forward.

The coach had rumbled out of York long ago. They were bowling through darkness lit only by the faint glow cast by the carriage lamps. Mulley and Brenda had already settled, curled up in their respective corners, eyes closed; Mulley was softly snoring.

Beside her, Dominic was still awake. She didn't need to look to know he was; she could sense his alertness, although it wasn't focused, just there in case of need.

Midnight was upon them, the witching hour ahead.

She sat still for a moment more, letting sleep draw near, then she yawned, shifted, and drew up her legs, curling them on the seat and tipping sideways to pillow her head against his upper arm. "You don't mind, do you?" she mumbled, then stifled another, perfectly genuine yawn. It truly had been a long day.

She felt him staring down at her, sensed his surprise, and perhaps a touch of suspicion, but she wasn't the least surprised when he whispered, "No." After a moment, he added, "Just sleep."

Lips lightly curving, she relaxed against him, and did.

They reached Berwick at ten o'clock the following night.

Descending from the coach, Dominic walked to the inn's open door, forcing himself to allow Angelica to trail after him. The impulse to escort her properly—so she was within his sight and reach—had only grown after the previous night.

In the small hours, he'd finally given into temptation and had lifted her until her hatted head had been pillowed on his chest, and in her sleep she'd curled against his side, then he'd put his arm around her, closed his eyes, and, to his surprise, had got a few hours' decent sleep.

Other than that, however, he'd yet to decide how to react to her unexpected breaching of their invisible wall, or if, indeed, he should react at all. As an indication that she was willing to draw closer, it was all well and good, but was it enough of a declaration to be taken as an invitation to proceed to intimacy? He suspected not. Regardless, now was not the time for that.

Sitting alongside her as their group rapidly accounted for a supper of soup, bread, cold beef, ham, pickles, and assorted condiments, he pretended not to notice her thigh touching his.

Not that he moved away. Not that he imagined she didn't know he felt every inch of the sleek feminine limb she pressed against him.

As usual, she ate less than anyone else, but politely filled the gap with conversation. "I have to admit I've had enough of traveling on the mail. I can't wait to stretch out in a bed."

He looked up and met her eyes as the others voiced their agreement. He swallowed, then said, "Sadly, we have one more night to endure."

"Hmm." She studied him. "As I'm the smallest of the group, I suppose I can't complain—or at least not too loudly." She allowed her gaze to sweep the others before returning to him. "I truly cannot imagine how you're all faring, there being so much more of you than me."

"Oh, it's not that bad," Brenda said, oblivious to the undercurrents on the other side of the table.

"For me," Mulley said, "it's that 'one more night.' I hold a vision in my mind of my bed at the Edinburgh house as incentive—as what I'll have tomorrow night if I can just make it through tonight."

The others all agreed.

"Edinburgh Mail! Passengers back on board, please. Hurry, now—we've a schedule to meet."

With a sigh, they all rose, and after Dominic paid their shot, they trooped out and climbed back into the coach or clambered up to their seats on the roof. They'd dropped the pretense that they weren't all one party after York.

He followed Angelica into the coach and sat beside her.

From being on tenterhooks at the Bull and Mouth, then living in expectation of running into some hurdle at every halt until Newark, once they'd reached York, he'd started to hope. Now, with Scotland three miles up the road, he was no longer concerned enough to growl at Angelica to keep her hat tilted down as she scanned the yard.

In the press and crush of the crowds around the coaches, in the yards, or in the taverns at which they'd stopped, no one had yet looked closely enough to detect the subtle differences, still vividly clear to his eyes and vibrantly apparent to his senses, that revealed her true gender.

With luck, they would make Edinburgh without leaving any trace.

Once they were away again, they all settled to get what sleep they could. Dominic waited only until Brenda's and Griswold's heads started to nod, then raised his arm, reached around Angelica—who, he was well aware, had been waiting for the gesture—and drew her against him again.

She came readily, sighed and curled close, settling under his arm.

Tipping his head back against the squabs, he closed his eyes.

Later—he didn't know how much later—he heard her whisper, "Are you holding in your mind an image of your bed in Edinburgh as incentive for suffering through tonight?"

All but asleep, he tried to think, couldn't, so answered truthfully. "Yes."

She gave a little hum in her throat, patted his chest lightly. He heard the sultry, well-pleased smile in her voice as she confessed, "So am I."

It took a full minute for the connection between her question, his answer, and her response to register. Abruptly awake again, opening his eyes, he glanced down at her, but all he could see was her hat . . . had she really said what he thought she had?

Tipping his head back, he wrestled with that question—whether she'd meant *her* bed in *his* Edinburgh house, as distinct from *her* in *his* bed under the same roof . . . with her weight a soothing warmth against his side, he fell asleep.

London's bells were pealing the midnight hour when, having been summoned posthaste from a ball, Celia and Martin Cynster arrived on the doorstep of St. Ives House. Sligo, Devil's majordomo, opened the door before they reached it.

Ushering Celia inside, Martin fixed Sligo with a commanding glare. "What's happened?"

Sligo's lips twisted in sympathy. "News, but not of Miss Angelica—not as such." He waved them down a corridor leading from the front hall. "His Grace and the others are waiting in the library."

When Martin and Celia entered the long room, it was to discover that Sligo's "others" meant most of the family presently in London, barring only those of their grandchildren's generation. Even Aunt Clara and Therese, Lady Osbaldestone, were there.

"What is it?" Celia asked, unable to bear the suspense an instant longer. Sinking onto the chaise in the space Horatia and Helena made for her between them, she clutched their hands, one on either side, and fixed Devil, as usual seated behind his desk, with a determined look. "Just tell us, please, without any round-aboutation."

Holding her gaze, clearly choosing his words, Devil said, "It's not necessarily bad news, but it is disturbing. I've waited for you to arrive so I can explain to everyone at the same time." He picked up a letter. "I received this from Royce earlier this evening—he sent it by courier. He and Hamish finally located the band of reivers who had collected the body from the base of the cliff." Devil raised his gaze from the letter. "Body. Singular. According to the reivers, there was only one body, no sign at all of a second, and by all accounts the body they found and conveyed to a magistrate for notification and burial was that of Scrope. From the descriptions we have of the laird, it definitely wasn't him."

Silence reigned for a full minute, then—

"How the devil did he survive that fall, let alone walk away?" Jeremy Carling was dumbfounded. He glanced at Eliza, seated beside him. "We saw the cliff. We saw the laird disappear over the edge." Looking back at Devil, he shook his head. "I can't see how he could have survived."

Devil looked grim. "Royce went to the spot and found a narrow ledge, barely wide enough for a man to stand on, about twenty feet down. Royce thinks it's possible a man of immense strength, with significant experience of climbing sheer cliff faces, and absolute cold-blooded courage, could have managed it—and by the signs at the site, Royce is now convinced that the laird did, indeed, climb up and walk away."

Tossing the letter on his desk, Devil glanced at the other men standing behind the chairs and propped against the bookcases.

It was Gabriel who ground out, "So the laird is still alive—still at large. Is it he who has kidnapped Angelica?"

No one answered, but then Helena, head tilted as she considered, said, "I am wondering if this piece of news has, perhaps, a golden lining."

Devil looked at her. "It's usually silver, but I'll settle for gold. In what way?"

"Why"—hands rising expressively, Helena appealed to the ladies around her—"is it not true that whenever this laird has taken one of our girls, he has always given the so-strict orders that she is not to be harmed? Not in any way? So is it not reasonable to suppose that if it is indeed he who Angelica is with, that he will take excellent care of her?"

"Yes—you're right." Celia seized on the point. "We don't know his motives, of course, but at least we know that much—she will be safe."

The males of the family said not a word.

They did exchange glances.

"Dear Angelica's a survivor." Aunt Clara reached across to pat Celia's hand. "She'll do."

"Indeed, when has she not?" Lady Osbaldestone observed.

The ladies gathered around Celia, exchanging positive opinions on the likelihood of Angelica's being hale and unharmed.

"No matter how it appears, I—we—think she's definitely pursuing a goal of her own." Eliza, chin firm, swept the faces of the older ladies, many of them among the most powerful in the ton. "When she disappeared, she was wearing the necklace from Catriona—the one supposed to assist us in finding our husbands, our heroes." Eliza glanced at Henrietta, standing behind her mother, Louise. "Henrietta saw it."

All gazes swung to Henrietta.

Louise reached back and caught one of Henrietta's hands. "How did she seem when you saw her?"

"She was in good spirits . . ." Henrietta frowned, glanced down, then touched the bridge of her nose, a habit when thinking. She looked at her mother, then at the others. "Actually, now I think of it, she was . . . well, hunting, for want of a better word. I don't know whom, but I got the distinct impression she had someone in her sights."

The ladies exchanged glances, then Helena stated their collective thought. "That puts quite a different complexion on this episode, no?"

Horatia nodded. Celia did, too, even more definitely.

Heather and Eliza exchanged a vindicated glance.

Lady Osbaldestone thumped her cane. "If you want my opinion, I would have to say that if this laird has inveigled Angelica away, then it's *he* who should have a care for his future. She's neither a child, nor weak. Naturally one cannot approve of such a situation, but until we know her role in this drama—and I'm sure none of us will make the mistake of imagining her a passive pawn—then there's no reason I can see to panic, much less to lose hope."

"Indeed." Honoria nodded decisively. "We should wait on more certain news—preferably from her—before leaping to any conclusions."

That decided, the ladies looked across the room at their menfolk, all gathered around Devil's desk, arguing the merits of this or that action.

Patience shook her head. "There's no point trying to make them see sense."

"Sadly, no." Alathea sighed. "We'll just have to leave them to run as they will. On a brighter note, out of all this, we'll get to see Phyllida and Alasdair's latest addition. Alasdair went home to fetch them both, and they're on their way up from Devon."

While the ladies turned their minds to family matters, the gathering about the desk focused on the one new aspect that offered some hope after a week of totally futile searching. None of the men present were accustomed to failure, especially not when it came to protecting one of their own, and the laird had transgressed and successfully invaded their territory not just once but three times.

Feelings were running high.

"I accept that just because he's still alive, it doesn't necessarily follow that it was the laird who seized Angelica," Vane said, "but for my money, it's him behind this."

Devil nodded. "The coincidences are too many and too great to swallow. I believe we should assume that it is indeed he behind Angelica's kidnapping."

"But *who* is he?" Gabriel growled. "And how could he have got his hands on Angelica?"

"Let's list what we know," Vane suggested. "His description alone should make him stand out."

"That and being a Scottish peer." Devil glanced at the other men. "I suggest our first step in catching up with this gentleman is learning exactly who he is, and there aren't that many Scottish peers in town, or who might have been here recently, and every single one of them will be known to someone we know."

Gabriel nodded. "I'll check my sources in the City."

"I'll ask at the House of Lords," Devil said.

"Meanwhile"—Demon exchanged a glance with Vane—"we'll check at the clubs."

"Arthur, George, and I can help with that," Martin said. "The older men might know of a younger nobleman not so well known in town."

"And we"—Breckenridge looked at Jeremy and received a nod in reply—"will search everywhere else we can think of."

Devil nodded. "If any of us discover a Scotsman fitting our man's description, don't engage. Send word here and we'll call a meeting to decide what our best—and most satisfying—course of action will be."

The others all agreed.

Seeing their ladies preparing to depart, the men went to assist, all feeling rather better now that they had something to do that held real hope of catching up with their elusive enemy.

Chapter Nine

Angelica woke as dawn was painting the sky in washes of rose and gold. The others in the coach lay silent, still asleep. For long moments she listened to Dominic's heart thud softly beneath her ear, then she slowly eased his heavy arm from around her and sat up.

She straightened, stretched, settled her hat, then looked out of the window. Ahead to the right, the rock on which Edinburgh stood rose above the plain, its outline softened by wisps of mist wafting off the nearby firth. As she studied, assessed, expectation and enthusiasm, curiosity and interest stirred, then slowly welled.

Dominic shifted, then leaned nearer and looked past her shoulder. "Almost there."

He drew back and she glanced at him. "You must be happy to see it again."

"Truth to tell, I'm still struggling to accept that we've got this far without tripping over your family, either in person or via an agent or hireling."

"I told you they'd never think of the mail." For good reason; she felt literally rattled to her bones.

Turning back to the window, she watched the town draw nearer.

They swung under the arch of one of the main coaching inns a few minutes before seven o'clock. After tipping the coachman and guard, Dominic hefted his bag and joined an eager Angelica, waiting with the others in the street. In a group, they set off, walking up the rising street into Auld Town.

"This is South Bridge Street, isn't it?" Angelica asked.

He nodded. "You said you'd been here before."

"With Mama and Papa for some social event—some old friends of theirs." She looked around. "We weren't here long, but I remember this street, and the church with the big spire." She pointed ahead. "What's it called?"

"Tron Kirk. It's on High Street. East to west, Cannongate, High Street, and Lawnmarket make up the main street, running from Holyrood Palace to the castle."

She peppered him with questions as they strode up South Bridge Street, then turned right along High

Street and continued on into Cannongate. She slowed to peer through shop windows; eventually waving the others on, he waited until, her curiosity appeased, she rejoined him. With more questions.

That he'd expected. What he hadn't anticipated was her energy, her enthusiasm, the unbridledness of her curiosity. Her interest radiated from her, lit her eyes and face . . . made him wonder if, now she'd decided to step past her nervous filly stage, if—

He cut off that line of thought. Later. He'd decided it would be later. Through the journey his libido had stepped back, giving way to the greater need to protect her; he didn't need it reemerging and slipping its leash now.

They reached the corner of Vallen's Close. He tipped his head down the street. "This way."

Angelica followed him down the cobbled street. Eyes wide, she looked back, to the side, then forward again, taking in everything she could. No youth was likely to evince such open interest, but she no longer considered her disguise important. Not as important as learning and absorbing everything she could about Dominic's life.

The life that henceforth she would share.

The houses in Vallen's Close were the largest she'd thus far seen. She assumed they belonged to the aristocracy; the palace was not far away.

Halting before a grand old house, Dominic opened the gate set in the wrought-iron railings. He caught her eye, then walked up the short path and climbed the five steps to the raised stone porch. He waited until, eager to see what lay behind the dark oak front door, she joined him; he studied her for an instant, then reached for the latch—just as the door swung open.

A benevolently benign white-haired butler looked at Dominic and beamed. "Good morning, my lord. Welcome back."

The simple joy in the words declared beyond question how Dominic's staff saw him.

"Thank you, MacIntyre." Dominic glanced at Angelica. "And this is Miss Angelica Cynster."

MacIntyre transferred his blue gaze to Angelica. Wishing she hadn't been dressed as a youth, she smiled and inclined her head. "MacIntyre."

The butler's gaze remained on her face for an instant longer than it should have, but then a smile creased his cheeks and he bowed. "Welcome, Miss Cynster. We're delighted to welcome you to Glencrae House."

Dominic waved her in. She crossed the threshold half expecting cobwebs and dust over everything. Instead the place was not just clean but polished; she smelled the lemony scent of good beeswax.

Looking around, eyes widening, she drew in a long breath, then slowly exhaled. *Oh, yes!* She could definitely see herself as mistress of this.

Walking forward several paces, then halting, she slowly pirouetted, taking in all aspects of the wide hall. MacIntyre quietly closed the door, then both he and Dominic stood watching her. She let her delight color her expression, let her pleasure light her eyes. "This is just *lovely.*"

The room was an exhibition of linen-fold paneling, and more generally of the woodcarver's art. A strip of plastered wall a yard wide ran between the upper edge of the paneling and the cornice, and that was filled with paintings and portraits in ornately carved gilded frames. Other than that, the walls were paneled or encased in wood in one way or another, and all the furniture—the central round table, the two high-backed chairs flanking the fireplace, and various side tables and wall tables—was of the same rich, glowing oak. The carving decorating the balustrade and newel posts of the wide stairs that led upward from the hall echoed the frieze decorating the mantelpiece.

Despite having so much wood of a single hue, the room was vibrant with color. A fire leapt in the grate, throwing golden light over jewel-toned tapestries and crimson velvet curtains and cushions, the ruby hue echoed in the Oriental rugs spread over the flagged floor. The result was warm and welcoming.

A door at the rear of the hall swung noiselessly open. Dominic glanced that way and smiled. "And this is Mrs. McCutcheon, who with MacIntyre keeps this place in order."

A tall, thin, pleasant-faced woman, Mrs. McCutcheon swiftly scanned Dominic, then bobbed. "Welcome back, my lord."

Turning to Angelica, Mrs. McCutcheon curtsied. "And a welcome to you, miss. We hope your stay here will be comfortable."

Angelica smiled. "I'm sure it will be." She watched a small procession line up behind Mrs. McCutcheon.

MacIntyre stepped forward. "This is Cora, miss, she's our first parlor maid. And this is Janet . . ."

Dominic might not have informed his staff of her pending status, but presumably the others had passed on their assumptions. Regardless, her strategy of not yet agreeing was a matter between her and him alone. With appropriate grace and sincere interest, Angelica allowed herself to be conducted along the short line—three maids, two footmen, a cook, a scullery maid, and an errand boy. When she reached the end, Dominic stepped to her side and together they faced the assembled staff.

"Mrs. McCutcheon, if you could show Miss Cynster to her room, and then"—glancing at Angelica, Dominic caught her eye—"perhaps breakfast in an hour?"

"Of course, my lord." Mrs. McCutcheon came forward. "The rooms are prepared and we've everything ready." She turned to Janet. "I'm sure Miss Cynster would like more hot water to top up the bath."

A bath? Angelica beamed. "That would be lovely." She would kill for a bath.

Mrs. McCutcheon nodded approvingly and waved to the stairs.

Starting up them, Angelica saw Dominic with MacIntyre in attendance walk across the hall and into a corridor leading deeper into the house. Curiosity tugged, but for once she held it back. She would explore later. First . . .

She slowed so Mrs. McCutcheon came alongside. "I can't thank you enough for thinking of a bath, let alone having it ready and waiting."

"Och, weel, I couldn't imagine you wouldn't be wanting to sluice the dirt of travel away, and nothing does that better than a bath."

"I do so agree." Looking toward the top of the stairs, Angelica asked, "Which rooms have you prepared for me?"

"Why, the countess's suite, of course. His lordship told us on his way down to London to have all ready for his bride-to-be."

So that's how they'd known. The man did like to plan.

He also tended to assume that all would go exactly as he planned.

Reaching the head of the stairs, Mrs. McCutcheon led the way to a pair of doors at one end of the gallery. There, she halted and faced Angelica.

Halting too, Angelica met the older woman's eyes; still lightly smiling, she arched a brow.

Mrs. McCutcheon studied her, shrewdly and frankly evaluating her.

Not entirely surprised, Angelica waited patiently under the scrutiny.

Then Mrs. McCutcheon's lips eased. "I do believe you'll do. He needs a wife with fire and a will to match his." She lifted her gaze to Angelica's hair. "Reckon he's found one."

Angelica laughed. "Oh, yes, indeed. Rest assured, Mrs. McCutcheon, that much is true."

"Aye, weel, in that case, you'll do nicely." Struggling to look severe and failing, Mrs. McCutcheon threw open the doors and waved Angelica in. "So let's see what we can do about that bath you're wanting."

A little more than an hour later, Angelica descended the stairs, once again in her turquoise silk ballgown, fichu in place. Brenda had washed and ironed both gown and fichu, but while Angelica now felt blissfully clean and presentably neat, she wasn't at ease over wearing such a gown during the day. If anyone called—unlikely, but still—she would feel dreadfully silly.

"Gowns," she declared as, having followed Janet-the-very-helpful-maid's directions, she walked into the breakfast parlor; Dominic was sitting at the head of the table, a news sheet in one hand. "I need more gowns. We agreed I would get them here."

MacIntyre held the smaller carver at the foot of the table for her; with a smile, she allowed him to seat her. Then she looked up the table and caught Dominic's gaze. "I believe you can direct me to some suitable modistes?"

Dominic looked into her greeny-gold eyes. "I'll make a list."

"Excellent." She reached for the toast rack. "So, what now?"

Laying aside the news sheet, he picked up his coffee cup, sipped as he ordered his thoughts. "Our stay here needs to be as short as we can make it while getting all we need in place for the journey to the castle and our stay there, and arranging anything else that might make convincing Mirabelle to return the goblet easier." He focused on her. "So you need to get your gowns and anything else you might require. Meanwhile, I'll organize a horse for you and attend to those business matters I can't avoid. I'm hoping to clear my slate so I can devote the coming weeks to reclaiming the goblet."

She crunched her usual slice of jam-laden toast, swallowed, then asked, "From here, how long will it take us to reach the castle? Incidentally, what's it called? I don't think you've ever said."

"Mheadhoin Castle. It stands on an island in Loch Beinn a'Mheadhoin, in the eastern part of Glen Affric. How long it will take us to reach there . . ." He looked down the table at her. "That will depend on how well you ride."

"Assume well. In fact, assume I won't be the laggard of the group." Angelica fixed him with a level gaze. "So how long will it take if you and the others go as fast as you can?"

From the way he hesitated, his gaze on her, she felt certain he hadn't accepted her assessment of her equestrian abilities, but she could educate him along the way.

"If we leave first thing one morning, while alone I can make the distance inside three days, as a group we'll reach there on the afternoon of the fourth day."

"That long?" She hadn't realized it would be that far.

"It's mostly reasonable road, but we won't be able to get remounts, so it's not simply a matter of speed but also of spelling the horses, and that means we ride from dawn to as long as the light permits. Every day."

The prospect didn't bother her. "Hmm. All right. As we need to leave as soon as possible and getting new gowns is going to take time, I should start on that immediately. However"—she waved at her ballgown—"I can't be seen in public like this, not during the day, and I can't borrow a gown from anyone in the house, not to visit modistes." After a moment's reflection, she said, "Janet, the maid, is close to my size. I could send her to buy a ready-made walking gown, and once I have that, I'll be able to visit the modistes and arrange what I need."

"If you can instruct Janet well enough to be happy with her purchase."

"I'm sure she and I will manage." She caught his eye. "So . . . what's my dress allowance?"

He held her gaze. Eventually said, "If I give you carte blanche, will you buy something outrageous just because you can?"

"Of course not. I'll bear your dignity in mind, I promise."

He softly snorted and looked down. "Just tell the modistes to send the bills to me here, at Glencrae House."

"I take it they'll know the direction?"

He looked up and met her eyes, and didn't say anything more.

"All right." Sobering, she calculated. "How long do you think we'll be here?"

"I assume that will depend on how long you take to assemble your wardrobe."

"A challenge?" She widened her eyes at him. "Have I told you how much I enjoy challenges?"

"No. But I feel sure I'm going to find out."

"So! One more day—that's all we'll need." Allowing Dominic to seat her at the foot of the dining table in the smaller of the two dining rooms—the principal dining room could seat thirty comfortably—Angelica felt absurdly triumphant. "This afternoon I visited all three modistes on your list, and each swore they'd have the gowns I commissioned from them ready by tomorrow evening at the latest."

She flicked out her napkin. "The first gown from each should be delivered tomorrow morning, so I'll be able to go out and purchase the other things I need." As he settled in his carver, she looked up the table at him. "Tell me—is there any reason that, dressed as a young lady, I need to avoid notice here, or can I walk and shop freely?"

He considered the question while the soup was served. "Your family will have accounted for your absence—they won't have allowed your disappearance to become public knowledge."

"Definitely not. I did ask them to concoct a suitable tale, and we've grown rather experienced in that skill of late."

He inclined his head. "Precisely my point. So there's no reason to assume that if anyone not in the know sees you here, they'll think it odd. They'll assume you're here with family or visiting friends. The only reason to hide and race back here is if you spot anyone from your family, or anyone who might be close enough to know of your disappearance and raise an alarm."

"All right—so I can roam freely, but I should keep my eyes peeled."

That decided, they gave their attention to the meal.

Angelica was particularly pleased with the standard of the dishes. She'd already won over Mrs. McCutcheon, and Janet, and was working on MacIntyre, but overall the staff had proved very ready to embrace her as their soon-to-be mistress and accord her the control due to Dominic's countess.

In some respects, the household reins were already in her hands, but she was being judicious in how she managed them. She'd always viewed controlling any reasonable-sized staff as similar to managing a team of horses; one needed them all running in stride and in the same direction, but the best results were invariably gained through having a light hand on the reins.

As the meal progressed, her satisfaction mounted. She wondered if Dominic would notice any change.

Eventually, with the end of the main course in sight, he leaned back in his chair and regarded the remains of the guinea fowl on his plate. "That was excellent. I can't recall ever having better. I must remember to compliment Cook."

She smiled delightedly. "Please do. Then Cook can pass your compliments on to your new undercook, who will then decide that this is an excellent household in which to work, meaning one where her skills are appreciated."

Dominic paused, then asked, "I have an undercook—a new one?"

The angel at the end of the table nodded, transparently pleased with herself. "While I was waiting for Janet to return with the walking dress, I met with Mrs. McCutcheon and MacIntyre. We agreed that in order to cope adequately with all future requirements, the household needed an undercook, and Cook knew of an excellent candidate who was trying to make up her mind which of several offers to accept." She grinned, her green-gold eyes alight. "So you've stolen the French-trained undercook the Earl and Countess of Angus thought they'd successfully wooed."

There was competition for undercooks? "I didn't realize . . ." He waved a hand. "No, forget I said that. You may rule the household as you deem fit as long as I have no mutinies in the ranks."

"Of course there'll be no mutinies." She humphed, but her dimples assured him she wasn't offended.

He'd never shared such exchanges with any other female. Back-and-forth comments about ordinary day-to-day things, quick verbal jousts spiced with challenge, laughter, and the camaraderie of shared goals.

Mitchell had been gone for nearly four years; no one could ever take his cousin's place, but Dominic's unexpected countess-to-be seemed to be carving out her own niche in his otherwise closed and very private world.

That she had so eagerly, efficiently, and effectively stepped into the shoes of his countess-to-be here, too, was reassuring.

He studied her while dessert was being served; when all but MacIntyre had withdrawn, he asked, "Do you enjoy organizing staff, and so on?"

"Of course. It's—" She paused, then went on, "If your role is to manage the estate and all that entails, then my role is to manage your households, and all that's associated with that." She waved her spoon. "It's what I've been trained for—exactly what I expected to do with my life. And now I'm doing it." She looked up and caught his eyes, her own shining. "I did mention that I thrive on challenges, although to give your staff their due, I've thus far found them all very able."

She was in her element and knew herself to be. Any lingering guilt over having pressured her into helping him and through that marrying him—over having kidnapped her and taken away her choices, even taken her away from a life she might have preferred—faded. By luck, or fate, it seemed he'd offered her one thing, at least, that in terms of her future she'd wanted, needed, and had most likely been searching for. Being his countess would, indeed, give her the life she'd anticipated, and he was relieved by, and content with, that.

Licking the last of an especially creamy crème anglaise from her spoon, Angelica sighed, then looked up and caught Dominic's eye. He'd already cleaned his plate and was sitting back, his gaze on her, as it often was.

She wasn't surprised by the scrutiny; he was trying to learn to read her, to understand her, preferably to the point of being able to predict her, and so control her. She smiled. "Assuming that, as it now appears, we'll be able to quit Edinburgh on the day after tomorrow, what's our route to the castle?"

He hesitated, then uncrossed his long legs and rose. "Let's go to the library. Or would you rather sit in the drawing room?"

"No—I like libraries." And she wanted to see his domain.

He waved MacIntyre back, drew out her chair, then offered his arm. Delighted, she placed her hand on his sleeve, registering the steel beneath it, and allowed him to conduct her out of the dining room, across the front hall, down the corridor, and so to the library.

She hadn't lied; she did like libraries, and this one epitomized all she thought best in them—beauty, functionality, and comfort. The walls were lined with glass-fronted bookcases filled with leather-bound tomes; the lettering on the spines winked gold and silver, while the covers created a random patchwork of soothing colors. As in the rest of the house, golden oak prevailed. Spaced along one wall, three pairs of long velvet curtains, presently drawn against the night, testified to wide windows that during the day would let in plenty of light. She wondered what the windows overlooked;

she hadn't yet ventured into the gardens at the sides and rear of the large house.

A fire burned cheerily in the large fireplace opposite the windows, the flames throwing golden light deep into the room.

The desk gracing one end of the room was larger, more ornately carved, and also showed more evidence of use than the one in the London house, its surface all but obliterated by papers of one description or another; legal papers, letters, orders, invoices—she glimpsed examples of them all as Dominic led her to one of the two armchairs angled toward the desk.

Twin lamps, one on either end of the desk, were already lit.

Drawing her hand from his sleeve, she sank into the chair and watched while he circled the desk. He bent, opened a drawer, pulled out a map, then walked back around the desk. Grasping a nearby side table, he drew it between the armchairs, sat in the other chair, and spread the map out so they both could see. "This is our route—from Edinburgh via the ferry across the firth and on to Perth, then via Pitlochry, Drumochter, and Kingussie to Inverness. From there, we head west, through Eskdale and Strathglass. Cannich is the last town of any description before we reach Loch Beinn a'Mheadhoin and the castle."

Dominic sat back and gave her time to familiarize herself with the route. When she looked up, he caught her gaze. "You said you ride well, but how well? Be honest—this is important. I can't organize a mount for you if I don't know your ability in the saddle, and once north of Edinburgh, the odds of finding a decent replacement are next to none."

The look she bent on him was exasperated. "I'm a Cynster. We all ride and ride well—it goes with the name."

He held her gaze. "Eliza."

She pulled a face. "She's the exception that proves the rule. Truly, I know of no other Cynster who isn't an excellent rider."

He hesitated, then inclined his head. "Very well. I'll assume you'll at least be able to keep up with Brenda and Griswold—they're the slowest of our group, but they aren't slow." He got the distinct impression that she bit her tongue, but after a second she nodded, and he went on, "Thankfully, that means we can ride the whole way, which will be faster—having to use a gig or curricle on those roads would slow us significantly."

"You'll be hiring a horse for me from a stable here?"

He nodded.

"In that case, I want a mount at least fifteen hands high, sleek and nimble rather than overly muscled, and with some degree of spirit." The gaze she leveled at him was serious and direct. "Given we need to ride fast, you won't be inclined to hire a slug, but do bear in mind that the fleeter the horse, the faster I'll go."

She was lecturing him on horseflesh? "I'll bear your preferences in mind and see what I can find."

"Good." She looked back at the map. "Where are you planning to stop for the nights?"

"Perth, then Kingussie if at all possible, although reaching it within the day will be very hard riding, and then Inverness. From Inverness, it'll take us three to four hours to reach Cannich, and about an hour more to the castle. Naturally, that's dependent on the weather, but it seems to be holding—the roads should be dry."

Angelica studied the map; when she set out on a journey, she liked knowing where she was heading. Dominic glanced at the papers on his desk, but remained in the chair, watching her.

Once she was satisfied she had a firm grasp of their geographical direction, she turned her mind to their personal direction. If he needed to work on his papers tonight, she should leave him to it, but having decided that they needed to move forward in the physical sense now, before they reached the castle, what was her best next move?

The answer seemed obvious.

Raising her gaze from the map, she met his eyes. "I believe I'll retire—none of us got all that much sleep over the past nights." She rose.

As she'd expected, he got to his feet, too. He bent and moved the side table toward the desk, out of her way, then straightened with the partly folded map in his hands. The desk was behind him, the side table to one side.

She had to pass him to reach the door. She stepped forward, and paused. Close.

Tipping back her head, she met his eyes, smiled as if intending to wish him a good night. Instead, she stepped closer, reached a hand to his nape, and drew his head down as she stretched up to the very tips of her toes and pressed her lips to his.

She had an instant in which to savor his shock, then—

Fire.

Heat erupted—between them, around them. Searing flame welled, swelled, then raged through her, through him, and burned.

And she was no longer kissing him—he was devouring her.

One large hand had speared into her hair, cradling her head and holding her to the kiss, holding her captive while his lips crushed hers in urgent, greedy, ravenous hunger.

The force of that unleashing transfixed her, caught and held her senses—as if he'd been waiting for this moment, anticipating and wanting, but had held back, just as she had.

Now all restraint was gone.

His tongue cruised the seam of her lips, blatantly tempting, aggressively challenging; instinctively, she parted them and felt novel pleasure surge as his tongue boldly thrust into her mouth and laid claim.

Hard and commanding, his lips moved on hers, supping, taking, hungrily savoring; his tongue caressed, explored, branded and incited, impressing stark passion and searing desire on her giddy senses, setting them and her wits spinning ever faster.

She might have been brazen in initiating the exchange, but there was nothing reluctant about his response. He kissed her like he wanted and intended to devour her inch by sensual inch. He could not have made that statement more clearly—more boldly, more ruthlessly—and while her heart sang, her body and her senses gloried.

His other hand had spread over the back of her waist, his touch a heated brand even through the silk of her gown. She felt him shift, moving them both, then the angle of the kiss changed to one less strained; some dim, distant, still lucid part of her mind realized he'd sat on the desk, reducing the difference in their heights and pulling her between his thighs.

Perfect, her inner wanton purred. Now she could kiss him back, could with more firmness return his flagrant, diabolically sensual caresses. She might not have had much experience to call on, but if he could, then she could; taking that as her guide, she set about returning his every favor.

She remembered her hands; after that first moment, they'd fallen limp on his shoulders. Raising them, she speared her fingers into his black locks—and was momentarily distracted by the silky softness. She played, clutched, used her hold to press a boldly deliberate kiss on him, then she eased her grip and sent her hands wandering. Over his cheeks, fingertips lightly stroking down, learning. Down past his hard jaw and over his collar to sweep across the width of his shoulders, and savor.

Then he edged the kiss into new, deeper, more intimate territory, ruthlessly jerking her attention back to the increasingly heated communion of their mouths. She'd never kissed a man like this—had never known she could, never even guessed that a kiss, simple or otherwise, could descend into this, an exchange so laced with latent passion and desire that like ambrosia it addicted her, mind, body, and senses completely, and rendered anything else—all and everything else in the world—secondary, of little import.

This—what they shared, what was welling and swelling and burgeoning between them—was all that mattered.

This, and the conflagration spreading like wildfire beneath their skins.

Distantly she wondered whether it was entirely her imagination that beneath her fichu, the necklace burned hot, and the pendant between her breasts grew heavy.

Dominic hadn't seen the kiss coming, but regardless, not even in his wildest and most wary dreams had he ever considered that she—with just one kiss—could undo the control he'd spent the last decade and more perfecting. But the first touch of her lips had struck straight through his defenses, had connected directly to that inner self he normally kept well leashed, and tripped the lock. And the hunter had responded, shouldering his rational and logical self aside in an overwhelming drive to capture and seize, seduce and possess.

Possession—possessing her—currently burned as the central critical focus in his mind.

He'd thought that she would run and save them both, but no. Far from being sensibly frightened by the raw power of the passion they'd between them evoked, the witless wanton was urging him on, as if she couldn't wait to lie spread beneath him.

If neither of them came to their senses soon, she would, most likely on his desk.

The thought made him groan, the sound trapped in the kiss.

She heard, and only kissed him even more seductively.

When had angel transformed into siren?

Relegated, as it were, to a corner of his brain, he was reduced to battling to regain his own reins.

The taste of her—sugar and spice had never been so nice—didn't help.

The warmth of her body, lithe and elementally feminine, pressed flagrantly to his helped even less.

As for those tracing, tantalizing touches that laced fire over his skin . . .

For long moments, the battle hung in the balance; his lips and tongue engaged with hers, his senses ravenous for more of her in whatever way more might come, he feared he wouldn't win—wouldn't be able to draw back before . . .

He dragged in a breath, searched desperately through his mind and hauled two images to the fore. Bryce and Gavin in one, the castle and his clan in the other.

And he was suddenly in control again.

Able to block out the compulsive desire thudding in his veins and ease back from the kiss, finally to break it.

He raised his head. His breathing ragged, he stared into her face.

Waited to see what she would do, how she would react; he honestly had no idea.

Her lids slowly rose, revealing emerald eyes glittering with gold. Her gaze steady, she looked into his eyes, searching them as he searched hers.

Then her lips, swollen and slick, gently curved.

"I'll leave you to finish with your papers." Her voice was low and husky. She held his gaze for a moment more, then stepped out of his slackened hold.

He straightened from the desk as she glided to the door.

Reaching it, she glanced back at him. "I'll see you in the morning."

She opened the door and stepped through, then gently closed it behind her.

Leaving him standing, stiff and hard in every possible way, staring at the door—and fighting another battle not to follow.

That there had been no further sirenlike lure embedded in her parting words was quite possibly the only reason he won.

Jaw clenching, he finally managed to get his feet to move and carry him around the desk. Easing down into his chair, he stared at the numerous papers awaiting his attention.

But all his senses, all of his mind, continued to be filled with her.

And the next step she'd clearly decided on.

He'd been waiting for her to declare her wishes, to issue an invitation impossible to misconstrue; he should have known she wouldn't do anything by half measures.

He would have liked nothing better than to oblige her, whenever and wherever she wished, but . . . if he'd needed any demonstration that his decision to defer broaching the physical aspect of their pending union until later, until after they'd reclaimed the goblet and saved the clan, was not just wise but now critical, she'd just provided it.

Fingers tapping the desk, he tried to think of a way around that conclusion—tried to convince himself his loss of control had only come about because she'd taken him by surprise. That next time would be different.

The truth was it might not be. How long it would take him to be certain of his control with her he couldn't claim to know.

What he did know was how deeply immersed in those heated moments, in her, he'd been. The Cynsters could have come tramping through his house and he wouldn't have noticed.

Long minutes ticked by, then he reached for a fresh sheet of paper. "Damned female!" She'd shattered his control once; he needed to remind himself why she couldn't be allowed to do so again.

Picking up his pen, jaw clenching, he dipped the nib in the inkwell and wrote down all the reasons he couldn't—shouldn't—bed his countess-to-be *yet*.

Angelica lay in the beautiful bed in the countess's bedroom and stared at the canopy overhead.

Self-control was a trait she understood well and applied constantly, yet she hadn't been in control through that kiss. Not that that concerned her in the least; it hadn't at the time, and didn't even now, but he . . . he hadn't been in control at the start, nor through most of that wild exchange, but he'd seized and exerted rigid and absolute control at the end.

And she wasn't so sure about that.

Especially given he'd let her go, had let her slip from his arms without any sign of wanting to prolong the moment.

"Hmm." Fingers twisting the rose quartz pendant, she wondered what that meant.

Regardless, she was content with her progress. She hadn't intended matters to go even as far as they had, not tonight, and, indeed, she was grateful he had exerted control and drawn back—because she had a sneaking suspicion she never would have, and after three nights in a mail coach, she wasn't at her best, and she wanted to be at her best for her first time.

But now that she'd learned their route to the castle, how long the journey would take, and where they would be halting each night, she was even more convinced of the rightness of her decision. She needed to be established as his countess in all but name *before* they reached the castle. Once they walked into his keep, he and she both would focus on what they needed to do to get the goblet back—that was simply the way they were made; they both understood duty and the necessity of getting the most important things done first. Once at the castle, they wouldn't have time to establish the physical side of their union; if they didn't arrive with the connection already in place, neither of them would be able to draw on the inner strength she was convinced would flow from the consequent deepening of their regard.

From the love their lust would transmute to.

"So . . . tomorrow night." Tomorrow night she would make her bid to storm his castle. Tonight's interlude had been highly encouraging; it had also shown her the way. "Surprise. If I don't want him shortchanging us, I'll need to shake the arrogant Earl of Glencrae to his very large boots."

The idea made her smile. "Yet another challenge."

Smile deepening, she turned on her side, snuggled down, and gave herself over to catching up on the sleep she'd recently missed, and the sleep she intended to miss the next night.

Chapter Ten

It was much easier to deal with passion and desire in the cold, hard light of morning.

Dominic waited until Angelica joined him at the breakfast table, then signaled MacIntyre to leave them.

Once the door had closed, he looked down the table; she was slathering jam on her customary slice of toast. He waited until, sensing his regard, she looked up, then he caught her gaze and evenly said, "Our exchange last night was unwise. As you instigated the incident, I'm not going to apologize, but regardless of my compliance last night, given how important reclaiming the goblet is to us and to so many others, it will be best if we avoid any further intimacies until after we've achieved that goal."

She looked levelly at him; for a long moment, she didn't react. Then she blinked, and searched his face, as if examining not his words but him. "Was that your considered and previous opinion? Or is this declaration *because* of what occurred last night?"

He tried to keep his frown from his face, but didn't entirely succeed. "Last night provided a perfect demonstration of why we should keep a reasonable distance. I—we—cannot afford to be distracted from our currently overriding and critical purpose. Conversely, later, we'll have plenty of unencumbered time in which to give such matters our full and undivided attention."

"Hmm." She arched her brows. "There is that—the prospect of us applying our full and undivided attention to the matter."

He set his jaw; now was not the time to respond to such taunting. He waited, but, her gaze now distant, she merely crunched her toast, apparently lost in considering . . . he didn't want to imagine what.

After another full minute of crunching, he gave in and prompted, "So you agree? No more intimacies until later—until after we have the goblet in our keeping."

She blinked. "What?" She refocused on his face. "Oh. Well, if that's your declared position"—she shrugged—"far be it from me to argue."

He looked at her, at her expression, which had remained devoid of any strong emotion. They might have been discussing some minor social issue for all that showed in her face.

And he had absolutely no idea what that meant.

Frustration rose; he couldn't be sure he'd successfully corralled her sirenlike tendencies, but he had no wish whatever to discuss the matter further, especially not with her. Pushing back his chair, he stood. "I have business in town, close by the castle. I'll see you at luncheon."

"Yes, all right." She peeked under the teapot lid. "Can you send MacIntyre back—I could do with more tea."

Jaw clenched, he walked out of the room, entirely unsure who had won that round.

He next set eyes on his countess-to-be as he strode back from a discussion with his Edinburgh-based agent. She and Brenda were standing on the pavement of High Street opposite Tron Kirk, apparently examining the construction of its spire.

She spotted him as he crossed the street. Her face lit—and his lingering irritation over their morning's encounter fled. She had a smile like an angel and eyes to match, and she used both shamelessly, yet as long as it was him she was beaming at he felt it would be churlish to find fault.

On reflection, he'd concluded that their exchange over the breakfast table had been a clash without the clash; she hadn't specifically agreed with his stance, but at least she'd acknowledged she now knew what it was. What she did next . . . wasn't in his control. He'd have to wait and see, then counter whatever move she made, which, given he was highly experienced in that particular field and she wasn't, shouldn't prove too difficult.

Discussing whisky sales with his agent had had a calming effect.

"Have you completed your business?" Tipping up her red-gold head, now crowned in a fetching bonnet, she studied him as he halted beside her.

"Yes. I'm on my way to see about the horses. The stables I use are near the palace, so I can walk you home." He glanced at her new finery, which included a finely wrought parasol, presently furled. "If, that is, you've finished shopping and are headed that way?" It was only eleven o'clock; if she wanted to shop more, she had time.

"Yes, indeed. I managed to find everything I needed. I sent the parcels to the house with a delivery boy so Brenda and I could stroll."

"In that case . . ." Taking her hand, he wound her arm in his. She smiled and they set off, strolling through the crowds ebbing and flowing up and down the High Street.

She was wearing a new gown in fresh spring green that showcased her figure exceptionally well and complemented both her complexion and her stunning hair. He was aware that passersby were surreptitiously staring, but she seemed oblivious. While she clearly appreciated what beauty she had, and would, he felt sure, use it as a weapon against him or any other male in her sights, and although she clearly liked fashion and pretty things as much as the next lady, he was starting to suspect she had no truly vain bone in her body.

They'd crossed North Bridge Street and resumed their progress along High Street when she slowed, then glanced at him. "From what Eliza said, the house she was held in was somewhere near here."

Looking into her eyes, he saw nothing more than her usual curiosity. "It's in Niddery Street." He tipped his head across High Street. "Over there."

Her eyes lit. "Can you show me?"

He didn't bother asking why; the answer would be that she simply wanted to know. He was starting to understand what drove her—not all that difficult, as it was similar to what, given the same situation, would have driven him.

They parted from Brenda, her presence unnecessary now that he was escorting Angelica. When they started down Niddery Street, Brenda walked on.

Halting opposite Number 23, Dominic tipped his head across the street. "That's it."

Angelica studied the façade, remembered what she'd heard of Eliza's rescue. "Eliza and Jeremy told me about the . . . vaults—is that the term?"

Dominic nodded.

"Do you know where they are—these vaults?"

"Yes. But no, I won't take you to see them."

She frowned. "Why not?"

"Because you're not dressed for it." When she blinked at him, he continued, "Did your sister and Mr. Carling tell you the story of the vaults?"

She shook her head.

He turned her back up the street. "They were originally the spaces between the foundations of the two bridges—South Bridge and North Bridge."

She allowed him to lecture her about the vaults and their occupants, and why as a lady she couldn't visit, and pretended not to notice that he was leading her back into High Street and on toward his house; she hadn't expected him to take her into the vaults, but she'd wanted him to deny her something before she asked for what she really wanted.

When they reached the top of Vallen's Close, she halted and looked up at him. "Where are these stables you use, and is the massive chestnut you often ride there?"

He hesitated, then said, "The stables are on Watergate, and, yes, Hercules is there."

She beamed. "In that case, I'll come with you—I've heard rather a lot about your very large horse."

His eyes on hers, he hesitated some more, clearly uncertain over what she might be up to. Confident that nothing of her machinations, much less her intentions, showed in her face, she waited for him to probe. Instead, his lips firmed and, with a barely detectable air of resignation, he nodded. "Very well."

Resettling her hand in the crook of his elbow, he turned and they continued along Cannongate to Watergate and the stables.

Dominic's suspicion that his not-so-innocent intended had some ulterior motive in wanting to accompany him to the stables proved well founded. After duly admiring Hercules, her interest clearly genuine, and simultaneously charming old Griggs, the stable master, she demanded that she choose her own horse.

Well, not demanded, precisely, but she insisted on both having her say and sticking to it in the teeth of his opposition, implied as well as stated, and with Griggs on her side, and Dominic not having any grounds on which to deny her horsemanship other than his own prejudices, he was driven back, step by dainty step, until he discovered himself with his back against the wall and not a leg to stand on.

Hands on his hips, he looked into her face, at her expression—one of unflinching and unwavering determination. Stubborn didn't come close to describing the resolution burning in her eyes.

He saw it all now, saw their excursion down Niddery Street for what it had truly been, but she'd backed him literally and metaphorically into a corner and left him with no choice. Lowering his head so his face was closer to hers, he gritted out, "All right."

Triumph flashed through her eyes, but she was wise enough not to crow.

Keeping his voice low so Griggs, waiting further down the aisle in the expectation of making an unexpected sale, wouldn't hear, he said, "You can have the damned filly, but you will leave the negotiations to me."

She beamed. "Thank you." Stepping back, she left him with a clear path down the aisle.

He considered Griggs, then, without looking at Angelica, said, "Come with me, but don't say a word. However, make sure Griggs knows how much you've set your heart on that horse."

She brightened even more and did as he asked, allowing him to use Griggs's dual wishes—to sell a horse that few riders could handle, and to ingratiate himself with the future Countess of Glencrae—to drive down the asking price on the spirited black filly his devilish angel wanted for her own.

After more than an hour of manipulation—hers, his, and Griggs's—as well as the inevitable bargaining, Dominic quit the stables with the horses for the following morning organized, a brilliantly beaming Angelica on his arm, and an unsettling suspicion that in warning him to be wary of her, his instincts had been nothing but right.

They reached Cannongate. He glanced down at her.

She looked up, studied his face, his eyes, then smiled—a much more unnerving, understanding smile. Then she patted his arm, looked ahead, and murmured, "Don't worry—you'll get used to it."

He nearly snorted. He would have loved to deny the assertion categoricaliy . . . except he had a sinking feeling she was right.

"The long and the short of it," Devil said, "is that although we've located all the Scottish peers known to have been in London on and around the night of the Cavendish soiree, not one of them looks anything like the laird, nor is there any reason to suppose that kidnapping Angelica, let alone the other two, ever entered any of their heads. More, I had a chance to speak with Cavendish and managed to introduce the subject of Scottish peers—he assured me no such gentleman attended his wife's soiree."

Vane grimaced. "That is indeed the sum of it."

A brooding silence fell over the library where Devil, Vane, Demon, Gabriel, Breckenridge, Jeremy, and Martin had gathered to pool all they'd learned.

Alasdair, better known as Lucifer, Angelica's other brother, had only just returned to London after fetching his wife, Phyllida, and their tiny baby daughter, Amarantha, from Devon. Phyllida had not approved of not being in London to support Celia, and she had the added advantage of being able to distract her mother-in-law with her new grandchild. Lucifer now sat in a chair before the desk, fingers steepled before his face. "Perhaps we're approaching this from the wrong angle."

"There's another?" Martin asked.

"Yes." Lucifer spread his hands. "Who was it who inveigled Angelica out of Lady Cavendish's salon?" He looked around, but no one answered. "She wouldn't have gone off on her own. Even if we credit the substance of her notes, that she's gone to help a friend desperately in need, someone must have contacted her at the soiree—given her an urgent message, at least. Something of the sort, otherwise she wouldn't have left. And that someone doesn't have to be the laird—he might still be behind it, but as with Heather and Eliza, he might have used some pawn, in this case someone who had the entrée to Cavendish House."

"You're right," Gabriel said. "Whoever contacted Angelica and got her out of the house is the key. We leapt to conclusions about the laird and Scotland— which may yet be true—but we overlooked that."

"Well," Demon said, "it's harder to get at that point without talking to other guests who attended the soiree, which we didn't want to do because we don't want Angelica's disappearance made public." He studied the others' faces, his gaze coming to rest on Martin's. "Are we going to risk it getting about that she's vanished, or . . . what?"

Martin considered, then grimly shook his head. "That's the one thing she asked in her note—that we conceal her absence from the ton. And our ladies have done a magnificent job doing just that. If we act to overturn their good work—"

"We'll never hear the end of it." Devil grimaced.

"Wait a minute." Vane sat forward. "There's one source of information that might prove sufficient for our needs." He looked around the circle. "The ladies themselves. The grandes dames, too. Whoever was there that we can safely interrogate."

Gabriel snorted. "*Safely* interrogate? With grandes dames, there's no such thing. However, I take your meaning—they might have seen something without realizing its significance, and it's perfectly possible that between them they might well know who Angelica spoke with just before she disappeared. So . . . Helena was there, Celia of course, and Louise must have been because Henrietta was there, too."

"Who else?" Devil picked up a pen and started making a list.

In the end, the list numbered six. Devil agreed to speak with his mother, Helena, and his duchess, Honoria, both of whom had attended. Demon volunteered to pin down his mother, Horatia, and Gabriel similarly agreed to approach Celia. Lucifer was deputed to ask Louise and, if he could manage it, talk to Henrietta, too.

"Which," Vane said, casting the others a jaundiced look, "leaves me with Lady Osbaldestone."

"It could have been worse," Martin told him. "But luckily for me, Aunt Clara didn't attend."

Vane humphed, but couldn't argue. Unraveling his great-aunt Clara's peripatetic discourse would give anyone a headache.

"Right." Devil set down his pen. "We'll all go and request audience and enlightenment, and if whoever we speak with can suggest any others who we might in safety approach, do that, too. It's only the middle of the afternoon, but finding our targets at home, in a state to speak with us privately, may mean waiting until tomorrow . . . let's reconvene here on the morning of the day after tomorrow."

The others nodded or grunted in agreement. Rising, they left the library, still unwaveringly determined on their hunt.

Angelica swept into the drawing room that evening in an extremely mellow mood, further gilded by anticipation.

She was wearing one of her new evening gowns in a delicate shade of violet; she'd convinced the modiste to dispense with all ruffles, ribbons, and bows, and felt justifiably pleased with the result.

Dominic had been standing before the hearth, staring at the blaze; hearing her, he turned. If the arrested look on his face was any guide, her sartorial arrow had found its mark.

His gaze raced over her, then returned to linger on her breasts, the upper swells enticingly revealed by the sweetheart neckline. As she halted before him, he blinked, then raised his gaze to her face, to her eyes. "I thought . . ." He blinked again, then frowned. "Isn't that rather . . . unfussy?"

She smiled. "You mean plain—and yes, deliberately so. As I'm sure you've noticed, I'm neither tall, nor over-endowed, so frills and furbelows make me feel—and look—weighed down. Simple and elegant, however"—she waved a hand down her figure—"is more flattering, and serves to display but not disguise, thus shifting the focus from the gown itself to what's in it."

Looking into his eyes, she let her smile deepen. "And as you see, it works."

His eyes narrowed; she could see him toying with some response, but in the end, he only grunted.

"My lord, miss, dinner is served."

They both looked across to see MacIntyre standing just inside the door.

Dominic glanced at her, then offered his arm. "Dinner, my lady."

She smiled, serenely confident, and set her hand on his sleeve.

As he led her into the dining room, Dominic inwardly shook his head—at her, and himself. Despite his declaration of the morning, she was clearly intent on playing the age-old game. Her tactics, however, were not exactly flirting, but rather an engagement more subtle and definitely more potently provoking—witness the fact that he was responding.

Why, he didn't know; just seeing her left him half aroused—he didn't need further stimulation.

He sat her in her chair, then walked up the table to his. MacIntyre and the footmen brought in the platters and the meal began.

Contrary to his expectations—he was starting to suspect that she delighted in confounding them—her conversation held no hidden agenda but was wholly focused on their upcoming journey.

"Brenda's packing everything she can this evening so we won't keep you waiting in the morning." She wrinkled her nose at him. "Are you truly set on leaving at dawn?"

He nodded. "First light—as soon as there's light enough to ride safely." After a moment of debating whether he really wanted to know, he asked, "How many bags do you have?"

"Only three—and one bandbox, of course."

"Of course."

She registered his dry tone, but only smiled. "I know you ordered sumpter horses, so there won't be any bother with only that much luggage."

He grunted—a non-reply—but he knew that, for a lady of her station, three bags and a bandbox was traveling very light.

They talked of this and that, touching on and re-assessing all the preparations for the trip, but neither he nor she uncovered any lack or oversight. The inter-action, however, necessarily drew his gaze again and again to her face—to her lips, to her eyes, to the shad-ows her lashes cast on her cheeks.

At one point, wine sleeked her lower lip; he watched, unwillingly fascinated, as her tongue came out and swept over the full curve. He thought of his own tongue doing the same, then . . .

He looked away, surreptitiously shifted in his chair, and had to wonder if she was doing it deliberately—purposely stoking his lust. He assumed she was, but although thereafter he watched her closely, he never caught her out in any too-open, too-deliberate, inten-tionally arousing act.

Even when her fingers played with her necklace and the pink crystal pendant that hung from it—focusing his unwilling mind and his all too willing libido on her breasts, on the valley between the firm mounds—he couldn't tell if her actions were artless, or artful.

Regardless, they were effective.

By the time they rose and he walked with her to the li-brary, he was aching, but even more determined than he had been that morning to adhere to his declared position.

Angelica led the way into the library and made for her usual chair. She'd earlier asked Brenda to fetch the book she'd brought from the London house and leave it in the library; it was sitting on the table by the chair.

Hefting the weighty tome in both hands, she sat, laid it in her lap, and opened it to the last page she'd read. From the corner of her eye, she saw Dominic pause at the end of his desk and study her through narrowing eyes, but then he moved to his chair, sat, and focused on his papers. There seemed a few he hadn't yet dealt with, but the desk was almost clear.

Relaxing in the chair, she settled to read a few more pages, if only to distract her from what she had planned for the rest of the night. What she hoped she'd successfully organized to bring about.

Given the challenge of his morning's declaration, she felt buoyed by what she'd accomplished through the day. Convincing him to buy her the black filly had been an additional, unexpected victory; she hadn't known the horse would be there to be bought, but the result had confirmed that she could indeed manage him, albeit not easily. But her gowns had affected him exactly as she'd hoped, and all her other lures, heavily disguised though they'd been, appeared to have sunk home.

She had his measure now, sufficiently well to avoid any overt gambit at this point. Neither the setting nor his underlying watchfulness and resistance were in her favor, not here, not now; his will was simply too strong.

Even now, she wasn't at all sure, if they were to engage toe to toe, will to will, who would win. Wasn't sure if such a clash would end in triumph for either of them. But she'd planned for that, planned how to overcome the hurdles, indeed, to turn the setting, at least, to her advantage.

She tried to keep her mind focused on Robertson's words, but she remained intensely aware of the man behind the desk, and the excitement, anticipation, and sheer eager impatience building inside her.

Dominic found himself reading every paragraph, every sheet, at least three times before he could be sure all pertinent details had penetrated the sensual haze wreathing his mind. She was reading a book, for heaven's sake—admittedly a book about Scottish history—but why on earth his instincts, his awareness, wouldn't settle but remained expectantly fixed on her he couldn't fathom.

She was driving him demented without doing a damned thing—simply by breathing. By being.

By being anywhere near him, anywhere within his sight.

He wasn't foolish enough to pretend to himself that he wasn't, patently and painfully, deep in lust with her.

If he were truthful, he had been since first setting eyes on her in Lady Cavendish's salon, and the attraction had only grown more powerful by the day—sometimes by the hour.

Worse, it was lust with a new edge—with all the fascinating allure of a familiar urge made new and exciting. She would be his wife, ergo different—his relationship with her would be novel and new, and some unruly part of him was slaveringly eager to find out in what way. To sample—

He cut the thought off. Jaw clenching, he lifted the last of the documents he had to deal with and set it on the blotter. Forced his eyes—and his mind—to read it.

He'd reached the end, signed it, and was blotting his signature when she stirred.

He glanced at her and caught her stifling a yawn.

She met his eyes and smiled one of her gentle, easy, apparently uncomplicated smiles. "I think I'll go up."

Rising, she lifted the Robertson and tucked it under one arm. "I'll take this with me—I'm not even halfway through."

He nodded. Watched as she glided to the door, opened it, and went out.

The door softly closed.

He stared at the panels.

He'd been expecting something quite different. He'd expected her to make some attempt to overturn, at least to challenge, his declaration of the morning—to make some attempt to cross the line he'd drawn.

To capitalize in some way on his susceptibility to her subtle, but very real, seduction.

He'd been steeled to resist, to hold firm.

To not let her bend him to her will—or more accurately to recruit his libido to her cause, and so defeat him.

And instead, she'd retreated.

She'd gone upstairs, and left him not just aching but . . . deflated.

Oddly disappointed. He'd been looking forward to the tussle . . .

"*Gah!*" The damned woman was tying him in knots.

He ransacked his desktop, but he'd finished, finally finished, every document, every contract, everything he'd needed to deal with before they left.

But going upstairs now . . . in this mood, he didn't trust himself to pass her door, to continue walking on to his, rather than knocking on hers and instigating the very engagement that he'd been expecting, but she'd avoided.

"And that way lies insanity." With no other distraction offering, he opened the bottom drawer to his left and drew out the contract his father, nearly six years before, had negotiated with a group of London bankers.

If anything could refocus him on what was truly and immediately important, reading that contract was it.

Chapter Eleven

Half an hour later, his mind refocused, his thoughts revolving about the days ahead, Dominic lit the last candlestick left on the hall table and used it to light his way up the stairs.

He passed the door to the countess's suite without hesitation and continued to his own. Opening the door, he stepped into his sitting room—and halted.

There was a light in the bedroom. The door stood open, directly to his right, but from his present position he could see nothing beyond the front of an armoire. It didn't, however, take much mental effort to guess who was in his room.

For several seconds, he toyed with the notion of stepping back into the corridor, going to her suite, and sleeping there instead, but that smacked too much of cowardice.

And while his libido might be eager to discover exactly what she was doing in his bedroom, and what might come of that, he was not at all happy with her latest tack. He'd spent the last half hour recentering his thoughts on his primary objective, and now . . . jaw setting, already frowning, he shut the main door and stalked into the bedroom.

And discovered her in his bed.

Sitting propped up against the pillows, the covers to her collarbone, she was reading Robertson by the light of the bedside lamp.

He came to an abrupt halt a good three yards from the bed.

The lamplight washed over delicately rounded bare shoulders and set fiery glints flaring in the tumbled jumble of her hair, which fell in loose curls over said shoulders down to the line of her breasts.

She glanced up, smiled easily. "There you are. I wondered when you'd be up."

"What. Are. You. Doing here?" His voice remained low, but displeasure and more vibrated through it.

As if surprised by his tone, she arched a haughty brow. "Reading and waiting for you, of course."

He narrowed his eyes at her. Held onto his temper. "*Why* are you here?"

"Because I have several matters I wish to discuss with you that are more appropriately discussed here than elsewhere." She closed the book. "Now you're here—"

"Did you, or did you not, hear what I had to say regarding such 'matters' this morning?" Swinging away, he set the candlestick on the tallboy facing the bed. She was still wearing her necklace, and a silk robe lay over a chair beside the tallboy. He could see no evidence she'd removed her nightgown; presumably she was wearing a summery one with a drawstring rather than sleeves.

He turned to face her.

She met his eyes. "This morning you made a declaration based on your opinion. I don't recall you asking for mine."

She thought him fool enough to allow her to voice it?

His face a mask of implacability, he let the moment— the silence weighted with his annoyance and anger— stretch; unmoved, unintimidated, she just watched him and waited. With a patience he didn't have.

Clearly this was one argument—one clash—they were destined to have.

"Very well." He nodded. "What is it—this opinion of yours?"

"It's perfectly straightforward. As your countess-to-be, I believe I should start as I mean to go on. As I have in picking up the reins of your household, as

I have in choosing a suitable wardrobe. And in the matter of our sleeping arrangements, sleeping in this bed."

"You expect me to sleep beside you and not touch you?" The incredulous words slipped out before he'd thought.

She held his gaze and calmly stated, "No."

The shackles he'd placed on his libido—that he'd spent the last half hour strengthening—shattered and fell away. Lust roared, not just to full life but to a rabid, ravenous hunger.

Her gaze remained steady, locked with his; there was absolutely no chance she didn't know—and mean—what she'd said. As an invitation to intimacy, it trumped any he'd ever heard.

There was only one reply he could make. "Not tonight."

Two swift strides took him to the side of the bed. Stooping, he thrust his hands under the covers to scoop her up and carry her back to her room—and encountered bare skin. "*Christ!*" He pulled back his hands as if they'd been scalded.

Quick as a flash, she grabbed his cravat, preventing him from straightening.

He could still have easily done so, but, eye to eye with her determination, he had no reason to think she would release him if he did, and the image of him pulling her, naked, free of the covers . . .

He closed his eyes, clenched his jaw so hard he thought it would crack. "You don't have a stitch on."

"I thought I'd save time. You, meanwhile, have far too many on."

He opened his eyes and glared into hers, less than a foot away. His hands tingled with the remembered feel of warm, silken skin; fisting them, he leaned them on the edge of the bed.

She misinterpreted and pulled on his cravat to draw him closer, to draw his lips to hers.

He didn't shift an inch. "Why are you doing this? The real reason." A test of wills, hers against his, in an arena where he was certain to fail?

She narrowed her eyes, her gaze boring into his as much as his was boring into hers . . . as if they could somehow see inside each other's minds. Eventually, without breaking the contact, she said, "I'll answer your question if you'll first answer mine."

"Which is?"

"Why are you resisting being intimate with me when you've already decided I'm your countess-to-be? What's the real reason behind that?"

The answer—the real, deepest, and most true— swam through his mind: Because for the first time in his life he had no idea where bedding a woman would lead. She was that different. He saw her, reacted to her, thought of her, regarded her in ways that were utterly unique, and no matter what he tried to tell himself, that was not just because she was to be his wife.

But he couldn't say that. Couldn't even suggest it.

He dragged in a long, slow breath. Keeping his eyes locked with hers, he said, "As you already know, retrieving the goblet is vital to me. At this moment, doing everything possible to ensure we get it back is, to me, more important than anything else. Commencing a liaison— with you or any lady—at this time would almost certainly distract me from that vital purpose." He paused, then amended, "Correction—commencing a sexual relationship with you at this point will definitely distract me, very likely more than usual precisely because you will be my countess, an ultimate outcome that, as we both know, isn't in any way in question regardless of when you formally consent to it. However, to indulge ourselves in that manner, one certain to lead to distraction, now, when my people are depending on both of us to recover the goblet and save the clan, would, in my view, qualify as an act bordering on betrayal." Gaze locked with hers, he stopped, shut his lips, and waited.

A long moment went by during which she remained locked in their mutual gaze, then she blinked, refocused, searched his eyes, his face, then returned her green-gold gaze to his. "I understand your position and can see why you wish to hold to it. However, I have two reasons to advance against that, and both directly impinge on us being able to do our very best to reclaim the goblet."

He gave up on impassivity and frowned. "You think we should become intimate so we'll be *better* able to trick my mother and reclaim the goblet?"

"Yes." She nodded decisively.

She hadn't eased her double-handed grip on his cravat. Grim-faced, he shifted to sit on the side of the bed. "First reason."

Angelica paused only to draw breath. "I, too, see our mutual distraction as a potential problem. On that issue, as it appears to have escaped your notice, allow me to point out that we're distracted—mightily—now. Do you really think this"—she almost took one hand from his cravat to wave between them, but stopped just in time, and instead locked her fingers more firmly in the linen and gave a small tug—"this unrelenting focus between us, me on you and you on me, is going to *lessen* as the days go by? That if we don't do something to satisfy it, but just keep putting it off, it will fade?"

She studied his eyes, then firmly stated, "Yes, it's distracting, but it's driven by curiosity, by constantly wondering about the prospect, how it will feel, what it will be like, and if we don't do what's necessary to sate that curiosity, it's only going to get progressively worse. If we continue to delay addressing the issue, by the time we reach the castle, I, for one, will be in no fit state to single-mindedly focus on our charade to trick your mother—how on earth could anyone expect me to be, when most of my mind will be focused on you? On us. On you and me together."

He remained silent for a full minute, then said, "There's distraction, and distraction."

"Possibly." Tilting her head, she tried to read his eyes, to gauge what exactly he'd meant, but she couldn't. "I concede that you know more about this than me. Never having been intimate before, I can't judge what level of distraction might continue subsequently, yet I cannot imagine it would be worse than the distraction we're currently subject to due to not having been intimate yet. In my experience, expectation and anticipation are always more powerful before one has done something rather than after."

His lips tightened. Before he could say anything, she hurried on, "And if you do see the sense in my reasoning, and agree that we'll be better off addressing the issue before we reach the castle, then the questions of when and where arise, and the obvious best answers to both are now and here—in the safety of your house and the comfort of this bed." She held his gaze. "If we're to commence an intimate relationship before we reach the castle, then I vote that we start it here, tonight, in this bed."

A moment ticked past. When he continued to stare silently at her, she widened her eyes. "Well?"

After another half a minute of consideration, he said, "As I see it, both our arguments regarding distraction are valid. Which is to say that they cancel each other out, leaving us with no good reason to act now, nor to delay." He held her gaze. "So . . . what's your second reason?"

Something much harder to explain. Looking into his eyes, she felt certain he'd guessed that she didn't really want to explain her second reason . . . but she would. To meet fate's challenge, and his, to convince him to take the next necessary step along the path to falling in love with her, she would dredge her thoughts, her emotions, and find the words.

She took a full minute to think, then, keeping her eyes on his, commenced, "When we reach the castle, neither of us can be sure of what it will take to convince your mother that I'm ruined. That's our aim, the goal we, together, have to achieve. Even though we haven't discussed what we might need to do, I'm sure you've thought of it, and I have, too. The part I'll have to play, the sort of charade I'll need to act out, won't necessarily be simple or straightforward. It might, very likely will be . . . difficult, on several levels. And not just for me, but for you, too."

She paused; locked in the storm-tossed sea of his eyes, she could only hope that he would understand. "In order to perform as I—and you—will almost certainly have to, we need to be . . . closer."

His brows fractionally rose; he was thinking, trying to follow her meaning.

That wouldn't be enough; increasingly sure she had to sway him, now, tonight, she searched inside, and found the truth—her own vulnerability—waiting to be owned, her real reason why. She drew a suddenly tight breath and, eyes still locked with his, forced herself to say, "To pull off our charade, to have the confidence to carry it off successfully, I'll need to have—and to know I have—complete and absolute trust in you, especially in the physical sense. And the only way I know of to reach that level of trust quickly, over the few days we have before we reach the castle, is for us to be intimate."

Something shifted behind the gray clouds in his eyes. It was tempting to say more, but she pressed her lips tight and, her gaze locked with his, waited.

Dominic searched her eyes and saw nothing but stark honesty. He'd asked, and she'd told him. Simply and sincerely. And he understood. He knew far more than she did about the act of intimacy, and her view was unquestionably correct; for a woman, especially with a man of his strength, trust was . . . utterly essential.

And he could see why she wanted that particular level of trust, could imagine what she foresaw of their required actions at the castle.

She wasn't wrong in that, either.

He looked at her, and saw a woman, a lady, who had agreed to aid him, a man she hadn't known other than by adverse repute, to save a clan she had no connection to or responsibility for. She'd done all and more than he could possibly have expected of her; to this point, she had given unstintingly.

This was something she was asking in return. More, it was something she needed.

This was what he was being called on to give in return for all she'd already given him, and all she was committed to giving as the days rolled on.

He couldn't deny her.

Even though he had reservations—severe reservations that had grown even more acute through the last hour—over how what had already flared between them would play out for him.

He certainly couldn't deny her to protect himself.

Her first reason had been a practical one, the second an emotional one. His resistance to the first had been on practical grounds, too, just as his resistance to the second was as emotional as her need.

He saw the parallels, but seeing changed nothing.

Drawing in a breath, he scanned her face, taking in her tension—the same tension gripping him.

Returning his gaze to her eyes, he studied the emerald-flecked gold, then asked, "You do realize that once we're intimate, there will be no going back—not even by any sleight of hand, no matter how far-reaching, practiced by your family?"

"Yes." She met his gaze with her usual fearlessness. "But I'm still withholding my agreement. I accept that we're going to marry, but I will not formally agree until later."

He let his frown—his distrust of her motives—show in his eyes. "Why?"

She considered him for a moment, then evenly replied, "At this point, that's something you'll have to take on trust. I believe I know what I'm doing, and that that is the right path. For us both."

The words didn't ease his suspicions; if anything, they grew.

But . . . hauling in a deeper breath, he exhaled, then nodded. "All right." He looked down to where the

Roberston still lay in her lap. He reached for it, lifted it, then leaned down and set it on the floor. Although her grip on his cravat eased, she didn't release it. Slowly, he straightened. "One thing." He met her gaze.

She arched a brow and, attempting a degree of savoir faire, inquired, "What?"

"As in a waltz, I lead." Raising his hands, he reached for her face; with his thumbs, he brushed errant red-gold tendrils from her cheeks, felt his pulse stir at the contact, sensed her attention shift to his touch. Sliding his fingers back into her hair, he gently framed her face, felt her delicate jaw against his palms. Saw her lashes flutter as he tilted her chin. "And you follow."

She parted her lips, doubtless to argue, but he gave her no chance. He bent his head and kissed her. Shut her up, and distracted her.

Shifting closer, he held her face tipped to his and slowly, thoroughly, kissed her.

To within an inch of her life—and his.

As it had the previous night, heat erupted—rapidly, searingly—between them. He made no effort to temper it but let it rage, imagining, in some distant, still lucid recess of his brain that the scalding wave of passion would shock her, melt her, and make her more malleable.

For himself . . . decision made, all thoughts as well as reservations set aside, he saw no reason not to take his time and savor the captivating taste of her, content enough to allow the welling urgency already drumming in her veins and his to grow. To recognize and appreciate that swelling response while her lips clung to his, while with his tongue he tempted hers, and slowly, commandingly, whirled her down the, to him so familiar, path into passion's embrace.

Step by step. Under his control.

But oh, those lips—soft, succulent, and lush—and the way she so readily yielded her mouth, his to claim, to plunder at will, with the unquestioning, arrogant ardor of a conqueror . . . her invitation could not have been more evocative, provocative, or blatant.

Through the kiss alone she told him she was his, declared it with a force more powerful than any words. The hunter within heard and understood; she was there, held and captured, already surrendered, in his bed, under his hands, so he didn't have to chase but could simply enjoy . . . all she offered. All she invited him to take.

He'd sunk so deeply into the heady rush, under the enthralling spell, that her tugging at his coat didn't register sufficiently to draw him back—to make him pay attention rather than glory in the pleasures of her mouth, in the feel of her cheeks against his palms, in the tantalizing trace of her silken tresses over the backs of his hands.

Then she nipped his lower lip, yanked hard at his coat, pushing at his shoulders. "*Mmph!*"

He broke the kiss, and she sucked in a breath and said more clearly, "Off!"

Bemused—amused—by her focused determination, he helped her wrestle off his evening coat, then while he undid his waistcoat, she fell on his cravat. His gaze tipped to the top of the sheet; courtesy of her sudden activity it was descending, giving him a tantalizing view of the smooth upper curves of her breasts, but the sheet hadn't yet fallen free of the pert tips.

His mouth watered. Shrugging off his waistcoat, he tossed it aside, toed off his shoes, bent to strip off his stockings, leaving her to draw the cravat free. She flung the strip of linen at his waistcoat and reached for his shirt. Abruptly realizing the danger of allowing her too much rein, he swiveled, put one knee on the mattress, then crawled over her legs and slumped alongside her.

His weight landing jostled her; she shrieked and grabbed the sheet back up to her neck.

Suddenly intent, he rose on one elbow and leaned across her. Capturing her gaze, holding it, he slowly closed his other hand on the sheet and tugged.

Fingers clenching, she held it in place.

Looking into her eyes, he arched a brow. "Aren't you going to let me see?"

Her eyes narrowed. "Isn't that something you're supposed to earn?"

If he hadn't been so focused on getting what he wanted, he might have laughed. Instead, he shifted more definitely over her, his weight more on one arm than the other, yet still caging her. "In that case"— with the fingers of one hand he played with a strand of her fiery hair—"let's see what I can do."

Eyes on hers, he bent his head, set his lips to hers, and kissed her . . . and as before she responded instantly, eyes closing as she yielded her mouth. His own lids falling, he dove in and claimed.

And the heat rose again, more potent, more powerful; a tidal wave of burgeoning need, it swamped them. He let the swell crash and roll through them, more than willing to harness and ride the tide.

Held beneath him, Angelica shifted, heated, flushed, restless, and impatient. She needed touch, wanted to feel the hard body propped above hers against her, needed relief from the urgency that was building, building, just beneath her skin.

She wanted more. More fire and fury, more of the wonderful heat—more flames.

More giddy, reckless excitement.

But his kiss was all sexual mastery, commanding, demanding, and controlling. Every heavy thrust of his tongue, every languorous caress, every artful pressure of his lips on hers held her senses locked in thrall, sent her wits spinning—and left her at his mercy.

Which wasn't how she'd imagined this would be.

She wanted to leap into the flames and take him with her. She wanted fireworks and passion, wanted to be wild and unrestrained, and she wanted him to be, too.

With an effort, she managed to drag enough of her consciousness free of his spell to peel her fingers from the sheet and set them lightly to his chest, to the fine linen still covering the fascinating expanse.

He stilled—she sensed it clearly through the kiss, that with just that simple touch she'd fractured his concentration—but then he deepened the kiss and poured heat down her veins as one hand swept between them and captured both of hers.

When her awareness resurfaced from the rapacious onslaught—when he broke the kiss, raised his head, and drew her arms up over her head—she discovered he'd shackled both her wrists in the hand of the arm he was leaning on, and her hands were now anchored in the pillows above her head.

Breathless, she tried to summon a frown, but her features wouldn't oblige. She tried easing her hands free, but his grip, although not painful, was unbreakable.

His eyes—now a clear pale green with very little gray—met hers, then his gaze drifted downward, to fix on her breasts, rising and falling dramatically beneath the sheet. His lips curved, but she wouldn't have described the gesture as a smile.

"Hmm . . . let's see."

Looking into his face, at the edge desire had stamped on the angular planes, she felt anticipation flare; prickling awareness raced over her skin.

Beneath the sheet, her nipples pebbled.

He saw; the curve of his lips deepened in blatant satisfaction, then he lowered his head, but not to take her lips again. With his free hand, he framed her jaw; with his thumb under her chin he tipped her head up and to the side so he could place a tantalizing, lingering kiss just below her ear, then his lips skated down the fine tendon in her throat, tracing down to where her pulse thudded. He pressed a hot, openmouthed kiss over the spot; her lids fell and she fought to quell a shudder.

His beard-roughened jaw lightly abraded the skin over her collarbone as, instead of releasing her face, he caught the edge of the sheet with his chin and slowly—oh, so slowly—drew it down.

His warm breath washed over the skin he exposed, a startlingly intimate sensation.

She couldn't breathe; expectation and anticipation cinched tight about her chest, held her lungs locked. Waiting . . . she felt her breasts swell, felt heat flare hotly beneath her skin as inch by inexorable inch he drew the fine sheet down.

Revealing her breasts, exposing them.

Despite the tumult of her pulse, despite her increasingly giddy senses, she retained wit enough to recognize that his every move, his every touch, was, and would be, orchestrated.

Even through the covers she could sense the heat of him, the hard, muscled strength of him, so close, yet not where she wanted him.

Lifting her lids, battling to steady her whirling senses, she looked at his face, at his focused, oh-so-intent expression as he edged the sheet down to where it caught on her painfully tight nipples.

She took in the quality of his resulting smile.

And knew beyond doubt that it was time to take a hand—to make a stand—to stake her claim to at least half the reins.

And drive them where she wanted them to go—into the heart of their fire.

She could almost feel the control he wielded, not just over her but over himself even more. She didn't simply sense but *knew* that there was a great deal more that he kept leashed, held back, held at bay—so much more that they could have, could experience, could revel in if only he would drop the reins and let them free.

Let them both simply be.

Before she could think of any suitable action, he bent his head, pressed his lips to the soft upper swell of her breast, then sent them cruising. Sensation flashed anew, leaving her breasts tight and aching. He released her face, lowered that hand, closed it about one aching mound, and kneaded.

A momentary relief, almost immediately superseded by another wave of escalating pleasure as his lips caressed and his fingers and hand shaped. Then his tongue rasped over the upper edge of her aureola and she sucked in a breath.

Held it as sensation sparked and flared.

As his tongue artfully circled and his fingers tightened on the sheet.

If she didn't act now . . .

He was lying on his hip alongside her, his legs stretched out alongside hers. Her hands might be useless, but her legs were free.

The sheet slid away as she raised her shoulder, twisting and rolling her hips toward his, raising one thigh, aiming to stroke it firmly over his groin—over the hard ridge of his erection.

Her arching movement raised her breast to his lips, an offering he instantly accepted; before her thigh made contact, his tongue rasped over her nipple, then he drew it into his mouth—just as she succeeded in caressing him where she thought it would do most good.

The result significantly exceeded her expectations.

Her caress made him jerk, stiffen, then he suckled fiercely—ripping a smothered scream from her throat.

Fire lanced through her, pouring down her veins. Struggling to breathe, she felt his grip on her wrists ease. She pulled her arms free; driven, she grasped his nape with one hand, held him to her as he suckled and licked and she gasped and clung—and reached for him.

A sensual tussle ensued.

He tried to roll her onto her back and pin her, but she fought, resisted, her hips and thighs pressing, pushing, sliding against his, her hand boldly caressing, stroking and shaping the iron-hard column behind the flap of his trousers.

On a hissed curse, he stopped pushing and rolled to his back, taking her with him. "For God's sake, woman—exercise a little self-preservation!"

She landed sprawled on top of him, naked and exposed, the covers tangled between them—with the placket of his shirt in front of her nose. Ignoring the erotically charged caress of cool air over her bare skin—over her shoulders, back, bottom, the backs of her thighs—she fell on the shirt's buttons.

Greedily undid them as he cursed again and tried to catch her hands.

Dominic's fingers tangled in her necklace, and even more in her hanging hair. The thick strands caught and clung as if they were alive. Alive and doing their mistress's bidding.

She yanked and tugged on his shirt, hauling it from his waistband; like a demon, she wrenched the buttons free, simultaneously squirming to block his attempts to stop her—

The last button slid free and with a sound of feminine triumph, she sat up and dragged the loose halves of the shirt wide—and stared down at what she'd revealed.

Her expression—one of excitement, enthrallment, and covetousness combined—suggested she'd found some El Dorado.

He registered it, but barely, too focused, too fixated, on what he could now see. Her, utterly naked, perched atop him, her sleek thighs to either side of his waist, her red-gold hair, fiery copper in the lamplight, falling in loose waves over her back and shoulders, those strands that had earlier trapped his hands falling to curl, a gilded frame, about her breasts. Between the mounds, caressed by the light, her crystal pendant hung, faceted and mysterious.

But those breasts . . . full and swollen, the mounds perfectly shaped to fit his hands, the peaks rosy and begging for more attention. His attention.

His mouth had long dried.

Her skin was flawless silk, fine and pale, now tinted with the telltale flush of burgeoning passion. The sight did nothing to cool his ardor; it called to his inner hunter, beckoned and provoked.

Oblivious to the stillness that had come over him, she released his shirt, and with a look of pure greed investing her lovely face, she set her hands to his chest, splayed her fingers, and caressed.

Explored. Devoured by feel. Claimed.

Ruthlessly holding back the urge to immediately respond, to reseize control and simply take, he lowered his gaze, skating over her midriff to the indentation of her waist, over the evocative flare of her hips, then inward to the thatch of browny-copper curls at the apex of her thighs.

Behind those curls, she would be hot, swollen, and slick . . .

All concept of control fled his mind.

He shifted them both to the left, then tipped her, flipped her to her back. The covers remained tangled and twisted between them, but left her legs, her arms, and her breasts bared. He came down on top of her, his weight on his elbows so he didn't crush her; her thighs instinctively parted to cradle his hips.

Momentarily distracting him.

"Wait—get this off!"

She was still struggling with his shirt, trying to get it off his shoulders. Her focus wasn't where he wanted it to be; with a grumbled oath, he raised up enough to, with her assistance, peel the garment off. She flung it away and refocused on his chest.

Swooping, he trapped her lips in a kiss expressly designed to curl her toes, to wipe her mind of all thought, and send her wits whirling. To have her loosen her grip on the reins of this engagement and cede them wholly to him.

The kiss was all he'd intended it to be.

The result wasn't what he'd planned.

Instinctively recognizing the tussle of wits and wills, the battle of experience against sheer enthusiasm—the fight for dominance—Angelica fearlessly leapt into the fray. She kissed him back, met his thrusting tongue with her own, and with reckless and giddy abandon gave him back every iota of passion he poured into her.

This was what she wanted—or at least the threshold of what she wanted. Them, together, rolling in the flames, and stoking said flames ever higher.

She reveled in the kiss, in the unrestrained mating of mouths it had become. Pulling her hands from their fascination with his chest—so wide, so hard, so warm— she slid one to his nape; she wanted—*needed*—to feel his chest against her tight, still aching breasts. She tugged; in response, he settled lower on his elbows, but his chest still hovered an inch above her breasts.

Her other hand had skated to his side, gripping the warm skin above his waist. Sending that hand roaming over his back, over all of him she could reach, she savored, almost purred through the ravenous, greedy kiss; his skin was smooth, pulled taut over rock-hard muscles and heavy bone.

And he radiated heat. A heat that beckoned and tempted her—nay, compelled her to rub her body against his, to tangle her naked limbs with his.

But no matter how she tugged, no matter the temptation she poured into the kiss, he wouldn't lower further—wouldn't give her the relief she sought.

So she brazenly took it. Using his rock-solid immobility as an anchor, she tightened her grip on his nape and arched upward against him, pressed her breasts to his chest, shifted and caressed.

Caught her breath at the sharp, lancing sensation, at the wave of intense pleasure that the black hair across his chest abrading her ruched nipples sent streaking through her.

Their lips were still locked, but she thought he'd gasped, too.

Then he stilled.

And she knew she'd won.

That she'd succeeded in convincing him to stop managing their reins and let them free.

The satisfaction had barely registered when he pounced.

One hard hand caught and held her face, then he kissed her—with an unrestrained ferocity that left her reeling.

Had she thought his kisses passionate before? This kiss laid her waste, left her with wits flown and her senses rioting.

Abruptly he broke the kiss and turned his attention to her breasts. His full, undivided, almost ruthless attention. Hard hands shaped and kneaded, weighed, seized, and claimed. His lips branded; his tongue savored and rasped, and drove her to ever greater desperation.

Then he took the tight bud of her nipple into his mouth, suckled hard, and drove her wild.

And she could no longer think, could only respond to the intimate pleasuring.

To every powerful suckle, every lick, every knowing squeeze.

The strength in his hands was undeniable, yet fear had no purchase in her brain. Anticipation did. Building inexorably, it licked her skin, lashed her flesh, shivered down her nerves.

Yes, yes, yes.

More, her body sang. She did everything she could to communicate that, to encourage and feed his desire, his passion, his urgency.

Until hers became his, his became hers, and want and need and passion and desire were one blazing conflagration.

Greedy and ravenous, aching and needy, addicted to the flames she undulated beneath him, savoring the alienness of his hardness against her softness, then she ran her hands down his back, down to slip her fingers beneath the back of his waistband, reaching further to stroke, to touch, to learn.

Dominic bit back a curse; heat erupted, arousal geysering as her delicate fingers brushed the skin of his lower back—skin only a lover would be likely to touch.

He didn't need any further reminders of what role she was intent on filling; the brutal impulse to claim her was pounding through his skull, through every part of his body, demanding. He was riding the edge of passion in a way he never had before; never had the hunter within been so intent on taking absolute possession.

On owning. On claiming. On making his.

But she was, if not innocent, still a virgin; he couldn't simply take her.

Instinct and impulse had him sliding down the bed so that he could with his hands claim more of her, so he could rain openmouthed kisses over her taut belly, could lick and taste her skin there, too.

Her breathing grew harried. She could no longer reach his lower back. Her small hands roamed his shoulders, caressed his upper arms, every touch openly inciting.

Shifting lower yet, he dragged the covers from between them and shoved the folds aside, revealing her beauty, her bounty, baring all the feminine delights he fully intended to claim.

It was her turn to still. He heard her breath hitch, felt expectation grip her.

His body held one of her legs trapped; his shoulders had kept her thighs wedged wide, yet he closed one hand about her free knee and opened her wider still.

And looked down at her ultimate delight, the pink pouting lips glistening with arousal, the tip of her clitoris just visible behind the screening curls.

His mouth watered.

Tracking his gaze slowly up her body, he glanced at her face.

Caught her gaze. Watched her eyes widen, held the emerald and gold splendor while anticipation heightened and her hands gripped, nails sinking into his arms. Eyes locked with hers, he released her knee, ran the backs of his fingers down the quivering inner face of her thigh, set his hand to her flesh, and cupped her.

Her lips parted; he felt the sensual jolt that shook her, heard her smothered gasp. Relaxing his hand, he trailed his fingers through the scalding wetness, set them to the plump lips and traced. On a shuddering sigh, her lids fell, but he continued to watch her expression, watched as she registered the novel sensations, the blatant intimacy, then he looked down.

And explored.

Her harried, increasingly ragged breathing was music to his senses.

He stroked and caressed, but neither he nor she had much patience left. Aware of the tension rising in her, evident in the flickering muscles of her thighs, he tested her entrance with one blunt fingertip—and discovered just how tight she was.

Leaving that hand where it was, he pushed back up the bed; rejoicing in the slide of his chest, skin to skin, over her sumptuous body, he settled over her again and, ignoring her faint frown, her restless questing hands, dipped his head and covered her lips, took her mouth again, filled it with a demand too rapacious for her to resist. Once she was caught in the exchange, he eased one finger into her sheath.

Angelica lost her breath—suddenly discovered she could only breathe through the kiss, through him. She clung to the exchange, to its heat, to the lifeline it provided while her senses spun. While her mind was overwhelmed by the sensation of him slowly, carefully, sliding just one finger into her.

His fingers were large, but courtesy of her earlier endeavors she now knew just how large the pertinent rest of him was. If this was how one finger felt . . .

With that finger finally buried inside her, he stroked.

And something within her quaked.

She pulled back from the kiss and hauled in a huge breath. Head pressed back into the pillow, eyes closed, she followed every flexion of his hand between her thighs, every press, every pressure, every subtle, knowing, repetitive glide of his fingers.

Heat flared, even hotter, more hungry, than before. It flashed beneath her skin, raced down her veins, pooled, welled, and swelled low in her body.

Compelling. Demanding.

She shifted beneath him, restless and needy; his lips returned to hers in a gentler kiss. He drew back, murmured, his voice gravelly and grating, "One step at a time."

If she'd had any doubt that he was as captured—as captive—as she was, his tone would have dispelled it. The harshness spoke of raw need, ruthlessly restrained, yet impossible to deny.

In her case, she couldn't—and saw no reason to— suppress her escalating need, but while she was determined to experience the full clamor of desire, his and hers, both unleashed, she could only be thankful that he retained sufficient wit and control to ease her through this, her first time.

Then he withdrew his finger; she sensed him glancing down. A protest forming in her brain, she clutched his shoulder, but then he replaced one finger with two, pushing both past her entrance, slowly yet deliberately working them deep and she forgot . . . everything else.

Forgot to breathe.

She remembered, and heard her shallow, ragged, desperate pants, but then he stroked again, more definitely, more heavily, and her senses expanded, then soared.

Her body grew hotter; tension coiled, tighter and tighter. She suddenly wanted something, needed relief. She arched beneath him, hips lifting, rising, riding the now regular, repetitive thrusts, reaching for something, searching for yet more—

Desperate, she reached for him, blindly caught his nape and pulled his lips back to hers and kissed him with wild abandon—with her own brand of command and demand; with her other hand she clutched his back and held tight, urged him closer.

Dominic kissed her back, met her and matched her, fought and battled for supremacy, for once a battle he couldn't seem to win.

She wanted, needed—so he gave.

Gave her what she—her body—was clamoring for.

With long, sure strokes, he brought her to the peak, to the point where her nails sank into his arm, her back arched and her sheath tightened inexorably about his fingers.

He broke the kiss, dipped his head, caught one of her nipples, took it deep into his mouth, simultaneously thrust his fingers deep. Suckled hard.

And she screamed.

And shattered. Shifting, his mouth still at her breast, he watched the glory flow across her expressive face— the wonder, the amazement, of her first climax.

Ripples of release washed through her; he stroked within her, prolonging the delicious pleasure, waiting until she eased.

Gradually, her body relaxed, all tension erased. The hand that had locked in his hair released, and slid to his shoulder.

He took advantage and shifted lower in the bed, settling his shoulders between her bent knees. He was hard and aching, but he had time for this. Had a need for this.

Splaying one hand over her belly, grasping her knee with the other and holding it wide, he bent his head and tasted her.

Licked, laved, and savored her.

Angelica came back to life on a shuddering gasp, on a shaft of intense, erotically intimate pleasure. For several seconds, her mind refused to accept what her senses were conveying—then she levered up her lids, glanced down her body, and watched him lap at her.

He felt her gaze, glanced up, and watched her watching him. His next long, slow, rasping lick shot pleasure so sharp through her that she gasped, eyes closing, spine bowing, as she rode the wave out.

But the wave didn't end. The pleasure built, and built.

Until she was writhing under his hand, her panting breaths just short of sobs, her head threshing, her hands fisted in the covers as he drove her relentlessly on.

This time the peak was higher.

Wielding an expertise that was little short of damning, he drove her straight to the pinnacle—then held her there.

Kept her there, her senses straining, her mind awash, nearly drowning in intimate sensation.

When he finally consented to thrust his tongue into her and let her fly, the soaring release propelled her so high she felt she'd touched some sensual sun.

For a moment, she knew nothing, could sense nothing beyond the blinding brilliance.

Dominic eased up from his position between her widespread thighs. For an instant, balanced on his knees, he looked down at her—at the sumptuous female flesh, rose-tinted with desire, spread before him like a feast. Well-pleasured and ready for the taking.

Her taste was on his tongue, fresh, tart, an undeniable lure.

One that had sunk barbs into his hunter's soul.

His fingers went to the buttons at his waist, slid them free. Seconds later, he'd wrestled his trousers off; he flung them away.

Returning to her, as he stretched over her, then lowered his body to hers, all he knew was a raw, driving, primitive urge to join with her.

To mate with her.

Courtesy of her actions and his reactions, passion now rode him so unforgivably he was close to blind with need. Close, very close, to losing all control. Desire was a raging torrent in his blood, more primal, more ravenous, more powerfully ungovernable than he'd ever known it. He had no option but to appease it, to sate the burning need.

Without haste yet with no hesitation, he wedged his hips between her thighs, set the blunt head of his erection at her entrance and, hanging over her, arms braced so he could watch her face, he pushed into her.

Slowly.

Her lids fluttered, then rose, and she looked up at him.

As the scalding wetness of her sheath closed around the head of his erection.

A heartbeat later, he met the expected obstruction, but she was already stretched to the limit by his size; one short, sharp thrust, and he was through.

She'd started; pain had flashed through her eyes, but one blink and it was gone . . . superseded by amazement and wonder.

Jaw clenched, muscles starting to quiver, he used what little control he had left to hold himself back from simply thrusting home.

Her gaze raced over his face, returned to his eyes, then her expression softened. She shifted, hips lifting, tilting, pressing nearer. Easing his way as best she could.

He fell on the wordless invitation and pressed deeper. Further. Halfway in, he halted and closed his eyes on a shudder. She was so damned tight.

She eased further beneath him, a welcome and an encouragement impossible to misconstrue.

Opening his eyes, he looked down into hers— and saw her welcome, her acceptance, and her need reflected there.

She reached up, caressed his cheek, then ran her fingers back into his hair.

Locked in her eyes, he pressed on, forged steadily deeper—until at last he was sheathed to the hilt in the hot, wet, wonder of her body.

And she sighed.

A sound of delight, of inexpressible sensual pleasure.

Her eyes a medley of emerald and gold, she used her hand at his nape to rise up enough to touch her lips to his jaw, then brush them across his mouth.

Holding herself there, meeting his eyes at close quarters, the curve of her lips deepened, and she whispered, her breath warm across his lips, "Now ride me. Take me. Show me." The last word he heard as her lips closed on his was "All."

And then her mouth was there, offered and surrendered, and he plunged in and plundered.

Withdrew and plunged into her body, and plundered there, too.

And surrendered to her fire and their flames.

Desire beat at him; passion raked claws over and through him, and shredded what remained of his control.

Some impulse even more powerful wiped his mind of all thought—and left only raging hunger behind.

But she was there—there to sate him, to take him in and mate him. To join with him and hold tight as their world spiraled into a frenzy of heat and passion.

She was there, as one with him in their greedy hunger, in the maelstrom they had together unleashed; hands grasped and clung and fingers sank deep as their breaths sawed and passion ignited and burned—all around them, in them, through them—cindering wits and searing their senses.

Until they raced up a peak impossibly high, until their hearts thundered and their senses turned inward and they knew nothing beyond the world bound by their locked bodies.

By their joined desires.

By their linked souls.

Wills aligned, wits long gone, they rode through the flames and headlong into ecstasy.

She shattered beneath him on a breathless scream.

He followed her over the edge, holding her close, reveling in the unprecedented glory as on a hoarse shout, his body emptied into hers.

For long moments, ecstasy held them, bright, sharp, overwhelming.

Then they fell. Into oblivion. Into a sea of boundless satiation.

Chapter Twelve

Dominic woke to the sensation of a warm female body snuggled against his.

And knew, instantly, even without thinking, who she was.

He tried to tell himself that it was because she was in his bed at Glencrae House, where he'd never brought any other woman, so who else would she be, but that was a lie. His knowledge had leapt from some instinctive place; something inside him recognized who she was. Not Angelica Cynster so much as his mate.

He'd always understood his primitive side, had worked with it all his life; it was the talents of that less civilized self that made him such an excellent hunter. He valued the heightened instincts; they'd kept him alive too often to count.

While that other side had naturally played some part in his previous sexual conquests, never before had that more primitive self stepped forward to claim a woman—to possess her as his. It was usually just the chase that mattered, not the claiming itself.

With Angelica . . . nothing had been all that "usual."

Certainly not the depth of satiation that later had held him in thrall.

He'd collapsed half on top of her, but she hadn't seemed to mind. Eventually, however, he'd lifted from her, untangled their limbs, found the covers and dragged them over their cooling bodies.

Without a word, she'd crawled back into his arms and settled her head on his chest; he'd fallen asleep with her hair caressing his chin.

She must have stirred and turned during the night. Her back was now to him, her curvy, heart-shaped bottom snuggled against his groin. One of his arms lay over her waist, his hand relaxed beneath her breasts; he could feel the tip of the rose-pink crystal touching the top of his hand.

He breathed in, and the scent of her wreathed through his brain.

Revisiting what had occurred after he'd surrendered and kissed her . . . throughout the engagement, he and she had fought for control, but neither had won.

Instead . . . he wasn't entirely sure what had happened instead.

His instincts had warned him that being intimate with her would be different, and, as usual, his instincts had proved correct. That left him . . . not understanding what was going on. Not knowing the pertinent factors, the relevant parameters, not knowing how to exert control.

He was accustomed to controlling virtually everything in his life, and in all things he most assuredly controlled himself. Yet last night . . .

He focused on her red-gold head. Wondered if, the next time he slid into her body, the engagement might be more amenable to his customary mastery.

There was only one way to find out.

Angelica awoke to the shiveringly intimate sensation of long, strong fingers stroking between her thighs, sliding over the already slick flesh from behind.

Even as her mind locked on the sensation, the fingers probed, testing, then opening her.

Before she'd caught her breath, before her wits had caught up with her senses, Dominic shifted behind her, and the blunt head of his erection parted her folds.

The fingers that had been preparing her splayed over her belly, angling her hips so that he could press deeper and fill her. His other hand had slid under her hip and now held her steady, anchored before him.

Eyes closing on a shuddering exhalation, she let her senses feast on the delicious, indescribably glorious sensations the intimate invasion sent pulsing through her. He pressed slowly, deliberately, in, and her flesh parted, gave way, surrendered—and claimed.

He filled her, and her body delighted.

Finally seated deep inside her, he curled his body around hers, his chest to her back, his legs behind hers. He bent his head; his lips cruised her bare shoulder. "There's no need for you to move. Just lie there, and let me show you."

He drew back on the words, then surged slowly in again. Sensation rolled in a long, dreamily somnolent wave through her. The feel of his hard body, naked and hot, cradling hers, the abrasion from the crinkly hair that decorated his chest, thighs, and groin as with every surging thrust his body shifted against hers, brought her pleasure, and a subtle, scintillating joy.

Smiling, eyes closed, she did as he asked and gave herself up to his expertise, to experiencing this slower, yet equally intimate, possibly more erotic, dance.

Appreciated what it revealed.

To be as she presently was, her body surrendered, his to use, to fill and pleasure as he would and from which to take pleasure as he willed, required precisely the sort of trust she'd wanted to find. That she'd wanted to learn to have in him.

In their veins, the thud of desire had steadily escalated, albeit, this time, to a measured and tightly reined beat. Lips curving, she felt confident such rigid control wouldn't last, not through the final, cataclysmic moments. Where that confidence came from she didn't know, but it was real and absolute.

Their fire had ignited and flared long ago; passion's flames had raced through them, claiming them both. Their skins were heated, yet still the internal conflagration built.

Soon. The end had to come soon.

She was already panting, nails digging into the forearm he had locked around her. Need raked her. Passion coiled, hotter and tighter, deep in her belly; his increasingly hard, deep thrusts fanned the furnace. She felt the end fast approaching. Could feel the inevitable coiling tension gripping his body, investing the heavy muscles surrounding her, holding her in passionate supplication.

Up to then she'd obeyed his injunction to just lie there, but that was denying herself the pleasure she most enjoyed—pleasuring him. Yet he had her in an unforgiving hold, one she didn't truly want to break . . . his next thrust brushed some point of such sensitivity that she gasped, senses spiking, and instinctively tightened about him.

Remembered she could. She did it again and realized she didn't need to move to caress him, to pleasure him. Blatantly, flagrantly.

He'd stilled at her first experimental attempt, breaking his rhythm of thrust and retreat, but then, at her back, his chest swelled, and he resumed, then picked up the pace, thrusting harder, more powerfully—and she found her own rhythm and matched him.

Head bowed, his breathing harsh, Dominic shuddered, felt the reins slip, tried to hold on. Couldn't. He let them fall, gave up his futile attempt to control the apparently uncontrollable, and let himself—his body, his senses, his all—ride the glorious tide.

Her intimate caresses were the last straw, but the firm press of her bottom to his groin as she accepted each hard, heavy thrust and pushed back to take more of him, wordlessly inviting even deeper penetration, was simply too much.

Too much temptation for him to withstand.

He held her and filled her and their senses spiraled, twining inextricably, merging and converging on some other plane.

Nothing else mattered but this—this pleasured joy, this profound togetherness.

Now he'd tasted it, and knew that it lay within him and her to create such glory between them, he couldn't hold back, couldn't deny his soul this ultimate bounty.

They crested and broke. She went first, but he was only seconds—two deep thrusts—behind her. The familiar cataclysm awaited them, but more intense, almost unrecognizable in its power.

Ecstasy caught them, held them, shattered them.

Utterly. Completely.

Wracked, broken, and emptied—of thought, of will, of self—they floated in that golden glory where the aftermath of pleasure spread like a benediction, soothing, refilling, overflowing.

Then satiation rolled in and pulled them down, into oblivion, and sated slumber.

His last thought before he succumbed shone beaconlike in his mind.

He'd bedded Angelica Cynster, his countess-to-be, and life as he'd known it had changed irrevocably.

They left Glencrae House at nine o'clock to walk to the stables in Watergate.

Angelica glanced back at their little procession—Brenda, Mulley, Griswold, Jessup, with Thomas walking alongside one of the footmen, who was dragging a hard-cart piled with their bags, her bandbox perched on top.

Facing forward, she glanced up at Dominic, striding beside her, her gloved hand in his. Not on his sleeve, not tucked into the crook of his elbow, but firmly locked in his grasp.

Shifting her gaze ahead, she kept her smile within bounds. This morning when Griswold had tapped on the bedroom door, then called to wake them, Dominic had grunted, but had made no attempt to hurry her back to her rooms or to hide her presence in his bed. He'd risen, donned a robe, waited until she'd reclaimed her own robe and the slippers that had slid under the big bed, then had shown her the private door that connected their suites. After waving her through, he'd shut the door. She'd listened, and had been pleased that he hadn't relocked it.

The first and biggest hurdle in getting him to fall in love with her had, she judged, been successfully overcome.

Further heightening her excellent mood, her emerald velvet riding habit had lived up to her expectations; when she'd swept into the breakfast parlor arrayed in it, Dominic had paused, rendered momentarily speechless by the sight, then had complimented her, patently sincerely, before continuing with his meal. The modiste who'd supplied the severely cut habit, with its contrastingly delicate, frothy, lacy blouse, would remain on her list of Edinburgh modistes to be favored with her patronage.

Reaching Cannongate, they turned toward Holyrood Palace. In society's terms, it was still early; there were few people about in the more well-to-do streets, few to see their little procession marching along.

She looked around, breathed deeply, then exhaled. The morning was fresh and clear, with a light breeze scudding fluffy white clouds across a cerulean sky. According to Jessup, the weather looked set to remain fine through their days of riding to the castle. All in all, she was looking forward to the day, to the start of this last leg of their journey.

They reached the stables to discover their horses saddled and waiting.

Dominic checked the girth of the sidesaddle on the prancing black filly, then lifted Angelica up. Having her lithe body between his hands instantly evoked memories of the night; grimly blocking out the distraction, he set her in her saddle, then held the bridle, watching as she efficiently curled her leg about the crook, slipped her feet into the stirrups, then rearranged her skirt.

Picking up the reins, she nodded, the feather in her cap bobbing above one eyebrow. He released the bridle, holding himself ready to seize it again if she couldn't manage . . .

The filly sidled but, without apparent thought, Angelica brought the skittish black under control, then turned her and walked her to where the others were gathering.

Jessup appeared by Dominic's shoulder; eyes shrewd and keen, he nodded at Angelica. "Thought you'd taken leave of your senses, but she has excellent posture, and her hands are good and steady."

"Hmm." Dominic watched for a moment more, then said, "I'll keep a close eye on her nonetheless."

Jessup nodded and headed for his own horse.

After checking that all the baggage—including her bandbox—had been loaded securely on the sumpter horses, Dominic accepted Hercules's bridle from Griggs and swung up to the saddle.

It felt good to settle into his own saddle again.

To, at least in this, be in control again.

Picking up the reins, he had to admit that, despite the not-entirely-to-his-liking outcome of the night, he was feeling remarkably positive. That said, he couldn't understand *why* he was feeling so damned at ease. Last night hadn't been a victory, not for him, yet his instincts were reacting as if they'd stumbled on some new, unexpected, but excellent way forward and were now focused on exploiting what had fallen into his hands.

Even though he was, clearly, going to have to learn to share reins that, until now, had been solely his.

Inwardly shaking his head, he walked Hercules toward the other horses.

Angelica turned; her gaze swept over Hercules, then slowly rose over Dominic, until she met his eyes. She smiled. "He really is a magnificent specimen."

He narrowed his eyes at her, but inwardly preened.

Her smile deepened and she turned back to the others.

Drawing Hercules up alongside her, he spoke to the group. "We'll go down Holyrood Road onto Cowmarket, then on through Grassmarket and past St. Cuthbert's."

Everyone nodded. Wheeling their mounts, the others fell in behind as, with Angelica beside him, he led their company out of Edinburgh.

Ten miles out, they reached South Queensferry on the banks of the Firth of Forth.

Riding beside Dominic as they picked their way down a steep street running from the High Street to the shore, Angelica said, "I read about Queensferry. It was named after your Queen Margaret, the one who married one of the Malcolms. She was very religious and used to go back and forth from Edinburgh to Dunfermline Abbey, and so set up the ferry. Hence, Queensferry."

Dominic nodded. "It was originally operated by monks."

They emerged from the street onto the road following the shoreline. Several piers were located at various points around the cove.

"There." Dominic pointed to where a large ferry was tied up at the farthest pier. He nudged Hercules in that direction. "They use whichever of the piers best suits the prevailing conditions."

The ferry was still loading. Dominic bought their fares, then their small cavalcade dismounted and walked their horses on.

They didn't have long to wait before the ferrymen cast off and the ferry started its slow journey across the choppy waters.

Standing at the railing beside Angelica, Dominic glanced down at her. Small hands gripping the rail, she was looking ahead, the brisk breeze whipping loose tendrils of her hair about her cheeks. Her face glowed with eagerness.

The ferry pitched. Catching her elbow, he steadied her, anchored her. The ferry righted and forged on; he released her, but shifted closer, locking one hand on the rail to one side of her and angling his body so that if she lost her grip, she'd bounce against him and he could catch her.

He glanced at her face. "Not queasy?"

She looked up at him, smiled, and shook her head. "Mind you, I've never been on such open water before—it's much rougher than the Solent, at least during summer, and that's the largest stretch of water I've been on. Then again, we're not going that far." Raising a hand, she pointed ahead. "At least, if that's the other side?"

Dominic glanced ahead. "Yes, that's Fife. The ferry runs here because it's by far the narrowest part of the firth."

Overhead, seagulls wheeled, raucously cawing. The wind strengthened, bringing with it the scent of the open sea. Together they remained by the railing and watched as the opposite shore drew nearer.

Several times, Dominic checked her face, her expression, for any signs of malaise, but she remained unperturbed, unconcerned, caught up in enjoying the moment, the adventure. The third time he looked, he caught himself, realized why he was looking, checking. Why he was standing as he was, with her literally within his protection.

Facing forward, he waited for some inner recoil, some instinctive resistance to his changed focus . . . instead, all his instincts remained in accord over how he was dealing with and reacting to her, as if accepting as natural that his well-being should now be contingent on hers.

After several long moments of dwelling on that, he shook aside the distraction. He'd never been attached to anyone else as he now was to her; doubtless he'd grow used to the ramifications.

Just over an hour later, they landed at North Queensferry. Walking off the pier and halting beside Dominic as they waited for Jessup and Thomas to bring their horses, Angelica looked around in some surprise. "It's barely a hamlet."

Dominic, who'd been watching Jessup lead Hercules off the ferry, glanced at her, then turned and surveyed the scattered roofs lining the road north. "People rarely stop here, not overnight. Everyone off the ferry is on their way somewhere else, just passing through. However, there are several taverns that serve excellent lunches. We'll stop at one before riding on."

Jessup and the others arrived with the horses; remounting and forming up once more, they clattered up the street.

Dominic halted at the second of the three taverns the town boasted. The Wayfarer's Halt had fed him many times; he felt confident their food would pass muster. Dismounting, he handed Jessup his reins, then lifted a waiting Angelica down. While Jessup and Thomas led the horses to the yard behind the inn, with Angelica on his arm, he led the rest of their party into the tavern.

The tavern keeper, Cartwright, looked up from behind the bar, then smiled hugely and came hurrying forward. "A pleasure to see you again, my lord." Halting, Cartwright's eyes went to Angelica, rounded a trifle in surprise, then he bowed and looked inquiringly at Dominic.

"Good morning, Cartwright. I know it's early, but we require a full luncheon, in the parlor for myself and the lady, and at a table here for my people." Dominic glanced at Brenda, Mulley, and Griswold, who had followed him and Angelica in. "Jessup and my groom are stabling our horses and will be joining the others."

Cartwright beamed. "Of course, my lord. Your people are welcome to take the big table in the window, or the one closer to the fire if they prefer. And if you and the lady will come this way . . ." Bowing several times, Cartwright ushered Dominic and Angelica into a parlor overlooking a small garden. "Very quiet and private, you'll find it." Cartwright, his gaze, a little dazed, fixed on Angelica, backed toward the door. "I'll send the missus in to lay the table."

"Thank you." Dominic dismissed Cartwright with a wave, then drew out a chair at the round table for Angelica.

Her gaze on the closing door, she sat. The instant the latch fell, she looked at him. "I just realized. Me not wearing my disguise might be a mistake. I hadn't thought of it, but clearly I'm going to attract attention—-people will remember I passed this way."

Drawing out the chair opposite hers, he looked down at her and couldn't fault Cartwright, or the other three patrons in the main room, for staring. It wasn't often that a lady of her quality graced their lives. He sat and shook his head. "I thought of it, but on balance it's preferable that you appear as you are."

She frowned. "Why?"

"Because as you just saw, I'm well known along this road. I might not have been to London for years, but I travel to Edinburgh at least six times a year."

"Ah—which is why the Edinburgh house is in such excellent state."

"And the closer we get to the castle, the more well known I become, so trying to pass you off as my charge, a charge I'll be sharing a bed with, will raise more talk than the notion I've brought my countess-to-be home and happen to be sharing her bed. And once we're married, you'll be traveling this road frequently, too, so how you appear now will fix your status in the inn-keepers' minds—"

"And me appearing dressed as a lad, which might very well not pass undetected in such circumstances, would not be a good way to start my rule as Countess of Glencrae."

"Exactly. However, to ease your concern that your appearance along the road might lead your brothers and cousins to the castle gates, while I feel safe in guar-anteeing that no one who sees you is likely to forget you, I'm even more confident that, were your cousin St. Ives to walk through the door in the next minute and ask Cartwright if he'd seen a lady with red-gold hair"—he glanced at her crowning glory—"Cartwright and the other patrons out there would deny having seen any such being."

Angelica searched his eyes, but could see only the confidence he claimed. She widened her eyes in query. "Because Devil's English?" When he nodded, she frowned. "How can you—they—tell? You could be English—you fooled me and, apparently, all of the ton."

"I pass for English easily enough south of the border, even perhaps south of Edinburgh. North of Edinburgh,

however, not only am I known, but"—he shrugged—
"I've never been taken for anything other than Scottish, and a highlander at that."

"Hmm. Richard said that the men at the tavern at Carsphairn—the ones you asked about the manor—identified you as a highlander, without question."

"They were Scottish, and I wanted information. I didn't try to hide what I am."

"But your accent doesn't change."

He waggled a hand. "Not that much—no big, obvious change in my diction—but it's enough for anyone Scots to know I'm one, too."

The latch lifted and the door swung inward to admit a bustling woman carrying a tray. She bobbed a curtsy to Dominic, then to Angelica. "Lovely to see you again, m'lord. M'lady. I'll just set the table, and my girls will be in with the platters momentarily."

While quickly setting plates and cutlery on the table, Mrs. Cartwright constantly glanced at Angelica, open curiosity in her gaze. Angelica caught it and smiled; the woman blushed and set down the salt cellar. Lifting her empty tray, she held it to her bosom. "Can we get you anything to drink, m'lord?" She dipped her head to Angelica. "M'lady?"

Dominic looked at Angelica. "An ale for me. And . . . ?"

She hesitated, then asked Mrs. Cartwright, "Perhaps you make some wine?"

"I've got a nice perry, m'lady, if that would suit?"

"That will do nicely."

When the door closed behind the innwife, Angelica looked at Dominic. He returned her gaze, then they both smiled.

The door opened again and three girls carried in platters and covered dishes. Within minutes, an array of food was displayed upon the table.

"Mmm." Angelica breathed in. "So many delicious smells."

The girls, who had been surreptitiously staring at her, smiled shyly. They bobbed and withdrew.

With a wave, Dominic invited Angelica to make her selection. She did. Mrs. Cartwright arrived with their drinks, set them down, preened when Angelica complimented her on the fare, then curtsied and left them.

Angelica sampled everything she didn't recognize. While they ate, she quizzed Dominic about the dishes, and whether there were local delicacies she was likely to be served at the castle. As she'd expected, he was well versed on the subject of food.

The meal concluded, he was eager to get back on the road. "It's four hours and more to Perth." Rising, tucking his fob watch back into his waistcoat pocket, he circled the table to draw out her chair. "It's only just one o'clock, but I'd prefer to be certain of reaching there in full daylight."

What he meant, she surmised, was that he would rather she wasn't riding a horse she didn't yet know, over roads she didn't know, once the light started fading, but she had no real argument with that. Rising, she picked up her gloves. "I have to admit it's been months since I rode any great distance, so leaving now and taking our time will undoubtedly be wise."

He stilled. His eyes locked on hers, then he searched her face. "Are you . . . all right?"

For a moment, she stared up at him blankly, then understanding dawned.

He grimaced. "I didn't think to ask—"

Gripping his lapel, stretching onto her toes, she silenced him by brushing her lips over his. As she sank back, she murmured, "I'm perfectly all right." Looking into his eyes, she smiled. "It's nice of you to think of it, but I'm very well indeed." She emphasized the last three words. When he still seemed unconvinced— still worried over whether, courtesy of their night's activities, she was too sore to ride—she patted his lapel and turned toward the door. "Truly, in that respect, I feel utterly wonderful." She arched a brow at him. "In extremely fine fettle, in fact."

When he didn't move, but continued looking down at her with a still considering but somewhat different light in his eyes, she couldn't stop herself from smiling even more delightedly. She raised her brow higher. "Perth, my lord? Or . . . ?"

He actually debated it, but then snorted and waved her to the door. "Perth, my lady." He held the door for her. As she passed him, he murmured, "The rest can come later."

She had to fight to dim her smile as she walked out into the main room.

They gathered the rest of their party. While Dominic settled with Cartwright, Jessup and Thomas left to fetch the horses. Angelica followed them out of the front door. Jessup and Thomas headed down the alley to the rear yard. Halting on the narrow front step, she turned to look back down the road to the firth.

Just as three riders trotted up from the ferry.

Three aspiring bloods was her immediate assessment, borne out when, seeing her, the three drew rein, setting their showy mounts prancing and dancing.

All three raked her with too-familiar gazes.

"Well, well," the nearest drawled, "what have we here?"

Viewing them with mild amusement, she debated her answer.

The nearest rogue took her pause as encouragement. He wheeled his horse nearer. "Come along, sweetling—I can't imagine what you're doing in such a place, but you'd be very much better off coming with us . . ."

She knew Dominic had arrived when the rogue's gaze went past her, then rose, and rose, to fix above her head.

Watching the younger man's face, she wished she could turn to see what Dominic's expression looked like, but even she could feel the palpable aura of sheer menace that reached for the hapless gentleman before her.

"Are these . . . gentlemen disturbing you, my dear?" Winter ice was warmer than her husband-to-be's tone.

She considered—saw the younger men swallow— then shook her head. "No. I believe they were just passing."

A pause, then, "Is that so?"

All three horsemen nodded. The nearest tried to speak, had to clear his throat and try again. "We'll . . . er, be off then."

With that, the three took off like the hounds of hell were after them. One hound, at least.

Amused, Angelica watched the trio disappear up the road.

Hauling back and restraining the possessive highlander he truly was behind his more civilized shields, Dominic waited for her to comment on what she was sure to have seen as an overreaction to three patently silly whelps.

Jessup and Thomas came around the corner leading the horses. The others stepped out of the inn.

Angelica finally turned. Lips curved, she shot him an openly appreciative glance, then swept up her heavy trailing skirt preparatory to stepping down to the street.

He grasped her hand, stepped down, and steadied her to the roadway. He released her, but, unable to help himself, set his hand to the back of her waist as he escorted her to her mount, then he lifted her to the saddle.

She smiled. "Thank you."

He could see nothing but approval in her green-and-gold eyes. With a nod, he turned, caught Hercules's reins, set his boot in the stirrup and swung up to the saddle, then wheeled the big chestnut up the road.

She brought her flighty black alongside. As they trotted out of the hamlet, she said, "I've been thinking of what I should call this fine girl." She patted the horse's sleek neck. "I haven't yet discovered anything suitable. Is there a female version of 'hellion'?"

Angelica. "I don't know. How about 'Buttercup'?"

She laughed. "I'm serious. I need something appropriate."

He thought. " 'Black Lightning'?"

They headed north, trading names.

They rode steadily on, past Kelty and on toward Loch Leven. Dominic held the pace to a canter overall; they didn't need to rush along this stretch, and he wanted to allow Angelica time to settle with her new mount. Initially frisky, the black filly, now glorying in the name of Ebony, grew increasingly accepting, increasingly responsive to Angelica's hand on the reins. By the time they saw the gray waters of the loch ahead, his attention had lost its honed edge.

At least with respect to the black filly.

Her rider was a different matter; all in all, he had a better chance of predicting the black filly's behavior than he had of predicting hers.

Witness the incident outside the tavern; while his protectiveness hadn't come as any shock to him, he'd expected her to jib, not to smile gratefully. His previous experience of ladies of her ilk, not inconsiderable, had taught him that any overtly possessive behavior was likely to earn significantly more than a frown. Instead, she'd seen, smiled, and been the soul of reasonableness.

How he should interpret that he had not a single clue.

The skies remained clear. As they rode, he surveyed the countryside, instinctively scanning for any threat.

"Tell me more about the castle." She edged the filly nearer. "About the people and how the clan works."

An eminently sensible question; he put his mind to answering it.

She was attentive and intuitive; her questions led him into a wide-ranging and detailed explanation of how the clan system worked, of the community dynamics within both castle and keep, and who was who at the castle.

"So the vast majority of those serving in the keep are clan, or at the very least connected?"

"Griswold is the only exception."

"Hmm. At some point, once we decide exactly how to trick your mother into believing what she wants to believe, we'll have to define what help we'll need from which staff, who we trust with what, and so on. But for now, what about those in the castle overall? How many live within the walls?"

They rode on and he gave himself up to answering her every query as completely as he could; her clear focus on learning all she might need to know once they reached the castle was both encouraging and reassuring. He felt increasingly confident they—he and she together—would succeed in hoodwinking his mother and reclaiming the goblet.

That growing confidence eased the burden weighing on his shoulders.

"All right." Deciding she'd absorbed all she could about the castle and its occupants for one day, Angelica turned her mind to another area she needed to know more about. "What are the primary sources of income to the clan?" She met his eyes when he glanced at her. "I saw the contracts and legal papers you've been dealing with. There's obviously enterprises other than just farms involved."

He cocked a black brow at her, but his lips remained relaxed. "Do you know much about farms?"

"A bit. My parents' estate is all farm-based—farms, orchards, sheep, cows—all those sorts of things."

He nodded and looked ahead. "We have the farms, too, but the additional, not so usual to a Sassenach enterprises are . . . well, there's at least three major ones, and various cottage-based businesses as well."

She listened, drawn into his world as he described a raft of agriculture-based industries she'd known must exist, but of which she'd had no real understanding. The horses cantered on, hooves drumming as their long strides ate the miles, while he talked, and she questioned and learned.

Later in the afternoon, they reined in as they approached a bridge spanning a decent-sized river, then walked the horses across the bridge, their hooves clopping sharply on the stone.

Angelica studied the range of hills that ran across the horizon ahead of them. "Is Perth this side, or the other?"

"The other." Dominic had swiveled to look back at their company. Facing forward and settling in his saddle, he said, "This is the river Earn. We're about five miles from Perth. The road takes us through a pass up ahead, then on into the town."

She straightened. "Perth! I just remembered."

He looked at her warily. "What?"

"The Fair Maid's house is there, isn't it? I mean, it's real, so we can see it." Enthused, she looked at him, saw his nonplussed expression. "Catherine Glover's home in *The Fair Maid of Perth.*" He still looked blank. "Sir Walter Scott's latest novel."

"Ah." His expression cleared. "I haven't read it."

"It's only been out for a little while, so you're excused, but do you know where the house is?"

He hesitated, then said, "I heard some talk of it in London. We can check at the hotel, but if it's the house I think it must be, then yes, we might be able to take a look at it."

"This evening? If Perth's only five miles on, we'll be there in less than an hour."

"Possibly." After a moment, he said, "We'll need to leave at the crack of dawn tomorrow—I want to reach Kingussie tomorrow night. So as you've set your heart on seeing the place"—he glanced at her—"it would be as well if we went this evening, before the light fails."

"Excellent!" Facing forward, she saw the end of the bridge nearing. She lifted her reins. "Do we trot on?"

"Not just yet. The horses need a spell."

She grimaced, but resisted pushing. His huge chestnut was the strongest horse she'd ever seen and looked like he could gallop for hours, but Dominic had been careful of all the horses, slowing to trot, or jog, and sometimes walking for stretches to rest them.

She'd wondered if he might become more autocratic and dictatorial in the aftermath of last night. However, she'd seen no sign of it, although he was still watching her, studying her—learning her ways. She didn't mind that at all.

Indeed, in all practical aspects she felt they were making commendable strides in determining how their union would work. Accommodating each other's foibles was crucial, and learning how to do so—when to stand firm and insist, and when to give way—would take time.

She had, she thought, done well thus far in accommodating his protective tendencies. Even if there was a possessive vein creeping into his protectiveness, it would be wiser, she felt, to work with him rather than directly oppose him. She'd always understood that learning to cope with possessive protectiveness was the necessary price a lady had to pay to be the wife of a certain type of gentleman—if she wanted him to see her as his, she couldn't complain when he acted as if he did.

However, as she'd learned at her mother's, aunts', sisters-in-laws', and cousins' wives' collective knee, there were ways to cope with, meaning manage, that unavoidable outcome. Namely by giving way when one could reasonably accommodate it with no real loss of freedom or will, but holding firm when matters threatened to cross that line.

He picked up the pace to a jog-trot, then a canter. Fluidly adjusting, she shifted Ebony to the faster pace.

With the rising breeze in her face, and him riding beside her, her heart rose, buoyed, light. She felt confident she knew in which direction they were heading. Perth was merely their immediate destination.

Chapter Thirteen

"That's it." Dominic halted on the pavement at the point where Blackfrairs Wynd met Curfew Row, and tipped his head at the house across the street.

On his arm, Angelica all but jigged. "It's *exactly* as I imagined it."

Her pleasure shone in her face, reward enough for his efforts in hunting down another guest at the hotel, an old lady's companion who was a devotee of Scott and who had confirmed the site of Scott's Fair Maid's house.

"I must write to Henrietta and Mary—they're such champions of Scott's work. They'll be eager to visit us just so they can stop and view this house." Having changed into a walking dress and put on her bonnet, she tipped her head back to look up at him. "Can we cross and go closer?"

He obliged, escorting her across the narrow street. The house stood directly on the street, allowing her to walk along the front wall, covertly glancing in through the window.

Halting before the door, she looked up at the stone lintel. "'Grace and Peace'—just as Scott said. That's the motto of the Glovers' Guild, apparently." She sighed.

"Back to the hotel." He steered her on. "It's quite a walk."

"But it was worth it." She hugged his arm, leaned closer. "Thank you for bringing me here."

He squelched the urge to kiss her, there in the middle of the street, blocked his awareness of her breast brushing his arm. "It was probably wise to walk after half a day and more in the saddle."

And even that perfectly innocent statement set his libido slavering, evoking the sensation of him lying in the saddle of her silken thighs.

He fixed his gaze ahead. "This way." He hoped she didn't hear the deeper tone in his voice.

They strolled back into Castle Gable, past Horse Cross and the remnants of the old city wall, into the top of Skinnersgate, then turned into Barret's Close.

She looked up and around. "It's like Edinburgh, isn't it? All these narrow, twisting lanes."

"Mmm." He was hoping Perth would be like Edinburgh in another way, as well. Throughout the day he'd fought to keep his mind from dwelling on their previous night's activities; riding when aroused had never been high on his list of acceptable tortures. Courtesy of her questions and the physical separation of riding, he'd managed well enough. Until they'd arrived at the King's Arms and he'd organized rooms for the night.

He'd taken two large bedchambers—one for her and one for him. He was reasonably well known at the hotel and had no wish to generate unnecessary gossip; as Angelica had a maid with her, and they were traveling with a group of his staff, the image he'd arranged to project was that he was escorting his chosen bride to his home.

Of course, having separate rooms didn't mean they would be using both beds.

It was at that point, when she'd retreated to her room to change, and he'd gone into his to change his coat and had seen the huge bed, that his libido had broken free of all restraint and proceed to run amok, playing havoc with his concentration.

Slowly filling his lungs, he lectured himself that he was no stripling to be led by his cock. Emerging into George Street, he escorted Angelica across, then down

George Inn Lane and into the long cobbled yard that led to the King's Arms . . . as he set eyes on the hotel's façade, his rampant libido threw up an image of the four-poster bed in his room, with Angelica, clad only in her silken skin, lolling upon it.

They changed for dinner; it was that sort of hotel. He waited outside her room, and when she emerged in another new evening gown, this one of pale blue and white, with her silk shawl over her elbows, he offered her his arm and led her down to the private parlor he'd hired.

He seated her, then, clinging to impassivity, retreated to the safety of the opposite side of the round table. It was ridiculous; he'd managed to keep his impulses regarding her in check, libido subdued and under his control, for all their days in London, and even through the journey to Edinburgh. Yet now, having had her twice, his more primitive self was literally champing at the bit to have her beneath him again.

Unsettling wasn't the half of it.

Luckily, at an establishment of this caliber there were always serving staff in the room, private or not. He could, of course, send them out, but he wasn't that stupid. At present they provided the only real bulwark against his primitive self breaking loose and suggesting that Angelica replace the dishes currently decorating the table.

The first course came and went; she instituted a discussion about Perth, the River Tay, and the town's history, all of which he knew enough about to keep the conversational ball rolling.

The second course passed with a quick sweep through Scottish history, a cursory one given she knew so little and needed to start with the bare bones; her inquiries bolstered the image that she was his willing and eager Sassenach bride-to-be, keen to know more about her new country.

Then the dishes were removed and dessert, a trifle topped with clotted cream, was placed before them.

He sampled a spoonful and finally looked directly at her, something he'd avoided since they'd met upstairs, and found himself gazing into green-gold eyes that already looked more intensely emerald . . .

Could she read his mind?

Or . . . the notion that she was experiencing the same compulsion he was roared through him.

Even as he watched, she put out her tongue, passing the tip over her lower lip, swiping up a sheen of clotted cream.

The image of her spread upon the table flashed back into his brain; if he asked . . . looking into those emerald-gold eyes, he doubted she would refuse.

Looking down at his plate, he wondered how quickly he could make the dinner end.

She pushed her barely touched trifle away.

He met her eyes, arched a brow.

Her smile was determined. "I've had enough food."

Glory be. Setting down his spoon, he stood. Waving the footman back, he walked to her chair and drew it out, offering his hand to assist her to her feet.

She laid her hand in his and rose; clasping her fingers, he set her hand on his sleeve and turned her to the door.

Bending his head, he murmured, "I assume you don't wish for tea?"

She met his eyes. "I was thinking of something more . . . enthralling."

His answering smile felt tight. "We're going to walk through the foyer and up the stairs as if we're merely intent on getting an early night. Nothing more exciting than that."

He straightened.

Facing forward, Angelica nodded. "An unenthralling, unexciting, early night."

Nothing was further from her mind. She'd never felt like this before, as if she was burning from the inside out, consumed by fiery wanting. Her breasts had swelled beneath her bodice and she'd grown unaccountably warm. She'd forgotten to bring a fan, but in the dining parlor she'd needed one more than she ever had in any ballroom. She hadn't realized that a single night's excursion into physical intimacy could lead to an addiction, but that was what this felt like—a driving craving to have his hands on her again, to have him deep inside her again. To feel the pleasure rolling through her as . . .

Cutting off the thought, she fought down her impatience, ignored the urge to hurry, *hurry*, and matched her pace to his as he strolled through the foyer; with an easy nod to the clerk behind the desk, he started them up the stairs. She battled a near-overpowering impulse to drop his arm, pick up her skirts, and race up to her room . . . if she did, he'd be on her, on her heels and capturing her, in an instant; the arm beneath his sleeve was steely hard, locked with a tension she now recognized as a symptom of desire.

Intense desire.

She'd been thrilled, beyond delighted, and enthralled by his attentions over the previous night. Now she knew the basics, she was eager to explore further, yet from the moment he'd escorted her to the countess's suite that morning, she'd had so much else to fill her mind . . . aside from the moment in the tavern parlor, she hadn't entertained a single heated thought all day. She'd noticed that his touch, along with his attitude, had grown more possessive, but the flare of heat whenever he touched her—to lift her to her saddle, in taking her hand, or when his hand brushed the back of her waist in that peculiarly male, proprietorial fashion—seemed, not muted, but easier to deal with.

Her equanimity had been perfectly even-keeled, until, dressed for dinner, she'd walked out of her room and had seen him leaning on the gallery balustrade, waiting for her.

He'd turned his head, seen her, and straightened. She'd walked to him—and the only thought in her head had been to get him out of his evening clothes and have him sprawl naked in her bed so she could have her wicked way with him.

Tamping down the eruption of desire had taken all the self-control she'd had.

Now . . . her self-control was running decidedly thin. Frayed, and fraying.

They reached the head of the stairs and he turned them along the gallery.

She locked her gaze on the door to her room. Just a little further—

"In here."

The gravelly order brought her up short. She heard a click, then he drew her across him, steering her through an open door. He followed; his hands grasping her waist, he pressed her back against the wall while he pushed the door closed with one foot.

And then he was there, hard, muscled, and radiating heat, his heavy body trapping hers against the wall, holding her captive. For one fleeting instant, their eyes met, then he bent his head and his lips captured hers.

Searing, demanding, the kiss was nothing short of incendiary; it instantly set their passions alight.

Within seconds the blaze was roaring.

She reached up, sank her hands into his hair, held tight as the kiss raged, as desire, freed, erupted and raced through them.

When he released her lips and bent his head to press fire along her throat, her hands sunk in his hair, she hauled in a shaky breath and managed to get out, "My room. Shouldn't we—"

"No. Here." He laved the spot where her pulse pounded. "The bed."

He closed his mouth over the same spot and she shuddered. Forcing up her lids, she glanced across the room . . .

Whispered, "Oh, my."

The hotel had given him the best bedchamber, a stateroom containing a massive four-poster bed hung in the royal colors of crimson and gold. The wide expanse within was large enough to accommodate even him. Large enough for them to roll in, wrestle in, without any danger of falling off.

His hands slid up to close about her breasts, to knead with an urgency impossible to deny, to possess by touch laced with unassailable right; lids falling, she bit her lip against a moan at the surge of heat his masterful, blatantly possessive caresses evoked.

He found her nipples and squeezed. Her knees turned to jelly; if he hadn't been holding her up she would have slid down the wall. She clutched at his shoulders; after seeing that bed, the only coherent thought left in her head was to get them out of their clothes and rolling naked on the silk sheets.

Raising his head, he took her mouth in a kiss so openly ravenous she gasped. His tongue plundered, stroked, claimed; she seized his shoulders and returned his fire, sent her tongue to tangle, to duel with his.

The engagement spun out of control; passion spiraled and desire shrieked.

Abruptly the mating of their mouths was not enough.

Nowhere near enough to appease the demand thundering in their blood.

His hands released her breasts and streaked over her body, claiming, provocatively shaping.

Finding strength in desperation, she slid her hands from his shoulders, reached for his lapels.

He broke from the kiss, brushed her hands aside—so he could set his fingers to the buttons closing her bodice.

Letting her arms sag, she struggled to catch her breath.

Something ripped.

He swore.

"Never mind," she got out. "You paid for it—I have others."

He glanced up, caught her gaze; his eyes were crystal clear, burning with intent. "You're sure?"

"I'll have the modiste make another. Just get it off—"

He closed his hands and ripped. They both stilled, for a fraction of a heartbeat frozen by the unmistakable, unexpectedly arousing sound.

Then he wrenched his hands apart and buttons rained to the floor.

Releasing the hanging halves of her gown, he seized her by the waist and pulled her to him, away from the wall. He stripped the gown's remnants and the folds of her shawl away; the instant her arms were free, she wrapped both about his neck and levered herself high enough to capture his lips—to kiss him with all the pent-up passion in her soul.

Dropping the ruined gown, Dominic closed his hands about her waist, held her up on her toes as she ravaged his mouth, transparently bent on issuing an entirely unnecessary sexual challenge.

Intent on ravaging her back, intent on doing much much more, he looped one arm under her bottom and hoisted her up; she immediately wrapped her legs about his waist, levered herself higher against him, and applied herself to frying his brains with her ardor.

All she had on was a filmy chemise, silk and so fine it concealed nothing; no real barrier to his touch, it became a tantalizing, shifting layer between his hands and her skin. But her new position left the heated haven between her thighs riding just above the head of his already fully engorged erection.

And as she shifted against him, pouring her passion into the kiss . . .

He mentally cursed, then with his other hand palmed the back of her head, held her immobile as he wrenched control of the kiss back, then settled to devour her. To claim her mouth, her lips, to sup and seize with unrestrained hunger, to fill her mouth with the heavy repetitive thrust of his tongue, evocatively mimicking the possession to come.

Once she was caught, her senses snared, he walked to the bed.

His legs hit the side. Holding her to him, still captured in the kiss, he reached blindly with one hand, felt and found the top of the covers. With one yank he hauled them back and flung them to the end of the bed.

Bracing his legs against the bed's side, he bent forward, pried her hands from about his neck, broke the kiss, and let her fall onto the bed.

She sank into the ivory silk sheets, but her gaze was locked on him. She waved at his clothes. "Take them off." She started to shift as if intending to curl her legs under her and sit up.

Gripping her thighs behind each knee, he lifted both, tipping her back, keeping her where she was. "No time." His voice was a gravelly growl. "Later. After."

Her eyes flared.

He drew her toward him until her hips rested on the edge of the mattress, then he pushed her thighs wide, dropped down to one knee and set his mouth to her.

She shrieked, tried to swallow the sound, then pressed a fist to her lips as he licked and laved, and drove her frantic.

But he was already too far gone himself to take the long road; glancing up, watching her head thrash, her hair spilling from the elegant knot to whip about her shoulders, the drive to be inside her escalated to near-brutal force.

Rising, licking her nectar from his lips, feeling it, an arousing drug, add its note to the clamor of his instincts, he released her legs, cupped her slick flesh, and with two fingers tested her entrance while with his other hand he undid the placket of his trousers.

Breasts heaving, Angelica struggled to fill her lungs, watched, mesmerized, as he released his engorged staff. Her eyes locked on the wide, bulbous head; her mouth watered—she wanted to reach out and touch, claim, to run her fingers down the thick, heavily veined shaft.

Before she could summon enough wit or strength to move, he slid one large hand beneath her hips and raised them as, with his other hand, he guided his erection to her entrance.

She felt him there, through the slickness seeking entry. Her lids fell; her breathing snagged, seized, as her senses focused and she felt him push in just a little way.

Then he shifted; the mattress beside her shoulder sank. Forcing up her lids, she looked up, into his face. He'd splayed his left hand on the bed by her shoulder; arm braced, he was leaning over her, the hand beneath her hips keeping them tilted so he could, inch by inch, impale her.

She watched him as he did. Took in the intense concentration that etched his features as, eyes closing, he eased himself slowly, steadily, into her body. Absorbed the incredible, deeply erotic sensation of him, hot, hard, and heavy, pushing deep within her. She couldn't breathe. Couldn't think. Could only watch and feel—and in some deeply instinctive corner of her soul, know.

Even under his coat, under his shirt, she could tell his muscles were locked, that they'd turned to steel and the control he was exerting to ease into her so slowly—so carefully—was no small effort.

But he did it. Until, at the last, he was fully seated inside her.

Then he expelled a breath, opened his eyes, and looked down at her.

His eyes blazed with a raw need that gripped her, held her, fascinated and mesmerized . . . then he spoke, guttural and low. "All right?"

She looked into those predator's eyes, then gracefully lifted her legs and wrapped them about the solid core of his body, just above his hips. She held his gaze, dragged in a breath, let it out with, "Yes. Now—"

He moved. Flexed his spine, withdrew, then surged in again.

She caught her breath, fought to keep her eyes on his, to meet his burning gaze. He set a slow, deliberate pace, one that escalated as she gasped, as she found the rhythm and rode with him.

Locked together, they rocked, their lower bodies parting and coming together, intimately joining, but other than the brush of his clothes against the sensitive faces of her inner thighs and along her calves, they weren't touching.

Which somehow registered as excruciatingly erotic to her avidly greedy senses.

And he was watching her, watching her every reaction to his increasingly powerful, increasingly forceful possession.

And possession it was. He filled her completely, the hand beneath her bottom holding her body anchored to receive each thrust. To take him in, take him deep.

And she could do nothing but lie there and let him have her. Let him fill her.

Let him possess her.

Her shallow pants filled her ears; her senses reeled, overloaded and overwhelmed.

His thrusts rocked her, would have shifted her on the sheet if he hadn't held her in place.

Reaching up, she pushed the halves of his coat aside, spread her hands on his chest, then gripped his sides and tried to tug him down, but he didn't budge.

He briefly shook his head. "Not this time."

She slumped back, looked up at him, and saw his lids lower. Felt the hand beneath her tighten, gripping harder. Sensed the change, the escalating urgency of their joining, recognized the start of the climb.

If he could watch her, she could watch him.

Could—between fighting for breath, between panting and writhing and riding her own race, between
clenching the sheets as passion and desperate desire
welled and ecstasy beckoned—watch him gasp, watch
him shudder, watch the flow of expressions, dramatic
and intense, cross his face as he thrust harder, deeper,
ever more powerfully.

Her inner dam broke. Distracted with watching
him, it caught her unawares, an explosion so shattering
she lost touch with the world.

Her body bowed, a breathless scream on her lips,
and then she couldn't see.

All she knew in those instants of searing pleasure, of
incandescent heat, was the feel of him within her, the
need to have him there, to hold and grip and caress and
keep.

He gave a hoarse groan. With one last, shockingly
powerful thrust he buried himself inside her, then
shuddered.

Glory closed around her, smothered her wits, gilded
her senses. Her heart thundered in her ears; she felt his
heartbeat, solid and strong, an echo deep inside her.
Pleasure rolled over her in boundless waves.

A minute passed, and all she could hear was their
labored breaths.

Unable to open her eyes, she reached up blindly, with her fingers gently traced his face.

He turned his head and pressed a long, slow kiss to her palm, then, moving very slowly, he unwound her legs, let himself down alongside her, and drew her into his arms.

They rode out of Perth as the sky started to lighten, Dominic riding alongside Angelica, Hercules pacing easily beside Ebony.

After half a mile, Dominic nodded at the filly. "She's settled more rapidly today."

Angelica leaned forward and patted Ebony's neck. "She's learned to keep pace with Hercules, I think."

Just as, in the space of three lessons, her mistress had learned to keep pace with him.

"She's a fast learner," she proudly informed him.

He nodded and looked ahead, and prayed his day wouldn't again be peppered with unintended double entendres; he most definitely didn't need the distraction, especially after last night. He couldn't recall being so driven to be inside a woman, not since his distant youth . . . in fact, not even then. He'd gone into the engagement with no thought in his head beyond sinking his member into her body and finding the fastest, most satisfying route to heaven. Which he'd found; the intense pleasure and consequent, unbelievably deep satiation had been the stuff of male dreams.

But he was used to being in control of his appetites, not being controlled by them. He was accustomed to tempting and pleasuring his bed partners until they begged him to take them; with Angelica . . . if she'd held back, he would have been the one begging.

Luckily, she'd been driven by her own desires, her own fierce passions, and had been no more in control than he.

Last night . . . had matters been normal, he would have had her at least once, if not twice, more. Instead, after their admittedly cataclysmic effort, he'd eventually stirred enough to withdraw from her, strip off his clothes, shift her so she lay with her head on the pillows, then he'd stretched out alongside her and dragged the covers over them both. She'd turned to him, pushed her way into his arms, settled her head on his chest, then pressed a kiss to his skin and slid back into slumber. He'd followed her under, dragged deep by satiation more complete than any he'd previously known, and had slept like the proverbial baby until Griswold had tapped on the door at five o'clock.

He and she had woken, blinked sleepily, then she'd grumbled something about having to leave so early and tossed back the covers. With her gown in ruins, she'd commandeered his robe; he'd dragged on his breeches, shirt, and boots, then checked the corridor before seeing her safely into her room.

After a sizeable breakfast—she'd eaten rather more than her usual tea and slice of toast with jam—they'd gathered their bags, and the others, loaded the horses, and set out.

They rode on as the sun climbed the sky; the day remained fine, with high clouds screening the bite of the sun and a cool wind blowing off the Obney Hills.

He took care to spell the horses, walking them more frequently now the road had started to climb. They passed through Dunkeld in good time; when they were clear of the town, and the dark stretches of Craigvinean Forest closed around the road, he picked up the pace.

Angelica shifted Ebony to the longer stride, taking care not to let the filly imagine it was a race. There was plenty of energy under the glossy black hide; she suspected the horse had a good dose of Arab in her.

As she drew level with Hercules, Dominic caught her eye. "We'll ride straight through the forest. It's usually safe, but there are clanless men who call it home."

She nodded and looked around. The road they were following was straight enough, but the forest was thick, and back from the road grew sufficiently dense to prevent much light from penetrating. They'd crossed a ridge of hills outside Dunkeld; since then the road had been steadily rising. Leaning toward Dominic, she raised her voice over the drumming of the horses' hooves. "Have we crossed into the highlands yet?"

"We passed the boundary a little way back."

Resettling in her saddle, she surveyed the country with greater interest. The highlands were frequently described as dramatic and romantic; she was looking forward to judging for herself.

Dominic noted her expression and felt one of his concerns ease. Not every lady would view an excursion deep into the highlands with eagerness. Looking ahead, he tried to see the scene through her eyes, tried to imagine what was going on in her head . . . admitted he had not a clue. But as the road rolled beneath their horses' hooves and the way ahead remained clear, he increasingly felt infected by her buoyant, expectant mood.

He could count on the fingers of one hand the few whose moods had ever swayed him—Mitchell, Gavin, Bryce . . . and now Angelica. Somehow she eased him; she brought sunshine into his day and made his heart lighter.

She teased him and made him smile, reminding him he'd almost forgotten how to do so spontaneously. The years after his father had died, and Mitchell and Krista soon after, had been filled with hard work and few reasons to smile or grin. The last six months had been hellish. When with the boys, he made an effort, but the fact he was conscious of it told its own tale.

That Angelica had such an effect on him, had grown that close to him so easily, so quickly, and courtesy of her need for intimacy, was daily growing closer still, was, beneath his apparent outward acceptance, making him increasingly uneasy.

He didn't know why she wouldn't yet agree to marry him, didn't know what she had in mind regarding their future union. He still didn't know what, with respect to him, had from the first motivated her, why at the soiree she'd set out to hunt him even before she'd met him.

Those questions, and the uncertainty they spawned, were there, in his mind, yet while he rode beside her, even with the metaphorical clouds he could see massing ahead, while she remained content he was willing to leave tomorrow's problems until tomorrow, and instead enjoy the day by her side.

They emerged from the forest and he slowed, once again walking the horses. Pulling out his fob watch, he checked the time. Tucking the watch back, he saw Angelica's questioning look. "We're making good time. We'll be early into Pitlochry, but we'll stop for lunch regardless."

"As I recall from the map, we've a long afternoon's ride."

He nodded. "On to Blair Atholl and up the length of Glen Garry, but after that the pass at Drumochter will slow us significantly. Where we spend the night will depend on how soon we can get over the pass and out on the other side, so the sooner we leave Pitlochry the better off we'll be." After a moment, he added, "You'll be seeing the real highlands from Pitlochry on."

She smiled. "I'm looking forward to it."

A hare, startled, skittered off the verge. Ebony pranced, but Angelica immediately drew the filly in.

He hesitated, then said, "Your sister Eliza." When she met his gaze, arched a brow, he asked, "Exactly how far does her antipathy toward horses extend?"

Angelica laughed, the sound like bells pealing. Eyes shining, she replied, "Let's just say that you should feel extremely lucky Jeremy rescued her. Some deity was looking out for you that day."

"She really can't ride?"

"She can sit a horse and is comfortable enough at a walk—which is really all she needs in London. She might manage a slow trot for a short distance in the Park, but at a brisk trot, she'll gradually lose confidence, and then she'll panic, and that sets off the horse, and"—she waved—"disaster ensues." After a moment, she added, "Mind you, she's always been lucky and as far as I know has never truly been thrown."

"I take it you have?"

"Several times." She met his eyes, confidence in hers. "But I always get back on."

He bit his tongue against any salacious riposte his libido might think to make.

A moment passed, then brazenly she said, "You should be very glad you ended with me instead."

"Believe me"—he held her gaze—"despite having to go to London and fetch you myself, despite the ordeal of the pit at the Theatre Royal, I am, indeed, exceedingly thankful that it's you rather than either of your sisters riding into the highlands with me."

Her eyes searched his. He'd meant every ambiguous word, and she saw it.

Suddenly, she grinned. "Have we walked enough?"

He glanced at the others, then nodded. "For now."

"Good—because Ebony and I need to run."

With that, she just went—streaked off, straight into a gallop.

Before Dominic had even thought, Hercules was thundering in her wake.

As he followed her down the road, admiring her seat, more specifically her heart-shaped arse as she leaned forward and urged the filly on, he wondered whether this was how his life henceforth would be—her leading and him chasing after her.

He assumed he would feel revolted by the thought.

Instead, he discovered he was smiling.

As arranged, the Cynster men of the current generation, and several males related by marriage, returned to St. Ives House to piece together the information they'd gleaned from the various grandes dames they'd managed to interview.

It was midmorning when Sligo shut the door behind Martin, the last to arrive. The others were all present, lounging about the room.

"So." Martin sat in the vacant armchair facing Devil's desk; his face looked older, more drawn. "Do we have any clues?"

Devil nodded. "Several of the ladies reported seeing a gentleman they described as a friend of your family introduce Angelica to a very tall, very large, black-haired gentleman during the soiree. Said gentleman was leaning on a cane, but beyond that, his general description bears a striking similarity to that of our elusive laird."

Michael Anstruther-Wetherby, perched on the wide windowsill to Devil's left, started. "You're not telling us the blackguard came into the heart of the ton and whisked Angelica off under everyone's noses?"

"No." It was Vane who answered. "Despite the similarities, Lady Osbaldestone named the black-haired man as Viscount Debenham. I checked with Horatia, and a few minutes ago I spoke with Helena. All of them saw Angelica speaking with Debenham, and while all agree he's in general terms a good fit for the laird, he's definitely English and, most telling, has a bad limp—hence the cane. He's apparently had the injury since he first came up to town more than a decade ago. And, of course, they've all known him for that long, at least to nod to. His principal estate is Debenham Hall, outside Peterborough. None of the ladies could immediately supply his family and background beyond that, but they all know who he is."

Lucifer leaned forward. "So he's not the laird. However, he does seem to be the last man any of the ladies saw Angelica with—I got the same description from Louise this morning."

"Yes, *but*," Demon said, "this morning I asked Mama—Horatia—if she'd noticed when Debenham left, and she was quite clear in her recollection that he was there, in the drawing room, chatting as calmly as you please, long after they'd realized Angelica had vanished."

"I had some luck with Lady Osbaldestone and Helena in that regard—they both said Debenham left much later, with a friend." Vane glanced at Devil. "Rothesay."

Silence followed while they considered the possibilities.

Gabriel looked at Vane. "Who was the family friend who introduced Angelica to Debenham—do you know?"

"Horatia and Helena named him as Theodore Curtis," Vane replied.

Gabriel and Lucifer exchanged glances. "We know him," Lucifer said.

"Perhaps"—Gabriel looked at Devil—"Lucifer and I should pay a call on Curtis and see what we can learn, even if all it does is rule out Angelica's speaking with Debenham as being of any consequence."

Devil slowly nodded, then glanced at Vane. "Vane and I will run Rothesay to ground and see what he can tell us of this very large viscount." Looking at the others, he said, "Debenham's is the only name we have at present—if, as seems likely, all we accomplish is to rule him out, we'll need to look further."

Breckenridge, leaning against the back of a sofa, said, "Jeremy, Michael, and I will keep searching, especially for any hint of a mysterious Scotsman being in town, and possibly around the Cavendish residence that night."

Jeremy nodded. "The street-sweepers or one of the jarveys might have heard an accent, might have driven a fare to some address—who knows?"

Demon sighed. "I have to go to Newmarket to check on things—I'll be back later tomorrow." He glanced around. "Don't do anything rash without me."

A round of frustrated snorts answered him.

Devil pushed back from the desk. "Should anyone find anything, even the merest whiff of a scent, send word here."

Nodding, the others rose, and headed, a herd of dissatisfied males, for the door.

Chapter Fourteen

Because they reached Pitlochry so early, they had the inn's dining room to themselves. Their party sat together about a large rectangular table; given they were in the highlands, that raised no eyebrows.

Angelica wanted to avail herself of the opportunity the larger group posed. She waited while the inn's staff laid a substantial repast before them and withdrew, then held her plate for Dominic, on her right, to serve her slices of roast beef, and said, "As you all know, I intend assisting the earl to convince his mother, the countess, to return the goblet she's taken. To do that, I need to know more about her—for instance, how she spends her days. What she does, where in the castle she goes, where she doesn't. Who she visits, who visits her—that sort of thing."

Turning her head, she met Dominic's gaze. "If I don't know what to guard against, and what framework we have to work within, it'll be much more difficult to succeed."

He held her gaze for a second, then nodded. "Ask away."

She looked across the table at Brenda. "So how does the countess spend her days? Start in the morning."

While the others served themselves, Brenda said, "She's rarely up before midmorning—usually closer to noon. She comes down to the great hall for meals and sits at the high table with the laird. After lunch, she goes to her sitting room—far as I know she spends most all of her day there. She embroiders a lot and sometimes plays an old clavichord. She calls for tea midafternoon—religious about that, she is, always has to have scones and a big teapot, very fussy about exactly how it all has to be on the tray. She's . . . well, finicky—about who can set foot in her rooms, what can be touched, and so on. She changes her gown for dinner, and afterward sits in the drawing room and embroiders, or has Elspeth read to her. Her ladyship calls Elspeth her maid-companion, but there's never been much companionship to it, if you take my meaning. Then about ten o'clock or so, her ladyship goes up to her bedchamber, and that's that, until the next day."

Brenda accepted the plate Jessup had piled with beef and vegetables for her.

Swallowing a mouthful, Angelica frowned. "She must go wandering the castle, or at least the keep, sometimes."

But Brenda and all the others shook their heads.

"Her ladyship is rarely seen outside her sitting room during the day, or the drawing room of an evening," Griswold said.

"She doesn't ride?" Angelica looked at Jessup.

"Never has to my knowledge." Jessup glanced questioningly at Dominic.

Who shook his head. "I assume she could, but hasn't while she's been at the castle—I can't remember her ever having a horse. In fact, I can't remember ever seeing her in the stables."

"What about visiting? She must drive out to visit other ladies in the district? Tenants? The sick?" When that elicited nothing more than head shakes, Angelica stared. "I can't believe she never sets foot outside the castle."

"Och, but you asked about visiting," Jessup said. "As to venturing forth, her ladyship goes to church every Sunday morning. I drive her and Elspeth in the carriage, there and back, never any stops or detours along the way. No visiting involved. And Scanlon mentioned that he's occasionally seen her walking the paths on the loch's shores. Sometimes with Elspeth, or the old steward McAdie, other times alone."

"That's all?" Angelica could barely credit it, but they all agreed that the countess otherwise did not stir from the castle. "Well, then—what about visitors?"

"None that I know of." Dominic looked at the others, but all shook their heads.

"Good Lord, she might as well be an anchoress."

No one argued.

After several minutes of eating and thinking, she said, "I'm not as yet sure exactly how we'll convince the countess to do as we wish"—*to believe that I'm ruined and hand back the goblet*—"but whatever our eventual plan is, I'll need to know where in the castle and around it I might encounter her or be within her sight." She glanced around the table. "Never having been to the castle, I need you to help me and think of all the possibilities. Where will I be safe, out of her sight, and where will I need to be on guard?"

Dominic shuffled several platters aside, then set the salt cellar and the mustard pot in the cleared space. Mulley retrieved the salt and mustard from another table and handed them to Dominic; he set them down to represent the four towers of the keep. Between them, the others gathered and arranged various condiment pots, then set cutlery fetched from a nearby sideboard to join the pots in the outer circle.

Angelica pointed. "Those pots are towers in the castle wall, and that's the gatehouse, and those four represent the towers of the keep?"

Dominic nodded. "This"—he placed a fingertip on the salt cellar representing the keep tower most central to the castle as a whole—"is the north tower in which Mirabelle has her rooms. Her bedchamber is on the upper floor, her sitting room below it. From her bed-chamber she has a decent view over much of the bailey, an excellent view of the gatehouse, and a reasonable view of a section of the castle walls. However, she rarely looks out that way—the curtains on that side are often left closed. She prefers the view on the other side, over the loch to the forests. As for her sitting room, where, as Brenda said, Mirabelle spends most of her day, that only has windows to the gardens."

"So," Angelica said, "she's unlikely to see me if I'm in the bailey, or at the gatehouse, or up on the battle-ments . . ." She looked at him. "I'm assuming you have battlements, walkways along the top of the castle walls?"

The others all smiled.

He kept his lips straight and nodded. "The castle wall has battlements all the way around."

"What about the keep? Does it have battlements that she might go up to and so get a wider view?"

Mulley leaned forward. "The keep towers and the keep itself have battlements all around, but I was up there recently, checking the doors were locked against our scamps, and I'd take an oath the door at the top of the north tower hasn't been opened in years."

"All right. Let's assume she isn't likely to suddenly decide to go up there." Angelica considered the structure, the layout. "From what you've said, outside the keep, other than there"—she pointed to the area overlooked by the countess's sitting room—"I should be safe."

Dominic waved at the area she'd indicated, the space between the north and east towers. "That's the danger area—the gardens. The kitchen garden is at the back, against the castle wall. I can't imagine Mirabelle would ever go there, and I'm not even sure she can see into it from her sitting room. The rose garden circles the east tower—where my rooms are—and the northwestern half of that is clearly visible from her sitting room. All the rest is the Italian garden, which stretches between the towers and can be reached from the drawing room via the terrace that runs between the bases of the towers. On the rare occasions when she decides to get some air, Mirabelle walks in the Italian garden, and all of that garden is visible from her sitting room."

Angelica nodded. "So no strolling the gardens for me, not unless I want her to see me." Elbows on the table, chin propped in her hands, she studied the model. "So tell me about inside."

Together with Mulley, Griswold, and Brenda, Dominic figuratively walked her through the main rooms on the ground floor—the foyer, the great hall, the long galleries running around it, the drawing room, his study, the library, the breakfast parlor, the huge kitchens, the armory—and then through the towers. His rooms were in the east tower, those of the boys in the west. The south tower was the province of the senior household staff, several of whom she'd yet to meet. The floor above the gallery and reception rooms, kitchens and armory, circling the vault of the great hall, contained guest chambers and, above the kitchens and armory, more accommodations for household staff.

"In addition," Mulley said, "there are two lower levels, but even in the towers, those rooms are used for storage. I've never seen her ladyship venture down there."

Dominic caught Angelica's eye. "In winter we can be snowed in for months."

She nodded. She stared at their "castle," picturing it in her mind and placing Mirabelle within it.

They'd finished their meals. The serving girls came up, hovering, wanting to clear the table.

Feeling Dominic's gaze on her face, Angelica glanced up, read his impatience to get on, and nodded. "Yes, all right." She eased her chair back.

The girls swooped and commenced clearing. Dominic rose, drew out Angelica's chair, then went to pay their host. Underneath his impatience he was pleased, not just by her focus on gathering the information necessary for her to help him reclaim the goblet but also by the way she interacted with his staff. She might not have been born to any clan, yet she'd absorbed the dynamics and had already gained the acceptance and support of those with him. Admittedly, she was working to assist him and they would die for him, but they were all—even Jessup, a hard man to win over—starting to view her with not a little pride.

His people would have accepted whoever he had chosen as his countess, but that they were already viewing her as worthy of the role, and more, as theirs, was a testament to her true mettle, to the summation of her skills.

Fronting the counter at the rear of the room, he smiled at the innkeeper. "What do I owe you?"

Rising from the table, Angelica had joined the others. Jessup and Thomas strode out to fetch the horses; with Mulley, Brenda, and Griswold, she walked more slowly to the door. Halting before it, she glanced at them. "One last question. How much control does the countess exert over the household?" When they looked at her uncertainly, she elaborated, "Does she decide the menus, oversee the household accounts, interview and select new staff?"

"Oh, no, miss, m'lady." Brenda appeared scandalized by the thought. "She might've done afore I came to the castle, but in the five years I've been there, she and Mrs. Mack, they've barely exchanged a word."

"Aye," Mulley said. "Mrs. Mack runs the household, and John Erskine, he's steward, and the rest of us take care of anything else that needs doing. No need for the countess to bestir herself, and I can't remember that she ever has."

"Nor me," Griswold said.

Angelica got the distinct impression they were all perfectly happy with the countess's aloofness. "So she, the countess, has no real idea what goes on in her own household. No, wait, what about her maid-companion?"

"Elspeth?" Brenda looked at Angelica as if she'd missed some vital point. "Elspeth's one of us—clan.

Poor girl has to make her way, but she'd never tell her ladyship anything she wasn't asked about."

"And not even then," Griswold muttered. More loudly he stated, "Her ladyship is not the sort to inspire devotion, much less confidences."

Angelica shook her head. "This is sounding all too easy, and I know it won't be . . . what about the boys? The earl's wards?" Little boys were fonts of information, which usually spilled from them with no discretion at all. "The countess might not involve herself with their day-to-day activities, might not approve of them, might even actively dislike them, but out of duty, if for no other reason, she must take an interest in their welfare . . . at least spend a little time with them?" In her experience of small boys, a little time was all it took.

"No." The word came from behind and above; Dominic had rejoined them.

She swiveled to face him.

He met her eyes. "My mother has no contact with the boys, and that's the way I, and the two of them, prefer it."

She studied his eyes, then nodded. Turning, she followed the others out of the door.

Stopping on the step to pull on her gloves, she said to Dominic, who'd halted by her shoulder,

"Despite living in a crowded castle surrounded by an entire highland clan, your mother is living in total seclusion. And that's going to make our task much easier."

"How so?"

"Because if she'd had any friends, any confidantes at all, we would have had to convince them—or at least convince her enough for her to convince them—as well. Your mother doesn't sound entirely rational, so convincing her will be easier if she has no one else's shrewdness or insights to fall back on, to use as a guide in judging me ruined."

He didn't reply, just set his hand to the back of her waist and guided her to where Ebony was dancing. Thomas held the filly's bridle. Reaching the horse, Angelica turned, raised her hands, and let Dominic close his about her waist and lift her to her saddle.

She loved the instant of being effortlessly lifted, then gently, so gently, set down; her lips curved with the simple pleasure.

When he didn't immediately release her, she looked at him, saw the deadly serious expression in his eyes and arched a brow.

"Mirabelle may not be rational on certain subjects, but she's not lacking in wits. She's clever, clearly cunning, and in her own fashion intelligent—fooling her for long enough for her to deem herself convinced won't necessarily be easy."

Angelica looked into his eyes, then picked up her reins. "You'll have to tell me all you can about her before we reach the castle."

His lips tightened, but he nodded, then turned to Hercules.

Jessup, who'd been talking with a group of riders just dismounting, came striding back. "The road's clear from here to Dalwhinnie. With luck and hard riding, we'll make Kingussie like you wanted."

"Good." Dominic planted his boot in Hercules's stirrup and swung himself up to the chestnut's broad back. "Let's get going."

Angelica brought Ebony alongside Hercules and they walked out of the yard. When Dominic paused, waiting for the others to form up behind, she asked, "Why Kingussie?"

"You'll understand when you see the other so-called towns on the other side of the pass. They're drovers' towns, often with nothing more than a hedge tavern for travelers. Once through the pass, Kingussie's the next decent halt—stopping anywhere else . . . only if we're desperate."

"Ah. I see." And she unquestionably agreed. Whatever else their halt for the night provided, she needed it to have a good bed.

They thundered down from the pass at Drumochter with enough daylight in hand to make for Kingussie. Hours later, they entered the small town with the sun dying in a blaze at their backs.

Angelica was still practicing saying the town's name when they drew rein in the forecourt of the one and only inn. "King-eeu-sie. No—King-*ew*-see." Halting Ebony alongside Hercules, she regarded the sign above the inn door. "The King-*ew*-sie Inn."

Set in a clearing beside the road, the inn was neither large nor distinguished, but having now seen the alternative accommodations, she was even more grateful Dominic had made them ride the hideous distance to reach there.

"Better." Having already dismounted, Dominic came to lift her down. "But no one will ever believe you're a native."

"I'm not concerned with being taken for a native, just in being understood." Set on her feet, she stroked Ebony's nose, then walked with Dominic to the inn door. "As I can't make out half the place names—can't relate the sounds when Scottish folk speak them to the way the names are spelled—I assume the reverse is true, and they won't understand me if I ask for directions."

They reached the inn's front stoop; Dominic opened the door and held it for her to precede him. Pausing, she glanced up at his face, expecting some response. When he simply looked back at her, his expression impassive, she narrowed her eyes at him. "Let me guess—the notion that, if I do decide to bolt, I won't be able to get very far meets with your unqualified approval."

He smiled. With one arm he swept her over the threshold and followed her in.

He spoke with the innkeeper, organizing rooms and meals. Their requirements arranged, Dominic waved her to the stairs; she inclined her head graciously to the bobbing innkeeper, then let Dominic escort her to the best bedchamber the inn possessed.

Jessup was leaving the room as they neared. Entering, she noted Dominic's bags sitting by the tall-boy, while her bags and bandbox had been left by the dressing table. Pulling off her gloves on her way to the dressing table, she heard the door shut. "Only one room tonight?" Her tone was purely curious, not in the least disapproving.

Dropping his gloves on the tallboy, Dominic shrugged. "They don't have many rooms, and—" He broke off at a light tap on the door.

Returning to it, he admitted two girls, each carrying an ewer and basin. After depositing their burdens on the washstand, the girls bobbed and hurried out. Dominic shut the door behind them, then, very deliberately, slid the bolt home.

Turning, he strolled—in the manner she always thought of as a predator's stalking prowl—toward her; his lids were low, his lashes screening his eyes. "As I was about to say, now that we're well into the highlands, there's no reason to hide our connection." Halting before her, he looked into her upturned face. "To bother concealing that we're sharing a bed." He searched her eyes. "Does not concealing that worry you?"

"No—not in the least." She studied his face. "Just as long as no hint of our intimacy reaches your mother, and given what you and the others have told me, I can't see how it would."

His lips slowly curved, but the tension she could sense in him eased not a jot. "Good." His gaze caressed her face, then fixed on her lips. "In that case . . . do you need help getting out of those clothes?"

They were late down to dinner, not that anyone mentioned it. Indeed, the others seemed to view their tardiness in a manner that suggested they considered the reason for it entirely acceptable, as an understandable outcome of how things should be.

Seated by Dominic in the chair beside his, Angelica strove to ignore the understanding in the others' expressions; highlanders, she was fast learning, were far less reserved over matters of the flesh than peoples further south.

Despite the water in the ewer being cold by the time she got to it—or perhaps because of that—she was feeling refreshed, and also hungry. The innkeeper's wife laid a simple but hearty repast before them. While they ate, they discussed their plans for the following day.

"I spoke with the stableman," Jessup said. "No one passing through has mentioned any difficulty along the Inverness road."

"Regardless, we'll have to stop there for the night." Dominic glanced at Angelica. "No matter how quickly we make Inverness, the castle is at least five hours further on, and I'd rather not arrive in darkness."

She nodded. "Indeed." Quite aside from wanting to get a clear first look at her new home . . . "I'd prefer to see the place in daylight and get my bearings from the first."

The others talked of the route, about which inn they could stop at for luncheon. After due consideration—and a glance at her—Dominic declared that they could take the time for a decent breakfast before departing at nine o'clock. "We should still make Slochd not long after midday."

Mulley asked Jessup about their sumpter horses; Dominic joined the resulting discussion. Angelica listened with half an ear, absorbed with the topic the others hadn't, and wouldn't, broach: exactly how they were to convince the sometimes-rational, sometimes-less-so countess that she, Angelica, was ruined.

The others didn't know what Dominic's mother had demanded beyond having a Cynster sister brought to the castle and paraded before her, but they would follow Dominic's lead without question; that, however, presupposed that he and she had come up with a workable plan.

From beneath her lashes, she studied his face. They had only two more days, two more nights, before they reached the castle; they needed to work out their strategy, define the details, and agree on them before they arrived at the gates.

They needed to make a start on their plan tonight, but they needed privacy for that.

She bided her time until, all decisions for the morrow made, the group rose and headed up the stairs. Dominic turned her to their door, opened it, and ushered her inside. She walked to the armchairs flanking the fireplace, heard him lock the door as she sat and settled her skirts.

Looking up, she discovered him standing by the door regarding her.

She waved to the chair opposite. "We need to discuss how we're going to pull the wool over your mother's eyes."

Dominic hesitated. He'd been putting off the moment, more or less since the night she'd agreed to help him. Despite his desire to regain the goblet, he'd wanted to keep his mother's madness from in any way touching Angelica . . . irrational, given the situation, but when it came to her, his protectiveness was difficult to deny.

But she was right—they needed to face the approaching challenge and decide how to meet it. Walking to the other armchair, he sat. "What did you have in mind?" Evidently, she'd been thinking of it, even if he hadn't.

"Me, ruined—that's what your mother wants. The most straightforward approach is to determine what she will accept as proof of my ruination, and then deliver that to her in as convincing a manner as we can, so that she accepts it, believes it, and hands over the goblet." She met his eyes. "Has she ever *specifically* told you what she means by 'ruined'?"

"No. I was to bring you to the castle, thus effectively ruining you—that was how she and I both phrased it." After a moment, he added, "As I told you in London, she appears to believe that the mere fact of you being kidnapped and brought to the castle will be sufficient to ruin you."

"Which it would if I wasn't me, a Cynster."

"Indeed." When she compressed her lips, her gaze growing distant, he said, "I would suggest that our most straightforward plan will be to do exactly as she's asked—for me to turn up at the castle with you in tow, parade you before her—and see what happens."

"Yes, but how likely is she to clap eyes on me and . . . wait, *wait*." She looked at him. "How will she know I'm me?" She blinked. "For that matter, given her seclusion, why didn't you just hire an actress to impersonate one of us rather than go to all this trouble?"

Abandoning impassivity, he grimaced. "My apologies. With all the rest I had to tell you that night, I forgot that point." He met her eyes. "When my father lay dying, while I was sitting by his bed, Mirabelle ransacked his private papers—he kept them in his study. By the time I realized all his journals on your family were missing, more than a month later, there seemed little point in retrieving them. I assumed she would eventually destroy them, but according to Elspeth,

Mirabelle still had them when she stole the goblet." He paused, then went on, "I could have taken them back then, but as she'd apparently been studying them preparatory to making her demand, I decided it would be wiser to let her keep them. The collection contains artists' drawings—in the case of you and your sisters, my father had commissioned sketches of each of you on or around your fifteenth birthdays. I've seen them, years ago, and although I can't recall enough to be certain, I think we can assume that Mirabelle will be able to recognize you by sight."

Angelica stared at him. "You're telling me she knows chapter and verse about my family?"

"Up to five years ago. She knows more than enough to ensure that I couldn't use an actress, that the lady I bring her has to be one of Celia's daughters. I reasoned that whichever of you I persuaded to help me, you would be able to correctly answer any question she chose to ask."

"In other words, you left her with the means to assure herself that I am, in fact, Celia's daughter." She nodded. "Yes, that was sensible."

"So I thought." After a moment, he went on, "But as to your interrupted question, How likely is Mirabelle to clap eyes on you and instantly hand back the goblet?—" He paused, then admitted, "I can't tell. It's possible. However, I suspect we should assume you'll have to weather a catechism at least, and perhaps a day or two of supposed ruination while she convinces herself that she's truly got what she wanted."

"That she's truly gained her revenge. Yes, I agree. So!" She rose as if compelled to do so. Brow furrowing, she paced before the fire, back and forth between their chairs. "Let's say I have to remain ruined for three days. The most critical point is that if Mirabelle ever guesses the truth—that what we present to her is a charade and I'm not ruined in the least—then, if I understood you correctly as to her character, she's malicious enough, vindictive enough, to withhold the goblet beyond the first of the month purely out of spite." Pausing, she glanced at him. "Is that a reasonable assessment?"

"Yes."

She studied his face, then, still frowning, resumed her pacing. "So we have to convince her that I'm ruined, and until you have the goblet literally in your hands we can't afford any mistakes. We'll have to have an agreed fiction and be consistent in ensuring she sees only that." She glanced at him. "Does she have any correspondents in London?"

"No."

"You're sure?"

"I would have to frank any letters she sent, and if she received any, I would be told, so yes, I'm certain. Why?"

"I'm trying to define what sort of young lady she'll imagine I am. If the last information she has about me is from five years ago, when I was sixteen and not yet out, then she can't have any idea what I'm really like." Swinging around, she met his eyes. "Answer me this— how will she make up her mind that I'm ruined? On what will she base her conclusion?" When he didn't immediately reply, she spread her hands. "All she'll know, all she'll see, is my behavior, and yours." Halting before him, she locked her eyes on his. "How I behave, and how you behave toward me while we're in her sight, is going to be the key."

He fought to keep his expression impassive even though his instincts were already bristling. "What sort of behavior are you envisaging?"

She heard the warning in his voice, but chose to pretend she hadn't. "*I* have to play the part of a gently reared, well-bred, delicate and sensitive English young lady kidnapped from her home, cruelly and frighteningly wrenched from the bosom of her family, and hauled unceremoniously to Scotland. She knows I'm twenty-one. She'll expect me to be near-terrified, overcome and overwhelmed, timid and fearfully cringing and shrinking from all risk of exposure, wanting to flee but without a clue what to do or where to go." She paused, frown deepening. "Not a ninnyhammer—I couldn't manage that—but in terms of getting out of the situation, I'll have to be in a panic, but at a total loss, and positively *devastated* over being ruined."

Warming to her theme, she went on, "I should be constantly bemoaning my lost prospects, indeed, be almost prostrate with grief over the life I've lost." She glanced at him. "I need to construct a character who can believably wail"—flinging out one arm, she touched the back of her other wrist to her forehead—"I'm ruined . . . *ruined!*"

Dropping the pose, she looked at him. "If I can't do that convincingly, if I can't make Mirabelle believe beyond all doubt that *I* believe I'm ruined, then she'll never believe it, either."

He held her gaze for a long moment, then asked, "Do you think you can pull that off? The persona you've described is nothing like you."

"My part in this will undoubtedly qualify as a stellar performance, but if we want that goblet back, we have to pull off the necessary charade."

There was more, he knew, namely the part she hadn't yet broached. "As you've noted, it's 'we' who have to pull off this charade." He held her gaze. "So what's my role?"

She looked into his eyes, hesitated—and he knew beyond question that he wasn't going to like her answer.

Confirming that, she adopted her most earnest, most reasonable and persuasive tone. "This is, I admit, supposition—I can hardly claim to know your mother's mind—but my interpretation of her demand is that she wants to *see* me ruined. She wants to be there, a witness, while I cope with the painful and devastating realization." Pausing, she arched a brow at him.

Lips thin, he let a moment tick by before conceding, "I can't say you're wrong."

She nodded. "So Mirabelle will expect me to be a quaking-in-my-slippers virgin, otherwise my ruination won't ring true. And the only way I'll be able to quake believably, well enough for her to swallow, is if *you* appear to be a potential threat, at least to my quaking persona."

He let a moment slide past, then clarified, "A sexual threat?"

She nodded. "Don't forget—in our charade you feel nothing for me. I'm just the irritating and troublesome ton female you've had to seize and drag all the way from London to the highlands in order to save your clan. You can't show any softness or partiality toward me, and you can't act protectively, at least not in any way that Mirabelle might see. If anything, you need to treat me with contempt, disdain, even disgust. To you, I'm dispensable, of no real account, otherwise you would never have done what you supposedly have, and on top of that, I'm a reminder of what you've had to do, had to become—a dishonorable kidnapper.

"Precisely *because* you violently dislike what your mother has forced you to do—and from what I understand, that's a part of her scheme, too—you aren't at all pleased with me. I'm the living embodiment of your failure to live up to your family motto. I'm a symbol of your personal disgrace. You'll need to pretend to feel darkly toward me, an antipathy that will allow me to cringe and to be as fearful of you as I need to be to convince her that *I* believe there's no hope for me—that I'm a disgraced and ruined woman, socially worthless and forever beyond the pale, and that I see and fear every possible repercussion of that." She considered, exhaled, then glanced at him.

He captured her gaze, held it. After a long, drawn-out moment, flatly stated, "You'll need to think again."

She sighed, but the sound held more resignation than surrender. "Yes, well, I realize you're not going to *like* behaving like that, but I don't think we can avoid it."

To his surprise, she refocused on his eyes, her gaze sharper, more intent, her expression unusually sober. "You haven't told me this, but reading between the lines I feel sure that part of what Mirabelle wants is to see you bending to her will, and the most emphatic demonstration of you bowing to her is if she successfully forces you to act dishonorably. To turn your back on the family motto, and on the character you've held to despite everything she's forced you to do. She wants to hurt you, to pay you back for not supporting her against your father, and thus far she's been denied. She's forced you to kidnap three Cynsters sisters, but by sheer luck, or fate, or whatever you will, you've been able to do so while escaping any permanent stain on your conscience. Fate has protected you. But this time . . . even though you haven't stepped over that invisible line, you have to convince her that you have. That *you* believe you have, so that there's no longer any point in holding to any moral line, because you believe yourself already damned."

She held his gaze unwaveringly. "You need to convince her that you will do *anything* to satisfy her demands, up to and including that you'll force yourself on me."

He'd grown colder and colder. An icy rage howled inside him—with no outlet; it wasn't the woman who stood before him he was furious with. It took him several long moments before he could draw breath and, his gaze still locked with Angelica's, anchored by hers, quietly state, "In other words, that if it were necessary to reclaim the goblet, I'd rape you."

She didn't like the word any more than he did, but she didn't back down. "You need to give the *appearance* that you would. That you don't care—that you no longer have morals or honor, and all you want is the goblet back regardless of what it takes."

Unflinchingly, she held his gaze. "In this charade you have to make her believe she's won, that she's beaten you into submission. If you don't, if she suspects you're still unbowed, that you're still working to thwart her in some way, she'll resist, or push you further—or in the end, not hand back the goblet anyway." She looked down at him, seeing more than anyone else ever had. "This has never been solely about Mirabelle getting her revenge on Celia—it's equally, or perhaps even more, about her getting her revenge on you."

Silence fell.

For a moment, he remained unmoving in the chair.

Abruptly he came to his feet, driven by an overpowering impulse to fling away across the room and refuse to deal with this anymore.

Startled, she took an involuntary step back.

Instantly he stilled, without thought put out a hand, gently grasped her arm. "Sorry."

She dragged in a breath, lifted her chin. "No—I'm sorry. I'm pushing you, and I know I am."

He hung his head. Let his hand remain on her arm, holding, but not tightly.

After a moment, he drew in a breath and looked at her. Locked his gaze with hers, searched her eyes, then, slowly, shook his head. "You may be an excellent actress, but I'm not that good an actor. I cannot conceive of behaving in a way sufficient to convince Mirabelle that I would harm you. Not so much as a hair on your head."

She studied his eyes, then pulled a face. "Yes, well . . ." She exhaled, then drew a huge breath, straightened to her full height, and tried to look down her nose at him. "In this, you and I don't have a choice."

"We always have choices."

"Indeed, and that's precisely what I'm suggesting. None of this will be real. Our choice is to *pretend,* to trick and deceive someone who deserves to be tricked and deceived. In order to win back the goblet, we need to *pretend* to give Mirabelle everything she wants—we can't afford to make a mistake in that, and we're running out of time."

Before he could respond, with a swish of silk skirts she stepped closer and set her fingers across his lips. Looked into his eyes. "Enough for tonight. No—don't argue. Just think about it. I will, too. We have tomorrow, and tomorrow night, to refine our plan. If we can come up with something else, some other way, we will. But for now . . . enough talking."

In that moment he wanted, more than anything else, to be distracted—to forget the impossible ugliness she'd described. "What, then?"

She smiled, her inner siren peeking out to tantalize him. "Come to bed."

He'd thought her invitation meant that he should take her to bed, but it was she who took him. She who, with a small, seductive smile, took his hand and led him across the floor, who, with a blend of threat and promise, forced him to stand by the side of the bed and let her disrobe him.

Unclothe him.

Then she damned near unmanned him by going to her knees and taking him between those rosebud lips, and with innocent skill tormented him until he sank his fingers into her fiery mane and instructed her in what she wanted to learn.

When, head back, every muscle locked, he managed to ask, in a voice hoarse and gravelly, how she'd known to do what she was doing, she looked up at him, her eyes almost all emerald, and murmured, "Imagination."

If he'd thought it was distracting, overwhelming, when he took her, he discovered it was even more so when she took him. When she wove her enchantments with hands and lips, with a delicate skill he knew was instinctive, driven not by thought but by simple desire—the desire to pleasure him.

She overwhelmed him.

And when she finally rose up and took him in, sheathing him in the hot, slick bounty of her body, he knew nothing beyond the moment, beyond the sheer glory and the unrelenting pleasure of her body rising and falling, riding his.

The end came slowly, yet still too soon.

He saw stars and touched heaven, and she did, too.

Spent, she collapsed upon him. His arms around her, he held her close.

And for those moments, let the benediction they'd wrought soothe his soul.

Angelica woke in the dark of the night. He'd disengaged their bodies, untangled their limbs, and drawn the covers over them. He lay on his back with her snuggled against him, cradled in one arm, her head on his chest. She could hear his heart thudding, slowly, evenly, beneath her ear, and knew he wasn't asleep.

Without shifting her head, she murmured, "Why are you awake?"

His breathing, soft and deep, paused, then resumed. "I'm thinking."

"About our plan to trick your mother." Statement, not a question.

He sighed. "I honestly don't think I can do it. I'm simply not capable of behaving in such a way, not believably. Not to any woman, but especially not to you." After a moment, he added, "I'm too much me, and you're too much you."

She sighed. "I'm sorry."

Dominic glanced down at her gilded head. "For what?"

"I pushed for us to become intimate in part because I wanted the . . . bolstering of knowing how you felt about me while going through with our necessary charade. Because I felt I needed it, that having an intimate connection between us would reassure me through whatever we had to do. But in pursuing that, I didn't think of you. I didn't think about how us being intimate would make our charade that much harder for you."

Pushing up from his arm, she leaned on his chest, looked into his face. Through the dimness, she met his eyes. "For me, our closeness is like armor, a shield that will protect me no matter what happens with your mother—no matter what she might say, no matter what you and I might be forced to do. For you . . . now we've been intimate, you see me as yours to protect, and acting as you'll need to is now something that will . . . cut at you. Something that will go drastically and hurtfully against your grain. And for that I apologize—I didn't think it through. I didn't intend to add to the pressure your mother has already subjected you to."

He didn't know what to say. That she saw that, saw him, so clearly . . . slowly reaching out, he cupped the back of her head, drew her close and gently kissed her, a grateful, unarousing, unashamedly tender kiss, then he settled her against him again. Finally found words through the turmoil inside him. "We'll find a way— you and I. Together, we'll manage, and together, we'll win."

He heard his tone, knew he meant every word, that inside him such confidence yet remained. Dipping his head, he brushed a kiss to her forehead. "Sleep. We have tomorrow and tomorrow night to finalize our plan."

She exhaled and relaxed against him; within minutes, she was asleep.

He listened to the soft huff of her breathing, felt the inexpressible comfort of her soft body against his side, closed his eyes, and unexpectedly slid into slumber, deep, dreamless, complete.

Inside the keep of Mheadhoin Castle, the delicate French clock on the side table in the countess's bed-chamber whirred softly, then chimed.

Mirabelle lay slumped on her stomach in the rumpled billows of her bed, her face turned away from her lover while she regained her breath, and her composure.

Her lover lay beside her, his large, heavy, naked body dark against her ivory sheets. One hard hand idly stroked her hip. "Have you had any progress reports from Glencrae?"

She pouted. "No. I told you—he never tells me anything." She considered, then made a sound of disgust. "I fully expect him to return empty-handed *yet again*." Her lips curved in vindictive anticipation. "And then it'll be all over for him, and all the rest of his precious clan. All the people of the castle and estate who've never given me my due. If he doesn't turn up with a Cynster girl in tow, I swear I'll forget where I've hidden the goblet, and then they'll *all* be out on their ears."

"And what a shame that'll be." Rolling toward her, leaning over her, her lover nuzzled the sensitive spot where her throat met her shoulder.

Mirabelle couldn't see her lover's eyes, couldn't see his coldly calculating expression. After a moment, his breath washing over the bare skin of her shoulder, he murmured, "Incidentally, where have you hidden the goblet, my clever sweet? You've never said."

She laughed. "Don't worry—they haven't found it yet, and they never will."

Her lover's lips thinned, but in dealing with her he'd learned not to push; if he did, she would dig in her heels just for the hell of it.

If he'd thought his own plans stood in any danger, he would have more than pushed, but as matters were unfolding . . . he really couldn't see how he could lose. One way or another, Dominic Lachlan Guisachan was going to be ruined, and that was all he cared about.

Well, the first thing he cared about. But once Dominic and his clan were evicted from the Guisachan holdings, he would be there with the goblet in hand, waiting to step in and claim all his old foe was going to forfeit.

And that would be his final and ultimate victory. His clan would triumph, and the Guisachans would be gone. Making that vision a reality was worth any

price—certainly the relatively mundane one of seducing and servicing Dominic's ageing mother.

She hummed and shifted against him, rubbing her
hip against his groin. Insatiable bitch. Returning his
mind to the matter at hand, he slid down in the bed and
set his mouth and his hands to keeping her amused.

As things stood, that was all he needed to do, until
Dominic disappointed her one last time, and the goblet
fell into his own hands.

Chapter Fifteen

They departed Kingussie and rode on beneath brisk breezes and overcast skies. Dominic kept them to a decent pace; Inverness was close enough that he didn't need to rest the horses as he had through the previous days.

Alongside him, perched on Ebony, now a reliable mount, Angelica looked about her with undisguised interest.

He watched her drink in the choppy waters of Loch Insh, the wide sweep of the sky, and the hills filling their horizons. The northern slopes of the Cairngorms lay to their right, while the bleaker heights of the Monadhliaths loomed on the left. Directly ahead the road curved north through the pass above Aviemore. An indefinable beat in his blood told him he was nearly home, but Angelica seemed gripped by a similar eagerness to reach their destination. Or at least to look upon it.

The challenge they would face once they gained the castle lay like a black cloud ahead of them. He wasn't surprised that his protectiveness toward her had grown to the extent that he shied from even the pretence of harming her; in accepting her agreement to help him, he'd expected that, as he grew to view her as his bride, his countess-to-be, his protectiveness would rise to embrace her. What he hadn't expected—what he'd realized the previous night when she'd laid her plan before him—was how deeply attached to her he'd grown. How irretrievably ensnared by feelings he'd never expected to feel, and so hadn't thought to factor them or their power into his calculations. He hadn't dreamt that not even the threat to his clan would be enough to allow him to mute, if not suspend, his protectiveness toward her, not even temporarily, not even for a charade.

Her vision of how to trick his mother into handing over the goblet . . . if he had allowed himself to formulate a plan, he would have come up with something similar, albeit less focused on her. Her strategy was sound, but as for his part in it . . .

He cast her a glance, then looked ahead before she noticed.

If he hadn't been so profoundly and inextricably attached to her, he could have done it, but even before she'd invaded his bed, she'd captured him, his hunter self, in myriad ways; he was now so deeply in thrall there was no hope of him drawing back, of stepping back to the point where he could deal with her charade as if it were some game.

Like father, like son. Evidently certain Cynster females were the equivalent of sirens to Guisachan men, irresistible and unrenounceable.

They swept on, up and over the pass, and the repetitive drum of their horses' hooves underscored the continuing refrain of his thoughts: How *did* a man like him allow the woman he loved to go into danger? To risk being harmed.

To invite being treated as badly as his mother might very well treat Angelica.

They clattered into Inverness in the late afternoon. They reined to a walk as their road descended toward the banks of a river, then curved to the right. Looking ahead, Angelica beheld an ancient castle.

Dominic saw her surprise. "Inverness Castle. They're talking of demolishing and rebuilding it."

"So they should—it looks decrepit."

He pointed beyond the looming pile. "Our hotel, unimaginatively called the Castle Hotel."

Unimaginative or not, the hotel was an exclusive, luxurious establishment, more so than she'd expected to find in the wilds of Scotland, and the staff clearly knew the Earl of Glencrae. Their accommodations were swiftly arranged, and if the superior manager, McStruther, harbored any curiosity over the lady Dominic escorted upstairs to the stateroom overlooking the rear gardens, he kept it to himself.

She glanced at Dominic's face as he followed her up the stairs. "Do you stay here often?"

Looking around, he answered, "Often enough. It's the closest major town, and Inverness is effectively the capital of the highlands—whenever there's any business the clans as a whole, or even a few of them, need to agree on, it's here that we meet."

Gaining the head of the stairs, he paused to scan the foyer below. When he turned and took her arm, she asked, "Is that why you're searching the shadows— because there might be someone here who will recognize me?"

"I don't think there will be, but until Griswold has a chance to check, there's no sense taking chances."

Two boys had already brought up their bags; while Dominic gave them some coins, she crossed the sitting room to the wide window. The sun hung in the western sky shedding golden light over the scene below. Beyond the hotel's leafy gardens and a narrow street, a decent-sized river ran down to the nearby sea. Dominic joined her and she nodded beyond the glass. "Which river is that?"

"The Ness. The body of water to the right is Moray Firth, while that"—he pointed left—"is Beauly Firth. Our road tomorrow follows Beauly's shores, until we come to the Beauly River. We head upstream—west—from there."

"So the castle is west of here."

"West, and a little south. We're facing north, more or less."

A tap on the door heralded Griswold.

Closing the door behind him, Griswold bowed and reported, "None of the other lords are in residence, my lord. Only a few businessmen from Glasgow, and an old lady and her companion up from Perth to visit a friend."

"Good." Dominic glanced at Angelica, then looked back at Griswold. "Inform McStruther we'll dine early, in the private parlor."

"Indeed, my lord. And I'll have the maids bring up some hot water."

They had time to wash and change, to shake out their clothes and leave them for Griswold to brush and make ready for the next day.

Clad in a new gold satin evening gown, Angelica sat at the dressing table to brush and arrange her hair. Dominic came to stand behind her, using the mirror to tie his cravat; studying his reflection, she couldn't help but feel pleasantly domesticated. When Brenda had asked permission to visit family in the town, Dominic had referred the question to Angelica; while she had, of course, agreed, the apparently instinctive courtesy had only underscored his view of her as his de facto countess.

For tonight, she was more than content to play the role and savor it; once they reached the castle, only when he had the goblet in his hands would she be able to safely resume it.

Elegantly clad in regulation black-and-white, he escorted her downstairs to a small, private dining room. Cozy and intimate, they dined by candlelight, eating off the finest porcelain, with silver and crystal gleaming. She passed the time by asking him for stories of Gavin and Bryce, a topic on which he had few reservations.

At one point, Mulley came in; he bowed to them both, then bent and murmured in Dominic's ear.

Dominic nodded. Once Mulley left, she caught Dominic's eye, arched a brow.

"Mulley, Jessup, and Thomas are heading off to a tavern they favor. They don't often get the chance to visit Inverness."

Half an hour later, Dominic having denied any wish for port or whisky, and she for tea, they climbed the stairs.

Dominic had intended to turn his mind to the question hanging over him—their necessary charade and how he could possibly play his part—but his mind simply wouldn't budge. Wouldn't let go of, wouldn't shift from the moment, from the simple contentment the evening had wrought that had somehow sunk to his bones. He was following at her heels . . . and for tonight, that was enough.

For the first time in six long months, he could see past the moment when he had the goblet once more in his hands. Past the moment when he handed the coronation cup to the bankers and reclaimed the deeds to his lands. Even past the time when he and Angelica married.

To a time when, for one reason or another, they would be here, like this, climbing the stairs to the Castle Hotel's stateroom as husband and wife.

As laird and lady, a lady who would be his helpmate—a true mate in all ways, in every sense of the word. He didn't need to think to know that she would accept nothing less; what surprised him was his willingness to embrace that vision. To share not just his life but his care for his people, something he'd held solely to himself for the past five years, and in truth for some years before that.

They reached the stateroom. He opened the door, ushered her in, and followed.

Reaching out, he twined his fingers with hers, delaying her while he closed the door, then he turned and faced her. Freeing his fingers from hers, with both hands he framed her face, tipped it up, and kissed her.

Neither gently nor ravenously, but simply, openly, sharing the moment. The caress. The impulse behind it.

She responded without guile, without hesitation parted her lips and welcomed him in. The pressure of her lips encouraged; her tongue tangled with his and boldly returned the pleasure he was intent on pressing on her.

For long moments, they stood in the soft light and spoke of no more than that; time stood still while they savored the beauty of what they already had.

Eventually, chest swelling, he broke the kiss. Watched her face, saw her lids slowly rise, read the question in her eyes. Closing his, he leaned his forehead against hers. "I know what we have to do tomorrow. I haven't yet made up my mind how to deal with it—how I will deal with it—but for tonight, I want . . . to just be with you. For you to be you, and me to be me, with nothing else allowed to interfere." Raising his head, he looked into her eyes.

Lifting a hand, Angelica brushed a lock of black hair from his forehead. She searched his eyes. "Just you and me, as we wish to be?"

He nodded.

She didn't know why, what had provoked the request, but . . . she smiled, took his hand, turned out of his arms, and led him toward the bedroom. Picking up the lighted candelabra from the side table as they passed, he allowed her to tow him inside, then he shut the door.

Placing the candelabra on the high tallboy, when she presented him with her back, he obliged her by undoing her laces, then he left her to slip the gown off while he eased off his evening coat, set it on the stand left ready, then unbuttoned his waistcoat.

They undressed without haste, without rush; after letting down her hair, brushing out the long strands, she stripped off her chemise, laid it over a chair, walked to the bed, and slid under the covers.

Lying back on the pillows, she watched as he tossed his shirt over the clothes stand, toed off his shoes, then unbuttoned his trousers, drew them down, stepped out of them. Her eyes caressed the long lines of his body, the sculpted muscles, the heavy bones. Without looking at her, he shook the garment out, laid it on the stand, then he crossed to the tallboy and snuffed the candles.

She blinked, waiting for her eyes to adjust to the sudden dimness. A large, dense shadow, he walked to the bed, lifted the covers, and slid in beside her.

The mattress sank; she let herself roll into him.

Into the arms that were waiting to catch her. Waiting to embrace her.

To his hands and him, waiting to make love to her.

He settled her alongside him; instinctively she wrapped her arms about him, sent her legs to tangle with his. He nudged her face to his; one hand curved possessively over her naked hip, through the dimness, he searched her face. Then he bent his head and kissed her, set his hands to her skin, and with a simplicity she hadn't expected, an honest courage she hadn't foreseen, ripped away every veil, every screen and shield that had been or might ever be between them.

Within the cocoon of the covers, desire and passion bloomed, yet in the dark, in the heated silence, no reality existed beyond his body, hers, and what drove them.

What hung in every gasp, what invested each and every caress.

Once she grasped his intent, she reciprocated as freely, as unreservedly, as he. While the heat of desire and the flames of passion rose, as always, to their call, this time there was no rush, no overwhelming haste. No desperation, no driving urgency; they took their time, deliberately and unhurriedly savoring each touch, each caress. Each heartbeat of togetherness.

Together they strung the moments out like pearls beyond price.

He was an excellent rider in this sphere, too; he knew how to set the pace. Knew how to hold back their desires while they built and built, knew exactly how far he could push her, how far she could push him, before they had to move on.

To the next potent pleasure.

Caught up in the magic, enthralled beyond recall, she had never imagined the simple act could be this elemental, that when passion and desire were stripped to the bone, their stark radiance could be so powerful, so mesmerizing.

He opened her eyes.

About him. About herself.

She hadn't fully comprehended what he'd meant, what he'd asked for in wishing them simply to be as they were, but now she saw. Through his eyes, through his touch.

Through the tactile reverence he brought to every moment.

Through her responses.

She saw herself through him, through the unstinting worship he lavished on her. Saw him even more clearly and responded in kind, showing him all that she felt for him, letting that drive her reactions, infuse her touch, letting her joy in it color their every exchange.

It was as if through their hands, through the communion of their bodies, they spoke on some different plane, in a language distilled from passion and desire, in voices that came from deep within, in words shaped by emotion.

That carried emotion, clear and strong, in every touch, every heartbeat, every gasp.

Until the moment was all.

Until he slid into her body and she closed around him and they clung to the scintillating pleasure of that second.

Everything they were, him and her together, was captured there, shining and bright, for them both to see. To savor, to appreciate and know.

To understand that it was theirs, now and forever. Theirs to hold and cherish.

Also theirs to lose.

This was what they would fight for.

Their mouths melded and he moved upon her, slow strokes that filled her completely, his hard body embraced in her softness. She met and matched him, accepted and held him.

Loved him as he loved her.

Making love. This was what it was supposed to be—this simple, shining, unadorned yet brilliant truth. All that had gone before had been leading to this; all before had been them finding their way to this.

The friction between their bodies built, built; the flames racing over them, through them, flared.

And then the cataclysm was upon them.

And nothing else mattered but their race up and over the peak.

Nerves unraveling, senses spiraling, fingers sinking deep, she bowed beneath him, and with one last powerful thrust he sent her winging.

He followed a second later.

Into the blinding, bone-melting delight of ecstasy.

Into a nova of pleasure so intense it shredded their senses.

For long moments they hung, suspended in the glory, one in body, hearts thudding in time, souls merged.

Slowly, slowly, clasped and clinging, they drifted back to earth.

To the warmth of the bed, the rumpled covers, the tangle of their limbs.

He disengaged and slumped heavily beside her.

She curled toward him, nestling into his arms.

Relaxed, sighed, closed her eyes.

Her returning wits wandered. Through a landscape stripped of all pretence.

And she realized why now, why tonight.

Tipping her head back, she peered through the dimness. Her eyes had adjusted; she could see his face. His features were lax, his eyes closed.

Shifting within his encircling arms, she stretched up and brushed her lips over his. Saw his lashes rise, caught the gleam of his eyes. Fixing her eyes on his, she said, "No matter what happens, I will never forget that this is how we truly are. That this is how *you* truly are. What we found tonight is our truth, and nothing you might be forced to do to save the clan will ever tarnish it. Could ever tarnish it."

Beneath her palm, his chest rose and fell. His eyes remained locked with hers.

Eventually, he murmured, "I hope not."

There was none of his habitual arrogance in the words, only a quiet, understated vulnerability.

She wondered if she should belabor the point, if she should reassure him even more emphatically that no matter how he behaved toward her while they were working to fool his mother, she would never doubt him. Or would he hear that as her protesting too much?

He stirred, raised a hand, brushed back her hair, then urged her down. "Sleep. Tomorrow is going to be a very long day."

She searched his face, then acquiesced.

Sinking back into the warmth, into the inexpressible comfort of his arms, she let body and mind slide back beneath the lingering blanket of satiation.

He was right. Tomorrow would be a watershed on several counts.

They rode out of Inverness at eight o'clock the next morning. After clattering across the bridge over the Ness, Dominic led his party along the road to Beauly. Soon, they were riding by the shores of Beauly Firth. The day was cloudy, the skies gray; the wind whipping off the water made conversation impossible.

That last suited him; he needed time to think. To sort through the conflicting emotions ruling his head, to separate them enough to decide which should dominate.

This morning, once the soul-stealing wonder of what they'd shared had receded, he'd discovered the answer to his question of yesterday starkly etched in his mind.

How did a man like him allow the woman he loved to risk being harmed?

By trusting her.

And Angelica was, in every way, worthy of his trust.

As they rode on, the wind ruffling his hair, the scent and sounds of the firth so familiar, he wrestled with that realization and what it meant he would have to do.

After an hour, the road left the firth's shores and wended through flat fields with the mountains a distant backdrop. An hour later, they crossed the old stone bridge over the Beauly River and turned onto the road to Kilmorack. The further they rode inland, trees and tall shrubs increasingly crowded the road, blocking the wind. The sun struggled to break through, eventually sending sunlight shafting down, painting the distant hills a pale gold.

Perched on Ebony, Angelica rode with confidence in her heart, and an unshakeable determination. Last night, her highland laird had *shown* her that he had fallen in love with her. Even though he hadn't used words, she couldn't have asked for a more definitive declaration. He'd given her every assurance she would need to carry her through their charade, and while he hadn't yet confirmed his acquiescence and agreement to it, she knew he would.

She also knew well enough not to press him. Instead, she looked about with unfeigned interest, absorbing all she could of the countryside, the lanes, the hamlets, the environs of her new home. And the air! Brisk and bracing, yet softened by the warmth of approaching summer. Breathing in deeply, she exhaled, smiled.

She saw deer and asked what sort they were. Dominic spotted a hawk; she watched the bird ride the currents, then stoop and drop like a stone out of sight. Jessup directed her attention to a highland hare, watching from the top of a bank, ears twitching as they rode past.

Now the wind had died, they could converse easily enough. She threw herself into learning all she could; soon the others were volunteering information and pointing out sights. It was a pleasant way to fill the miles, and a useful distraction.

She knew she shouldn't again speak of Dominic's role in their necessary charade, not until he did, but it was difficult to rein herself back. She was unreservedly certain he and she would triumph, but she couldn't simply tell him that he could and would perform as required, that she had unshakeable confidence that even if he couldn't suppress his protectiveness, he would at least conceal it well enough for their purpose. That even though the charade would constantly abrade his protective instincts, now fully engaged where she was concerned, he *would* rein in his instinctive, more primitive self well enough to fool his mother—because he had to.

Because it was vital for his clan's survival.

She knew he would meet whatever challenges they encountered, but he had to come to that realization himself; he wouldn't believe her if she told him, and she didn't know how to hold up a metaphorical mirror to show him his own strengths.

Strengths like loyalty, like self-sacrifice. Like devotion.

Like doing whatever needed to be done because others were relying on him.

He and she could and would pull off the charade, recover the goblet, and save his clan. She knew it beyond question, believed it to her soul.

Buoyed and eager to get her teeth into the challenge, she rode gaily through the morning, steadily eating up the miles to Mheadhoin Castle.

Chapter Sixteen

Devil Cynster surveyed the crowd gathered in the drawing room of St. Ives House with what, in a lesser man, would have been frustration. As it was . . . impotent resignation was nearer his mark.

He'd expected the males; they'd been scheduled to reconvene to share what they'd learned and decide what next to do. As for the ladies, he'd invited only his mother, Helena, and Therese Osbaldestone, in the hope one or other of the elderly pair, both of whom knew the ton root and branch, Therese especially, might recall something relevant. But inviting two such ladies involved giving them due notice, which in turn had given them time to notify the entire female half of the family.

Vane prowled to where Devil stood before the fireplace. "Even Great-aunt Clara is here." Jaw set, Vane glanced around the assembled multitude. "What do they think they're doing?"

"Helping," Devil replied. "In their own inimitable fashion. And, of course, they want to know what we've learned." He straightened and raised his voice. "If everyone could cease talking . . . ?"

Instantly, the ladies fluttered and settled, perching like so many brightly plumed pigeons on the sofas, chaises, and chairs that had been grouped in the center of the room. Once all eyes were expectantly turned his way, Devil said, "We should first share what we've learned from our inquiries. Gabriel?"

Gabriel straightened from the wall against which he'd propped. "Lucifer"—his mother caught his eye and he smoothly amended—"that is to say, Alasdair and I spoke with Curtis—it was he who introduced Angelica to Debenham. According to Curtis, it was Angelica who instigated the introduction."

Alasdair, as the females of the family insisted he be called, added, "Curtis had been speaking with Debenham and his circle, but then moved away. A few minutes later, Angelica found Curtis in the crush and demanded he introduce her to Debenham."

"So she approached him," Breckenridge said.

Gabriel and Lucifer nodded. "Curtis," Gabriel went on, "has known Debenham for over a decade, since they both first came on the town. They're both thirty-one. Curtis confirmed that Debenham's estate, Debenham Hall, is near Peterborough, outside Market Deeping. As far as Curtis and Debenham's other friends—and there seems a fair circle of those—know, Debenham hasn't been in town for at least the last four years. He was summoned home at the end of one Season, four or five years back. They'd all expected him to return long since, but until recently, he hadn't been seen. When they inquired over his absence, he said he'd been caught up in estate matters. As for the limp, Debenham's carried the injury since he was twenty, apparently from some near-fatal accident."

"One thing Curtis was absolutely certain about," Lucifer said, "was that Debenham is English, not Scottish."

"So he's not the laird," Jeremy said.

"Apparently not. However," Lucifer went on, "according to Curtis, when a waltz started, the other gentlemen in the circle asked the young ladies who by then had joined them to dance, leaving Curtis, Debenham, Ribbenthorpe, and Angelica. Curtis quit the group at that point but remained close enough to see and hear what happened. Ribbenthorpe asked Angelica to dance, but she declined and steered him to some other lady. Curtis assumed Angelica was simply going to chat with

Debenham, who can't waltz because of his limp, but some minutes later, when the dancing was well underway, Curtis overheard her suggest to Debenham that they—Debenham and she—stroll on the terrace. Curtis saw them leave the salon and step out onto the terrace."

"Wait a minute." Lord Martin frowned. "You're saying *she* asked *him*?"

Gabriel nodded. "From everything we've learned, it was Angelica who set her sights on Debenham, not the other way around."

"Doesn't sound like any kidnap attempt I've ever heard of," Demon muttered.

"No." Devil frowned. "However, Curtis's is the last sighting of Angelica we have. No one saw her after she stepped out onto the terrace with Debenham." He swept his gaze over the assembled ladies, inviting any of them to contradict him; none did. "Just so. So let's finish with Debenham, even if only to rule him out once and for all. But first"—he looked at Gabriel and Lucifer—"has Curtis any inkling that Angelica's disappeared?"

"No," Lucifer replied. "He assumed—reasonably enough—that Angelica is forming some attachment to the man and we're doing the expected checking."

"Good. So back to the elusive viscount." Devil glanced around the circle, directing his words to the men standing behind the chairs, sofas, and chaises. "Vane and I finally tracked down Rothesay, who left Cavendish House with Debenham that night—we've just come from speaking with him. He, too, has known Debenham for years—he confirmed everything Curtis said, and added his assessment that Debenham is a capital sort, very straight, without a duplicitous bone in his body. He, too, thought we were asking for the obvious reasons."

"So neither Curtis nor Rothesay had a bad word to say about Debenham?" It was Honoria who asked the question.

Devil set his jaw. "No. However, neither Curtis nor Rothesay have seen Debenham since that night. They assume he's been called back to his estate, but they don't know, and both are a little perturbed that he's vanished again. Yet Debenham is the last person we know to have seen Angelica that evening—if we can locate him, he should be able to shed light on what she did next, where she went after their stroll in the moonlight. As many have confirmed, he was at the soiree long after she'd disappeared."

Demon's brows rose. "Very cool if he'd had any hand in kidnapping her."

"Indeed, but"—Devil shifted before the mantelpiece—"by luck, Rothesay walked home with

Debenham that night. Debenham was staying at the Piccadilly Club. He and Rothesay parted on the steps—Debenham went in and Rothesay walked on."

Lucifer and Gabriel stepped forward. "The Piccadilly Club isn't far," Gabriel said.

Devil nodded. "Go and see what you can learn. And if by chance the gentleman in question should happen to be in, present my compliments and invite him for luncheon."

Lucifer flashed Devil a grim grin. "We will."

The two strode from the room; the door closed behind them.

"Before we go any further," Demon said, "I should report what I've learned, which is a little . . . contradictory to what we've been hearing of Debenham thus far."

"I thought you went to Newmarket?" Vane said.

Demon nodded. "I did. But Newmarket isn't all that far from Peterborough, so . . ."

His older brother sent him a disapproving look. "And you told us not to do anything rash."

Demon shrugged. "I was there, and you were all running around here unearthing the local clues, so I took a look." When Devil gestured for him to continue, Demon reported, "Yes, Debenham Hall is there, and Debenham is known to own it, but no one has set eyes on him for years. But those who could remember him gave the same description as all the others, so it is him—the same man, the right estate. Which is where things start not adding up. All the land attached to the estate is under cultivation, but all by tenant farmers—and yes, I asked, and they liaise via a local agent, who sends his reports, accounts, and the funds collected to a solicitor in London. That was strange enough—given Peterborough is so close to London, why would Debenham be running the estate like an absentee landlord? So I called at the house. It sits in its own park, is in excellent condition, and is rented to a family unconnected to Debenham." Demon paused, then went on, "So I checked with the agent, who also collects the rent. He told me Debenham has never resided at the Hall, not in the thirty years he's been the agent."

Silence fell as everyone digested that. Devil put his finger on the most glaring oddity. "If Debenham is thirty-one, but hasn't lived there for thirty years, where the devil has he been?"

Vane said, "Rothesay said that through the years he and Curtis and the others knew him, Debenham had lodgings in Duke Street."

"But where did he spend his childhood, and all the years to that point?" Alathea asked.

"The man's a nobleman," Therese Osbaldestone stated. "Ergo he has a family, a father, a mother. Where were they?"

Discussion ensued, noisy enough to drown out Clara's wavering, "If I recall aright . . ."

Significantly older than Therese Osbaldestone, next to whom she was sitting, Clara was accustomed to no one hearing her frail voice, her rambling sentences. But . . . "I vaguely recall something about the Viscounts Debenham." She tipped her head, thinking. "Yes, I'm sure it was they. Something about the title itself?" After a moment, she nodded, and cast her eye over the available males.

Sylvester—Devil—her usual first choice, was absorbed in an argument over whether Debenham could, after all, have kidnapped Angelica, possibly to raise funds, which didn't seem likely given Harry's—Demon's—assessment of the return from the farms he'd seen.

Clara's old eyes wandered on. Her nephew Martin was too perturbed, and she didn't feel she knew that nice new boy, Jeremy Carling, well enough to ask. Besides, he wasn't yet officially family. Michael Anstruther-Wetherby she might have asked, but he was caught up in a discussion with that other viscount, Breckenridge . . . Clara's eyes halted on the down-bent fair head of a tall, gangling male in his early twenties, who was listening while propping up the wall.

It never occurred to Clara to ask one of her many grand-nieces, all within easier reach; she was of the generation that held firmly to the notion that one sent young men to run one's errands—that was what young men were for.

Clara fixed her gaze on Simon and waited.

Eventually, he looked up, glanced around, and met her eyes.

She smiled and beckoned. She saw the fractional hesitation while he debated if he had to obey, then he surrendered with good grace, pushed away from the wall, and walked over to where she sat.

Simon bent and gently took the birdlike claw Clara held out to him. "What is it?"

She beamed up at him; he really was very handsome, but then all the men of her family were. "If you would be so kind, dear, could you fetch that nice new book . . . not Debrett's, that might not have what I want in it, but the newer one that lists all our families—what's it called?"

"Burke's Peerage?" Simon asked.

"That's the one. I'm sure Sylvester will have a copy in his library."

Simon nodded. "Do you want me to bring it here?"

Clara squeezed his hand and released him. "Please."

Simon left on his errand, and Clara turned her inadequate hearing to the closer conversations; the ladies around her were dredging their memories for recollections of the Debenhams—of the present viscount's father or anyone connected to the title at all.

Therese Osbaldestone was growing quite irate. "Devil take it, I *ought* to remember, but I cannot for the life of me recall even a family name."

"Maybe they were the Debenhams," Phyllida suggested.

"No," came from several throats. "If that were the case we would remember," Helena declared, "and the mystery of it is that none of us can."

Simon reentered the room, carrying a heavy, leather-bound tome.

Clara's eyes lit. She *thought* she knew what the key to the mystery of Viscount Debenham was, but there was no point saying so until she checked and had something in black-and-white to convince them all that she wasn't simply rambling again. She did ramble sometimes, memories mixing dizzyingly with the present, but today . . . no, she was quite clearheaded today.

She beamed at Simon as he carefully placed the book in her lap. "Thank you, dear. So kind." With that, she waved him off and carefully opened the book. "D," she murmured. "I do hope it's under D, and not just under wherever it landed, for that title I do not know." Carefully leafing through the pages, she said, "One can only hope that dear Mr. Burke was thorough in his listings."

Therese Osbaldestone heard; she looked and saw the book. "*Excellent* idea!" Therese turned to help, but Celia asked her something and she looked back to reply.

Clara slowly turned the pages, hunting down Debenham.

The door opened and Gabriel and Lucifer strode in. Conversation died. The tension in the brothers was evident to anyone with eyes, the grim set of their lips a further warning. Every male in the room straightened. "What?" Devil asked.

"We inquired at the Piccadilly," Gabriel said. "Debenham isn't a member, and he definitely didn't stay there on the night of the Cavendish soiree."

"The mystery deepens," Michael Anstruther-Wetherby said. "This man is turning out to be a phantom."

Clara placed her finger on the entry she thought was the right one and fumbled for her lorgnettes.

"Debenham told Rothesay he was staying there, so that's an outright lie to a friend—a friend who swears to Debenham's good character." Martin shook his head. "This isn't making sense."

Clara focused on the tiny print. Read the details—the creation, the successions, the . . . she stared. It was as she had remembered, with one shocking twist. "Oh, dear."

She looked up—across the room to where Celia sat in an armchair, with Martin leaning on its back.

This time, Clara's words had fallen into a silence—everyone had heard. Everyone turned to stare at her.

Therese saw Clara's finger on the page. "Finally. Well done, dear."

Clara struggled for words to explain. "My dears . . ." She broke off and looked down at the page again. "Oh, dearie me."

"What is it?" Therese asked more gently. When Clara didn't reply, Therese reached over and lifted the book to her own lap. "Here. Let me see." She squinted at the page. "Debenham. Damn—I can't read the rest."

Clara handed over her lorgnettes and pointed to the bottom of the paragraph beneath the title. "There. I *thought* I remembered something about the specific line dying out and the title reverting back . . ."

Therese read the relevant lines. "Good God!" She scanned them again, then raised her head and looked at Celia and Martin, for the first time in her long life struck speechless.

"What is it?" Devil demanded.

Therese drew in a huge breath, glanced down at the book, then started rapidly flicking over pages as she said, "The title of Viscount Debenham was created and conferred on a secondary branch of a noble family in Elizabeth's day. During the last century"—she paused to consult another entry, then resumed—"the secondary branch died out, and the title passed to the nearest male, and that happened to be up the tree and across, to the principal line."

Martin was frowning. "What's the family name?"

Therese looked him in the eye. "Guisachan."

Martin was no wiser, but Celia gasped, then paled.

Therese nodded at her. "Yes, my dear, I fear this is a case of your past returning to haunt you. You know the head of the House of Guisachan as the Earl of Glencrae."

That name Martin most definitely knew; he shot upright. "*He's* behind this?" He ran a hand through his thick hair. "After all this time?"

"No," Therese returned with asperity. "Not him, not least because he's dead. Five years ago, as it happens." Lorgnettes to her eyes, she read further. "The present Earl of Glencrae, also Viscount Debenham— the man everyone in the ton remembers as Viscount Debenham—is Mortimer Guisachan's son, Dominic Lachlan Guisachan, now the eighth Earl of Glencrae."

While that information was clearly a cataclysmic revelation to most of the older generation—Clara, Therese, Helena, Horatia, Martin, and Celia—all the others, including Louise, remained unenlightened. They glanced at one another, wordlessly asking for clarification, but none had any to offer. Meanwhile, those who understood looked stunned, disbelieving, but with concern rising behind their eyes.

Horatia leaned across to lay her hand on Celia's. "Glencrae—he was the one . . ."

Celia swallowed, nodded. "All those years ago . . ."

The entire room waited, but nothing more came.

Devil finally gave in. "What," he demanded, in a voice that warned against any dallying, "happened 'all those years ago'? What the devil is all this about? And how in all that's holy does Dominic Lachlan Guisachan, eighth Earl of Glencrae, come into it?"

It took a while to extract the story in anything re-sembling a coherent whole, but eventually, the others grasped the gist of it. Before any of them except Devil and Vane had been born, Celia, then Celia Hammond, a beautiful young lady, had fallen in love with Martin Cynster, the fourth son of a duke, but Celia's parents had preferred the suit of a wealthy Scottish nobleman, one Mortimer Guisachan, seventh Earl of Glencrae. The earl had been considerably older than Celia and she hadn't been in love with him, but her parents had stood firm and had insisted she marry him, so Celia and Martin had eloped and married over the anvil at Gretna Green.

"Good Lord." Breckenridge, held as captive as any by the tale, glanced down at Heather, his soon-to-be wife. "Is that why he had Heather taken to Gretna Green? To marry her there in some sort of parody?"

Reaching up, Heather closed her hand over his. "Let me state it again—I'm so very glad you rescued me."

For long moments, silence reigned. That Celia and Martin had eloped and married over the anvil had never been a secret, and, indeed, had always been deemed highly romantic, but not even Gabriel and Lucifer had known the background to the elopement; it had never seemed relevant before.

Then Martin, tight-lipped and pale, shook his head. "No, it still doesn't make the slightest sense. Why would anyone be kidnapping our daughters? Mortimer himself didn't kick up a fuss, not at all. He behaved in a perfectly gentlemanly fashion, gracefully bowed out, and went home to the highlands. And as he obviously subsequently married and had a son, at least—"

"Only child," Therese put in.

Martin inclined his head. "But he married and had an heir . . . why would his son be kidnapping our daughters now?"

"Daughter, one at a time." Breckenridge glanced at Jeremy.

Jeremy nodded. "And as soon as he saw that the girl he'd kidnapped preferred some other man, he drew back, and at least with Eliza and me, did his best to save us and, at great risk to his own life, succeeded." He looked around the room. "Whatever else Dominic Lachlan Guisachan might be, he most definitely isn't a madman, nor is he without honor."

Devil studied Breckenridge and Jeremy, and Heather and Eliza, too, then nodded. "I can't disagree. Which means there's something critical to all this that we don't yet know."

"True," Gabriel said. "But there is one, or by now most likely two, people who know the whole story." He glanced at the faces that turned his way. "The earl and Angelica." He looked at Lady Osbaldestone. "Where's Glencrae's principal seat?"

Therese located the relevant part of the entry. "Castle Mheadhoin, Glen Affric."

"In the highlands." Lucifer nodded. "That's where he'll have taken her—that's where she'll be."

"Let's go." Demon headed for the door. Most of the men went to follow.

"Wait." Devil's order halted them. For several silent seconds, he stared at the book on Lady Osbaldestone's lap. When he spoke, his words were measured and sure. "We need to start giving the earl his due. He risked returning to London, risked appearing in the ton. He couldn't have known Angelica would all but arrange her own kidnapping—he couldn't have been prepared. Yet he improvised, whisked her out with no one the wiser—and we all know she wouldn't have simply let herself be taken. One wrong move and she would have screamed the place down. But he didn't make a wrong move. Instead, he returned to the soiree and stayed for an hour or more—which bought him time. We've been stumbling over that piece of icy daring all along. Then he walked out with a friend and went to a club . . . but he didn't stay there that night." Devil lifted his gaze to Therese Osbaldestone's face. "Does he have a London residence?"

She consulted the fine print, then snorted. "Glencrae House—in Bury Street."

"So close . . ." Devil smiled intently. "He took her there, and I'd wager they stayed there, a block or so from Dover Street, and waited while we searched every carriage bound for Scotland and virtually sealed off the roads to the north for five days. They waited us out." He realized he'd used "*they*," and not "*he*," but on reflection suspected that no correction was needed. He looked at the others. "Before we hie ourselves to

Scotland, let's have a look in Bury Street and see what we can learn."

Bury Street was so close that they walked, splitting up into twos and threes the better to avoid attention.

Glencrae House wasn't hard to find; in iron scroll-work, the name graced the twin carriage gates, shut and locked with a massive chain and padlock.

"I could probably get it undone," Gabriel said, squinting down at the padlock, "but the gates look like they haven't been opened for decades. There's inches of dead leaves behind them."

"Leave the gates." Devil ambled on down the street. "That's not how they came and went—let's try the back."

They found the mews. Found the garden gate. Demon checked the adjacent stables. "Empty, but in good shape—recently used and left tidy and clean."

The lock on the garden gate took Gabriel less than a minute to open; in a long single file they walked up the path to the house. Devil knocked on the kitchen door. When no one arrived to let them in, he stepped aside and waved Gabriel on. Two minutes later, they walked into the servants' hall.

Vane went into the kitchens beyond, and returned, saying, "All neat and clean, no dust anywhere. They've been here."

They followed the corridor to the front hall.

Halting, Lucifer looked up and around. "Lovely old place."

Devil grunted. "We'll split up—two or three to each level." He glanced at the holland covers visible through the open doorway to the drawing room. "Let's see if we can determine how many were here."

They spread out through the house. Devil, Vane, and Lucifer remained on the ground floor, checking through the reception rooms.

In the drawing room, Lucifer crouched before a sideboard he'd opened. Reaching in, he drew out a candelabra, studied it, then sighed and put it back. "I have a strong feeling this house was decorated for my mother—it's her taste." Rising, he glanced at the walls, at the deteriorating silk, then headed for the door. "It appears Mortimer did just give up, close this place up, and go home. He let her go."

"No—she was never his. She was always Martin's." Devil followed Lucifer out.

Vane, who'd been surveying the dining rooms, joined them in the hall. "Only the breakfast parlor's been cleaned. Two settings of cutlery and crockery recently used, and whoever ate there sat at either end of the table."

Devil nodded. "Angelica and the earl." He pointed down a corridor leading off the hall. "That way."

They found the library. Found the paper Angelica had used to blot the letters she'd sent them.

Lucifer prowled the room, checking the window locks, looking at the square of garden outside, gauging the wall.

The door swung open and the others trooped in.

"Two rooms—two suites—used on the first floor," Gabriel reported. "And it looks like a maid slept on a truckle bed in what appears to be the countess's dressing room. The rooms in that suite are the only ones that have been recently decorated."

"Four bedrooms in the attic look used," Breckenridge reported. "All on what I imagine is the male side of the divide."

Devil stood behind the desk. There were no papers left lying on the top, or in the drawers. He would own himself surprised if there wasn't a large safe concealed somewhere in the room, but even from the remnants on the desk—the ink still in the ink pot, the sharpened nibs, the sealing wax still waxy—he could tell that the earl had been using the desk for business while he'd been there with Angelica.

"There's a book missing." Bent over, Jeremy was studying a gap on one shelf. Straightening, he looked at Devil. "Recently removed—I can tell by the dust. And if I had to guess which book it was, I'd say it should be Robertson's *History of Scotland*."

Devil raised his brows. "I can't see Glencrae consulting that at this point in his life."

"No," Jeremy agreed. "I'd say Angelica took it, and as it wasn't upstairs, that she's taken it with her."

Gabriel frowned. "She's studying Scotland?"

"So it appears," Michael said. "Which raises the question of whether she went north willingly, or under duress."

Lucifer sighed and leaned against a bookshelf. "She went willingly."

Devil looked at him. "I don't disagree, but how can you be so sure?"

Lucifer waved at the windows. "This place is old. Old locks, no bars. None of the windows upstairs have bars either. Most of the interior doors have no locks." He glanced at Gabriel. "Upstairs?"

"The same. And the window in the countess's bedroom has recently been opened. For a tomboy like Angelica, getting out and down the thick creeper, across to the wall and the ivy growing over it, climbing over the wall, dropping into the street, then walking home, would have been ridiculously easy." Gabriel stood stiffly for an instant more, then the tension in his shoulders eased. He met Devil's eyes. "Lucifer's right—we're all right in what we're thinking. For whatever reason, Angelica became a party to her own abduction, which makes it no longer an abduction, I suppose. There is no way she could have been held captive here—we've found no evidence that she was restrained, she dined freely, and she's never been slow to use her wiles. And her wits, as we all know, are razor-sharp."

He glanced around the room. "If they were here for several days, she had ample time to escape, and she had to have known she was still in Mayfair. If she'd been held against her will, she wouldn't have hesitated to clout whoever was guarding her over the head—she could have been down in the garden and over that wall in under ten minutes, and home five minutes after that. But I can't see any sign that she tried."

Bringing his gaze back to Devil, Gabriel concluded, "You were right—there's something going on, something major, that we know nothing about."

Devil drummed his fingers on the desktop. "We could—as I'm sure our better halves will argue—sit on our hands, possess our souls in patience, and wait until Angelica or the earl sends us word." He paused, then went on, "On the other hand, we could hie ourselves to Scotland and see what all the fuss is about. Who knows? They might need our help."

Lucifer straightened from the bookcase. "I vote for option two."

"As do I," Vane said.

"And me," Demon added.

Gabriel, Jeremy, and Breckenridge nodded. Martin had remained with Celia at St. Ives House; no one imagined he would ride north at his age.

Michael Anstruther-Wetherby pulled a face. "Much as I would love to join you, I'm too caught up in matters of state to leave."

Devil nodded. "You can be our contact here. If anything unexpected occurs, send word."

Michael arched a brow. "To where?"

Devil grinned. "To Castle Mheadhoin. As it appears the earl has joined the family, he can start dealing with the inevitable outcome."

Michael grinned, nodded.

Quitting the desk, Devil headed for the door. "I'll send a courier to Richard—he would never forgive us if we left him out of a venture like this so close to his territory. He can join us along the road."

Pausing at the door, Devil glanced at the determined and eager pack at his back. "We shouldn't be seen riding in a troop out of Mayfair—some will wonder where we're going and why. Let's meet at the top of Barnett Hill at three o'clock, and be prepared for frequent changes of horses along the way." Facing forward, he led the way out. "We're going to race up to Scotland and *politely* ask Angelica and her earl to explain what this is all about."

Alongside Dominic, Angelica rode on as the morning waned and the clouds closed in. After passing through Kilmorack, the road followed the Beauly River, passing several tiny hamlets before veering southeast down the length of a long valley she was told was Strath Glass. Visible only occasionally through thick trees, rounded mountains closed in on both sides; those to the north were appreciably higher and their crests more barren, brown even under the summer sun. But the valley of the river Glass was lush and green; she cantered along, noting the diversity of trees that closed around the ever-narrowing road—birch, holly, the occasional beech or oak, and others with which she was less familiar. Highland cattle, with their shaggy coats and long, curving horns, ambled in verdant meadows, their occasional lows echoing almost mournfully between the hills.

"Cannich." Dominic nodded to where a cluster of cottages stood in a clearing flanking the road. "There's a small inn we can stop at—they have a private room."

"What time is it?" Angelica looked at the now solidly gray sky.

"Nearly noon." He consulted his fob watch. "Fifteen minutes before."

She glanced back. The others had fallen a little way behind, enough for them to speak in private. Meeting his eyes, she said, "We need to tell the others what we're going to do. If we don't, they'll very likely react in some way that will bring us undone."

His reluctance was palpable. She waited, didn't argue. Eventually he said, "You're right. We'll need to explain what we're trying to portray."

"And that it's the only way to satisfy your mother's demands and convince her to return the goblet."

Jaw setting, he nodded.

Minutes later, they drew rein outside the inn. In short order, they were shown into a tiny private room, low-ceilinged and windowless, but with a table large enough for eight with bench seats along both sides. Once they were seated, Dominic to Angelica's right, Jessup beside him, with Thomas, Griswold, Brenda, and Mulley opposite, the old man who'd welcomed them and a woman Angelica took to be his wife brought soup and bread, saw them all served, then withdrew. All talk subsided while they ate. The second course, duly presented, proved to be large slices of an excellent venison pie. She ate her fill, then nudged the sizeable remains Dominic's way; she couldn't eat much, not with her nerves tightening with anticipation.

Accepting the offering, he glanced at her. Catching his gaze, she glanced at the down-bent heads about the table, then arched a brow.

He hesitated, but then nodded, gestured with his fork for her to proceed, and looked back at the pie he was attacking.

She cleared her throat. The others glanced up. "The laird and I"—she liked the sound of that; it had a certain ring—"need to explain the tack we're going to take to convince the countess to hand back the goblet she's hidden."

Five forks hung suspended, the others' attention all hers; only Dominic kept eating.

Folding her arms on the table, she leaned on them. "As you know, the countess's price for returning the goblet was that the laird kidnap me and bring me to the castle. Apparently she imagines that the abduction and subsequent journey will socially ruin me. Why she wants that isn't important. What is important is that to meet her demands and regain the goblet, we—the laird and I, and all who wish to see Clan Guisachan survive—must work to convince her that I am, indeed, socially ruined."

She paused, then continued, "The criteria for me being ruined aren't important, because to convince the countess, all I need to do is to make her believe that *I* believe I'm ruined." She spoke to the five pairs of eyes fixed on her face. "The countess will focus on me and on the laird. My behavior, and his toward me, will be critical, crucial to us getting the goblet back. It will be a pretence, a charade—play-acting to the highest degree—but it has to look real."

Surveying their faces, she went on, "So once we reach the castle, the laird and I are going to behave oddly toward each other, and in my case, toward you and everyone else, too. For our charade to work, I won't be me—not the me you've come to know—and the laird won't be the man you know, either."

Mulley set down his fork. "So you need us and the others to play along and help you pretend to be ruined?"

"I hope there won't be much for you to do, but if the countess is watching, you mustn't show any respect or liking for me. The major thing we need from you five in particular is for you not to be surprised by anything the laird and I do. You need to react as if any odd behavior is merely more of what you've seen since I joined you in London."

Dominic pushed away his empty plate. "It may be necessary for me to pretend to be . . . harsh with Miss Cynster. How harsh"—he glanced at Angelica—"we don't yet know." He met the eyes of his closest staff. "I've explained to Miss Cynster that you and all at the castle will know I would never treat any woman as I might be forced to *appear* to treat her, but Miss Cynster has agreed, and I have agreed, to do whatever we must to regain the goblet. To go as far as we must, to continue our act as far as is necessary for my mother to be satisfied and hand over the goblet."

He saw the glances of approval, respect, admiration, and gratitude the others directed Angelica's way and felt marginally better. "We believe our charade is the only way forward, especially as we're running out of time. What Miss Cynster and I need from you, and all at the castle, is for you to behave as if whatever you see is regrettable, but expected. You cannot show surprise, much less shock. Whatever you see, whatever you hear, you must act as if it's real, the truth and not pretence, and also that you accept what you see as the way things must be. You cannot rush to Miss Cynster's defense, nor can you be seen by my mother to actively aid her."

Angelica took over. "For instance, for my arrival at the castle, I have to appear bedraggled, weary, and with my spirit crushed. I can't wear this habit. Brenda and I will crease and dirty my old ballgown, the one I was wearing when I joined you. I'll disarrange my hair. We want it to look like you've held me in harsh confinement all the way here. I can't ride Ebony––we'll switch her with one of the sumpter horses." She glanced at Jessup. "As the countess doesn't go into the stables, if Thomas holds Ebony at the rear until you can take the horses to the stables, that should be safe enough, but we'll need to make the switch as close to the castle as possible, because Ebony won't like being kept from Hercules."

Jessup and Thomas nodded.

"And you'll need to tie me to my saddle on the sumpter horse."

Dominic frowned. "We don't need to go to that extent."

"Yes, we do." She met his eyes. "If the countess sees you lifting me off the horse, trussed like some bedraggled prisoner of war with my hands tied before me, she'll assume you've been treating me like that all along—which will imply that I've tried to escape at some point. She needs to believe that I tried but failed."

Dominic's frown grew black, but Mulley volunteered, "There's some hemp in the bags, but I'm afraid it will redden your wrists, miss."

"Perfect! My wrists will heal, and it'll only be for a few miles." Before Dominic could object, she rattled on, "We'll need to hide my bags and the bandbox. The countess will be better pleased if I appear with nothing more than what I stand up in."

Brenda readily said, "The bags will be easy enough, and we can wrap a horse blanket around the bandbox, make it look like a parcel."

"Excellent." Angelica looked at Griswold and Mulley. "There are two other things we should decide now. First, who at the castle should we take into our full confidence?"

On that point, the others had a tangential view, one with which Dominic agreed. "You can't tell when you might find yourself in a situation where some clan member knowing what's going on will prove vital. Clan works best when we're working together." It was decided that all those at the castle should be made aware of the charade; Dominic deputed the others to quietly spread the tale.

"Then the last thing we need to decide," Angelica said, "is where in the castle I should be held. It must be a believable prison, but preferably not where the countess can gain ready access."

"Not the dungeons," Dominic growled.

"What about the room at the base of the east tower?" Mulley met Dominic's eyes. "The one the secret stair from your chamber runs down to. There's nothing in it but old furniture and boxes."

"And a rickety bed." Dominic straightened. "Yes, that will do nicely."

A secret stair? How convenient. The words burned Angelica's tongue, but she swallowed them. "Right, then." She looked at the empty plates. "It's time to get our charade underway." She gathered her skirts to rise.

"No—wait!" Brenda waved her back and looked at Dominic. "There's one thing we haven't settled— well . . . two. The boys."

Dominic didn't swear, but from the way his jaw clenched it was a near-run thing. "I don't want them witnessing even a minute of Miss Cynster's and my pretence." His tone was chilly, his gaze cold. "I won't have them seeing me behave like that." He looked at Angelica. "And I won't have them seeing you behave like that, either."

She laid her hand over his. "Of course not." She sent a *help me* glance across the table.

Brenda grimaced. "You've been gone for weeks, so as soon as the gatehouse guards spot us and call down, the scamps will be up there, watching us ride in—"

"No, they won't." Jessup met Dominic's gaze. "Day like today, those two will be out with Scanlon. I'll go and meet them before they reach the castle. What should I say?"

"Mumps," Angelica said. When the others all looked at her, nonplussed, she went on, "Mumps, measles, some contagious childhood ailment. Tell them the laird has brought a friend to stay, but said friend has developed some pox or other, and to make sure the boys don't catch it, the laird wants them to stay in their rooms for the next few days, until the danger is past. They can go outside as they usually do, but they mustn't go wandering inside the keep." She looked at Dominic. "Will that do?"

He raised his brows. "It should." He looked at Jessup. "Tell them I'll come up and see them tonight, and explain."

Jessup nodded.

Dominic looked at the others. "Anything more?"

Everyone paused, everyone thought, then they all shook their heads.

"In that case"—Dominic rose and held out his hand to Angelica—"let's get on to the castle."

Letting her confidence show, she smiled, placed her fingers in his, let him help her to her feet and over the bench, then, settling her hand in his, she walked out beside him.

They halted just beyond a hamlet called Tomich.

Dominic dismounted and came to lift Angelica down. "A hundred yards further and the gatehouse guards will see us."

She leaned into his hands. "I won't take long to change."

Setting her down, he nodded south. "Go that way. Less chance anyone will see you."

She handed him her crop and gloves, unpinned her jaunty cap and set that in his hands, too, then glanced to where Brenda was rummaging among the bags, searching for the pale teal ballgown and fichu. "I'll start getting out of my habit."

Turning, she picked her way into the trees bordering the lane; they grew so thickly that within a few yards she was effectively screened from the lane or anywhere else. Getting lost would be embarrassing; reaching a small clearing, she stopped and started unbuttoning her jacket.

She'd stepped out of her skirt and was hanging it over a branch when she heard a *crack* behind her. "Thank you." She turned.

It wasn't Brenda who'd brought her gown.

Dominic, his face rigid, halted a yard away. He held out his clenched fist, then opened his fingers. Her crinkled gown slithered down to hang from his thumb, the fichu crumpled with it. When she blinked, he said, "Brenda said you wanted it crushed."

She nodded. "I did." Reaching out, she rescued her poor gown, held it up. "That's . . . very nicely crushed." Rather than hand it back, she hooked it on a nearby branch.

Returning her attention to unbuttoning her blouse, she pretended not to notice that his gaze had lowered to her legs, presently clad in sheer stockings and her boots; with her chemise's hem riding a few inches above her garters, there was a strip of naked skin on display . . . she wondered if it would distract him from his transparently less than happy mood.

He didn't say anything. When she shrugged out of the blouse and glanced his way, he was watching her, but she couldn't read anything from his face. "Here." She held out the blouse. When he took it, she pointed to her jacket and skirt. "You can carry those, too, but they don't require crushing."

His lips thinned, but he gathered her clothes, draping them over one arm.

She wriggled into her gown, settled the bodice, reached for her fichu, then walked to him and presented him with her back. "Can you do up the laces?"

After a few seconds, she felt the first tug.

"I'm agreeing to this only because there is no other way." His words reached her, low, frustrated, but also deliberate. Committed. "But that doesn't mean I approve, or that I'm not . . . torn. Never in my life has there been anyone or anything that has meant as much as clan to me. You do. Having to choose between you and clan—"

"You don't have to choose." His fingers paused, and she went on, "As your countess-to-be, I consider myself clan—clan is now as important to me as it is to you. Just like you, I will do whatever is needed to ensure the clan thrives—that's what clan is about, isn't it?"

A silent moment passed, then his fingers tugged at her laces again. "I don't deserve you."

Her heart swelling, she smiled. "Actually, you do—you just haven't fully realized it yet."

"Be that as it may, although during this charade there'll obviously be times I'll have to follow your lead, I will do whatever I must to keep you safe."

"I know you will—I would expect nothing less from you."

"We're agreed on that, at least." He pulled the laces through, started to tie them. "I know I have to trust you in this, trust you to know what you're doing, and I do, *but . . .*" He paused, hands stilling, then she heard him drag in a breath. "It would help if you would promise that the instant you want to pull back, the instant anything frightens or offends you too deeply for you to go on, that you'll tell me."

He knotted the laces and released them. She turned as he lowered his hands. She looked into his face, an impassive, impenetrable mask, but the real man—the man who loved her—looked back at her from his storm-sea eyes. "I promise. If things get too bad, I'll tell you."

He exhaled. "Thank you." He held her gaze. "There's one more thing." When she arched her brows, he said, "I can't protect you if I'm standing behind you."

She studied his eyes, considered what he was really saying. Negotiation being their key, she offered, "You can step in front of me, but only if there's no other way. *No* other option. Agreed?"

He held her gaze for a long moment, then curtly nodded. "Agreed." His features eased not one jot, but he stepped back and waved her through the trees.

Five minutes later, wrapped in a rough wool cloak Jessup had produced, the hood pulled low over her head and face, and with her boots changed for her ballroom slippers, she sat with her hands bound as loosely as possible to the crook of her sidesaddle, now perched on the oldest sumpter horse. Beneath the hood, loose strands of her hair wreathed her face and neck; she and Brenda had dusted her gown here and there with dirt, and used grass to stain it in several places.

With every element of her disguise in place, eyes locked on Dominic's broad back, she watched as her wild highland laird led the sumpter horse and her on the very final leg of their journey, and into the battle to wrest the goblet from the dragon holding it, him, his castle, and his people to ransom.

Chapter Seventeen

The castle was far larger than she'd imagined.

Her first glimpse was of the top of the battlemented keep, then the lane curved north and a break in the trees revealed the massive gatehouse—twin cylindrical towers flanking a huge drawbridge, presently down. The clouds had thinned, allowing a suggestion of sunlight to filter through. The further they rode, the more of the fortified castle wall became visible, the expanse of gray stone exuding a sense of solid, rocklike permanence.

The castle reminded her of its owner—large, immovable, utterly dependable when it came to safety and security, and impressive in a viscerally powerful way.

The more she stared, excitement and delight welled, tinged with a certain awe. Also like him, this would be hers; this henceforth would be her domain.

A distant halloo rolled out over the trees. Dominic raised a hand in acknowledgment.

He'd told her the castle stood on an island and was reached from the loch's southern shore via a smaller island; lowering her gaze, she saw reflected sunlight dappling the base of the castle wall. "Is the drawbridge in working order?"

Without turning, he replied, "Yes, but we rarely raise it. At night we lower one or other of the portcullises."

Thinking of their charade, she schooled her body into a defeated slump but continued to survey all from beneath her hood.

Ten minutes later, they reached the loch's shore and crossed a wooden bridge to the smaller island, the clop of hooves echoing loudly over the water. Unable to help herself, she looked around more openly, using apparent panic to disguise her curiosity. Shaped like a rounded crescent moon sailing in the lee of the castle walls, the smaller island was covered with grass, a smattering of low shrubs, and a few stray trees. The bridge from the shore gave access to the eastern end, while the castle's drawbridge met the western end, forcing anyone who wished to enter the castle to parade the entire length of the smaller island in full view of the castle walls.

While they did precisely that, she surveyed the island the castle dominated. Far larger than the smaller island, it appeared a heavily wooded, elongated oval with the castle occupying its center, the stone walls vertical to the waterline, leaving treed areas to either side, not sculpted parks but wilderness. The wilds of Scotland came right to the castle's door, a fact emphasized by a majestic backdrop of mountains, their peaks barren and brown, the lower slopes thickly timbered.

Surrounded by the primitive glory of Scotland, the castle was one of the most romantic sights she'd ever seen.

As far as she could tell, these were the only two islands in the loch. Since they'd turned off the main lane several miles back, she'd glimpsed no habitations for either man or beast.

They were approaching the drawbridge. Dominic glanced at her, met her eyes. "Ready?"

From within her hood's shadows, she flashed him a grin, tipped up her chin, but didn't alter her dejected pose. "Lead on."

He held her gaze for a moment, then faced forward. Seconds later Hercules's hooves drummed on the drawbridge's planks. The sumpter horse followed, carrying her into her new life. She looked up as the cool shadow of the gatehouse's arch engulfed her, and suppressed a shiver, a premonition, but of what she had no clue.

They emerged into the faint sunshine bathing the bailey.

Never on returning to his home had Dominic felt so alert and tensed for battle. Yet the familiar sounds and scents greeted him; familiar faces swarmed around, bright and cheerful, all pleased to see him as he walked Hercules across the bailey to the keep.

He tried to smile and nod in response, but before he'd covered half the distance to the steep keep steps, the brightness dimmed as those in the bailey noticed the bedraggled figure lashed to the saddle of the horse he was leading. Their expressions, at first curious, grew puzzled, questioning.

Leaving the others to provide the answers, resisting the urge to glance back at Angelica, he rode to the steps, dismounted, and handed Hercules's reins to the groom who'd come running.

Features set, he glanced up at the raised porch— just as his mother came hurrying out through the open double doors. Halting in a swirl of dark skirts at the top of the steps, she stared—in surprise, in disbelief—at his captive.

Turning, he walked to the side of the sumpter horse, reached up, and lifted Angelica down. Whispered,

"That's her at the top of the steps." Setting her feet on the cobbles, he released her.

She stumbled against him—an act—then wrenching back with a choking sob, she looked wildly around as if contemplating fleeing.

Gritting his teeth, he set his hand to her back and turned her to the steps.

She stumbled as if he'd pushed her, nearly falling.

He caught her elbow, had to grip more tightly when she ineffectually struggled. Didn't have to feign the irritation in his "Stop it, you witless woman!" He thrust her at the steps, then was forced to haul her up them while she pretended to resist, to hang back, flashing her bound wrists in case anyone had missed them. Courtesy of her struggles, her cloak fell open, revealing her soiled gown.

She'd warned him she was an accomplished actress; he hadn't realized she'd meant she was this good. She almost had him believing . . . which made it easier for him to play to her lead.

With a flourish, he swung her onto the porch and released her so she staggered to a halt facing his mother. He looked at Mirabelle. "You wanted a Cynster sister kidnapped and brought here. Allow me to present Miss Angelica Cynster."

Mirabelle's gaze locked on Angelica's face, still shadowed by her hood. "Indeed? You'll permit me to verify . . ." Reaching out with both hands, Mirabelle pushed back the hood.

Angelica sniveled, then looked up, displaying a tear-stained, abjectly terrified face. She stared at Mirabelle.

Mirabelle's eyes widened. Her gaze swiftly scanned Angelica's features, then lowered, taking in her wrecked gown, her bound wrists, before rising once more to Angelica's face, to her eyes. Mirabelle smiled. "My God. You've actually done it."

The quality of her smile turned Dominic's stomach.

Angelica flung herself at Mirabelle, grasping Mirabelle's hand between hers and breathlessly imploring, "My lady! Countess! You have to make him see sense." She bobbed a crude curtsy, deftly converting it into a supplicant's begging pose. "You *have* to make him let me go!" Her weak tone suggested she'd endured horrors and was likely to faint from the effects of her travails.

Dominic shifted and she shrank away from him; clenching his jaw, he glared, stepped behind her, caught both her elbows and dragged her up and away from his mother. "You don't understand, sweetheart." Holding her in front of him, his voice harsh, beyond cynical, he said, "The countess is the reason you're here."

Swinging her around, he pushed her toward the gloom of the keep's foyer. Ignoring their utterly fascinated audience, he stalked after her.

His mother, overjoyed and avid, scurried after them. "That's really Angelica Cynster!"

"In the flesh." Reaching his captive, ineffectually dithering on the threshold, he prodded her on.

Obligingly she staggered into the foyer. Stumbling to a halt in the middle of the wide, high-ceilinged entryway, she started to clumsily pirouette as if searching for a way out.

Having no idea what she might next take it into her head to do, he grasped her arm, anchoring her. "Angelica Cynster, third daughter of Lady Celia Cynster. Kidnapped, brought here, and now paraded before you—as you demanded."

Mouth falling open, Angelica stared, first at him, then at his mother, dawning horror in her face. "*What . . . ?* It was *you . . . ?*" After a second, she very creditably shrank away, blinking back tears. "But . . . *why?*"

Mirabelle's vindictive smile deepened; malice glittered in her eyes. "As to that . . . you'll learn soon enough, my dear."

Dominic drew Angelica further from his mother, effectively interposing himself between them. "I've fulfilled my part of the bargain—now where's the goblet?"

Her gaze fixed on Angelica, Mirabelle's face suffused with gloating triumph. She stared for several moments, then looked at him. Eyes narrowing, she searched his face. After another long moment, she all but purred, "I honestly didn't think you would do it—that you had it in you."

"In which you were clearly wrong. The goblet?"

She stared at him for a minute more, then said, "Don't be so hasty. You've surprised me—I need a little time to convince myself this is real and to absorb the implications. To"—her gaze swung to Angelica—"savor my victory."

"That wasn't our bargain."

"I never said I'd hand over the goblet the *instant* you brought me one of Celia's daughters." Her face hardening into its customary spiteful lines, Mirabelle looked back at him. "You will have to allow me a day or two to confirm, and then relish, my revenge. God knows, I've waited long enough for it, and you'll still get your precious goblet back in time." Returning her gaze to Angelica, Mirabelle beckoned. "Come with me, child."

"No." Dominic held Angelica anchored where she was, half behind him. "Until you surrender the goblet, Miss Cynster stays under my control." He held Mirabelle's gaze. "I wouldn't want her escaping, or in any other way disappearing, not after all the trouble I've gone to to get her here."

A muscle leapt along Mirabelle's jaw, then her eyes flashed. Without another word, she swung around and stalked across the foyer to the door to the north tower.

Once she'd disappeared, he cursed beneath his breath.

"You didn't imagine she'd hand it over just like that," Angelica whispered from behind him.

"I'd entertained a wild hope that on setting eyes on you she would be so overcome with delight that she might hand it over without thinking."

After a moment, Angelica poked him in the side. "Patience. We've only just arrived, and needs must when the devil drives, so come and show me this room you're intending to lock me in."

He closed his eyes, clenched his teeth against another oath, then exhaled, opened his eyes, grasped her arm, and significantly less forcefully swept her on into the great hall.

Shown to her temporary apartment on a lower level of the east tower, Angelica was pleased to discover small windows set high in the walls, and at the base of one wall a fireplace, albeit presently unused. If she had to spend hours there, it could be made pleasant enough. Circling the room, she tried to spot the door to the secret stair while Dominic, in a mood she equated with an irritated but restrained bear, growled orders to Griswold and Mulley, who had appeared with her bags; Brenda had taken her bandbox away to hide.

"Send John and Mrs. Mack here," Dominic eventually said, "and organize guards in the corridor in case the countess decides to come looking for Miss Cynster."

"Aye, my lord." Mulley bowed and departed.

"I'll make sure all's in readiness above, my lord." With brief bows to them both, Griswold followed.

Dominic swung to face her, then glanced around the room. "We'll make a show of setting this room up for your use, but in reality you'll be using my chambers."

"Where's the hidden stair?"

He pointed. "Over there." He picked his way across, around and over various obstacles. "We'll leave all this here—it'll make it seem more like a basement cell."

She nodded and joined him by the outer wall; she'd assumed the stairway would be in the inner wall.

"Give me your hand." Gripping her fingers, setting his own over them, Dominic guided the pads of her fingertips over and then into a shallow depression in one stone, then pressed.

Click. A section of the stonework popped forward an inch or so. Releasing her, he showed her the finger grip worked into the exposed edge of the stone, then waved her to try it; expecting that she wouldn't be able to shift such a weight of stone, she nevertheless pulled and dis-covered the secret door was exquisitely balanced. Easy to swing, but the hinges shrieked horrendously.

The door behind them opened, admitting an older woman with iron gray hair pulled back in a tight bun, and a soberly dressed man a few years older than Dominic.

"My goodness." Bobbing a curtsy, the woman pulled a face. "I'll have one of the lads in with some oil within the hour." Straightening, sparing an expectant, but welcoming, glance for Angelica, the woman clasped her hands, fixed her bird-bright gaze on Dominic, and smiled warmly. "Good day to you, my lord. It's a plea-sure to see you back."

"Indeed." The man had glanced at Angelica, then executed a neat bow, and now fixed an inquiring gaze on his master. "You wished to speak with us, my lord?"

Dominic introduced her to his housekeeper and steward as his bride-to-be—a revelation that left them openly delighted and predictably curious. Angelica responded with smiles and polite nods, but left it to Dominic to explain their scheme while she observed Mack's and Erskine's reactions.

From the way the pair reacted to him, and him to them, she suspected they'd both known him all his life. As with the others, both were immediately supportive.

Reassured, she glanced at the stairs. Listening with half an ear to the ongoing discussion and Dominic's orders regarding her comfort, she inwardly smiled. She'd thought she'd been prepared for the impact of his home, but her imagination, usually more than able, had for once fallen short of the mark. If the castle was impressive, the keep was magnificent. The soaring ceilings, the graceful arches, the fluting and carving of the stone were beautifully balanced against the solid simplicity of the stone walls. The windows in the rooms she'd seen were leaded and diamond paned, framed by velvet drapes, and perfectly set to themselves frame the views.

Given the tenure of the cold-eyed, black-hearted witch she'd just met, it seemed nothing short of miraculous that the inside of the keep exuded warmth and comfort, security, and, above all, peace, as if those qualities were embedded in the stone. Dominic's grandmother had decorated the Edinburgh house; Angelica suspected that it was her influence that still lingered, still dominated, here. That had proved strong enough to hold against Mirabelle's bleakness.

Angelica had thought she'd been prepared to meet Dominic's mother, but the moment she'd first looked into Mirabelle's eyes had been a shock. One thing to think one knew; another to know.

Mirabelle might have insane ideas, but that didn't mean she wasn't intelligent, cunning, and calculating.

Dominic had warned Angelica, and he'd been correct; their charade wasn't going to be as easy to pull off as she'd hoped.

"I'll send some girls in to make up the bed and set things to rights, at least enough to look as if you are staying in here." Mrs. Mack looked at Angelica. "If that won't disturb you, miss?"

Dominic glanced at her. "I'll be showing Miss Cynster around between now and dinner."

"As to that, my lord," Erskine said, "do you wish us to move dinner back?"

When Dominic paused, Angelica asked, "What time would you normally serve the meal when the laird is in residence?"

"Six o'clock, miss," Mrs. Mack replied.

Angelica caught Dominic's eye. "It would be best to adhere to your usual schedule. There's no reason to convert to ton hours because I'm here."

He nodded and looked at Mrs. Mack. "So we dine at six."

"Thank you, my lord. Miss." Mrs. Mack bobbed, Erskine bowed, then they left.

Dominic turned to Angelica. She smiled and waved to the secret door. "Why don't you show me where this leads?"

Crossing to her, he took her hand, opened the door fully, and led her through.

A few minutes after the clang of the dinner gong faded, Dominic propelled an apparently fearful and cringing Angelica into the great hall and onto the dais. He steered her past his mother, seated at the high table in her accustomed place to the right of his great chair, past his own chair to the smaller chair on its left. He drew the chair out and pushed Angelica into it. "Sit."

Wild-eyed, she collapsed as if her legs had given way; the damned woman had a histrionic streak a mile wide.

Jaw clenched, he dropped into his own chair. He didn't look out over the familiar faces gathered about the lower tables, but instead scowled at his plate as the footmen served the three of them the soup course.

The emotion fueling his scowl was real, although he doubted his mother, shooting sidelong glances at him, would guess that it was the necessity of Angelica having to appear before his people as a weak and near-hysterical female, his cowering captive to boot, that was its cause. And gads, the woman could act.

Every second of her public charade was rubbing some part of his psyche raw, but he had to put up with it; she needed his support, not his reluctance.

Luckily, his black temper fitted the persona he needed to show his mother. She would never believe he was happy with the situation, but she might believe—

and had thus far seemed to have accepted—that he'd been pushed to the limits of desperation and had surrendered to her demands, and was now darkly brooding over his lost honor.

Well and good.

Setting down his soup spoon, he raised his napkin to his lips and glanced at Angelica.

She'd hunched over her plate, somehow pulling in her shoulders so she appeared more frail, more pitiable. Eyes wide, she was casting furtive glances about the room, and stirring her soup spoon around and around the plate, from which she'd taken no more than two mouthfuls. Her other hand was clenched tight, crushing the napkin in her lap.

If he didn't know better . . .

"Which cell did you put her in?"

Angelica jumped at his mother's question, releasing the spoon with a clatter. Clenching both hands on the napkin, she stared at the soup.

Slowly, Dominic turned, took in the cold joy in Mirabelle's face as she looked across him at Angelica; she was all but salivating. "I'm keeping her in the store room beneath my tower." Mirabelle didn't know of the secret stair.

"Why not the dungeons?" She frowned at Angelica. "The lower levels are cold and dank, and so dark— *perfect* for her."

"No." When Mirabelle looked at him, he stated, "As I said earlier, after going to such lengths to get her here, I wouldn't want to lose her before you deem yourself adequately revenged. I'll keep her where I think it's safest—close enough that I or the staff will know if she escapes."

A mulish expression settled over his mother's once beautiful countenance. After searching his face, she narrowed her eyes. "I think you're right to take such care—indeed, you should restrain her. Tie her up so she can't escape."

"No."

Mirabelle's lips thinned. "At the very least hobble her—she's supposed to be a prisoner, isn't she?"

Resisting the urge to glance at Angelica, he lowered his voice to a warning growl. "I'm the laird here. Do you seriously imagine she could make it outside without anyone stopping her?" He wouldn't, in fact, put that feat past his bride-to-be, not least because all the interested spectators seated at the tables in the body of the hall were eagerly listening, and not one of them seemed anything other than interested in seeing what happened next. Which meant Mulley, Jessup, and the others had spread the word widely and well, so if Angelica did suddenly bolt for the door, everyone would just watch, and wait for the next act in the drama to unfold.

Luckily Mirabelle had never paid attention to his people; she neither saw nor sensed their interest. So it was she who backed down from their staring contest. With a sniff, she sat back as a footman retrieved her empty plate. "Very well. As you wish."

Noting the platters being ferried out from the kitchens, he turned and studied Angelica, then added as if in an absentminded aside to Mirabelle, "Don't worry. She won't escape." He met Angelica's green and gold eyes—for a fleeting second saw a smile reflected there—but then she looked down, and he concluded, entirely truthfully, "Believe me, she won't get away."

"She wants to gloat."

"Well, of course she does." Lying on her back beside Dominic in his now thoroughly disarranged four-poster bed, Angelica settled the covers over her breasts and stared up at the canopy. "But she'll grow tired of that soon enough, then she'll hand over the goblet and all will be well. Did you glean any insight into what she's looking for in terms of me being ruined?"

"No." Turning onto his back, Dominic raised his arms and crossed them behind his head. After dinner, having informed his mother that Angelica was not a guest to sit in the drawing room with her, he'd dragged his cowering captive back to the tower store room. The bed had been made up and a candle left burning on a crate. She'd rummaged in her bags, hidden among the room's other debris, hauled out the Robinson, and declared she would be comfortably occupied for several hours. He'd intended escorting her straight up the secret stair so she could wait in the comfort of his rooms, but she'd insisted that it was better she be in the store room in case, while he visited the boys, Mirabelle came knocking.

With the vision of the wicked witch in the fable of Snow White haunting him, he'd locked Angelica in, taken the key, and gone to see Gavin and Bryce.

She turned to him. "How were your wards? You didn't say."

He grunted. "Ecstatic to have me back, but predictably much less pleased by their confinement."

"I assume they normally have the run of the keep?"

He nodded. "They'll toe the line for a little while—I just hope Mirabelle deems you ruined enough, soon enough."

He'd been returning from the boys' room in the west tower when Mirabelle had waylaid him in the foyer. She'd been strangely—even more strangely than usual for her—enthused, expectant. Her eyes had glittered in the darkness. She'd been on her way to see him to tell him that she intended inviting Angelica, "the poor ruined child," to sit with her the following morning. Mirabelle had sworn to "keep an eye on" Angelica to ensure she wouldn't escape.

He hadn't wanted to agree, but he'd known Angelica would want to seize the opportunity, so he'd nodded, and then stalked to the staff's quarters to make suitable arrangements. "I've spoken with Elspeth and Brenda. Brenda will escort you to the sitting room and remain with you while you're there. If Mirabelle does anything too particular, anything you don't like, just look at either Elspeth or Brenda, and one of them will come and get either me or one of the others."

Settling on her back again, Angelica smiled; her knight's armor was still shining through the mire he was certain he'd smeared all over it. "Don't fret. This will play to our advantage. Having a sniveling young miss wailing 'woe is me' at her is sure to grate on her nerves. Leave her to me, and I guarantee it will."

He huffed, but didn't argue, which made her smile all the more.

"Meanwhile . . ." In her opinion, he needed further distraction to take his mind off his mother's behavior so he would sleep. "You have to admit that my performance today was nothing short of brilliant."

Another, stronger huff answered her.

Smile deepening, she rolled to her side, then, lifting up, shifted until she was perched across his waist. As naked as he, her hands splayed on his chest, arms braced, she looked into his face.

He opened his eyes wide. "Now what?"

"Now, my lord, it's time to pay the piper."

"In that case, my lady, consider me entirely at your service."

She took the statement literally, and over the following half hour, held him to it.

Chapter Eighteen

"So. Tell me about your first ball."

Angelica blinked. "M-my first ball?"

"Yes." Seated in an armchair before the window in her sitting room, Mirabelle waved imperiously. "Your first ball, miss—where it was held, what you wore, whether you danced every dance, everything you can remember."

Shifting on the uncomfortable, straight-backed chair Mirabelle had insisted she take, set facing the window and the armchair as if she was a maid applying for a position, Angelica frowned. "You mean my come-out ball?" While technically considered her first ball, it hadn't been the first she'd attended.

Mirabelle frowned. "Yes, that one—the big one."

"Oh. Well . . ." Fingers twisting a fold of the drab gown that Mirabelle had had delivered to her that morning, a dampened handkerchief clutched in her other hand, Angelica clung to her teary, wilting, helpless persona. "All the balls are big, of course, but that one . . . it was held at St. Ives House—my cousin, Devil Cynster, Duke of St. Ives's London residence. His duchess, Honoria, was co-hostess with my mother."

"Of course." Mirabelle's eyes glittered.

Keeping her eyes wide, Angelica paused as if frightened.

Her face contorting, Mirabelle gestured irritably. "Get on, girl! Tell me more about it."

Angelica swallowed. "Well, it was big, as you say." She let her voice hitch—as if remembering something lovely that was lost to her. "A very large number of the ton attended, and I wore a white gossamer silk gown over white satin, with tiny teal rosebuds around the neckline and waist, and about the edges of the hem and sleeves." What lady ever forgot her come-out gown? "I wore teal ballroom slippers, and carried a teal silk reticule, and there were teal silk roses in my hair, anchored by pearl pins. I had on my grandmother's pearl necklace and earrings, and a pearl armlet and ring my father gave me." She paused to draw a shaky breath, then rushed out, "And I definitely danced every dance." That was all but obligatory at one's come-out ball.

"Who was your first partner?"

Impressed by how thorough Dominic's father's informers had been, she sniffed, then nearly wailed, "His Grace, the Duke of Grantham. Oh, my heavens—I should have accepted him when I had the chance. I'll never get a better offer, not now!"

Gulping back sobs, she mopped her eyes with the handkerchief and kept her head bowed. From beneath her lashes, she watched Mirabelle eye her coldly.

"Stop sniveling." Mirabelle shifted in her chair. "Now tell me about your sisters. What gowns did they wear to their come-outs?"

Angelica managed to drag the information from her memory, but was relieved when, from there, Mirabelle's attention, albeit increasingly avid, deflected first to her brothers and their offspring, then to ton events, and from there to the customary pattern of tonnish ladies' days.

Such questions she could answer without thought, but judging that she'd satisfied Mirabelle as to her identity, she seized every pause, every opportunity, to weep and rail against fate, and turned every question to her own purpose, bemoaning the loss of the life she'd led— the very life Mirabelle seemed so keen to hear about.

Mirabelle grew increasingly restive, eventually becoming sufficiently irritated by Angelica's whining to dismiss her.

Angelica quit the sitting room in Brenda's charge. She and Brenda exchanged a speaking glance, but said nothing as they walked back to her store room-cum-cell.

The gong for luncheon sounded as they reached the door, and they diverted to the great hall. Angelica slipped into her shrinking, cowering role as they entered the cavernous room, allowing Brenda, her supposed jailer, to roughly escort her to her chair.

Dominic appeared, nodded to Brenda, and dropped into his chair. Without looking at Angelica, he murmured, "How did it go?"

"I passed the identity test, but she was even more interested in hearing about ton life, how we live in London, that sort of thing. And no, I have no idea why she's so interested in that." She'd kept her head down, murmuring at her plate.

Beside her, Dominic shifted. "Here she comes."

Angelica clung to her pose of weak, wilting, crushed violet. At one point Dominic glanced at her, then asked his mother, "So, are you satisfied?"

"I congratulate you," Mirabelle said. "She is, indeed, Angelica Cynster. However, to fully realize my enjoyment of my revenge, I believe I'll need more information from her. I'll have to think about it, but not this afternoon. I'll speak with her again tomorrow."

Angelica inwardly frowned, perfectly certain Dominic was doing the same thing. What was in his mother's twisted mind? Deeming that a question impossible to answer, Angelica shifted her attention to the hall and its occupants. Reasonable enough that, having been forced to stay, she should at least look around.

No one was paying any particular attention to the three occupants of the high table . . . except for two small boys who had slipped into seats at the far end of the hall. The pair's big round eyes were fixed on her. She let her gaze sweep over them before returning it to her plate. From beneath her lashes, she watched the pair observe, then talk to each other—back and forth, punctuated by glances at her. She debated warning Dominic that his wards' anticipated step over the boundaries he'd set had already occurred, but she was curious to see what they might do and was reasonably certain that, if explanations had to be made, the pair would understand the concept of a necessary make-believe.

Lunch ended. Dominic glanced at her. She didn't meet his eyes, but ducked her head in a cringing manner and whisperingly offered, "I suppose I'd better go back to my room."

He momentarily closed his eyes, then opened them and mildly glared at her. Then he looked up and summoned Brenda with a nod. She came; in her charge, Angelica slipped out of her chair and, giving Dominic a wide berth, scuttled past and out of the hall, back to her room.

Safely inside, she made herself comfortable on the bed, propped Robertson's tome open, and settled to read.

Two hours later, when Brenda looked in to ask if she wanted tea, Angelica shut the Robertson and stated, "Prisoners are customarily allowed to take the air. Let's go for a walk on the battlements."

Brenda readily agreed. She led Angelica through the corridors, away from the north tower and the witch therein. Angelica glanced into the library, but Dominic wasn't there. Skirting the kitchens, she passed numerous castle staff, all of whom beamed and bobbed curtsies or bows, murmuring a polite "miss" or, more often, "m'lady." Clearly the entire castle, barring only Mirabelle, knew of their charade.

Angelica had to admit that made her feel a great deal more comfortable. Having Dominic forced to portray himself as a violently aggressive, dishonorable man hadn't sat well, no matter how essential.

Brenda led her to the battlements along the castle's south wall. "Even if her ladyship gets some bee in her bonnet and looks out of her bedroom window over the bailey, she still won't be able to see you here."

"Good." Climbing the steep steps beside Brenda, Angelica admitted, "It'll be nice to stand straight and stride about a bit. That hunching is making my shoulders ache."

"Don't know how you do it, myself." Brenda looked at her with admiring amazement. "You really do look like a weak feeble thing, so spineless you'll collapse if her ladyship blows hard at you."

"Yes, well, let's hope that's all she sees until she hands over the goblet. Once she does"—stepping onto the battlements, Angelica smiled—"she'll rapidly learn her error."

Pausing, she stretched her arms over her head, then out to her sides, breathing deeply, savoring the tang of the forests and the crisp, bracing air. Then she and Brenda set out, swinging along the empty walks.

When Angelica asked about the lack of personnel, Brenda replied, "There's only guards at the gatehouse, two older clansmen, just to keep watch. If anyone they don't know approaches, they come along here and hail them as they reach the bridge." Brenda tipped her head beyond the wall.

Angelica stopped to peer out between the crenellations at the bridge from the loch's shore to the smaller island; it lay directly across from where they now stood. She considered the two swiftly running stretches of water, one separating the shore from the smaller island, the other the smaller island from the castle. "I've seen a few castles, and this would rank as the most defensible. Is it possible to swim across?"

"Possible, but difficult, and risky, too."

They heard footsteps and turned. Angelica smiled as Dominic joined them.

He nodded to Brenda. "I'll see our prisoner back to her cell."

"Aye, m'lord." With a curtsy and a grin, Brenda headed back to the steps.

Dominic fixed his gaze on Angelica's face. "What brings you out? Boredom?"

"Not so much that as frustration." She turned to look over the roofs of the numerous buildings hugging the walls, over the bustling bailey to the keep. "There's so much I want to learn about this place and the people in it, but I have to hold back until we're finished with this charade."

"Sadly, that's true."

Raising one hand to hold back her hair, drifting in the light breeze, she looked up at him. "One thing I wanted to check—is there anyone in the castle who, while they might remain loyal to the clan, might also feel sympathetic to your mother? If there is anyone in that category, I should be more careful around them." Her gaze went past him, then her eyes widened. "Oh."

Hearing the clicking claws, he swung about.

"What *lovely* dogs!"

About to step in front of her and halt the charging beasts, he pulled back and let the three water spaniels romp up; they barely paused to lift their dark heads to him for a pat before, tails waving, heads bobbing, pushing past to greet the new person.

Holding out her hands, then ruffling their ears and ruffs, she laughed as the three dogs—any of which could easily bring her down—cavorted around her. "They're beautiful. What are they?"

"Water spaniels." Pushing the three back, he commanded, "Sit."

They thought about it, but eventually all three obeyed.

"This is Gwarr, the eldest, and this is Blass, and the lady is Nudge—for obvious reasons." Nudge was already leaning heavily against Angelica's legs, looking up in blissful adoration. He'd never seen the dogs so readily accept anyone . . . but he and Angelica were sharing a bed; they might be able to smell his scent on her.

He stood and watched her speak with each dog, solemnly telling them her name and repeating theirs, and felt a lightness in his chest that, after a few moments, he identified as simple happiness. His lips curved . . . then he realized that where the dogs went . . .

Raising his head, he looked back along the battlements. Sure enough, two small figures stood watching from twenty feet away.

Gavin met his gaze. "Is she your friend we can't come near?"

He nodded. "Her name's Miss Cynster."

"But you can call me Angelica." Still patting the dogs, Angelica smiled at the pair.

Both regarded her steadily, then the one who hadn't spoken earlier asked, "Why can the dogs go near, but we can't?"

"Because dogs can't get illnesses from people, just as people can't get sick from dogs." She pulled a funny face at them. "I'm sorry, but I hope we'll be able to get to know each other soon."

They seemed to accept that at face value.

Dominic walked back to them; standing behind them, facing Angelica, his face softer, his expression one of pride and unabashed love, he put a hand on each shoulder. "This is Gavin." He whispered something, and Gavin smiled shyly and executed a small bow. "And this is Bryce." The younger boy bowed more jerkily.

Patting both shoulders, Dominic said, "Take the dogs off, now. I'll come up tonight and read you the rest of that story, all right?"

Their eyes still on Angelica, the boys nodded. Dominic whistled—the boys did, too—and the three dogs, interested spectators to the little exchange, rose and obediently ambled to them.

Dominic saw the group off, watching as they ran back along the battlements, then clattered down the steps.

Angelica walked slowly to join him where he stood watching boys and dogs race away across the bailey. "They planned that, didn't they?"

"Almost certainly."

She grinned. "They're sweet."

He looked down at her. "Never tell any male that he's sweet. It's an invitation to be anything but."

She laughed, then she linked her arm with his and they headed back to the keep.

"You asked about any who might be sympathetic to Mirabelle." Dominic slid beneath the covers of his big bed; propping on one elbow beside Angelica, he looked into her face. "There's only one I can think of—McAdie, the old steward." He grimaced. "I replaced him after my father died—if I'd been here,

I would have had him replaced sooner. He's a good man, but ineffectual. Sadly, he never understood, and so I'm not his favorite person, but he has nowhere else to go, so he's still here, wandering the corridors and keeping an eye on Erskine, his successor, trying to find fault, which he never does because John's excellent in the role, but still McAdie gripes."

"Is he a little on the shortish side, round like a top, with gray hair that's like a tonsure, and he wears a robelike coat over his trews?"

Face hardening, he nodded. "Has he approached you?"

"No, but I noticed him watching me in a puzzled sort of way in the great hall. I don't think he's seen me out walking, or at any time when I've not been playing my crushed violet role."

Dominic considered, then said, "He is, ultimately, loyal to the clan, but he's always been . . . accommodating, possibly even a trifle toadying, toward Mirabelle, and I expect that's grown more marked in recent years. However, he's not generally out and about. He keeps to himself, mostly in the staff quarters, so you should be able to avoid him."

Angelica nodded. "I will. Regardless, now I know about him, I'll make sure he sees nothing but the crushed violet."

Settling beside her, he drew her into his arms. "I'm not that fond of your crushed violet. She's . . . irritating." He kissed her chin. "Weak."

She brushed her lips over his. "Helpless?"

"That, too."

"Just as well, then, that all you'll ever get is the real me."

"Promise?"

She smiled into his eyes. "Let me show you."

Inwardly smiling, he lay back and did.

A sense of being watched drew Angelica from the pleasured oblivion Dominic had left her to wallow in. He'd filled her early morning with a delicious bout of lovemaking, then had risen and gone about his lairdly duties, leaving her boneless in his bed; as Mirabelle was such a late riser, there had seemed little reason to cut short her pleasured peace.

Except . . . the odd sensation dragged at her mind, insistently rousing her.

She was lying on her back, the covers over her shoulders. To convince herself that there was no one there, she raised her lids a fraction—and saw two familiar faces solemnly studying her.

Blinking, she stared at them, then struggled up to her elbows. "Ah . . . good morning."

"Good morning," they politely chorused back.

"You don't have a swollen neck," Gavin informed her.

"So we thought it must be all right to come and talk to you now," Bryce said.

It took a moment to realize they'd been told about mumps. "Ah . . . yes." She was naked beneath the sheets. Holding the covers to her, she wriggled up so she could lean against the pillows. With a wave, she invited the boys to avail themselves of the foot of the bed; they eagerly scrambled up. "What did you want to talk about?"

"Who are you?"

"Where are you from?"

"Why are you here?"

"And why are you sleeping in Dominic's bed?"

She studied their small faces, saw the budding intelligence and native shrewdness. Decided that her wisest course would be to adhere to her usual tack of starting as she meant to go on. "To answer the last question first, I'm sleeping in Dominic's bed because he and I are going to get married—we've already decided, but it's a secret for the moment—and this bed is where his wife, his countess, should sleep."

Slowly, Gavin nodded, hesitated, then asked, "If you'll be Dominic's wife, will that make you our mam?"

Danger, danger . . . she searched their faces; as with their older cousin, she could read little in the planes, unformed though they were, but their eyes . . . the soft blue was more revealing, showing a longing that made her heart weep. She recalled they'd been babes when their mother had died; they wouldn't remember her. "If you want me to be, then I will be—but only if you want me as your mam. If you don't, I'll just be Angelica, your friend."

That was the right answer; their eyes widened, hope glowing.

"But," she said, "we'll need to keep that a secret, too, until Dominic and I get married. All right?"

They both nodded solemnly. Then Bryce asked, "Will we be allowed to be at the wedding?"

"Absolutely. I promise. In fact, I swear I'll refuse to say I do unless you're there."

They smiled hugely and bounced on the bed. "So," Gavin said, "tell us the rest. The answers to our other questions."

She thought back, nodded. "All right. But I need to get dressed." Her clothes were where she'd left them, neatly laid over a stool, but being a male, Dominic had no screen behind which she could retreat. She pointed to the uncurtained window, the one opposite Mirabelle's tower. "I want you to go to the window and look out, and not turn around until I say. It's called giving me privacy."

They immediately scrambled from the bed and raced each other to the window. Once they were in place, she slid from the bed and grabbed her chemise. "Now, as to where I come from . . ." While she climbed into her clothes, she answered their questions, those they'd voiced earlier, and the others her answers inevitably spawned.

When she was fully clothed, she called them, then sat on the bed so when they halted before her, her face was level with theirs. "Now, this is important." Reaching out, she grasped a hand from each boy. "You love Dominic, and I do, too. I'm here to help him take care of the clan, and I'm sure both of you will do whatever you can to help him do the same."

Both solemnly nodded. "What can we do?" Gavin asked.

"This is the hard bit—the best way you can help him at this time is to do what he asks you to without question or grumbling." She looked into their faces, met their eyes. "I'm not ill, but he wants you to, just for the next few days, keep your distance from both me and him, at least while we're inside the keep. Inside your tower, in your rooms, there's no difficulty, but otherwise within the keep, it will make it easier for him and me to do what we have to if you both play least in sight." She searched their eyes. "All right?"

They glanced at each other, then Gavin asked, "Just for a few days?"

She nodded. "It'll all be over soon." It had to be.

"All right," they chorused.

After another brief exchange of looks, Bryce gripped her hand and jiggled it. "Can we go for a walk all together? Outside the castle, I mean?"

She smiled and rose. "I can't promise, but I'll see what I can do."

On receiving the expected summons to attend Mirabelle in her sitting room, Angelica allowed Brenda to escort her thither, her tack for the day clear in her mind. Mirabelle again instructed her to sit on the straight-backed chair facing Mirabelle's comfy armchair; knowing the position was deliberately designed to demean her, even deep in her crushed violet role, Angelica still felt a spurt of temper. The instant she sat, clinging outwardly to her role, she launched into her prepared monologue, illustrating that the crushed violet had accepted her lot to the extent of contemplating how to make her way as a "ruined lady."

In between wheedling, imploring, and begging Mirabelle to help her escape, tossing out vague mentions of family gratitude—none of which, perhaps unsurprisingly, garnered any response—she subtly and consistently underscored her belief in her own ruination; every request, every suggestion of making a new life was firmly predicated on the assumption that she was already irrevocably ruined, and, in polite terms, beyond the pale.

"Perhaps in Edinburgh? I have a good eye for fashion and can sew—perhaps I'll be able to find a place with a modiste there?" She fixed weary, helpless eyes on Mirabelle. "Are there fashionable modistes in Edinburgh?"

Finally able to get a word in, Mirabelle snapped, "I have absolutely no interest in what you do with the rest of your life. What I want to hear from you is . . ."

The catalog of her questions was as well thought out and significantly more extensive than Angelica's preparations. Stuck with the inevitable, she answered Mirabelle's queries about the Cynsters' connections, the other major ton families, the wider nobility presently in London, the patronesses of Almack's . . . it finally dawned that the questions revolved about all the ton luminaries with whom the Cynsters rubbed shoulders.

Angelica found that a touch unsettling. She countered by embellishing her answers with breathless speculation of how those named would react on learning of her ruination, how shocked they'd be, how horrified . . . only to see Mirabelle's vindictive avidity reach new heights.

Of course—that's what she hopes will happen.

The longer they spoke, the clearer it became that Mirabelle took real pleasure, nay *joy*, in imagining the ramifications of Angelica's—Celia's daughter's—social ruination.

Finally the gong for luncheon sounded; Angelica couldn't wait to leave the room and the blackness that surged within it.

But over luncheon, Mirabelle continued to cast sly, expectant glances at her, continued to ply her with leading questions, no longer about individuals but about the wider ton's likely reaction to such a sensational case of a young lady of good family being ruined.

Dominic growled and put a stop to the interrogation.

Mirabelle got huffy and declared that she'd heard enough from "the little twit" anyway.

"Does that mean you're prepared to hand over the goblet?"

"Not yet. I have to digest what she's told me . . . but soon." Her gaze distant, her expression coldly pleased, Mirabelle nodded. "Soon, very soon, I'll have gained all the revenge I want." She glanced at Dominic. "And *then* you may have your precious goblet back."

Pushing back her chair, she rose and swept from the hall.

Dominic watched her go, then murmured, "Do you have any idea what she's thinking?"

Eyes on her plate, Angelica replied, "I haven't a single clue."

"Is it my imagination, or is she waiting for something specific?" Dominic paced back and forth along the crenellated wall at the top of the keep.

He'd let Brenda escort Angelica back to the store room, then had gone down the secret stair, led her up to his rooms, and from there up the main stairs to the top of his tower, to where the air was fresh and they could speak freely.

Perched on a buttress nearby, with Gwarr, who'd followed Dominic from the hall, slumped beneath her feet, Angelica shook her head. "I didn't get that feeling, at least not while talking to her in her sitting room. As for her later comments, she seems to think she'll come to a decision—the right decision for us— soon."

"So she intimates, but I'm not about to believe I'll have the goblet back until I have it in my hands." Halting before Angelica, he looked into her upturned face. "What did you and she talk about this morning?"

She told him, ending with, "Looking back, she seems to have accepted my ruination as fact—she didn't appear to doubt or question that. Her focus today was on the outcome of my ruination. Yesterday's gloating had transformed to something more like glee—and yes, it's an anticipatory glee, but it didn't seem to be contingent on any other happening. She wanted to dwell on the result as she imagines it will be."

Reading her expression, the distaste conveyed by the set of her lips, he guessed, "She wanted to dwell on the pain you being publicly ruined would cause your mother."

She met his eyes, then sighed and nodded. "Yes. It was . . . more disturbing than I'd thought it would be, listening to her, knowing what she was taking such delight in."

"I'm sorry."

"It's not your fault. If any fault could be laid, it would be at your father's door, but even then his obsession was innocent in itself. It's what Mirabelle has twisted it into that's so black and awful."

He hesitated, then asked, "Do you want to call a halt?"

"No." She looked up at him, determination and stubbornness infusing her features. "I'm not such a weak creature that confronting a little nastiness will make me cut and run. There's far too much at stake, and never doubt that in this, I'm now as committed as you."

He looked into her eyes, now flashing gold more than green, and smiled. Reaching for her face, he tipped it up and kissed her.

She kissed him back, one hand rising to cradle the back of one of his. He straightened and, wrapping one arm around her, drew her off the buttress and into his arms.

She sank against him; he angled his head and deepened the kiss, accepting the invitation that she, with her lips and tongue and the caress of her small hands, laid before him.

Beside them, Gwarr stirred.

Then the big dog barked.

They broke off the kiss. Both stared at Gwarr. He was on his feet facing the door they'd used to reach the battlements—the one at the top of the main east tower stairwell that gave access to Dominic's rooms.

A low growl reverberated in the dog's chest.

"Quick—behind the buttress." Dominic urged Angelica into the lee of the stone abutment.

She crouched down, out of sight of the stairwell door.

Gwarr barked again. She heard Dominic stride toward the door. Then he asked, "What is it?"

"I wanted to speak with you," Mirabelle said. "I looked in your study, then felt the breeze from up here."

"Let's go back to the study—we can talk there." A second passed. "Gwarr. Come!"

The dog had stayed as he'd been, on guard between Angelica and the door. He whined, but then went.

Angelica waited a few seconds, then peeked out from behind the buttress—just in time to see Dominic send Gwarr down the stairs and pull the door closed.

Exhaling, she rose. She couldn't risk going down the stairs, not until she knew Mirabelle had left the east tower; Dominic would come and fetch her when it was safe.

Strolling to the wall, she decided she might as well enjoy the enforced interlude. Leaning on the stone, she looked out over the rippling waters of the loch, over the green spires of the forests to the wild mountains beyond, and let her senses spread, drinking in the scents, the sounds, and the abiding peace of the place she intended, from now until forever, to call her home.

"Is that all you wanted?" Standing before the desk in his study, Dominic laid aside his mother's latest dressmaker's bill. Although her allowance was generous by anyone's standards, she invariably outran the constable and had to apply to him to bail her out.

Despite the fact she never attended balls, never went anywhere, every year she ordered the most expensive of the latest fashions and threw out the previous year's acquisitions unused. He'd long ago stopped caring; the women of the clan enjoyed the lovely blouses and skirts the castle's sempstresses fashioned from Mirabelle's castoffs.

"Yes, that's all." Mirabelle turned to leave.

He couldn't help himself. "When are you planning to hand over the goblet?"

Halting, she arched her brows, but didn't meet his eyes. "Soon." She paused as if calculating, then said, "It shouldn't take much longer—a day or two at most." Her eyes found his. "I know you still have time."

"We don't have that many days left—I still have to get it down to London." Even as he said the words, he knew he was playing into her hands—playing her game rather than his. Angelica had seen the truth very clearly; Mirabelle's scheme was at least equally driven by her wish to be avenged on him.

"Nevertheless, you'll have to wait." Her expression grew coy, almost girlish. "Tomorrow, or perhaps the day after. We'll see."

With a swish of her skirts, she turned to the door. This time, he didn't stop her.

She stopped of her own accord. Poised in the open doorway, she looked back at him. "Meanwhile, you might dwell on the fact that if you'd done as I urged you all those years ago, you wouldn't be facing ruin now."

If he'd done as she'd asked and acquiesced to his father's murder.

His expression locked, his face like stone, he made no reply, just waited until she'd left, then he slowly crossed the room and quietly shut the door.

"I'm increasingly wondering if she intends to hand back the goblet at all. Once she does, she'll have no Damocles's sword to hold over me, no lever or power to make me do her bidding—and she's so enjoying that. Admittedly there's no benefit to her in holding onto the goblet, but . . ."

"But you fear she's vindictive enough to do it just for spite." Lying cushioned amid the pillows on Dominic's bed, Angelica watched him, heart-stoppingly naked, cross the room toward her. Moonlight shone through the window overlooking the forests, limning his long limbs and the upper edge of his broad shoulders.

"Exactly." He climbed into the bed beside her. "I can see her happily letting the clan collapse." He slumped on his back; crossing his arms behind his head, he stared upward.

She wished she could dismiss his fears. Unfortunately, she shared them. Their plan was straightforward, but what if it didn't work?

Two seconds of thought convinced her that that was an outcome she didn't want to think about, or even entertain regardless of how matters at the moment looked. "We can't let her throw us off. We will succeed. Come hell or high water, we will get that goblet back and get it to the bankers in time."

He glanced at her, but, like her, seemed to draw ineluctable comfort from the belligerently stubborn statement.

Rustling about, she turned to him. "And in the spirit of focusing on the better times to come, I have something to confess."

He studied her face, then arched his brows. "Confess away."

She smiled. "I had to tell the boys about us—that we're going to shortly marry, and that I'm helping you with something, and until that's finished with, it would be best if they could avoid us both while we're inside the keep, except for their rooms."

"They didn't say anything about speaking with you when I saw them a few hours ago."

"Possibly because it was here that we spoke."

"Here. This room?"

She nodded. "Which was why it was necessary to promise them that they could attend our wedding."

"You promised them that?" When she nodded, his lips slowly curved, then he gave in and grinned. "I know they look sweet and innocent to you, but do you have any notion of just how inventive those two can be when it comes to getting into scrapes?"

"Of course. I have nephews, and Gavin and Bryce can't be worse than they are. Regardless, I assure you, we—the females of the family—have tried-and-true ways of ensuring weddings go off without a hitch, even with the involvement of multiple page boys."

"Page boys. Have you told them that?"

"Not yet. I'm saving it for later." She smiled into his eyes, felt her own happiness well from knowing she'd eased his cares for just a little while. "I have a proposition for you."

He arched his brows, inviting her to state it.

Spreading her hand on his chest, she held his gaze, softly said, "I suggest we concentrate on the here and now, on the pleasures and the joys of this night, these next hours, the coming moments. And that we leave tomorrow's cares for tomorrow."

He studied her eyes, then he unlocked his arms and reached for her. "All right."

His hands closed about her waist. Before she could think, he rolled, and then she lay on her back beneath him, the dimness of the four-poster closing around them as he settled over her.

The warmth of their bodies merged; her nerves stretched with awareness and anticipation.

He looked down at her and smiled, his eyes slowly tracking up to her eyes. He looked into them, then murmured, "As you wish. Tonight is for tonight, and these hours are for you and me."

He bent his head and she tipped hers up, let him kiss her while she kissed him back. Then let him whirl her into the primal dance, banishing all thoughts but those that led them ever onward, down the road to paradise.

Chapter Nineteen

They were late down for breakfast; other than Brenda, still in her role of guard, there were only a few stragglers at the lower tables.

As Mirabelle rarely emerged from her rooms until much later, Angelica was happily addressing a bowl of porridge liberally laced with honey when Dominic, similarly engaged in his chair alongside hers, suddenly raised his head, then looked at her. "She's coming."

Angelica met his eyes, blinked, then drew breath, closed her eyes, and reached for her wilting, crushed violet persona, drawing it around her like a veil, shrinking down, her head lowering, her shoulders hunching as if to ward off a blow.

A second later, Mirabelle walked into the room. She didn't immediately glance their way, but peered toward the main doors. Frowning, she turned to the high table. Spotting the news sheets Dominic had been leafing through, her expression eased and she crossed to the dais to take her usual seat.

One of the maids came hurrying up, but Mirabelle waved her off and reached for the news sheets. Wordlessly, Dominic surrendered them—the Edinburgh papers from three days before, and the London papers from a week previously; he had both delivered by rider from Inverness every day.

His heart sank as he realized what his mother was searching for.

Discarding the Edinburgh sheets, she pored over those from London, turning each over, flicking back and forth. Abruptly, she sat up and flung the papers back at him. "There's nothing there!"

He had to be sure. "What do you mean?"

"I mean that there's no mention of *her*"—viciously Mirabelle jabbed a finger in Angelica's direction—"disappearing. No mention of the scandal! How can she be socially ruined if no one knows?"

Turning his head, Dominic exchanged a brief glance with Angelica.

Before he could think of what to say, she leaned forward and, as if hugely relieved by Mirabelle's outburst, said, "Oh, *thank you*! I didn't think to look. I didn't know if they would, you see, or if they might be able to even if they'd wanted to, given the circumstances." She smiled weakly—a smile that wobbled into a sad expression. She looked down. "It's so . . . comforting to know they cared and managed it."

Dominic faced Mirabelle. "Obviously her family has hidden her disappearance. They will for as long as they can. You must have read enough of them to know that they could, and most likely would." He frowned at her. "Surely you didn't expect to read about Angelica Cynster being kidnapped in a news sheet?"

The look Mirabelle bent on him stated very loudly that she had.

She glared, then, her face hardening, shot a dark glance at Angelica's bowed head. "I wanted a scandal."

"No—you wanted her ruined. That was our bargain, and ruined she is, whether that's puffed off in the news sheets or not."

Mirabelle's jaw firmed. Lips compressed, she glared even more furiously—first at the papers, then at him. "*I don't care!*" She drew breath, reached for a modicum of calm, then stated, "I'm going to wait until the scandal breaks." Rising, she pointed at the news sheets. "Until I see it in black and white."

Dominic held onto his temper. "That wasn't our bargain."

Leaning closer, Mirabelle grated out, "Too bad!" She stepped back. "She has to be *socially* ruined. I'm going to wait." Swinging around, she stormed out of the hall.

Angelica watched her go, then, straightening, closed a hand on Dominic's arm. "Not here." To her senses, his spiraling temper registered as a volcano about to erupt; her temper was not far behind. She eased out a breath. "Let's go for a walk."

They were going to need something to anchor and, later, refocus them. Angelica sent Brenda to fetch the boys and the dogs, then to her surprise found herself in company with Gavin, Bryce, and the three gamboling water spaniels being ushered by a silent Dominic down into the bowels of the north tower below Mirabelle's rooms. They crept down the stone stairs, then Dominic opened a door and waved them past, into a store room. After shutting the door, he took her hand and drew her in the wake of the boys and the dogs—to another door set in the outer wall.

This door was heavy, solid oak, with massive iron bracing, big hinges, huge bolts, and a large lock. The key hung to one side. Dominic lifted it down, inserted it and turned, then shot back the bolts and heaved the door open—revealing a stone-faced tunnel leading away from the castle.

Angelica looked down the tunnel, then at him.

"The postern gate, so to speak." The boys and dogs had already charged ahead, leaping along with careless abandon. Dominic waved her on. "The tunnel runs under the gardens and the outer wall, then beneath the surface of the loch. The floor's level and it's not that far—it comes out on the side of a hillock on the shore."

Brows rising, she stepped out. He followed, pulling the door shut, cutting off what little light the store room had offered. She slowed. His fingers closed about her elbow and he guided her on. "You'll be able to see shortly."

A few yards further, her eyes did indeed adjust to the low light. She could see well enough to walk without tripping.

"The other end is a grille, not a door. That's where the light comes from."

As he'd said, the tunnel wasn't that long. The boys had known how to unlatch the grille; it stood pushed wide, and boys and dogs were galloping ahead along a narrow path.

Joining her in the weak sunshine, Dominic took her hand, settled it in his, then they walked on, following the boys' lead. "On this shore, there are no lanes, only the paths, but there are plenty of forks and offshoots.

Until you get to know them, you'll be safer walking out with others."

She looked around, turning to look back at the castle and loch to get her bearings.

"We'll soon be out of sight of the castle." Dominic nodded to their left. "That hill and the forest will come between us and the loch."

Hand in hand, they walked on and didn't speak of the matter consuming them both—not yet. The forests closed around them, the shade soothing, the pervasive silence broken by birdcalls, the boys' bright voices, and the burbling of a nearby brook.

Still looking about her, she asked, "Are these clan lands?"

"Up to the crest." He glanced at the surrounding trees. "This is Coille Ruigh na Cuileige forest. The stream down there"—he tipped his head at the slope rolling down to their right—"is Allt na h Imrich. This path will take us to the head of the waterfall close by its source."

"Do the boys speak Gaelic?"

"Yes." He glanced at her. "Why?"

"Well, clearly, I'm going to have to learn." She met his eyes. "You'll have to teach me—I'm generally a quick learner."

His lips eased a fraction. He squeezed her hand lightly. Content enough with that, she looked ahead and they continued on.

The climb to the head of the waterfall demanded her attention and successfully hauled her mind from all else. When she wasn't watching her own feet, she was casting glances at the boys, toiling just ahead of her and Dominic.

He saw, murmured, "Don't worry. They're more nimble than goats."

Eventually, they reached a ledge just below the lip of the cliff top from which the waters of the Allt na h Imrich fell in a long, graceful cascade to land on rocks far below. The ledge was more than a yard wide, safe enough even though fully half its rocky length was damp and slippery, kept wet by the spume thrown from the waters plummeting down at the ledge's far end. A large natural alcove at the back of the ledge housed a cairn with a bronze plaque, while a bench had been hewn out of the rock where the path reached the ledge, at the end opposite the waterfall.

She peered past the curtain of water. "The ledge doesn't go behind the fall, does it?"

"No. If it did, the dogs would be soaked, and so would the two terrors."

Both boys and dogs, still reasonably dry, had clambered up a goat track to the cliff top above. Settling on the lip above the ledge, the boys sat with legs swinging and looked out, lords of all they surveyed.

Smiling, she walked to where a large rock, midchest height for her, formed a natural barrier at the edge of the ledge a few feet from where the water thundered past.

"Careful. It's slippery there."

Nodding, she set a hand on the damp rock and very carefully peered past and down.

Between roiling clouds of misty spray she caught glimpses of jagged black rocks a long, long way down. "Definitely not the place to slip."

Stepping back from the edge, she turned and walked to the cairn, almost as big as the rock; the bronze plaque was set into the front face of the rough pyramid. "What's this?"

"It's in honor of my great-grandfather. It was he who kept the clan safe through the clearances."

With her fingers, she traced the words on the plaque, once again in Gaelic. "Say this for me."

He did. She listened to his deep voice rolling through the syllables, to their cadence and the emotion they carried. When he fell silent, she sighed. "That's lovely."

"Yes, it is."

Turning, she saw him easing down to sit on the rock bench. She walked over and joined him.

For a moment they sat in silence. The view over the rolling mountains, the dips and shadows of the valleys, the ruffled green skirts of the forests, was breathtaking; they both took a moment to savor the sight, the crisp air, the peace.

Eventually Dominic leaned forward, rested his elbows on his thighs, clasped his hands. "So . . . what are we going to do?" When she didn't immediately respond, he went on, "I'm at my wits' end, and close to the end of my patience. If she keeps changing her rules, we'll never—"

"No—don't say it." When he fell silent, Angelica went on, "She hasn't actually changed her rules—she's just told us what criteria she'd expected to use to measure my social ruination. That was the one thing we didn't know, and now it's tripped us up. You told me she wouldn't understand how families like mine operate, so of course she assumed there would be a public scandal. As there won't be . . ."

Turning his head, he looked at her, studied her face, her eyes. He could almost see her manipulative wheels churning. Holding silent, he waited, wondering if even she could find a way out.

She'd been staring into space, a slight frown dragging down her brows; slowly, the frown eased, vanished, then she refocused and looked at him. Consideringly, assessingly.

His instincts pricked. "What?"

She compressed her lips, studying him—his face, his eyes—some more. Finally, she said, "You're going to have to trust me. For today, leave her to me. Let me work on her—there just might be a way."

Sitting up, he tried to fathom her direction, but could divine nothing from her face. "How?"

"I need to make her see that expecting to harm my family through a public scandal is unrealistic— that, if anything, she's going to play into their hands . . . yes, that's right. That's how I'll couch it." She paused, then went on, "And once I convince her of that, I need to show her a way in which she can be assured of gaining her revenge—a way that you and I can successfully deliver, a way she'll accept and so be satisfied."

Meeting his eyes, she smiled intently. "We need to remember that that's what this has been about all along—her being *assured* of her revenge."

He could sense her returning enthusiasm; his instincts still jibbed. "What, exactly, are you planning?"

She met his eyes, considered for a long moment, then laid one hand over his and squeezed. "Let me see if I can get her to swallow my bait, then I'll tell you my lure."

He didn't like it, but he'd run out of options. And he couldn't *not* trust her.

He did trust her, but . . . grim-faced, he reined in his instincts and nodded. "All right."

"Thank you, *thank* you! I can't thank you enough for showing me the error of my ways." Subsiding onto the straight-back chair she'd fetched and placed before Mirabelle's armchair in the sitting room, Angelica clasped her hands in her lap, fixed her eyes on Mirabelle's face, and endeavored to cling to her crushed violet persona while leavening her previous dejection with budding hope. "I hadn't realized, you see—quite silly of me, but with being so frightened, indeed, at times quite terrified of your son and his intentions toward me, well, you can see how it was that it simply slipped my mind that of course my family would conceal my disappearance. *Of course* they would—and clearly they have, and successfully, given there's no mention of my disappearance in the news sheets. That's *such* a relief!"

She'd let hope glimmer from the moment she'd been escorted to the high table for luncheon; throughout the meal, she'd pretended to be absorbed with her own thoughts, allowing her face to reflect that said thoughts had not been the same dismal, dire, fearful ones that had consumed her before.

During the meal, Dominic had eyed her with unconcealed suspicion and a touch of wariness, unwittingly playing the part she'd needed him to play to perfection. Mirabelle had come to the table in a pouting temper, had shifted to scowling when Dominic hadn't noticed, but eventually she'd seen Dominic's suspicious looks, and had followed them, and then she'd grown suspicious, too.

Immediately the meal had ended, Angelica had heightened suspicions all around by literally begging Mirabelle for an audience. Mirabelle had pretended to hesitate, but, of course, had agreed.

Leaning forward, Angelica confided, "I realize, of course, that you don't approve of your son's actions— that no matter how it appears, or what you think of me, that you're working against him." Mirabelle frowned, but before she could interrupt, Angelica held up a hand. "Oh, I know there's more to it that I don't know—I don't understand very much, but I've heard about the goblet, and how, now that he's brought me here, you won't give it to him and so he'll be the one ruined . . . well, I just wanted to tell you how grateful I am, and how grateful and appreciative my family will be, my father and my mother especially. By ruining your son, you'll be striking a blow for them, giving them exactly the revenge and retribution they would want visited on him for kidnapping me. Why"—eyes widening, she managed an ingratiating smile—"you could be said to be acting as their champion!"

Mirabelle's face was a study in stunned confusion. "*What?*"

"Oh, I realize you might not see it that way, and I do apologize if you find the suggestion offensive—he is your son, after all—but I just wanted to thank you for being so kind this morning in drawing my attention to what I should have guessed—that my family will conceal my disappearance and so avoid any public scandal—and so giving me real hope that this ordeal will soon be over, and I'll be back home with my parents and all will soon be well." With a small nod, she sat back and folded her hands in her lap.

Mirabelle regarded her much as she might a dog with two heads. After a moment, she asked, "Why . . . ? No. What do you see happening now?"

Precisely the question Angelica had been angling for. She frowned slightly. "Well, as you won't give your son this goblet, and I gather that has to happen in the next few days, then once that deadline passes, he won't be able to stop himself being ruined, so I won't be of any further use to him—not that I understand why I was in the first place—but he'll let me go, and once I reach Inverness I'll send for help. Then someone from the family will come and fetch me and take me home to Somerset. The family will have put it about that I've been staying with friends somewhere, so there won't be any scandal to come out of this at all—and if anyone tries to claim there was . . . well, what evidence would they have that would stand against my family's word?

"And once I'm back at home, all will go on as usual." She smiled, transparently savoring the prospect. "I'm only twenty-one, after all—the baby of the family—so next Season, I'll go up to town and attend all the usual balls and parties with my mother, and find an eligible parti." She sighed happily. "Because of you, ma'am, and your brave stand against your son, nothing in my life will truly change. Despite this horrible adventure, I'll still be able to marry a duke, and Mama will be so relieved. I'm very close to her, you know."

Mirabelle's eyes had narrowed to shards; her mouth was pinched. "You're saying that, as things stand, your mother, and you, will more or less be unaffected?"

"Oh, no—Mama must be in a *terrible* state, shocked and so concerned because I've disappeared, but once I get back, hale and whole, all will be well again."

"I find it hard to believe, miss, that being kidnapped will visit no lasting damage on you or your mother."

Angelica shrugged, her certainty blatant. "It's just the way the ton is, you see. A kidnapping is ruination only if it becomes widely known, and even then, it's only ruination by implication."

"Implication?" Mirabelle stared. "What does that mean?"

"Well, because of the assumption that . . ." She broke off, fidgeted, then blurted out, "Not to put too fine a point on it, that a kidnapped lady no longer possesses her virtue. For a ton young lady, losing one's virtue is what true ruination is, because it will prevent us marrying well, thus truly ruining our lives, our dreams, and dashing all expectations." She didn't dare cross her fingers but willed Mirabelle to follow the trail . . .

After a full minute of staring at her, Mirabelle said, "Are you telling me that if you lost your virtue—by which I assume you mean you were no longer a virgin—then you would truly be ruined, and that that would be true *regardless* of whether your kidnapping ever becomes widely known?"

"Well . . ." Drawing back into her crushed violet persona, she let her voice waver. "If I lost my virtue and was no longer a virgin, that's not something even my family could fix. If I was"—she gulped—"ravished, that would mean irretrievable ruin for me, and Mama would be *devastated* . . ."

Letting fear trickle back into her posture, her eyes, she drew in a sharp breath, then nervously shook her head. "But that won't happen. Your son . . . well, if he hasn't yet, then he won't, will he? Besides, although he's been frightful and frightening, he hasn't actually hurt me . . . well, not more than a bruise or two. And I gather he prides himself on his honor—the family motto and all that—so despite appearances, I really don't think that's likely. He might have kidnapped me, but he won't stoop to *that*." She drew a tremulous breath. "So I don't think I need to worry about that. I just need to wait until the deadline for you giving him the goblet passes, and then this will all be over and he'll let me go and I can go home and forget this ever happened."

Drawing welling nervousness about her, she shifted on the chair, then hesitantly rose. "Thank you, ma'am, for your indulgence. I just wanted to let you know that I appreciate your support through this frightening time." She bobbed a curtsy, then glanced at Brenda, standing, guardlike, by the door. She hung her head. "I'd better get back to my room."

From beneath her lashes, she watched Mirabelle's expression grow inward-looking, more intense, the lines in her face more harshly etched; the countess's attention was no longer on her.

After a fraught second, Mirabelle brusquely waved. "Yes. Go. Get out of my sight."

Silently exhaling, Angelica left the room.

Angelica next saw Mirabelle at dinner, when the countess entered the great hall and stepped onto the dais on which the high table stood. Her expression was fixed, her blue eyes staring, but not, it seemed, at anything; she was not just absorbed but obsessed by her thoughts.

Sinking into her chair on Dominic's right, Mirabelle acknowledged neither him nor anyone else. The meal began, and she ate what was put before her, but her attention remained elsewhere.

Several minutes after the main course had been served, Dominic turned his head and arched a brow at Angelica. An accident on one of the farms had taken him out of the castle shortly after she'd gone into his mother's sitting room; he'd only just got back in time for the meal, so hadn't had a chance to learn what had transpired during their afternoon's talk.

The change in Mirabelle set alarm bells ringing.

Although he looked at Angelica for several minutes—more than long enough for her to feel his gaze—she made no move to meet it, which escalated his wariness dramatically.

At the end of the meal, Mirabelle abruptly stood. She looked at him, then at Angelica. A heartbeat passed, then, frowning, Mirabelle turned and walked from the room.

Dominic watched her go, saw Elspeth scramble to follow her to the drawing room. When, distantly, he heard the drawing room door shut, he turned to Angelica. "What was that about?"

She glanced at him, then pushed back her chair, rose, and laid her hand on his shoulder. "Go and put the boys to bed. I'll tell you all after that. I'll be in the store room reading—come and fetch me."

Reaching up, he closed a hand over hers. "And what if Mirabelle wants to speak with me?"

She grimaced. "Avoid her. You'll need to hear my explanation first."

Turning, he met her gaze. "So I supposed."

Her green-gold gaze didn't waver.

Releasing her, he rose. He glanced to where Mulley was waiting to escort her to the store room. "I won't be long."

He waited until she'd left, then headed for the boys' room.

Sitting on the narrow trestle bed in the store room, a two-armed candelabra on a box beside her, Angelica was deep in Scottish history when the door to the secret staircase clicked, then swung open.

Looking up and seeing Dominic ducking under the lintel, she smiled, shut the book, and set it aside.

Rising, she picked up the candelabra and trod the path through the boxes to where he'd halted just inside the room.

He arched a brow as she neared. "Here or upstairs?"

"Upstairs." She handed him the candelabra so she could better manage her skirts. "I think—hope—that she's going to want to speak with you, either tonight or more likely tomorrow morning."

"About what?" Turning, Dominic followed her up the stairs; shutting the door behind him, he held the candelabra high enough to light her way.

"Let me explain what she and I discussed, and all will be clear." Emerging into his bedroom, she crossed to the bed, turned, and sat. He'd passed through the room on the way to fetch her; the curtains facing Mirabelle's tower were drawn tight, and the candles on the side tables beside the bed and on the tallboy across the room were already lit. She watched while he closed the stair door. He paused, looking at her, then crossed to set the candelabra on the writing desk before prowling to a halt beside her.

He looked down at her; she looked up at him.

Then he turned and sat beside her. "Tell me."

She did, simply, concisely, and clearly. He heard her out in increasingly ominous silence; unperturbed, she concluded with, "I laid the situation out for her—if she holds off giving you the goblet, then she loses all chance of any effective revenge against Mama, and she also forgoes her best revenge on you. Oh, she may ruin you and the clan, cause financial devastation and hardship to all and hurt you through that, but that was never her real goal—that was merely a sword to hold over you to get you to enact her revenge. Her real goal, her most longed-for and true revenge, has always been directed against your father, via Mama, as he's dead, and against you for holding to your honor and your loyalty to him. For choosing him over her—you can be absolutely certain that's how she sees it."

Drawing breath, she went on, "So I've left her with the choice of sitting and losing all she really wants, or acting and gaining the revenge she truly wants by insisting you ravish me, thus hurting Mama unbearably, and hurting you beyond recall by forcing you to an act that is the pinnacle of dishonor. She wants to *know* she's succeeded in both, that nothing can lessen, make right, or circumvent the harm she causes Mama through me, and likewise that she's succeeded in irrevocably stripping you of the one thing you hold most dear."

She glanced at Dominic, not just silent but oh-so-very still, so contained she could feel the control he was exercising, a tangible, physical restraint. Elbows on his thighs, he was looking down at his linked hands. His profile was grim; she couldn't see his eyes. She waited. When he said nothing, she prompted, "So now it's up to her to choose, and I'm fairly certain which path she'll take. We need to decide how to respond when she lays her latest and ultimate demand before you."

He shifted but instantly stilled, as if the leash he held over that explosively strong side of him had momentarily slipped and he'd seized it again. Tense seconds passed, then he said, "That I don't like any of this goes without saying, but before we address that, did you know it would come to this—staging a rape—when we spoke in Kingussie?"

She shook her head. "No—I wasn't prophetic. I wasn't trying to pave the way for something I foresaw from then. I thought we would succeed long before we were pushed to this. But as my words then bear witness, once I'd thought the situation through I knew you ravishing me would qualify as her ultimate revenge—it gives her everything, you see. Until this morning, however, I hadn't dreamt we'd have to offer her that."

He remained silent for a full minute, then he unlinked his fingers, reached across, and took one of her hands in one of his. His fingers slid over, then twined with hers, gripped. When he spoke, his voice was low, but steady and even. "I . . . am going to hate every minute of this, but I also accept, as I know you'll tell me, that I—*we*—don't have a choice, and, against that, that it will, after all, be nothing but pretence. That it will simply be the climactic scene of our necessary charade." He paused, then looked sidelong at her, met her eyes. Stormy eyes, more gray than green, gazed into hers. "Have I missed anything?"

Holding his gaze, she squeezed his fingers. "Only that the reason you will do this is because you will always do whatever God and fate require of you to protect the clan—and that I will be with you, by your side, metaphorically, physically, and in every other way, through each minute. *We* will do this because we must, because clan is too important to let niceties of feeling stand in our way. We'll do it and succeed because together we can, because together we're strong enough to do even that without surrendering an iota of who we truly are, who we've together become."

Still lost in his eyes, she tightened her grip on his fingers. "Trust me, we'll win."

He said nothing for a long moment, then the line of his lips eased. "You're wrong, you know. About the one thing I hold most dear. It's not my honor. If it ever came to it, I would unhesitatingly trade my honor and all else for—"

He broke off, head turning to look at the door.

An instant later, a sharp *rap-rap* was followed by, "Dominic—I need to speak with you *urgently*."

Mirabelle.

He swore—in Gaelic; sliding his fingers from Angelica's, he rose. Softly said, "Wait here. I'm not going to let her in."

Unsure whether he'd been saved by fate, or cursed by his mother's timing, Dominic crossed the room and opened the door enough to step out onto the landing of the tower's main stair. His mother moved back and he shut the door behind him.

As he'd expected, she was carrying a candlestick, which cast sufficient light for them to see. She was still dressed as she had been at dinner, but her expression had changed to one of intense, almost shocking, avidity, her features invested with so much greedy eagerness he knew she'd come to a decision, one from which she wouldn't be swayed.

"What is it?" His tone was unwontedly harsh, but she didn't seem to register it.

"I'm prepared to let you have the goblet if you do one more thing."

"What thing?"

"I want you to ravish Miss Cynster."

The clear, definite, decisive demand damned her beyond recall. He scowled. "I've kidnapped her, brought her here—as you demanded. I've done what you wanted, and now this?" Lowering his head, he looked her in the eye. "Give me one good reason why I should—why I should do it, and why I should believe you'll hold to your word this time."

They argued; she would have grown suspicious if he'd simply agreed, but regardless he wanted to hear it all from her lips—her offer, her demands, her promises, and the malignant desires those revealed. He pushed her and heard it all—and it was exactly as Angelica had described it, as, in his heart of hearts, he'd known all along.

It wasn't easy to listen to the vitriol, to the blackness that spewed out, but he needed to hear his mother condemn herself before he acted—before, ultimately, he brought her down.

He'd already thought further than even Angelica had; once this was over and the goblet once more in his hands, he'd have to banish Mirabelle, imprison her in some comfortable place where she could do no more harm to herself or anyone else. And that place could not be in the castle, not even on clan lands, but that was a decision he didn't yet have to make. For tonight . . .

Finally, she glared and belligerently stated, "If you don't do as I wish, I swear on your father's grave that

I will *not* give the goblet back in time for you to save your precious clan."

His gaze on her face, in the corner of his vision, Dominic glimpsed movement in the shadows at the bottom of the stair, where it met the gallery. Head rising, drawing a tight, genuinely furious breath, he looked—and saw McAdie.

Dominic nodded. "All right," he said to his mother, "but I want a witness to our agreement." Raising his voice, he called, "McAdie—come up here and stand witness for the clan."

The forcibly retired steward might be Mirabelle's toady, but Dominic entertained no doubt as to McAdie's loyalty to the clan. When alerted by Angelica's earlier question, he'd asked his senior staff about the old man, they'd admitted that no one had told McAdie the truth about Angelica, which explained his puzzlement; he didn't understand why Dominic had brought her to the castle and imprisoned her. Letting the old man see the real caliber of the lady for whom he misguidedly entertained a certain regard might save McAdie from getting further involved in Mirabelle's schemes.

Mirabelle had whirled to look down the stairs. After a fractional hesitation, McAdie started slowly up. As he neared, she asked, "Were you looking for me?"

McAdie nodded. "Aye, my lady."

Dominic wondered why but wasn't about to ask. McAdie reached the landing and bowed slightly. Dominic nodded crisply. "McAdie, my mother and I are about to voice an agreement of great importance to the clan. I'm asking you to bear witness for the clan. Are you willing?"

McAdie straightened. "Aye, my lord."

Shifting his gaze to Mirabelle's face, Dominic stated, "I am only going to make this offer once. There will be no negotiation of terms—you either agree to the offer as I make it, or you refuse it. Understood?"

She hesitated, but she knew he had to give her what she wished. She nodded. "Very well."

"I, Dominic Lachlan Guisachan, Earl of Glencrae, will accede to your specific demand that I ravish Miss Angelica Cynster on the following conditions. One, you will not be allowed to witness the act, but I will agree to allowing you into the room immediately afterward to visually confirm. Two, the ravishment will be carried out in a place, and at a time, and in a manner of my choosing. In return for agreeing to your demand, *immediately* the deed is done and confirmed, you will surrender to me the Scottish coronation goblet."

Mirabelle opened her mouth, then shut it. She frowned, then said, "The goblet isn't in the castle, but it is close by and I can give you the directions to where it's hidden immediately the deed is done."

He nodded. "Immediately the deed is done and confirmed, you will surrender to me the directions to the goblet's hiding place." He paused, ran through his evolving plan in his mind, then asked, "Do we have an agreement?"

Eyes glittering, Mirabelle nodded decisively. "Yes. If you'll do as you state, I'll return the goblet."

"McAdie?" Dominic glanced at the old man. McAdie looked shocked; even in the poor light it was evident he'd paled. More gently, Dominic prompted, "Do you bear witness to the agreement?"

McAdie blinked, then nodded. "Aye. I do so bear witness."

Dominic looked at his mother. "Done." He turned his back on her and opened his bedroom door.

"When?" she asked.

He glanced back, saw again the stomach-churning eagerness in her face. "Tomorrow." He paused, then added, "After lunch."

Opening the door just wide enough, he went in, shut it, then locked it. Turning, he saw Angelica, still clothed, lying on the bed. She arched her brows at him. Walking to the bed, he halted beside it. "You heard?"

"Tomorrow, after lunch. But the door's so thick I couldn't hear any of the rest."

Sinking down beside her, he repeated the agreement. Meeting her eyes, he concluded, "So now we have to plan your ravishment."

Lolling beside him, she grinned. "I'm all ears."

He stretched out on the bed, like her still clothed, the better to think. Crossing his arms behind his head, he did, then grimaced. "In all honesty, I seriously doubt I'll be able to perform as required." He glanced at her, met her eyes. "We'll most likely have to fake it."

Her expression now serious, she arched her brows. "That would be seriously dangerous given your mother is hardly a virgin herself and we can't risk her even questioning that anything about this ravishment, not even the smallest detail, is fake. This is our last throw of the dice—if we fail in this, we won't get another. However . . ." Wriggling higher in the bed, she leaned over him and trailed her fingers down the center of his chest. "If you will simply surrender yourself into my hands"— fingers trailing lower still, she demonstrated—"then as long as we lock the door, and no one else can see, then I'm utterly, unassailably confident that I'll be able to convince you to have your wicked way with me."

Eyes closing, Dominic's lips curved, but all he said was, "We'll see."

"Is that another challenge?"

"Take it as you wish."

She chuckled, sultry and sweet, and set out to convince him that she was up to it.

Mirabelle and McAdie didn't speak until they reached the safety of her tower. Halting inside the stairwell, she swung to the old man and eagerly asked, "Well? Is he here?"

"No. A boy came with a message—apparently the gentleman has returned from his trip, but is unable to attend you tonight."

Mirabelle's face drained of all expression. "Damn him—I wanted to gloat. He didn't think I'd be able to force Dominic to do as I wished, but I've finally triumphed over my intractable son. I'm one step away from gaining my revenge . . ." Lips compressing, she paused, then slowly smiled. "But perhaps it will be even better this way. Come up." She started up the stairs. "I'll give you a note. You can take it across tomorrow morning, then he can join me for my moment of ultimate glory, when I'll have even more to share with him."

McAdie toiled slowly up the stairs in her wake. His head was spinning; he could barely believe the agreement he'd been called on to witness. He was shocked by what the laird had agreed to do, but he fully understood why. He couldn't claim any moral high ground; he knew full well the importance of the goblet. Beneath his long-held rancor over the laird's dismissal of his services, in his heart he held nothing but respect, albeit grudging, for the man Dominic had become.

A pity he hadn't remembered that sooner.

Before he'd told Mirabelle the combination to the safe.

While he was horrified by what the laird had been forced to agree to, he was even more horrified by his own unthinking role in the unfolding drama.

As for his role as go-between and doorkeeper for the countess and the "gentleman" she'd taken as her lover . . . he'd originally agreed because he'd felt sorry for her in her isolation, because he'd seen her and himself as both suffering from the neglect of the Guisachan in showing them far less respect than their due, but over the months he'd grown increasingly uneasy. Not because of the countess's interest in the gentleman; her motives were clear enough. But the gentleman's interest in the countess . . . to McAdie, the man's motives were worryingly suspect.

Of course, he wouldn't—couldn't—say anything. He stood beside the countess while she wrote out her missive at the pretty desk in her sitting room. He'd chosen the desk himself, long ago, smitten by her face, by her smile. She had been so beautiful when she'd first come there, he'd been agonizingly jealous of Mortimer, yet she hadn't once looked his way. She'd never seen him as a man, only as someone to give orders to, to use when she wished.

He hadn't minded, not until now.

Now . . . he was starting to wonder just how much of an unthinking old fool he'd become.

Chapter Twenty

Breakfast in the great hall was a tense affair. Dominic and Angelica stuck to their agreed roles. He had no difficulty behaving appropriately; anger and frustration rolled off him in waves. He deliberately lowered the shield he usually kept his temper screened behind, and let the chill touch of menace, of violence barely restrained, reach out and spread.

For her part, Angelica kept her head down. While she no longer cringed, she definitely shrank, projecting the image of a woman who knew herself to be weak and helpless, and potentially subject to unspeakable threat; she conducted herself as if her entire being was focused on slipping past a dangerous, ravenous animal unnoticed.

Hungrily, greedily, avidly and intently, Mirabelle watched and delighted, while everyone else saw and wondered.

Dominic had already spoken with Scanlon, Jessup, and Mulley, with Brenda and Griswold, with John Erskine and Mrs. Mack. He and Angelica had agreed that no one else needed to know that anything dramatic was afoot, and even those—his closest and most trusted staff—knew only that he and Angelica wanted the keep cleared of everyone but them, Mirabelle, and McAdie immediately after luncheon ended. Dominic had opted for that time precisely so that he would be able to ensure a clear field—one on which no one else would be involved in any way.

Immediately breakfast ended, Angelica slid out of her chair and found Mulley waiting to escort her back to the store room and lock her in.

Inside, she paced and thought, planned, and considered. Like any play ever staged, her ravishment would benefit from being plotted and structured, and Dominic had proved adept at following her cues. "Just as well." The skirts of the drab, dun-colored gown Mirabelle had provided swirling as she turned, she paced before the locked door. "Clearly one of us is going to have to lead, and given how he feels about this, it won't be him."

Dominic had elected to take the boys out hunting with Scanlon and his lads; he would leave the group and return to the castle in good time to meet with her before luncheon.

"So," she murmured, "I have three hours to come up with a workable script, and then decide how much of it to tell him."

Outwardly, luncheon was its habitual, unremarkable event, but about the high table feelings ran high. Frustration, anger, and building expectation mingled with heightened awareness and burgeoning uncertainty.

Mirabelle had disrupted Dominic and Angelica's plan to meet by insisting Angelica spend the latter half of the morning with her in her sitting room. Although until then Angelica had taken her meetings with Mirabelle in her stride, this time, knowing what Mirabelle had set in motion, what she'd demanded Dominic do, and that she was gloating over and savoring—indeed, all but salivating over—what she expected would be Angelica's upcoming terror, distress, and devastation, had literally turned her stomach.

She'd had no appetite to speak of when, in Mirabelle's all but triumphant train, she'd slipped into the great hall and, giving Dominic, slumped and glowering in his huge carved chair, as wide a berth as possible, had slid into the chair on his left.

Pushing food around on her plate, she found herself unexpectedly trepidatious; they had no plan, no agreed series of actions. In what happened next, they would have to play their parts spontaneously.

For the first time in the entire charade, she felt nervous.

This was their last gambit, the last and final act. They had to get every single little gesture right, and Mirabelle had just made their task harder.

By the time the plates and platters were being removed, an unfamiliar knot had formed in the pit of her stomach.

Then Dominic pushed back his chair and rose. Everyone fell silent; expectation gripped the hall. He glanced over the faces, his own a mask, then spoke to the assembly. "As some of you already know, I've declared the rest of today a minor festival day for the castle. There'll be archery and other contests in the bailey and in the forests to east and west. I want everyone outside, enjoying the afternoon—I don't want to see anyone back in the keep until it's time to get dinner ready. I've some business to attend to, but I'll join you all soon." Raising both arms, he waved everyone out. "Now go, and enjoy the afternoon."

Excited, happy chatter welled, engulfing the hall. Under cover of the noise and the rush of activity as people left the tables and headed for the main door, Angelica started to edge out of her chair.

"Stay where you are."

She froze at Dominic's growl; the final act in their charade had begun.

He remained standing, watching the others leave. Silent and still, fingers lightly touching the table, he waited . . .

Shrunk down in her chair, Angelica leaned forward enough to glance past him. Mirabelle, still seated, was looking up at him, her face all but radiant with expectation of a twisted, malignant joy . . .

Stifling a shudder, Angelica looked down. She'd performed in charades too numerous to count. Never before had her pulse hammered in her throat, had her nerves cinched to such excruciating tightness.

Finally, the last stragglers were shooed out by Mrs. Mack, who followed them outside into the weak sunshine. Gradually the keep fell silent, until the only sounds to reach them were distant, muted by the thick stone walls.

Dominic pounced.

He seized her arm, hauled her up and out of her chair.

The squeak he'd surprised out of her had been perfectly genuine. Shocked, as he tugged her forward instinct kicked in and she pulled back. "No! What—"

"Shut up. If you know what's good for you, you'll come quietly."

"No! Let me go!" She threw herself back and succeeded in knocking over her chair. It crashed on the flags, the sound reverberating through the hall.

Dominic's jaw set harder than stone. With more force, he yanked her forward, ducked his shoulder, and straightened with her caught over it.

She struggled furiously. "Stop! You can't do this. Let me go!" She pummeled his back with her fists, wriggled and bucked and tried to kick as if she didn't care if he dropped her; she knew very well he wouldn't.

Undeterred by her resistance, he strode off the dais and into the gallery. When she redoubled her efforts, he slapped her on her bottom hard enough to make her shriek. "Stop it!" he snarled. "You'll only end hurting yourself."

The slap was followed by a knowing, kneading caress, an arousing reassurance that made her gasp and momentarily distracted her.

Recalling her role, she hauled in as much breath as she could and screamed, "Help!"

With his shoulder pressed solidly into her lungs, the best she managed was a weak cry.

"Scream all you like," he said. "No one will hear you."

Her gaze fell on Mirabelle. His mother had leapt up from her chair and was trotting after them, her eyes drinking in their performance, her lips parted in delight.

Revulsion rolled through Angelica. She wriggled anew, dragging in breath to appeal to the manic countess, "Help me! You can't let him do this."

Mirabelle smiled, and every ounce of her maliciousness, of her vindictive spite showed. "Oh, yes I can—he's doing this for me. He's so big, too—I'm so looking forward to hearing you scream. My only regret is that your mother won't hear it, hear her darling being ripped apart, but I'm hoping that later you'll describe the moment to her in all its horror."

Angelica was struck speechless.

As Dominic swiftly climbed the stairs to his room, her struggles weakened, lessened.

She managed a realistic sob as he reached his door. "No, please—don't do this."

"Stop fighting, be sensible, just lie there and take it, and I'll make things as easy for you as I can. It shouldn't hurt too much." Dominic set the door swinging wide.

"Just follow the old advice: Lie back and think of England. It'll be over soon enough, and then you can go home."

Swinging around, he slammed the door in Mirabelle's face and slid the bolt into place.

And exhaled.

Walking further into the room, he halted and lifted Angelica off his shoulder, letting her slide into his arms.

She wound her arms around his neck, looked into his eyes. "Lie back and think of England?"

Inexpressibly relieved to see laughter in her eyes, he shrugged. "It seemed apt."

She searched his eyes, then, lips curving, arched a brow. "So . . . what now?"

"I was hoping you might have some suggestions."

"Oh, I do—I definitely do." She raised one leg, waited until his hands cupped her bottom and he lifted her, then she wound both legs about his waist. Levering herself up so they were face-to-face, eye to eye, lips to lips, she murmured, "Let's start with this."

She kissed him, and within three heartbeats he learned that his fears had been groundless.

They could do this. Together they could, and would, and all would be well again.

Between them, between his kisses and hers, between the artful tangle of their tongues and their slowly rising hunger, the fires ignited and the heat between them rose.

And filled them.

Supporting her with one arm, he raised his other hand to her breast, claimed, kneaded, and caressed.

She murmured something incoherent, then drew back from the kiss, looked into his eyes. "She's doubtless got her ear pressed to the door, but she can't hear us, can she?"

"No, but she'll hear a scream."

She licked her lips; her gaze fastened on his. "We're not usually that noisy, so we're going to have to make an extra effort." With a wriggle and a slow undulation of her spine, she pressed the heat between her thighs to the reassuringly rigid rod of his erection. "You're going to have to give me a reason to scream . . . with appropriate feeling."

He wouldn't have thought it remotely possible, but she'd made him grin. "Let me see what I can do."

He trapped her lips in a kiss, although who caught who was moot, and desire and passion flared anew, flared higher. Within seconds, their hands were everywhere, tugging this, unbuttoning that. He staggered the two steps to the bed and tipped her down. She let her arms slide from his neck, let herself fall back to the mattress. She was already nicely flushed, lightly panting.

"We can't take too long." She'd already tugged his shirt free of his waistband. Now she reached for the buttons there.

He blocked her and reached for the buttons closing her bodice.

"No—rip it."

He met her eyes.

She grasped his wrists and shook them. "She gave it to me."

Gripping the fabric, he hauled the halves apart, ripping both gown and chemise to her waist, exposing her breasts, unmarked but swollen. Swooping, he set his mouth to her flesh, set his hands and fingers cruising. She'd wanted him to make her shriek and moan; he set himself to the task with his customary devotion.

She exaggerated, of course, but she took her cues from his ministrations, from his deliberate and ruthless assault on her senses. The sounds that fell from her lips urged him on; within minutes they were creating the sort of racket that would have convinced even the most hardened and cynical listener that a ravishment of the first order was taking place.

His mouth on her gave them her first scream. Her second, when he thrust swift and sure deep into her body, was simply perfect.

Her skirts rucked to her waist, her hips gripped and anchored in his hands, her legs wound about his hips, he leaned over her and rode her hard and fast; eyes gleaming from beneath her heavy lids, she was with him every heart-pounding second of the way.

And she'd been right. Nothing could touch them; no charade, no pretence however sordid, could even reach, let alone mar, the reality they'd already created.

In perfect harmony, they focused on their joint goal. And raced for it.

She didn't hold back, and neither did he. He rode her up the slope at a breakneck pace, all the way to the peak, and sent her flying. Head back, body bowing, she screamed. Her sheath gripped, a scalding velvet vice, and pulled him with her. On a hoarse shout, he let go, let her take him—then let her pull him down, into her arms, and hold him.

For that one blissful second.

Then they both dragged in huge breaths. Pushing back, he disengaged. She reached up and ran her fingers through her hair, disarranging the long strands, leaving them tangling wildly about her face, throat, and exposed breasts.

Breeches rebuttoned, he turned to the bedside table, picked up the knife he'd left there, and nicked his thumb. Returning to her, he let the blood well, then smeared it down the insides of her thighs, mixing it with his seed so that it glistened damply.

"Thank God you remembered—I'd forgotten."

"Every little detail," he murmured.

Stepping back, he sucked his thumb and surveyed her.

She arched her brows. "How do I look?"

He reached for her skirts, artfully draped a fold over flesh he saw no reason to let his mother see, tweaked her ripped bodice so the rip was even more evident, then waved at her. "Look ravished."

She obliged, falling limp on the disarranged counterpane, head to one side, palms upward in helpless defeat, limbs in a boneless sprawl, her legs spread wide, hanging over the side of the bed . . . he shook his head in honest admiration. "Perfect. Don't move—I'm going to let her in."

He crossed to the door, took a firm grip on his temper, his revulsion, his protectiveness, and held them all back, then he slid the bolt free and opened the door.

Mirabelle stood immediately outside. The look on her face . . . for a moment, he closed his eyes.

Turning from her, he opened them, waved at the bed. "As you demanded—Angelica Cynster, thoroughly ravished."

Mirabelle walked toward the bed. He walked beside her, intent on ensuring she didn't touch Angelica—that, he wouldn't stand for.

But Mirabelle halted at the foot of the bed. She looked down at Angelica, who didn't shift an eyelash. Mirabelle's gaze raced over Angelica's lax features, her tangled hair, over the evidence of her ravishment . . . then Mirabelle smiled like a child who'd just unwrapped her most longed-for gift.

She lifted her head and looked at him. He fought not to register what he could see in her face, but if he'd harbored any doubt that his jettisoning all honor had been every bit as important to her as Angelica's ruination, the look in her eyes at that moment would have slain it.

"At *last!*" Her voice rang with something far beyond triumph. "I'll fetch the directions to the goblet—they're in my bedroom."

"Bring them to me in the hall." He wanted her out of this room, away from Angelica, away from him. "I'll wait for you there."

She nodded; after one last glance at Angelica, she walked quickly to the door.

He waited until her footsteps died away, then returned to the door and closed it. Locked it. He turned to see Angelica sitting up, a smile on her face that the glory of the sun breaking through clouds couldn't have competed with.

"We did it!" She kept her voice low, but her excitement was real. Bouncing from the bed, she started to strip off her ruined gown. "Quickly—help me change. I'll go around and into the kitchens, and watch from there. The instant you know where the goblet is, we'll go and fetch it."

Halting before her, he looked down at her for an instant, then he swept her into his arms, lifted her high, and kissed her soundly. Deeply. Inexpressibly gratefully.

"Thank you," he murmured as he set her back on her feet. "From the depths of my heart, forever and always."

She considered him for an instant, then patted his chest. "I could say 'thank you' in reply, but you won't understand. However, you have to admit we make an *excellent* team."

Naked to the waist after having freed her arms from the gown, she wriggled, then sighed. "Now either rip this off me, or undo the laces—choose."

He ripped. She cleaned herself, scrambled into a walking gown she'd left waiting, then together—him in the lead for once with her following—they headed for the great hall to wait for Mirabelle and the directions to the goblet.

Chapter Twenty-one

Dominic sank into his great carver behind the high table, looked out over the empty hall, and told himself it was nearly over. More than five months of plotting, planning, missteps and failures, and now, finally, thanks to his amazing angel, within minutes he would have the goblet in his keeping once more.

And his clan would be safe.

And he would owe it all to her.

And the prospect of spending the rest of his life in thrall to her didn't bother him in the least.

Lips curving, he glanced at the archway that led to the kitchens, saw her peeking out. Smiled at her, saw her smile back.

Knew he was besotted and didn't care.

Angelica all but jigged. Mirabelle had to have reached her rooms by now, and given she herself had taken such pains to show the countess why she shouldn't deny Dominic the goblet, she really didn't believe Mirabelle would resile from handing it—or at least the directions to it—back now.

She told herself she should follow her own advice and possess her soul in patience, but—

A shout, distant and muted by the walls, reached her. She could hear the gentler noises of the castle folk enjoying their afternoon in the bailey, but that shout . . . sounded familiar. A familiar cadence, a familiar ring . . . what was it?

Less than a minute later, a clansman—one of the older crew who mounted guard at the gatehouse—came running into the hall. "My lord! There's a group of Sassenachs at the bridge demanding to see you."

Dominic looked at Angelica, all good humor flown, then pushed back his chair. "I'm coming."

She stared at him as he strode down the hall. A familiar hail . . . turning, she raced through the kitchens and into the gallery circling the great hall—then remembered she couldn't risk running into Mirabelle. Skidding to a halt, she turned and ran for the kitchen door. "Damn them! Did they listen to me? No. And, of course, they've picked their moment—them turning up now is the *last* thing we need!"

Upstairs in her bedroom, Mirabelle stood by the window tying off and snipping threads from the embroidery she'd been working on for the past several weeks. It wasn't finished, but the part Dominic wanted was there. She could have simply told him where the goblet was hidden—any clansman would know the spot—but the embroidery was her final conceit. Embroidery was the one thing at which she'd always excelled; it had seemed appropriate to use the skill to communicate to her son, or to whoever she'd decided to gift the goblet to, where she'd hidden it, her so-useful Damocles's sword.

The last dangling thread fell to the floor. Setting her shears on the windowsill, she straightened the rectangle of fine linen and smiled at the picture she'd created. She was, she realized, happy. She'd finally found the way, seized the goblet, and used it to gain all she'd ever wanted—revenge on her husband, revenge on her son, revenge on Celia Cynster for all the long, wasted years of the mire of empty ugliness her life had become.

Never again would Dominic be able to take the high ground with her. She would never let him live down what he'd done, what he'd traded, to save his precious clan.

Her face relaxing into a long-forgotten expression—a genuinely happy smile—she turned to the door just as it opened.

Her smile grew wider when she saw who'd arrived. "You'll never guess! Dominic brought me Angelica Cynster, but oh, my dear, it gets *much* better than that." She wanted to crow with delight, with triumph.

His lips curving, her lover stepped into the room and shut the door. "I see. It looks like I got here just in time."

She beamed like a girl. "Just in time to share my celebration."

"Indeed." With long, stalking strides, he crossed the room to her side.

Dominic stood on the castle battlements opposite the bridge from the loch's southern shore and studied the eight horsemen who were squinting up at him; six had crowded onto the bridge, while two remained on the shore.

The six on the bridge had halted; any nearer and they would be within pistol range.

Angelica popped up beside him; from behind one of the crenellations, she peeked out.

"I assume that's them."

"Damn it, yes! All *six* of them—both my brothers, and my four older cousins. The other two, the ones hanging back on the shore, are Breckenridge and Jeremy Carling." Turning, putting her back to the high stone, she met his eyes. "If Mirabelle sees them, she'll balk. God knows what she might do." She glanced back at the bridge. "They're going to spoil everything!"

"Can they swim?"

Angelica looked at him. "What?"

"Can all six on the bridge swim?"

She stared, thought, then nodded. "Yes. Why?"

Dominic looked past her. "Ready?"

Swinging around, a little further along the battlements she saw three large men manning a massive lever that connected with a huge, notched wheel.

"Aye, m'lord," the men chorused.

Turning back, she saw Dominic glance at the bridge, then she peeked out again. Her brothers and cousins were still there, talking, scanning the castle, planning . . .

"Now," Dominic ordered.

She swung back to see the three men heave, strain, and slowly push the heavy lever over. Released, the huge wheel started slowly, ponderously, turning.

"What the—!"

Demon's yell had her whirling to look out at the bridge again.

Her jaw dropped. "Oh, my God." The entire surface of the wooden bridge was slowly and smoothly tilting from the horizontal, gently tipping horses and riders into the rippling waters of the loch. Mesmerized, she watched as, unable to turn their horses back to shore, one after another her six closest male relatives were forced to take the plunge into the no doubt very cold water. All slid out of their saddles; bobbing alongside their mounts, they swam a little way to where the shoreline dipped. One after another they emerged, dripping and cursing fit to turn the air about them blue.

She clapped a hand over her mouth, tried to choke back her laughter, felt her eyes tear. "Oh, Lord! They will never, ever, forgive you for that."

Dominic shrugged. "They're in London, I'm up here. I'll survive their displeasure." After one last look, he turned away. "The dip should cool their blood long enough for us to fetch the goblet. My mother and her directions should be in the great hall by now."

Angelica hurried alongside him as he strode along the battlements to the steps leading down to the bailey. They went quickly down and crossed to the keep, tacking through the crowds, thinning now as the keep staff and others returned to their abandoned chores. "Wherever you have to go to fetch the goblet, I'm coming, too."

Looking ahead, he nodded. "Just hang back until I have the directions in my hand. Don't let her see you until then."

She obediently slowed, letting him go up the keep steps before following. Reaching the porch, she hung back outside the doorway until he'd crossed the foyer and stridden into the great hall, then she slid into the shadows edging the foyer—

"*Aa-aahh!*"

The scream brought them both up short. Dominic swung around; eyes locking on her, noting it wasn't her who'd screamed, he strode back into the foyer.

Echoes reverberated off the stone, confusing the direction, but Angelica had heard the original sound. Stunned, she pointed. "Mirabelle's tower. Upstairs."

Dominic ran for the stairwell.

Picking up her skirts, she raced after him. Brenda and Mulley came hurrying along the gallery. Seeing them, Angelica pointed upward, then dashed into the stairwell. As she climbed in Dominic's wake, she could hear awful, hysterical, gulping sobs coming from one of the rooms above.

She followed Dominic and the sounds to Mirabelle's bedroom.

The door had been pushed wide. Elspeth stood to one side of the doorway, hands pressed to her mouth, staring in disbelief at the figure Dominic had crouched beside.

Dark skirts flared over the floor. One hand lay flung out, clutching a crumpled piece of embroidery.

Slowly, Dominic rose. Staring down at his mother, he shook his head. "She's gone." His voice was flat, empty.

Reaching him, Angelica looked at Mirabelle's empurpled face, her tongue protruding, her blue eyes vacant and staring, then she turned and waved Brenda to Elspeth; while the maid folded Elspeth, shocked and starting to shake, into her arms, and drew her away, Angelica gripped Dominic's hand and held on.

After an instant, he gripped her fingers—too hard, but he immediately gentled his hold. "She's gone, and we don't know where the goblet is." He shook his head. "But who killed her—and *why?*"

The embroidery in Mirabelle's hand drew Angelica's eye. She bent, eased the worked linen free of the clutching fingers. Straightening, she smoothed out the piece. Felt her heart catch. "It's a map."

"What?" Dominic glanced at her.

She showed him, turning him from his mother. "See—here. That's the goblet." She tried to orientate the design, but bits of the map hadn't been finished. "Can you tell where it is?"

He took the embroidery, walked to the window, studied it, then turned the fabric—and swore. "It's the cairn by the waterfall. She's hidden it there."

Angelica looked at his mother. "I suppose it'll be safe enough—"

"No, it won't be." Dominic glanced at the woman who had given him birth, then flung the map down and headed for the door. "Whoever killed her wants the goblet—that's why she's dead. Someone else knew she had it—and that someone else now knows where it is, and they also know that the future of Clan Guisachan rides on that goblet."

He met Mulley on the landing. "Take care of this—I'm going after the murderer and the goblet."

"Aye, m'lord."

Dominic went down the stairs three at a time. He heard footsteps behind him. "You can't come," he yelled back at Angelica.

"Don't waste your breath," she yelled back.

He swore again but didn't stop, going straight past the ground level to the lower level and the store room that housed the postern gate. Shoving open the door, he raced across the room—and almost tripped over McAdie.

"Oh, no!" Angelica dropped to her knees beside McAdie.

Dominic crouched on the old man's other side. McAdie had been stabbed twice, both strikes close to the heart, almost certainly ultimately fatal; he lay with his eyes closed, his lips parted. His breathing was labored.

Angelica's hands fluttered around the hilt of the dirk buried in McAdie's chest. "What should we do? Do we pull it out, or . . . ?"

"No. Leave it." Noting the worn crest on the dirk, Dominic clasped one of McAdie's cold hands in one of his.

McAdie's lids fluttered. "Is that you, my lord?"

"Aye. Was it Baine?"

"Aye." McAdie's features fleetingly hardened. "It was Langdon Baine."

"Thank you. I'll see you avenged." Dominic tensed to stand, but McAdie gripped his hand.

"No, wait. Have to tell you." Eyes closed, McAdie moistened his lips. "Baine was my lady's lover—it was he who talked her into stealing the goblet. He said just now that he was going to take it and rid the highlands of the Guisachans once and for all."

"Over my dead body." Dominic's tone was harsh. He gentled his voice. "Rest. The others are coming, but I must go if I'm to catch up with Baine."

McAdie's head moved in an infinitesimal nod; his hand slipped from Dominic's.

"Who's Baine?"

Dominic looked at Angelica. "The laird of a neighboring clan." He rose. "Fetch Griswold, Erskine, or Mrs. Mack for McAdie."

She scrambled to her feet and ran for the door.

Reaching it, she looked back—and saw Dominic disappear through the open postern door.

She swore—not in Gaelic—glanced at McAdie, then raced up the stairs. "Griswold! Erskine. Mrs. Mack!" She knew where Dominic was going; she could spare a minute to get McAdie help.

Dominic raced up the tunnel and straight past the grille Baine had left hanging open. Exploding into the small clearing beyond the tunnel's mouth, looking down as he concentrated on keeping his footing over the rocky ground, his mind already following Baine up the track, he didn't see the men in his path until he mowed into them.

Their presence shocked him more than his appearance had shocked them, but his momentum carried him well into the pack, forcing some of them back, but they didn't get out of his way.

He stopped; so did they. For one fleeting instant, they looked at him, and his brain caught up with who the hell they were—

They threw themselves at him, grappled, caught, and clung. Hands seized; wet bodies slammed into him. He flung them off, struggled to get clear, to get free and on up the path.

Punches were thrown, not by him, but he hardly felt the impacts to his torso, and he avoided the blows to his face. He tripped three of them, almost got away, but the rest flung themselves on him and nearly brought him down.

He had to turn and fight them off.

One on one, even two or three to his one, he might have managed, but eight to one was impossible.

Eventually, two men hanging on each arm, they trapped him, held him, forced him to still; all of them were breathing heavily.

"*What are you doing?*"

They all jumped at the ear-splitting shriek. All turned to look at the point from where the sound had come—the mouth of the tunnel—but Angelica was already streaking across the clearing toward the path to the waterfall.

Two of the men who'd been squaring up to face him turned and gave chase.

One, brown-haired, snagged her arm. "Angelica—"

She abruptly halted and slammed her elbow into his side. "Don't you *Angelica* me!" Her brother doubled over. She wrenched her arm free—and quick as a flash raced on and up the path, avoiding the dark-haired man who'd been circling to cut her off. Not knowing the lie of the land, he ended facing a rock wall and had to turn back.

While Angelica raced on.

"Oh, God." Dominic suddenly realized she was perfectly capable of confronting Baine on her own. "*Angelica*! Don't! Come back!"

The look she flung him as she sprinted up the rising curve of the path plainly told him not to hold his breath. Her brothers and cousins, bewildered and confused, hesitated, not knowing if they should follow—letting her get further ahead.

Dominic cursed, struggled again, but they hadn't loosened their grips.

Just before she would disappear from their sight, Angelica whirled and imperiously pointed at her brothers and cousins. "If you want to protect me, just let him *go* and you'll have done your job!" She paused to see if they would comply. When they didn't, she flung her hands in the air. "*Idiots!*" She turned and raced on.

Dominic stared after her. He'd had no idea she could run that fast . . . realized what waited for her at the end of the path.

Forcing himself to calm, to still, shackling his instincts and his emotions, he glanced at the men around him; a leader himself, he had no difficulty picking out the one who led them.

Pale green eyes flicked his way, curiosity and assessment in the glance.

He caught the man's gaze. "She's racing after the man who just strangled my mother, and stabbed my old steward and left him dying. We can settle this now and lose her, or we can leave this for later and get her back, but you won't find her without me." He paused. "Choose."

The black-haired man—Devil Cynster almost certainly—hesitated, but only for a second. He nodded to the others. "Let him go."

They hesitated, too, but did.

The instant he was free, Dominic charged up the track after Angelica.

The Cynsters followed at his heels.

Chapter Twenty-two

Angelica slowed as she neared the waterfall. The roar of the cascade drowned out her footfalls as she eased around the last curve in the rocky path, then crept the final yards to the ledge.

Regardless, the man kneeling beside the cairn appeared too absorbed to notice; his attention was locked on the stone pyramid, on its rear face. His shoulders were broad, but not as broad as Dominic's, his hair brown and curly. Although it was difficult to judge with him on his knees, he would certainly be much taller than she.

She seriously doubted rational discussion would get her anywhere.

Silently stooping, she picked up a rock, the biggest she could grip and heft. Placing her feet carefully, she inched steadily closer. Stepping onto the ledge, she paused, but she was still well out of the man's line of vision as he scrabbled and pulled rocks from the rear of the cairn. He was wearing a jacket made of sheepskin over breeches and riding boots. What she could see of his face was rough, craggy without being honed.

Unhelpfully, her mind chose that moment to remind her that Mirabelle was—had been—bigger, and possibly, at least in her final desperation, stronger than she was. And this man—Baine—had strangled Mirabelle easily enough.

Baine paused, then, still on his knees, leaned into the alcove, reaching around and into the cairn. "Yes!" Twisting and shifting, he gradually withdrew his arm, along with what he now held in his hand. Sinking back on his ankles, he held up a golden goblet.

Angelica stopped dithering. Raising the rock, she stepped forward and brought it down on Baine's skull.

He reeled.

Dropping the rock and grabbing the goblet with both hands, she wrenched it from his grasp.

He bellowed.

She whirled and ran.

He flung himself at her and caught her hem.

Swinging back, she tugged, yanked, but he didn't lose his grip. The material held as he pressed it to the ground, pinning her, while clumsily, woozily, he got his feet under him, then rose. With the back hem of her skirt crushed in one hand, he pulled her to him.

As he did, his gaze searched her face, then rose to her hair; his puzzled frown evaporated. "You're Dominic's Cynster whore."

She kicked him in the side of the knee, but he shifted at the last second and the blow glanced off his shin.

"Now, now." He seized the moment to let go of her gown and cup his fingers about the bowl of the goblet.

He tried to jerk it from her grasp, but she'd locked the fingers of one hand around the swirling stem. Slapping her other hand over them, she clung with all her might. "No—it's not yours."

"Ah, but it's going to be . . ."

He realized that if she was there, Dominic wouldn't be far behind; she saw the change in his dark eyes, the coalescing of evil. "Let go, you little fool." He raised the goblet as high as he could, shook it like a terrier with a bone.

Chin stubbornly set, she hung on; he wasn't quite strong enough to lift her off her feet.

He glanced aside, at the edge of the ledge, then looked at her. "A pity, but . . ."

Using the goblet, he swung her, dragged her, step by halting step, closer to the edge.

She resisted, pulled back, fought, but he kept far enough away that she couldn't risk trying to kick at him again.

Foot by foot, he drew her on. "Let go."

"No."

"How long do you think your grip will hold once you no longer have rock beneath your feet?" Abruptly, he jerked the goblet.

Caught off guard, she screamed.

She lost her balance and stumbled into him.

Absorbing the impact, he steadied and tensed to rip the goblet from her desperate grasp—

The primal roar that erupted over their heads had them both jerking back.

Dominic leapt from the cliff above the ledge. He'd taken a shortcut over rougher ground, had heard Angelica scream just as he reached the lip, had taken one glance at the figures wrestling below him—without thought for his knee, without any thought at all, he'd leapt.

He landed all but nose to nose with Baine.

Instinctively Baine had released the goblet, released Angelica, to face him.

He was a much bigger threat.

He didn't waste time. He went for Baine's throat.

As Baine went for his.

They wrestled, neither immediately getting a decent grip, one sufficient to throw the other. Even without looking, Dominic knew where Angelica was, knew she'd retreated to the cairn, the goblet clutched in her hands.

The goblet was safe, and so was she.

Leaving him free to turn the full ferocity of his strength on Baine, on avenging McAdie and his mother.

They teetered, each battling to seize that telling instant of supremacy, but they'd always been evenly matched. Even though Dominic had grown taller and had a longer reach, Baine was heavier, more solid, less top-heavy. But Dominic knew balance was his weakness; he guarded against losing it and prayed his knee would hold through it all. Thus far, it had.

Jaws clenched, eyes burning on the other's face, they shifted and swayed, neither willing to give ground, both intent on victory. Either Dominic would kill Baine, or Baine would kill Dominic. This was the end of a fight that had been going on since their teens. Why, Dominic had never understood; Baine was seven years older, and competitively speaking, their paths shouldn't have crossed. But they had, constantly.

Dominic's feet shifted, slid. His back was to the falls; the ledge beneath his boots was wet. The tussle remained inconclusive, but the longer it went, the advantage would slowly tip Dominic's way; stamina-wise, Baine couldn't match him.

Baine knew that, too. Eyes narrowed, he spat, "I should have finished you off when I sent you into that ravine."

The instant of shock—he'd never dreamt that long-ago fall had been anything but an accident—was all Baine needed. Instead of grappling, Baine stepped into Dominic and heaved, pushing him back.

Feeling his shoulders, his balance, tip too far, knowing his feet would slide from under him, Dominic flung himself back—trusting in his instincts, in what they told him lay behind him.

He landed against the upright rock on the waterfall end of the ledge—but he didn't let go of Baine's shoulders. The instant his spine met the solid rock, he swung Baine to the side—off the ledge—and let go.

The rest happened in a heartbeat.

Baine tipped past the point of no recall. On a panicked yell, he released one hand and flailed wildly—then fell.

But he'd left one hand locked in Dominic's coat.

The sudden wrench before Baine's weight ripped his fingers free spun Dominic around—out over the edge.

His feet had no purchase on the wet ledge.

Instinctively he flung his arms around the upright rock.

As his weight swung him out over the void.

On a scream he heard even over the falls' roar, Angelica appeared above him, reaching around and over the rock to curl her small fingers into his coat sleeves.

She'd flung herself against the rock, wrapped herself around it. Anchoring him.

Temporarily.

He dangled a hundred yards above the jagged black rocks on which Baine already lay broken.

Beside him the waterfall thundered past, drenching him, drenching the rock his wet fingers clung to.

His grip on the rock was tenuous. He tensed his fingers, felt several slip. Cursed and forced himself to relax them, to keep at least that much contact.

Searching the cliff to either side of the anchoring rock, he looked for toeholds, but the ledge was undercut. Unable to swipe the wet hair from his face, he hauled in a breath, blinked, squinted, and saw one little outcropping to his left.

His weaker side.

Even as he contemplated it, Angelica jerked. Caught her breath on a sob.

He looked up at her and realized her feet had slid.

She was helping support his weight, and his weight was too great; inch by inch, he would pull her over the rock, until they both fell.

He glanced at the toehold. In an effort that left his shoulders and hips screaming, he managed to lift his left leg without pulling against her and balance the toe of his boot on the protruding rocky knob.

The contact allowed him to brace enough to ease the pull on his arms a fraction.

Even as he did, Angelica slipped again.

Cold certainty rolled over him. There was no way she could hold him, and there was no way he could climb up.

"Angelica . . . angel, you have to let go." He refused to think of what he was saying, clung instead to the reason—the one reason above all else.

Pale, her features tight, she stared down into his face. "No."

He inwardly sighed. "Sweetheart, you can't hold me. If you try to hang onto me, you'll fall, too, and that's madness. Please, let go."

Her chin set in a way he'd grown to delight in but didn't want to see now. "You're not listening. No—I'm not letting you go. Not now, not ever. That's *not* how this is supposed to end."

He didn't know how much longer he had. His fingers were nearly numb. When his grip slipped, he'd fall . . . and take her with him. He dragged in a breath, looked up and met her eyes. "I love you. You are the sun and moon and all life to me. I told you I don't deserve you, and I don't expect you to love me back, but I know you care for me, so please, I beg you, *because* I love you, please let me go." He hesitated, lost in her eyes, then simply said, "I can face death, but I don't want to die knowing I caused your death, too."

"Then you better not fall—and you're not going to die!" She choked, slipped again, then through clenched teeth muttered, "Why are men such fools?"

He clung to calm. He couldn't last long. "Ang—"

"*No!*" The negative was ferocious. She glared at him. "You *dolt*—has it never occurred to you that I love you? Which means I will never, ever, not in a million years let you go?"

Angelica saw his slow blink. Realized that he hadn't, in fact, worked that out. "*Arrgh!*" If she could have, she would have hit him . . . suddenly remembered. "Where are my brothers and cousins?"

His lips twisted. "They were following, but I outstripped them. They're probably lost and well away from here. You can't count on any help—"

She filled her lungs as best she could, tipped her head back, and screamed to the sky, "Rupert!"

Filling her lungs again, she screamed, "Alasdair! *He-e-elp!*"

Her cries echoed back from the mountains all around, then faded into the roar of the falls.

And her body shifted forward again. She looked down, knowing that it was entirely possible that they both would fall and die. Her breasts were flattened against the rock, the front of her gown soaked, her leather-soled shoes wet . . . and only the balls of her feet were still in contact with the ledge.

Face set, Dominic grimly looked up at her. While she kept her fingers locked in his sleeves, he wouldn't try to let go of the rock—would do his best to hang on. She saw him open his lips, but before he could speak, she did. Fiercely. "Don't you *dare* argue! You have to hang on—we have a shared life to live, in case you've forgotten. You promised you would marry me if I helped you get the goblet back, and I have, so you can't renege and leave me a ruined woman."

He looked at her, and she saw the simple, unadorned light of love shining in his eyes. "Angel—"

"*No.*" She wanted to shake her head, but she didn't dare move even that much. "I decided you were mine the instant I saw you in Lady Cavendish's salon—I set out to make you fall in love with me from then, and now I've succeeded I'm not letting you go, not now, not

606 • STEPHANIE LAURENS

ever. As far as I'm concerned, not even death will part us, not yet—not for a very long time."

She heard rock crunch above them.

"Angelica?"

"Down here!"

Seconds later, her brothers and cousins, Breckenridge, and Jeremy were all there. And for the first time in her life, she wasn't going to trust them. She had something far too precious at stake.

"Let go, and we'll haul him up." Gabriel had fastened his hands about her waist, anchoring her.

Confident he—all eight of them—would never let *her* fall, she set her chin and shook her head. "No. I'm not going to let go. You can organize yourselves and pull him up, but I'm not letting go while you do it."

Dead silence followed that pronouncement. None of them were slow; they could follow her reasoning.

It was Devil, standing beside the rock, who, after exchanging glances with the others, looked at her, then exhaled through his teeth. "All right."

The organizing wasn't a simple matter. Dominic weighed more than any of them, and with the ledge so slippery they couldn't risk just having one man pulling on each of his arms. In the end, Devil was anchored by Richard and Lucifer, and Vane by Demon and Gabriel. Breckenridge and Jeremy held on to her while Devil and Vane, one on either side of the rock, leaned over and reached around until they each grasped one of Dominic's wrists. Slowly, they straightened, inch by inch drawing Dominic up until they stood upright and his chest was level with the edge. Once all of them were steady, braced, and ready, on a count of three, they all shifted first one, then two, then three paces along the ledge, away from the rock and the falls, to where the edge was clear and they could pull Dominic the rest of the way up and onto it.

With his feet finally on solid ground, Dominic drew in a huge breath, then nodded to the men who had saved them. "My thanks—"

Angelica flung herself at him, slapped her hands to his cheeks, hauled his head down, and kissed him.

Hard. Long. Deep.

He closed his arms about her and she all but wrapped herself about him—in full view of her brothers, cousins, and future brothers-in-law.

His head started to spin.

She finally pulled back, broke the kiss—then pushed out of his arms, drew back her small fist, and thumped him in the center of his chest. "What *is* this fascination you have with falling off cliffs?"

Puzzled, he rubbed at the spot. "I don't have any fascination—"

"Was that"—flinging out an arm, eyes blazing, she pointed at the sheer drop past the edge of the ledge—"or was that not the second . . . no, wait! What did Baine say—he pushed you off a cliff years ago, didn't he?"

"That was a ravine."

"Don't *quibble*. It was a cliff—another cliff. Which makes this the *third* cliff you've fallen off!"

Her voice was rising. Conscious of their audience, he tried to calm her. "This is Scotland. There are a lot of cliffs."

"But you don't have to make a habit of falling off them!" She pointed at the edge again. "That was the second time in as many months!"

Her voice quavered. If he suggested she was getting hysterical . . . she might cry. And that would be worse. Infinitely worse. So he nodded. "All right. I'll stay away from cliffs for the foreseeable future." He heard a muffled guffaw from further along the ledge, but he kept his gaze on her over-bright eyes. Arched his brows. "All right?"

She glared at him, but then lifted her chin and nodded. "Yes. Good. See that you do."

With that, she stepped closer. He put an arm around her and she leaned against him, resting her head on his chest.

Over her head, he looked steadily at the eight large men filling the other end of the ledge.

They looked back at him, then Devil Cynster turned away and stepped off the ledge onto the path leading down. One by one the others followed, some—most—with smiles he wasn't sure he understood curving their lips, until there were only her brothers left.

The black-haired one, Lucifer Cynster, continued to measure him for a moment more, but then Angelica shifted and looked at the pair; after a second of studying her, Lucifer's lips kicked up and he, too, turned away.

Leaving Gabriel staring, face impassive, at his youngest sister.

Angelica narrowed her eyes at her most protective brother in clear and unequivocal warning.

After a moment, Gabriel shifted. He lifted his gaze to Dominic's face, then shook his head. "She's all yours. Enjoy in good health."

As Gabriel turned away, Dominic murmured for her ears alone, "I intend to do just that."

Angelica looked up at him and smiled. Brilliantly. What had happened—*all* they'd won—was only just sinking in . . . she remembered and looked round. "Where's the goblet?"

They both looked toward the cairn. "There it is." She walked over and picked up the golden cup from where she'd dropped it when she'd rushed to help Dominic. Dusting it off, she carried it back to him. Halting beside him, she examined the round jewels set circling the bowl, the swirl of the stem, the finely etched interior, then she presented it to him.

He smiled, lifted it from her hands, then, one arm sliding around her, ushered her along the ledge, and they set off in her brothers' wake.

Lucifer glanced back, then predictably halted and waited until they reached him. He nodded at the goblet. "What's that?"

Dominic hesitated, but he knew of Lucifer Cynster's reputation. He handed the goblet over. "It's the Coronation Cup of the Scottish Regalia. It's what this saga has been all about."

"It is?" Walking beside them, Lucifer examined the cup. "How so?"

Dominic waved at the others walking ahead. "Let's get back to the castle, and we can tell you all there."

Handing back the goblet, Lucifer shivered. "I won't say no to a hot bath and dry clothes." He grinned at Dominic. "At least when we borrow your clothes, they won't be too small."

Dominic smiled.

Devil, Vane, and Richard were standing in a group a little way along. Devil pointed off the track as they reached them. "I assume that's the murderer you went after?"

Through a veil of roiling spume, they could just make out the body of Langdon Baine, sprawled face up on the jagged black rocks at the base of the falls. Dominic nodded. "That's him."

"He got to the goblet first—it was hidden in the cairn—and when I grabbed it he tried to throw me off the edge." Angelica glanced up at Dominic. "Dominic got there just in time."

Devil nodded. "We saw that part, but we got lost finding our way up." He looked at Dominic. "Who was he?"

"Langdon Baine. He's—he was—laird of Clan Baine. They hold the lands to the south of ours." Dominic nodded at the hills on the opposite side of the valley in which the castle stood. "Their lands are on the other side of the ridge, high and not particularly fertile."

"What did he have against you?" Vane asked.

"I don't know, but I suspect"—Dominic raised the goblet, considered it—"that it was more in the nature of an undeclared clan feud. He apparently wanted to wipe all Guisachans from the highlands."

Gabriel eyed the goblet. "And stealing that would have done it?"

"It would." Dominic caught Gabriel's eye. "I'll explain later."

He glanced back at the distant body, then they all turned and walked on.

Angelica caught his eye, arched a brow.

"I'll send a party from the castle to fetch his remains and take them to Baine Hall."

She nodded, then thought of the other bodies that waited for them in the keep, and sobered.

Bringing up the rear of their procession, they walked home in silence.

Home.

As they rounded the ridge and the castle came into view, rising majestically above the loch, surrounded by its forests, set within its mountains, she felt her heart swell, and marveled. She'd only been there for a few days, yet it was already home in her mind. Curious . . . but perhaps not surprising. She glanced at Dominic. It was the place he called home, the one place on earth where he truly belonged. And she, and her heart, now and forever, belonged with him. With his.

Looking down at the goblet, he paused, then handed it to her. "You get to carry it in." Putting it into her hands, he raised his gaze to her eyes. "Without you, I wouldn't have succeeded in reclaiming it."

She smiled and they walked on, with her cradling the goblet in her hands. "You might also say that without it—without your father pledging it, without your mother stealing it, without you seeking to reclaim it—you would never have found and claimed me."

Looking up, she met his eyes, saw the emotion she'd seen so clearly above the falls still softly shining in the cloudy green.

Reaching up, Dominic took one of her hands from the goblet and twined his fingers with hers. "Often in my life, I've seen the signs, read the trails, enough to know fate moves in mysterious ways . . . and she always has her own agenda."

Angelica laughed, a musical sound that echoed off the hills and filled his heart.

Smiling, he drew her on. As they walked down the slope to the postern gate, he dared to believe that, at last, fate had finally finished with him.

Explanations had to wait. The instant they stepped into the store room, curious Cynsters at their backs, there were decisions to be made, orders to be given, arrangements, and all manner of organization to be attended to.

However, by general consensus the first matter to be dealt with was the goblet. With her male relatives looking on, Angelica found herself by Dominic's side on the porch of the keep, holding up the goblet to the cheering clan.

Dominic looked down at her, then stepped back and closed his hands about her waist. "Here." He hoisted her up and sat her on his shoulder.

She laughed and raised the goblet even higher—and the clan roared its approval.

Later, they retreated to the great hall. Food and warming drinks were served while guest rooms were made ready and hot water was heated. Dominic sent Jessup and his grooms out through the postern gate and around the lake to collect the others' horses, then, with the Cynsters, Breckenridge, and Jeremy all trailing at his heels, went to oversee the resetting of the bridge so the horses could be brought to the castle.

Although curious herself, Angelica let them go and went instead to see Elspeth, who had recovered enough to demand to be allowed to help Brenda lay out the countess, then she checked with Mulley and John Erskine as to the likely funeral arrangements for Dominic's mother and McAdie. The old man had hung on long enough to hear the cheers from the courtyard. "After that," Mulley said, "he just smiled and let go. Reckon he's at peace now."

The next hours went in sorting out her relatives, each of whom, being so very male, insisted that she, courtesy of the falls every bit as damp as they were and a fragile female to boot, had the first of the hot water.

She wondered if they'd actually thought she would argue. Warm again, her hair dried, brushed, and arranged, satisfyingly garbed in one of her new teal silk gowns, she bustled about what she now thought of as her keep, and organized them.

At one point, she met Gabriel, Lucifer, Devil, and Vane in the upstairs gallery outside the rooms they'd been given; they'd been talking, but fell silent as she swept up to them. Halting before them, she studied each of their faces, then drew breath and simply said, "Thank you. If you hadn't been bull-headed enough to come racing up here . . ." Just thinking about what she'd nearly lost had emotion clogging her throat. Blinking, she waved a hand.

They all looked faintly horrified.

Gabriel reached out and hauled her into a hug. "If you want to thank us, for God's sake don't cry. Save that for him."

She sniffed. "All right." She jabbed his arm and he released her. "Just don't think I approve of *why* you came, but I am very grateful that you did."

She kissed each lean cheek, then left them shaking their heads, bemused and confused as ever.

Then dinner was upon them. The boys and the dogs had returned from their day's outing with Scanlon and his crew, with a buck for the kitchens and the story of the hunt on their lips. Discovering a host of men all very like their cousin suddenly in residence, and swiftly ascertaining that all those men—just like their cousin—were willing to engage with and humor young boys, Gavin and Bryce didn't know to whom to appeal first for information, and stories, and tales of life.

The dogs circled, then collapsed around Dominic's and Angelica's chairs. On walking up to the dais, Angelica hesitated, then looked at Dominic, waiting by his carver; realizing he wasn't going to push her either way, she thought, then moved to the chair on his right—the one his countess should take. He smiled and seated her, then waved Devil to the chair on his left. Gavin and Bryce, immensely proud, were invited to chairs at the high table, Gavin, as master, seated on Devil's left, with Lucifer taking the next chair along, while Bryce shyly slipped into the chair alongside Angelica. Gabriel smiled at him as he took the next chair along. The other Cynsters, with Breckenridge and Jeremy, were accommodated at tables in the body of the hall.

The meal passed in near-riotous good humor.

Looking out over the hall, Dominic registered how long it had been since his people had been not just this relieved, this free of care, but this free to be unrestrainedly happy. It was as if sunshine had suddenly slashed through clouds and bathed Clan Guisachan in warmth and light, and in all the emotions—joy, peace, and hope—that lifted hearts and set them winging.

He glanced at the woman beside him—his twenty-one-year-old angel who had stood by his side and met every challenge fate had thrown their way. He'd thought of her as his savior-cum-bride-to-be, and she had been, still was, and surely would be.

She was speaking with Bryce and Gabriel. Reaching out, Dominic closed his hand over hers, gently squeezed. Without turning to him, she shifted her fingers and squeezed back, then left her hand in his. He smiled, sat back, looked out over his clan, and quietly gloried.

At the end of the meal, they retreated to the library—Dominic, Angelica, her relatives, plus the boys and the dogs—and they finally embarked on the necessary explanations. The first revelation, however, had nothing to do with them or their adventure; when Dominic handed around cut-crystal glasses of the clan's whisky, an appreciative silence rolled over the room.

The other men sipped, paused, then slowly, reverently, sipped again.

Eventually, holding his glass to the light, examining the richly honey-hued liquid, Devil quietly asked, "Where does this come from?"

Glass in hand, Dominic dropped into an armchair flanking the huge fireplace. "The clan's distillery near the head of the loch."

The other men exchanged glances, then Devil clarified, "You own the distillery that makes this?"

"Me—the clan."

"Hmm." Devil sipped again, then murmured, "I have to admit that there's a great deal the males of the family, at least, would forgive for such a drop." Of course, he and the others had already seen enough of Dominic Lachlan Guisachan to know they'd be welcoming him into the fold with open arms and a certain relief. They'd been stuck on the track, helpless to do anything but watch as Angelica—having with her usual stubborn deliberation rushed directly into the jaws of danger—had come within a whisker of being flung to her death off the cliff. Dominic had raced far ahead, but to reach her in time he had to have made a superhuman effort—but he had, and he'd saved her. And her attitude toward him later had, for Devil and all the rest, set the seal on their approval. Henceforth, the bossiest, most stubborn, far-too-intelligent-for-her-own-good firebrand of the family was *his* responsibility. "Very well." Reluctantly drawing his senses from their preoccupation, Devil looked at their host. "So where does this tale begin?"

Dominic told them, explaining the background to their adventure much as he had to Angelica that first night. Given his pending connection to her family, and theirs to his, there seemed little point in over-observance of any social niceties. When they questioned, he answered, but in large part they followed his reasons without difficulty or dispute.

Before they got halfway through, the boys were asleep. Angelica slipped away and summoned Mulley and Erskine to carry the boys to their beds; with sleepy, mumbled "G'nights," they went.

As the story of successive months unfolded, first Breckenridge and Richard, and later Jeremy Carling, helped Dominic fill the narrative to the point where he'd traveled to London, kidnapping Angelica his goal.

"One question," Devil said, fingers now steepled before his face. "Why didn't you just ask us—the family—for help?"

Dominic met his gaze. "If I had knocked on your, or Lord Martin's, door, and asked to be trusted with either Heather, Eliza, or Angelica, in order to pretend to kidnap her, take her into the highlands, and pretend to ruin her so that I could convince my mother, who wanted revenge on Lady Celia for being my father's obsession, to return the long-lost Scottish coronation cup to me, because if I didn't have it to hand over to a coterie of London bankers on the first of July, I would lose my estates and my clan would be ruined . . . what would you have said?"

Devil held his gaze levelly, then winced. "I see your point." He waved. "Pray continue."

Dominic, now aided by Angelica, did, relating how he'd removed her from Lady Cavendish's salon and taken her to Bury Street.

At that point, Gabriel and Vane joined in, interspersing Dominic and Angelica's actions with reports of how the family had reacted, and how ultimately their great-aunt had solved the riddle of just who Viscount Debenham was. But once they reached the highlands, the tale was Dominic's and Angelica's to tell, and while they recounted all the salient points, there were others they left untold.

When it came to what they'd had to do to convince Mirabelle to hand over the goblet, Angelica merely stated that after several days of being exposed to her superb histrionic skills, Mirabelle had deemed her sufficiently ruined and agreed to hand over the goblet's directions, at which point Langdon Baine's role in the entire plot had come to light.

They discussed Baine and his earlier attempt on Dominic's life, and his likely motives, then moved on to the story of the goblet itself.

Lucifer was fascinated, and so, too, was Gabriel. "If you're agreeable, I'd like to see that contract with the bankers—I've never heard of such a thing, at least not couched in such a way. I'd love to study its structure for future reference."

Dominic agreed.

Demon, having at Dominic's invitation circled the room with the decanter, settled back in his chair. "Having heard so much about that huge horse of yours, I took a look in your stables. Your stableman showed him off to me—incidentally, that's a nice part-Arab filly you have there, too. But I was wondering if you have any other horses of Hercules's line?"

Dominic hesitated, then admitted, "I've managed to locate two mares." When Demon gave an excellent imitation of one of the boys expecting a treat, Dominic grinned. "They're not at the castle but on one of the farms. I'll show you them tomorrow."

Demon grinned back and toasted him. "Excellent."

Jeremy was already scouting the shelves. Breckenridge and Vane wanted to know about the crops and the herds. Richard asked about the hunting, which subject snared all attention for some time.

Smiling, Devil sat back and let the others do all the necessary interrogating, even though he, and they, too, had already made up their collective mind. While they couldn't openly approve of Dominic's plan to reclaim the goblet, had they been in his shoes, every one of them would almost certainly have done the same, and if they were truthful, they might not have been able to pull it off—finding the way forward through so many twists and turns while walking the fine line between honor and dishonor—as well as Dominic had. They might not understand clan, but every man there understood family, and that sometimes one had to bend the rules to pull everyone through to the other side unscathed. If that's what was needed, then that's what one did; they couldn't hold what he'd done against him. And wouldn't.

Sipping again, savoring the smooth, malty taste, Devil listened to the others, to Dominic and Angelica, watched the pair as they reacted to each other, and let his smile deepen. In "kidnapping" Angelica, Dominic Lachlan Guisachan had made his own bed, and the entire family, Devil judged, would be far too pleased with the outcome to do anything other than help him lie in it.

Finally, they came to considering the days ahead and making the necessary plans.

Angelica suggested, and her brothers and the others readily agreed, that they should remain at the castle for at least the next day before setting out to ride back to London.

Perched on the arm of the chair in which Dominic was sitting, she glanced at him. "We'll need to remain here for the funerals. Mulley said they'll be held three days from today."

His expression impassive, Dominic nodded. "If we leave the day after, we'll still have plenty of time to reach London by the last day of the month. I'll send word to the bankers to set up our meeting for the morning of the first."

"And we'll take your traveling coach from Edinburgh—*not* the mail." When Dominic's lips eased and he inclined his head, she informed him, "We'll need the larger coach because we'll have the boys as well."

His eyes grew wary. "We're taking them with us?"

"Of course. They need to meet the family."

Richard sighed. "Before I left home, I was informed that after whatever transpired here was settled, I was to ride back to the Vale, and then together with my witchy wife, I was to travel to London—with the twins." He looked at Angelica, arched his brows. "She said you would know why."

She looked around the circle, saw the same inquiry in most faces. "Well of course there'll be a family dinner, probably on the evening after we reach town. And then, after Dominic hands over the goblet to the bankers, on the evening of the first of July"—she looked at him—"Mama and Papa, and Honoria, of course, will be hosting our engagement ball."

Dominic looked into her eyes, then raised his glass to veil his reaction.

Eyes narrowing, Breckenridge pointed at Dominic. "You just sprung that on him." He looked at Angelica. "Doesn't he have any say?"

Angelica retorted, "He's already had his say. It's my decision as to when and where."

"But . . ." Jeremy frowned. "Surely there's no reason for it all to happen so fast?"

"But of course there is." Angelica frowned back. "First, everyone will be ready to quit town by the end of June—they'll stay because of the ball, but not for longer. If it were held later, having everyone travel back for one major ball would be inconsiderate, not that everyone wouldn't come, but that's just not how things are done. Then there's the summer celebration in August at Somersham, and we all go to that. Then in September, in case you've all forgotten, the family has three weddings, all of which need to be organized between now and then."

They all blinked; all looked a trifle stunned.

Several mouths opened, then shut.

She humphed. "Indeed. You know perfectly well that engagements and weddings are the province of the females of the family, and you can—" She broke off when Devil held up a staying hand.

Then he reversed his palm, waved like a conductor, and he and all the others chorused, "Leave it to you and our wives."

Breckenridge and Jeremy had said "wives-to-be."

Angelica smiled. "Precisely."

Gabriel looked at Dominic. "Welcome to the family."

Dominic drained his glass.

Later, when night had fallen and the keep had grown silent, Angelica lay in the big bed in the bedroom at the top of the east tower and watched her very own highland laird undress in the silvery moonlight—a sight she doubted she would ever grow tired of, not if she lived to be ninety.

The windows on both sides of the room were uncurtained; she'd opened the casements on both sides and discovered that the breeze that then blew through carried the heady scents of the roses blooming in the rose garden circling the tower's base.

Finally naked, Dominic turned and walked toward the bed, his stride fluid and graceful, and the moon paid homage, gilding his broad shoulders, skating over the broad muscles of his chest, rippling over his abdomen, and glinting off the dark hair adorning his magnificent body.

Lifting the covers, he sank into the bed alongside her; she let the dip in the mattress roll her toward him. Propping on one arm, he slid the other around her, gathering her close.

Placing a hand on his chest, she stopped him before he kissed her and all chance of conversation fled. "Your knee. I wondered if you'd injured it again when you leapt down to the ledge, but you haven't been limping."

Eyes devouring her face, he shook his head. "No. I thought it would jar again, but it didn't. It feels stronger than ever—well, at least since I fell into that ravine years ago."

She smiled. "Good." She had a reason for asking, something she was planning, but it wasn't yet time to tell him about that.

"I take it that you announcing to your relatives the date for our engagement ball means you have, finally, agreed to marry me."

"I can guarantee you'll be entirely safe in assuming that to be the case."

"Thank heaven for that."

"You never seriously thought I wouldn't agree."

"No, but I did wonder what your price would be."

She hesitated, then told him, "You paid it today. Abundantly, extravagantly, in more ways than one."

He continued to watch her, as if waiting for elaboration. She looked into his eyes, and even though his face was in shadow she could still feel the emotion investing, infusing, the gray-green. Quietly marveling, lifting her hand, she traced her fingertips down one lean cheek. "You would willingly have died to spare me today."

He turned his head, pressed a slow, heated kiss to her palm. "And I will die for you tomorrow if that's what fate demands." His lips quirked. "But you won't let me."

"Not today and not tomorrow. You're mine, and I have no plans to surrender you, not to fate or any other authority."

His lips curved. "I thought that was my line."

"It can be ours—I'm willing to share."

"So am I." He gazed into her eyes. "Forever and always, all I have, all I am, is yours, angel."

"And I'll be yours, and you'll be mine, to the end of our days."

He bent his head and she drew him down and their lips met in a slow, achingly tender caress.

In the silvery moonlight, with the scent of roses wreathing about them, they revisited all they were, all they'd already found and claimed, and boldly, brazenly, beyond joyously, set out to claim it again.

Confidently they reached out, and together touched love and made it theirs again. Drew it in, wrapped it about them, held it to their hearts again.

Drank it in and rejoiced, reacquainting themselves with each other's bodies in slow reverence and exquisite harmony.

With unwavering commitment, they reaffirmed their faith in all that had grown between them, in their togetherness, their closeness, their soul-stealing intimacy.

Their celebration was simple, but unrestrained. They had won all their hearts had ever desired, yet both knew their most stunning victory hadn't been on the physical plane.

They'd both needed and had sought, and had ultimately been rewarded with the greatest prize in heaven or on earth.

They loved.

Loved, worshipped, and strove until they reached that pinnacle where love itself, pure and sharp, shone like the sun.

And its beauty shattered them.

Broke them, fused them, forged and remade them.

Two bodies joined. Two hearts beating as one. Two souls in perfect communion.

Then the grace of love swept over them and filled them, settling to lie in the moonlit night the gentlest of benedictions upon them.

Sinking back to the bed, settling in each other's arms, they reached for love and held it close.

They had made love theirs, let it thrive in their hearts, acknowledged and accepted. They had ceded love free reign, of their hearts, their bodies, their souls, and through that act had been gifted with its shining truth: Love won and embraced was the ultimate joy, and the ultimate triumph.

Chapter Twenty-three

Three days later, Angelica stood beside Dominic in the tiny graveyard of the local kirk in the nearby hamlet of Cougie and watched three coffins lowered into three graves.

The new laird of Clan Baine, Langdon Baine's much younger brother Hugh, had arrived at the castle the day after the deaths. He'd been under no illusions as to his older brother's infamy. "He got it from some of the elders who'd always resented Clan Guisachan's better lands and greater wealth, and used to preach the old ways, saying we should simply take what we wanted." Hugh had shaken his head. "Even when those elders passed on, Langdon wouldn't listen to reason."

Hugh had thanked Dominic for sending his brother's body home. For his part, Dominic had offered to aid

Clan Baine should they require it, and Hugh, in particular, in taking up his unexpected lairdship.

They'd parted as neighbors resolved to the common good.

As part of that joint aim, they'd agreed to hold a combined church service, by mutual accord attributing the three deaths to an unfortunate pact between unstable personalities, thus, they hoped, limiting the scope for any further feuding.

Mirabelle, Countess of Glencrae, was buried first, in a plot beside her husband's stone-encased grave. The congregation then shifted to the Baine section, where Langdon was laid to rest, then everyone moved back to the Guisachan area to watch McAdie's coffin lowered into the ground.

His burial elicited the most tears.

Angelica stood beside Dominic and the local reverend, with Hugh and his young wife on the minister's other side, and thanked those who had attended, mostly locals, but a few from the surrounding glens and clans. That she was to be Dominic's wife seemed understood by everyone; she was deferred to as if she were already his countess. She had half expected her brothers to try to convince her to return to London with them, but although Gabriel had voiced the idea, he hadn't pressed, having by then grasped the reality of her position within the clan, and that it was more important to her and to others that she be there by Dominic's side.

She and Dominic were the last of Clan Guisachan to remount and ride back to the castle.

Dominic let Hercules set an easy pace along the narrow lanes, but when they reached the turnoff to the castle, he checked the big chestnut and glanced at Angelica, managing a dancing Ebony alongside. He met her eyes. "Let's go for a ride."

She grinned. "Lead on."

Hercules surged. With a laugh, she gave chase.

Dominic led her at an easy pace off the track and onto a long stretch of sward—then he let Hercules have his head. The big chestnut thundered down the familiar straight, then veered around to continue along the edge of the loch. Ebony flew alongside, black legs flashing, mane whipping back. Angelica let out a joyful halloo.

Pushing Hercules on, feeling the rhythm of the heavy hooves find an echo in his blood, Dominic rode hard for the end of the cleared shore, only at the last slowing the big horse. He sent Hercules into a wide turn, breathing deep and exhaling, feeling more alive, more free, than he had in years.

Angelica pulled Ebony up a little earlier, then walked the black filly until Ebony's shoulder bumped Hercules's.

She studied Dominic's face, then, reaching up, laid a hand against his lean cheek, looked into his stormy eyes, then drew his face to hers and kissed him, but lightly.

When she drew back, he stopped her, held her within one arm and touched his forehead to hers. "I can barely believe it's all over."

She smiled as he released her. "Let's go home."

They cantered back side by side through the glow of the summer morning, through the mild sunshine and the scents of the forests. As the castle rose before them, the stone softened by the golden light, the rich tapestry of the forests' greens and browns spread like a cloak to either side, the flashing waters of the loch adding movement to the scene, she looked, heard, sensed . . . and felt in her heart that peace, gentle and abiding, had returned, creeping slowly over the mountains, rolling over the trees and the loch, to settle over the castle and spread through the glen.

They may have reached an end, but inherent in it was another beginning—the start of their own story, the beginning of their shared tale.

Dominic glanced at her. When she looked his way, he arched a brow. "A guinea for your thoughts."

She smiled. "I was just thinking that these last months were in essence the epilogue of your father's life." She met his eyes. "And the prologue of ours."

He held her gaze for a moment, then nodded. "And from here on, the rest of this tale is ours."

"Ours to create—ours to live."

"Ours to enjoy."

She smiled and rode beside him over the drawbridge, into his castle, and on to the keep.

The afternoon continued with the same sense of new-found freedom, of new directions, and their first steps along their now joint road.

In midafternoon, Dominic and the boys found Angelica in the gallery and persuaded her to allow them to kidnap her again—this time for a long ramble through the wilderness to the west of the castle.

As she walked beside Dominic, her hand locked in his, she watched the boys range ahead, along with the three dogs. Nudge had apparently adopted Angelica as her person, circling back frequently to bump her along, before padding away to rejoin the boys and the other two dogs.

When they'd first arrived at the kirk that morning, Dominic had detoured to stand before a double grave by the wall in the Guisachan section. She'd gone with him, had stood beside him, and had read the inscription. "The boys' parents?"

He'd nodded. "Krista was swept away in a flood. Mitchell tried to save her, but was badly injured himself. He died a week later from his injuries. I swore I'd look after the boys as my own."

She'd merely nodded, but later, while Dominic had been talking with others before the church, she'd slipped back to the grave, stood at its foot for some time, then quietly made a vow of her own: *I will care for all three of them as my own. You can rest easy now, and leave them to me.*

As she walked through the dappled sunshine, the words of that vow echoed in her mind.

Eventually they reached the western tip of the island. She and Dominic sat on the raised bank and watched the boys and the dogs cavort in the shallows. The boys threw sticks into the water and the dogs dived in, retrieving and returning them, then shaking the water from their thick, curly pelts to shrieks of delight from Gavin and Bryce, who were soon nearly as damp as the dogs.

The sun was westering, still warm and golden, turning the summer air hazy.

"Stag," Dominic suddenly said. Both boys froze and looked expectantly at him. To Angelica, he whispered, "Don't move." Then he slowly raised a hand and pointed at the shore to their right.

Following the direction, Angelica saw the proud head and a massive set of antlers rise as the stag lifted its muzzle from the waters. Surrounded by thick forest, it looked across at them, at the dogs still milling about the boys, then looked at Dominic and Angelica, studied them for a long moment, then the beast turned, and with a rustle, was gone.

"Oh." She sighed. "He was magnificent."

Dominic glanced at her, smiled. Arms draped over his raised knees, he looked back at the boys. "I've hunted him for years. He knows me. I've had him in my sights countless times, but never taken the shot. He knows he's safe in our lands now."

Angelica leaned her head against his shoulder. The stag had reminded her of him. The animal had the same regal but wild beauty—visceral, powerful, untamed, and just a little dangerous. Her hero was a true son of the highlands.

Sitting beside him, she watched the boys, laughed at their antics as the sun slowly sank.

As the shadows lengthened, she breathed deeply in, felt her heart, her very soul expand, and knew she'd found her rightful place.

Fate and The Lady had brought her a long way, far from her birthplace, far from London and the life she'd known.

They'd brought her here—because here, with him, with his people and the boys . . . this was where she belonged.

Seven days later, Dominic followed Angelica into the front hall of Lord Martin Cynster's house in Dover Street.

As Dominic waited beside Angelica while the butler closed the door, he was conscious of nerves the likes of which he hadn't felt since his school days, and it wasn't the prospect of meeting her father that was to blame.

He and Angelica, along with the same five staff who had accompanied him to London earlier, plus several others and the boys, had arrived in town the evening before. Angelica had made no bones about her intention to reside with him in Bury Street; he'd shared her bed in the countess's suite last night.

That morning, while she'd set about transforming his house, he'd slipped away and called on her father. Lord Martin, primed no doubt by Gabriel, Lucifer, and most likely Devil, had been severe at first, but civil, and finally understanding, welcoming, and even congratulatory. The bottle of the clan's finest old malt Dominic had brought as a peace offering had set the seal on what he hoped would be a lasting accord with his soon-to-be father-in-law. Cynsters, he'd realized, were partial to good whisky.

So as the butler ushered them into a long drawing room, he wasn't feeling nervous about meeting any of the males. Following Angelica into the room, he swiftly took stock of the company.

Gabriel was there, smiling, a tall brown-haired lady, presumably his wife, Alathea, beside him. Lucifer stood beside her, a slighter, dark-haired lady, his wife, Phyllida, by his side; Angelica had provided the names and descriptions.

The lady standing beside Devil Cynster, his wife, Honoria, looked exactly as Dominic had pictured her—a duchess to her toes. Breckenridge was there with Heather on his arm, alongside Jeremy and Eliza.

The latter two ladies Dominic knew by sight, but neither had seen him other than at a distance. Both unabashedly surveyed him, then their gazes flicked to Angelica and they grinned. He didn't want to know what was going through their minds.

The last lady in the room was seated in an armchair to one side of the fireplace, but because of the arrangement of people, he couldn't get any clear view of her.

Gabriel was closest; Angelica stopped before her older brother, stretched up and kissed his cheek, then touched cheeks with Alathea before introducing Dominic.

Taking the hand Alathea offered, Dominic bowed over it and murmured a greeting. Straightening, he met a pair of shrewd hazel eyes; after a finite pause, those eyes twinkled and Alathea smiled.

"Welcome, my lord. I believe you'll do very well in this family."

"Dominic, please." He returned the smile with a semblance of charm, but his mind had fixed on the lady in the armchair.

But before he reached her, faced her, he had to run the gauntlet of introductions—to Phyllida, who smilingly bade him welcome and asked after his wards, to Honoria, Duchess of St. Ives, who considered him, then deigned to smile and welcome him to "our clan."

While Heather and Eliza were curious, and he found them charming and engaging, he left them feeling—as Angelica had told him—that in deciding the outcome of each of his attempts to kidnap one of Celia's daughters, fate had successfully served all their best interests.

Finally, Angelica drew him past Breckenridge and Jeremy to the lady in the armchair. Martin stood beside the chair; as Angelica with Dominic in tow approached, the lady rose to stand beside her husband.

Celia Cynster, Dominic judged, was a quiet matriarch, one of those strong women who by her natural demeanor seemed less forceful . . . but Angelica's spine of tempered steel hadn't come from her father.

Barely taller than Angelica, with graying hair that once must have been a similar if less intense shade as that of her youngest daughter, Celia stood rigidly upright, her chin tipped high—while her eyes devoured his face.

He halted before her and waited for her verdict. For her censure, her repudiation, if she so decreed.

Angelica sensed his tension. Beside him, she looked from him to her mother and back again.

Martin stepped in and performed the introductions. Both Celia and Dominic responded by rote, but when he would have released her hand, Celia gripped his. With her free hand, she waved the other two away. To him, she simply said, "Walk with me."

He very correctly offered her his arm. She laid her hand on his sleeve and together they walked down the long room to the alcove of a bow window.

There, Celia stopped and faced him. Closely studied his face. "You don't look anything like your father, yet I can see something of him in you."

He suppressed a grimace. "My eyes."

She looked again, then nodded. "Yes, but yours are . . . less simple. More complex." Her gaze again roved his face. "Do you take after your mother, then?"

"No. Or at least she didn't think so. Only the color of my hair." After a moment, he added, seeing she seemed so intent, "I'm said to be the image of my great-grandfather—my father's father's father—except for having black hair."

Her fingers still touching his sleeve, Celia drew back, head tipping in a gesture she'd passed on to her youngest daughter, lips slightly pursing—he recognized that, too. After a long moment of intense scrutiny, during which he had to force himself not to fidget, she said, "From all I've heard, and all I can see, you're not in the least like your father—and certainly not like your mother, either. I suspect you're a throwback to an earlier age, your great-grandfather's possibly, to the days when clan chiefs ruled with wills of iron and performed great feats . . ." Her lips slowly curved. "And if you're marrying Angelica, you'll need to be able to do both."

Stepping nearer, stretching up on her toes, she drew his head down and kissed his cheek. "Welcome to the family, dear—I do hope you don't find us too overwhelming. Just hold on to Angelica if you do—she'll see you through."

He blinked. Remained stock-still when she would have turned him back into the room. When she arched a brow at him, he said, "You don't . . . mind?"

"Not a bit of it." Gripping his sleeve, she turned him around and started them back toward the others. "I trained my girls well—Angelica would never have let you within arm's reach if you hadn't been a worthy man. And if you're thinking I might feel awkward about the past—and I can see how you might—then as it's very nearly time to go in to dinner, while we dine, I'll tell you and the rest of the company, too, the story they've never heard." She met his eyes. "Your father was a good, kind, possibly weak man, but he was never other than a gentleman to me."

She looked ahead, then halted.

Dominic, perforce, halted, too.

After a moment of studying the group directly ahead of them—Heather and Breckenridge, Eliza and Jeremy, and Angelica, who was looking their way—Celia blew out a breath. "And to be perfectly blunt, while I abhor your mother's actions, if out of all the machinations I gain my dearest wish to see all three of my girls happily and suitably wed, then I really cannot find it in me to complain."

Angelica quit the group and came up. She mock-frowned at her mother. "You've had him long enough—he's mine."

Celia laughed. "Indeed, my dear—and I'm very glad he is."

On the first of July, at eleven o'clock in the morning, Dominic walked into a wood-paneled room in a discreet building in the City. Elegantly gowned, her hair fashionably dressed, Angelica walked beside him, her hand on his arm.

Devil Cynster, Duke of St. Ives, Mr. Rupert Cynster, well-known investor, and Mr. Alasdair Cynster, renowned expert on antiquities, followed them into the room.

Standing about the head of the central rectangular table, the seven bankers representing the City's seven largest banks were simultaneously taken aback and suitably impressed.

Halting at the foot of the table, Dominic inclined his head. "Gentlemen. I'm here as agreed, on the fifth anniversary of my father's death, to hand over to you the last and final piece of the Scottish Regalia—the Coronation Cup."

On cue, Lucifer stepped forward, a royal blue velvet drawstring bag dangling on silken cords from one hand. Angelica took the bag, opened it, reached inside, and to a chorus of reverent aahs, drew the goblet free.

She handed it to Dominic.

Taking it, he balanced it on the palm of one hand and looked at the bankers. Arched a brow. "The deeds?"

His tone snapped the bankers from the trance the sight of the goblet had induced. Not entirely surprising; Lucifer had cleaned and polished it until its beauty shone.

Flustered, the bankers rummaged among several piles of papers set waiting on the table. One by one, they hurried down the room to present the deeds they held. Stepping forward, Gabriel received each document, swiftly scanned it, then laid it aside. After examining each one for the required stamp of release, he looked up at Dominic. "All accounted for, all cleared."

Dominic smiled. "Excellent." He set the goblet on the table, took the stack of documents from Gabriel, and slid them into a satchel hanging from his shoulder. Then he looked at the bankers. "The cup is all yours, gentlemen."

Taking Angelica's arm, he turned her to the door. "Use it in good health—yours and the king's."

As their group quit the room, Devil, Gabriel, and Lucifer falling in behind Dominic and Angelica, they all heard a rush of feet as the bankers converged on their treasure.

Angelica looked at Dominic, and grinned.

He looked at her, and a smile broke across his face. "Done. Finished."

"Free at last!"

Dominic halted on the pavement outside the building and shook hands with the other men. Gabriel grinned at Angelica and tapped the tip of her nose. She scowled at him, while Lucifer laughed and hugged her. Devil smiled and saluted them both, then the three Cynsters sauntered off, leaving Dominic and Angelica to hail a hackney back to Bury Street.

Dominic didn't immediately do so. He stood on the pavement, facing Angelica, letting the bustle of the street pass them by, then slowly, deeply, incrementally he filled his lungs; lifting his head, he exhaled on a long, deep, sigh. Then he looked at her, trapped her eyes. "It's truly over. It's all finally gone. The past, at last, is done with and behind us, buried and no more, and the future is all ours."

She smiled, stretched up, pulled his head down to hers and planted a quick, shockingly hot kiss on his lips. "Speaking of futures"—she dropped back to the ground and wound her arm in his—"I want to hire more gardeners. We won't be here for long, and I want to tame the wilderness before we head north."

He set his hand over hers. "Whatever you want—anything you need."

She widened her eyes. "Is that so? In that case, hurry up and hail that hackney so we can get back to Bury Street for an in-depth discussion of *all* my needs."

Dominic laughed, did, and they did, to their mutual satisfaction.

That evening, St. Ives House was a blaze of lights. Carriages jostled all around Grosvenor Square, liveried grooms and stable boys battling to keep order.

Coach after carriage drew up at the canopied red carpet, disgorging their richly dressed occupants to the delight of the crowds thronging the pavements, eager to see the flash of jewels, the sheen of satins and silks.

Inside the mansion, the huge celebratory engagement dinner, attended by every member of the family and all the senior connections, had just drawn to a rousing and noisy close, with three cheers being called for and enthusiastically delivered in honor of the glowingly happy affianced couple.

Angelica, with an emerald and diamond ring on her finger, and a suite of fabulous emeralds blazing green fire about her throat, left Dominic to the mercies of her aunt Helena, and Lady Osbaldestone, and Great-aunt Clara—he would have to learn to cope with them sometime—and quickly tacked through the stream of bodies heading for the door, the hall, and the stairs to the ballroom. Reaching out, she snagged Henrietta's sleeve and tugged.

When her cousin looked her way, Angelica tipped her head to the side of the room. "Over here—I have something for you."

Obligingly, Henrietta slipped out of the crush. She followed Angelica clear of the melee.

Halting by a sideboard, Angelica hunted through her tiny silver reticule. "There it is." Carefully freeing the links, she drew out the amethyst and gold chain with its rose quartz pendant. "This is now officially yours."

Handing the necklace to Henrietta, lowering it into her cousin's palm, Angelica said, "I have my hero now, and so have Heather and Eliza. Wear this, and the chances are that you'll find your hero, too."

Henrietta watched the delicate links fall and fold into her hand.

Reading her cousin's expression, and knowing Henrietta had a sometimes distressingly conventional streak, Angelica added, "That said, you most likely need to believe, at least a little bit, that it will work. If you will, if you do, then there's every likelihood it will work as well for you as it has for the three of us."

"Thank you." Henrietta opened her plum-colored reticule and dropped the necklace inside.

"Oh—and once you've found your hero and your betrothal is decided, Mary's the next in line, but as I understand things, she can't use it until after it's succeeded with you." Angelica frowned, then added, "If in doubt, ask Catriona."

"All right." Tugging the drawstring of her reticule shut, Henrietta looked around. "Come on—you'd better hurry. You need to take your place in the receiving line."

Angelica rushed upstairs; everyone smiled and gave way to her. Two minutes later, becomingly flushed, she was standing beside Dominic as the first guests—Lord and Lady Jersey—were shown in.

Dominic soon lost the battle to keep all the names and titles straight. He decided that as Angelica knew everyone, he would simply smile and trade on her knowledge—and her distracting beauty. She appeared utterly scintillating in a gown of coruscating, delicately watered silk in a shade of teal that echoed yet was distinctly different from her mother's favorite turquoise, the hue fractionally darker than she'd previously worn—more intense, more vibrant, more Angelica.

She smiled and laughed; she was clearly in her element. Yet time and again she would pause and talk to him, focusing solely on him.

He still wondered, worried. But when he asked her if she would miss it, she looked at him, genuinely puzzled, and asked, "Miss what?" and he smiled and waved his own question aside.

She was his, as devoted to him as he was to her . . . thinking back to the night he'd asked her to help him, he realized she'd been his from the first.

He heard the musicians tuning up, but so accustomed was he to ignoring the sound that the implication didn't register.

He didn't remember that, in the ways of the Sassenachs, he and Angelica were expected to lead the company in their engagement waltz.

Then the first chords floated over the burnished heads, and Angelica turned to face him. About them, the smiling crowd drew back, giving them room; within seconds they stood in a wide cleared space, just the two of them alone.

She looked into his eyes; if she saw his sudden panic, she gave no sign.

Instead, she smiled and held out her hand. "Trust me. I won't fail you, and you won't fail me. You will always be able to lean on me, just as I will lean on you. I will hold you, now and forever, and I will never let you fall."

Confidence and love shone in her eyes. He knew she'd planned this, but he also believed her every word.

The horror of what would happen if his knee gave out flashed into his mind.

He pushed it aside.

Lost in her eyes, in her love, he took her hand, drew her near, and as the music swelled, they stepped out.

Together.

Slowly, at first a trifle stiffly, but eventually with rising confidence and burgeoning, effervescent joy, they waltzed their engagement waltz.

So captured were they by the moment, by the meaning, that neither heard the resounding applause. They barely registered when, the dance half over, other couples, led by Celia and Martin, Heather and Breckenridge, and Eliza and Jeremy, joined them revolving around the floor.

Angelica's heart felt so full she wasn't sure she could contain the welling, swelling, surging emotions.

Then Dominic's lips quirked and she focused on his face. "What?"

He hesitated, then said, "Earlier, along our long road to here, I wondered if fate would really let me be this happy. By that, I meant as happy as I was then. Now . . . I have my answer, and it's clearly no—fate has it in mind to slay me with happiness. I'm not sure I can take much more."

She laughed and let her happiness soar.

She had everything she wanted, for now and evermore.

She'd succeeded in all she'd set out to do: She'd captured the Earl of Glencrae.

Epilogue

There was chaos in Dover Street on that morning in mid-September. Crowds of onlookers had gathered, eager to see the bridal party emerge, to see the distinguished father and his handsome sons, the older ladies in all their finery, and, above all, the brides.

Footmen and stable lads from various households had been drafted to keep the street clear. Some manned barricades blocking off a section of the pavement along one side of the street, while others did their best to hold back the swelling throng.

When three black carriages picked out with gold, with white plumes dancing on the roofs, each drawn by four prancing jet-black horses also sporting white plumes, turned into Dover Street from the Piccadilly end, the crowd surged, expectation rising, leaving the footmen and stable hands having to push people bodily back to allow the carriages to pull up, one after another, along the protected pavement outside Lord Martin Cynster's house.

"Wedding of the year, it is!"

"Won't ever be another like this one."

Such comments ran rife through the crowd. The event had fired London's imagination, ton, gentry, and the lower orders alike, and while only a select number of the upper echelons of the ton would have seats in the galleries of St. Georges and so be able to actually view the critical moments, all the rest of London was determined to see whatever there was to be seen, and given this was a triple wedding involving one of the country's foremost noble families, that was already proving, as many commented, "More'n worth the effort of coming along."

As for the atmosphere inside Lord Martin's house, bedlam was nearer the mark. His three daughters had insisted not only that they all be married on one day but also that they all be married at one ceremony. The logistics involved made Martin's head ache, even though, personally, he hadn't had to deal with any of it. Just the thought of the myriad things that could go wrong . . . but he'd been told to leave it to them—the females of the family—and like all Cynster males, he knew when not to argue.

He and his sons, equally dismissed, had retired to the library to sit at their ease savoring the latest bottle of whisky to arrive from the Guisachan Distillery. Neither Rupert nor Alasdair had any idea precisely where their wives or children were; when they'd inquired, their wives had rather snappily informed them that everyone knew what they were doing, and they didn't need to bother their heads. Not that that stopped them wondering, but they knew better than to ask again.

The door abruptly opened. Celia, resplendent in her signature turquoise, with gold, diamonds, and aquamarines, stood in the doorway. "Good—start timing from now. Wait exactly ten minutes, and then go into the front hall, and the girls will be coming down the stairs."

Celia glanced down to see her granddaughter Juliet, one of the three flower girls, peeking around her skirts. "Horatia, Catriona, and I are taking the children with us and going on to the church."

Martin frowned and glanced toward the street. "Is our carriage here?"

"It's waiting in the mews. Are you watching the time?"

"Yes." Rupert had his fob watch in his hand. "Nine more minutes."

"Come along, Juliet. We have to catch up with the others—but don't run!" Celia whisked off, following a bounding Juliet.

Rupert, Alasdair, and Martin exchanged worried looks.

Alasdair shook his head. "I can't recall it being anything like this bad when we got married."

"It wasn't." Martin sat up and set aside his empty glass. "But that was different. They're girls—brides—and for them, the world stops."

His sons snorted, but rose as he did. They settled their waistcoats, checked their cravats, then adjusted the sleeves of their dove-gray morning coats.

At precisely the right time, Martin led them out and into the front hall.

They heard footsteps and rustling on the stairs. All three turned and looked.

And their world stopped.

After a moment of staring, Alasdair murmured, "And we're their blood kin. How in all hell do they expect Breckenridge, Carling, and Glencrae to find their tongues enough to say 'I do'?"

Rupert shook his head, whispered back, "It'll be interesting to see if they manage it."

Martin was silent, watching his daughters, all smiling radiantly, descend the stairs—first Heather, then Eliza, then his baby, Angelica.

Their gowns were all white, but each was very different. Heather's had wide, sweeping skirts of the finest silk, the fitting bodice heavily embroidered with pearls, while Eliza's was more sheathlike, delicate lace over white satin, and Angelica looked like a fairy-tale princess in clouds of white tulle over which delicately embroidered gold leaves had been scattered. Pearls were the jewels of choice, but again each was unique. Heather wore an ornate collar fashioned of pearls, echoing the embroidery on her bodice, while Eliza had a long loop wound twice about her neck, then dangling almost to her waist, and Angelica wore only a simple pearl pendant about her throat, but had pearled combs scattered through her shining hair.

They were stunning.

Martin managed a smile, although it wobbled. "I have no words."

Heather smiled. "We don't have time for speeches, anyway, not here." She took Martin's arm and steered him to the door. "We need to get going."

Swallowing his resistance, Martin accepted that they, at least, were eager to leave his house. Rupert gave Eliza his arm, and Alasdair escorted Angelica. The three couples formed up before the doors, then Abercrombie, beaming delightedly, swung the front door open, and Martin led his daughters to their wedding.

The crowd inside the church knew when the brides arrived. The noise outside rose to a pitch just short of a roar.

Standing before the altar, the three grooms exchanged glances. There were no groomsmen as the three had elected to stand for each other. Besides, as more than a few remarked, even given the wide width of the nave, having three couples lined up before the altar was going to be cramped enough as it was, and groomsmen, of all those in a wedding party, were quite the most dispensable.

The big doors at the end of the nave had been closed, so no one knew of the last-minute preparations in the foyer. But the organist had a boy running from the foyer to the great organ loft. Just as the expectant fidgeting in the church reached fever pitch, the organ wheezed, then launched into a rousing march. Everyone turned to look at the doors. Everyone held their breath. Then as the first repeat of the chorus commenced, the double doors opened, pushed back by Henrietta and Mary in their role as attendants, then they stood back and let pass a procession of three flower girls and three page boys—Gavin and Prudence Cynster in the lead, followed by Bryce and Juliet, with the twins, Lucilla and Marcus, bringing up the rear. Each boy held a gold bucket filled with rose petals into which his partnered girl dipped her hands and flung the petals wide with a joyous abandon that had people smiling and laughing— effortlessly setting the tone for what was to follow.

As Henrietta and Mary fell in behind the three pairs, the organist switched seamlessly to a full-bodied wedding march, and Lord Martin Cynster led in his eldest daughter. The oohs and aahs, and the excited, whispered comments only grew as Eliza, and then Angelica, were also led in. The twittering didn't fade until long after all three brides had been led to the altar and given into the care of the gentlemen waiting there to take their hands and face the minister.

When the minister raised his hands, the crowd quieted.

In a sonorous voice, he opened the service, then led the couples through their vows. Each, one after the other, plighted their troth in clear, resonant voices that carried to the back of the now silent galleries and the boxed pews. Then the minister called on God and the congregation to bear witness, before leading the assembled through the hymns and the short lesson, after which the minister led the three couples into the vestry to sign the register. While the congregation traded whispers and complimentary remarks, the organist filled the church with a soaring display, and then the couples were back, and the minister commanded the assembly's attention once more.

Minutes later, he pronounced the benediction and the congregation rose as the couples turned, hand in hand, to face them.

And it was as if the congregation wasn't there; each pair had eyes only for each other. Those among the assembled close enough to see their faces sighed. Ladies groped blindly for their handkerchiefs.

Then all six looked ahead. Twining their arms, each couple walked ceremonially back up the nave in the reverse order to that of their arrival—Angelica and her handsome highland earl, then Eliza and her fascinating scholar, and at the last, Heather and her rakish viscount.

As they emerged onto the church's colonnaded porch, the crowd literally roared. Hats were flung, rice flew, and suddenly laughing, ducking and hurrying, the three couples ran to the carriages drawn up at the porch's side.

And then they were away.

A similar reception awaited them outside St. Ives House, but once inside, once they reached the room upstairs set aside for their use while waiting for the guests for the wedding breakfast to arrive, they all looked at each other, then collapsed on the three sofas.

Smiling, Heather blew out a breath. "That was . . ."

"*Simply glorious.*" Eliza reached for Jeremy's hand. "You all did very well."

Dominic met Breckenridge's eyes and quirked his brows. "As if we would have dared fail in even the smallest way today."

Angelica patted his thigh. "Oh, we would have forgiven you, eventually. Sometime."

Smiling, Dominic caught her hand and kissed it.

Sligo appeared with two bottles of champagne and a footman bearing crystal glasses. "Best of luck to you all from all the staffs."

They popped the corks, poured, then sat back, sipped, put their feet up, and relaxed.

Eventually Celia appeared to summon them. She looked almost as ecstatic as her daughters. "Well, my dears." Her motherly gaze included the three males as well as her daughters. "I fear it's time. Just remember, three more hours, and then you can slip away."

There were groans all around, but on the girls' parts at least the complaint was all for show. Leaving the door open, Celia left. Heather, Eliza, and Angelica rose, shook out their gowns, then, under the fascinated gazes of their husbands, who had also risen and were settling their coats, all three ladies, heads tipping together, headed for the door.

"How are we going to do this?" Angelica asked.

"I suspect we should consider the size of the ball-room," Heather said. "We need to split up, one couple down each side, and one going down the middle. If we don't, even in three hours, we'll never speak with everyone."

"Hmm, but will that satisfy?" Eliza asked. "Did either of you think to get Mama's seating plan?"

The three ladies walked out—leaving their husbands behind.

Dominic was the first to break—to shake his head and start laughing.

Just a look, a shared glance, and Breckenridge and Jeremy were laughing, too.

"You do realize," Dominic said, valiantly stifling his mirth, "that this is how it's going to be for all three of us from this day forth."

Jeremy caught his breath, nodded. "They lead—we follow. Apparently it's the Cynster way."

"Ah, well," Breckenridge said, "what can we poor souls do?"

So saying, with smiles of deep appreciation on their faces, the three stepped out, striding swiftly to catch up with their futures.

To follow at the heels of the Viscountess Breck-enridge, Mrs. Jeremy Carling, and the Countess of Glencrae.

HARPER LUXE

THE NEW LUXURY IN READING

We hope you enjoyed reading
our new, comfortable print size and found it
an experience you would like to repeat.

Well – you're in luck!

HarperLuxe offers the finest in fiction and
nonfiction books in this same larger print size and
paperback format. Light and easy to read, HarperLuxe
paperbacks are for book lovers who want to see
what they are reading without the strain.

For a full listing of titles and
new releases to come, please visit our website:

www.HarperLuxe.com